Basil Hall Chamberlain

**Things Japanese**

Basil Hall Chamberlain

**Things Japanese**

ISBN/EAN: 9783337385194

Printed in Europe, USA, Canada, Australia, Japan

Cover: Foto ©Andreas Hilbeck / pixelio.de

More available books at **www.hansebooks.com**

# THINGS JAPANESE

*BEING*

*NOTES ON VARIOUS SUBJECTS CONNECTED WITH JAPAN*

BY

## BASIL HALL CHAMBERLAIN

# PREFACE.

THE author is under obligations to many kind friends—
especially to Mr. W. B. Mason, of the Imperial Department of Communications, by whose unwearying assistance
and advice every page of the book has profited more or
less. The article on *Porcelain and Pottery* is from the
pen of Captain Brinkley, R.A., the appearance of whose
" History of Japanese and Chinese Keramics " is eagerly
looked forward to by all persons interested in that beautiful
art. The Abbé Félix Évrard, of the French Legation at
Tōkyō, has contributed the article on *Roman Catholic Missions*; Mr. H. V. Henson, that on *Trade*; Professor Milne,
F.R.S., that on *Geology*; Mr. Mason, those on *Telegraphs*,
*Chess*, and the game of *Go*. Mr. Y. Sannomiya, Vice-
Grand-Master of Ceremonies and Master of the Court of
Her Majesty the Empress, has furnished the materials for
*Decorations*; Mr. R. Masujima, of the Japanese Bar and
of the Middle Temple, London, the materials for *Law*;
Mr. K. Fujikura, Chief Commissioner of Lighthouses, the
materials for *Lighthouses*; Captain J. Ingles, R.N., for
*Navy*; and Mr. C. A. W. Pownall, for *Railways*. The
advice of Dr. Erwin Baelz, of the Imperial University

of Japan, has been sought on various points connected
with medicine, and Lieutenant T. H. James, R.N., has been
similarly applied to for what relates to shipping. The
Map is adapted from one of those in the "Atlas of the
Agricultural Productions of the Japanese Empire," by
permission of Professor T. Wada, Director of the Imperial
Geological Office in the Department of Agriculture and
Commerce. Various other kind friends have contributed—
one a fact, another a reference, yet another a counsel. To
all, best thanks.

*Imperial University of Japan.*
*Tōkyō, May, 1890.*

# INTRODUCTORY CHAPTER.

To have lived through the transition stage of modern Japan makes a man feel preternaturally old; for here he is in modern times, with the air full of talk about Darwinism, and phonographs, and parliamentary institutions, and yet he can himself distinctly remember the Middle Ages. The dear old *samurai* who first initiated the present writer into the mysteries of the Japanese language wore a cue and two swords. This relic of feudalism now sleeps in Nirvâna. His modern successor, fairly fluent in English, and dressed in a serviceable suit of dittos, might almost be a European, save for a certain obliqueness of the eyes and scantiness of beard. Old things pass away between a night and a morning. The Japanese boast that they have done in twenty years what it took Europe half as many centuries to accomplish. Some even go further, and twit us Westerns with falling behind in the race. Not long

ago, a Japanese pamphleteer refused to argue out
a point of philosophy with a learned German resident
of Tōkyō, on the score that Europeans, owing to
their antiquated Christian prejudices, were not capable of discussing such matters impartially.

Thus does it come about that, having arrived in
Japan in 1873, we ourselves feel well-nigh four
hundred years old, and assume without more ado the
two well-known privileges of old age—garrulity and
an authoritative air.  We are perpetually being asked
questions about Japan.  Here then are the answers,
put into the shape of a dictionary, not of words but
of things,—or shall we rather say a guide-book, less
to places than to subjects?  The old and the new
will ·be found cheek by jowl.  The only thing that
will not be found is padding; for padding is unpar-
donable in any book on Japan, where the subject-
matter is so plentiful that the only difficulty is to
know what to omit.

In order to enable the reader to supply deficiencies
and to form his own opinions, if haply he should be
of so unusual a turn of mind as to desire so to do,
we have, at the end of almost every article, indicated
the names of trustworthy works bearing on the subject treated in that article.  For the rest, this little

book explains itself. Any reader who detects errors or omissions in it will render the author an invaluable service by writing to him to point them out. As a little encouragement in this direction, we will ourselves lead the way by presuming to give each reader, especially each globe-trotting reader, a small piece of advice. We take it for granted, of course, that there are no Japanese listening, and the advice is this:—

Whatever you do, don't praise, in the presence of Japanese of the new school, those old, quaint, and beautiful things Japanese which rouse your most genuine admiration. The Japanese have done with their past. They want to be somebody else and something else than what they have been and still partly are. When Sir Edwin Arnold, the illustrious author of the "Light of Asia," was entertained at a banquet in Tōkyō by a distinguished company including officials, journalists, and professors, in fact, representative modern Japanese of the best class, he made a speech in which he lauded Japan to the skies— and lauded it justly—as the nearest earthly approach to Paradise or to Lotus-land—so fairy-like, said he, is its scenery, so exquisite its art, so much more lovely still that almost divine sweetness of disposition,

that charm of demeanour, that politeness, humble
without servility and elaborate without affectation,
which place Japan high above all other countries in
almost all those things which make life worth living.
(We do not give his exact words, but we give the
general drift.)—Now do you think that the Japanese
were satisfied with this meed of praise? Not a bit of
it. Out comes an article next morning in the chief
paper which had been represented at the banquet,—
an article acknowledging, indeed, the truth 'of Sir
Edwin's description, but pointing out that it conveyed, not praise, but condemnation of the heaviest
sort. Art forsooth, scenery, sweetness of disposition?
What care. we for art, scenery, and sweetness of
disposition, cries this editor?—and he is a representative man. Why did not Sir Edwin praise us for
huge industrial enterprises, for commercial talent,
for wealth, political sagacity, strong armaments? Of
course it is because he could not honestly do so.
He has gauged us at our true value, and tells us in
effect that we are pretty weaklings.

Yes, reader, we—we now mean our own little
"we," not the editorial "we" of the disappointed
Japanese journalist—we have seen this sort of thing
over and over again. We can even sympathise with

it, or at least try to do so. For after all, Japan must be modernised if she is to continue to exist. Besides which, our new European world of thought, of enterprise, of gigantic scientific achievement, is as much a wonder-world to the Japanese as Old Japan can ever be to us. There is this difference, however. Old Japan is to us a delicate little wonder-world of sylphs and fairies. Europe and America, with their railways, their telegraphs, their gigantic commerce, their gigantic armies and navies, their endless applied arts founded on chemistry and mathematics, are to the Japanese a wonder-world of irresistible genii and magicians. The Japanese have, indeed, little or no appreciation of our literature. They esteem us whimsical for attaching so much importance as we do to poetry, to music, to religion, to speculative disquisitions. Our material greatness has completely dazzled them, as well it might. They know also well enough—for every Eastern nation knows it—that our Christian and humanitarian professions are really nothing but bunkum. The history of India, of Egypt, of Turkey, is no secret to them. More familiar still is the sweet reasonableness of California's treatment of the Chinese. They would be blind indeed, did they not see that their only

chance of safety lies in the endeavour to be strong,
and in the endeavour not to be too different from
the rest of mankind; for the mob of Western nations will tolerate eccentricity of appearance no more
than will a mob of roughs.

Indeed, scarcely any even among those who implore the Japanese to remain as they are, refrain,
as a matter of fact, from urging them to make
all sorts of changes. "Japanese dress for ladies is
simply perfection," we hear one of these persons
cry; "only don't you think that gloves might be
added with advantage? And then, too, ought not
something to be done with the skirt to prevent it
from opening in front, just for the sake of decency,
you know?"—Says another, whose special vanity
is Japanese music (there is considerable distinction
about this taste, for it is a rare one),—says he,—
" Now please keep your music from perishing. Keep
it just as it is, so curious to the archæologist, so
beautiful, for all that the jeerers may say. There is
only one small thing which I would advise you to
do, and that is to harmonise it. Of course that
would change its character a little. But no one
would notice it, and the general effect would be improved."—Yet another, an enthusiast for faïence,

wishes Japanese decorative methods to be retained, but to be applied to French forms, because no cup or plate made in Japan is so perfectly round as are the products of French kilns. A fourth delights in Japanese brocade, but suggests new breadths, in order to suit making up into European dresses. A fifth wants to keep Japanese painting exactly as it is, but with the trivial addition of perspective. A sixth—but a truce to the quoting of these self-confuting absurdities. Put into plain English, they mean, " Do so-and-so, only don't do it. Walk north, and at the same time take care to proceed in a southerly direction."

And can it be wondered at that the Japanese are bewildered? On the other hand, must it *not* be wondered at that any one can expect either Japanese social conditions or the Japanese arts to remain as they were in the past? All the causes which produced the Old Japan of our dreams have vanished. Feudalism has gone, isolation has gone, beliefs have been shattered, new idols have been set up, new and pressing needs have arisen. In the place of chivalry there is industrialism, in the place of a small coterie of aristocratic native connoisseurs there is a huge and hugely ignorant foreign public to satisfy.

All the causes have changed, and yet it is expected that the effects will remain as heretofore !

No. Old Japan is dead, and the only decent thing to do with the corpse is to bury it. Then you can set up a monument over it, and, if you like, come and worship from time to time at the grave; for that would be quite "Japanesey." This little book is intended to be, as it were, the epitaph recording the many and extraordinary virtues of the deceased,—his virtues, but also his frailties. For, more careful of fact than the generality of epitaphists, we have ventured to speak out our whole mind on almost every subject, and to call things by their names, being persuaded that true appreciation is always critical as well as kindly.

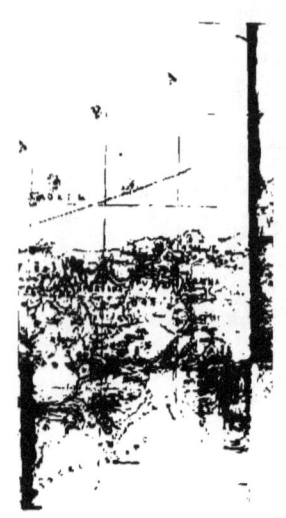

# THINGS JAPANESE.

**Abacus.** Learn to count on the abacus—the *soroban*, as the Japanese call it—and you will often be able to save a large percentage on your purchases. The abacus is that instrument, composed of beads sliding on wires fixed in a frame, with which many of us learnt the multiplication table in early childhood. In Japan it is used, not only by children, but by adults, who still mostly prefer it to our method of figuring with pen and paper. As for mental arithmetic, that does not exist in this archipelago. Tell any ordinary Japanese to add 5 and 8 and 7: he will flounder hopelessly, unless his familiar friend, the abacus, is at hand. And here we come round again to the practical advantage of being able to read off at sight a number figured on this instrument. You have been bargaining at a curio-shop, we will suppose. The shopman has got perplexed. He refers to his list, and then calculates on the instrument, which of course he takes for granted that you do not understand, the lowest price for which he can let you have the article in question. Then he raises his head, and, with a bland smile, assures you that the cost of it to himself was so and so, naming a price considerably larger than the real one. You have the better of him, if you can read his figuring of the sum. If you cannot, ten to one he has the better of you.

The principle of the abacus is this:—Each of the five beads in the broad lower division of the board represents one unit, and each solitary bead in the narrow upper division represents five units. Each vertical column is thus worth ten units. Furthermore, each vertical column represents units ten times greater than those in the column immediately to the right of it, exactly as in our own system of notation by means of Arabic numerals. Any sum in arithmetic can be done on the abacus, even to the extracting of square and cube roots; and Dr. Knott, the chief English, or, to be quite correct, the chief Scotch, writer on the subject, is of opinion that Japanese methods excel ours in rapidity. Perhaps he is a little enthusiastic. One can scarcely help thinking so of an author who refers to a new Japanese method of long division as "almost fascinating." The Japanese, it seems, have not only a multiplication table, but a division table besides. We confess that we do not understand the division table, even with Dr. Knott's explanations. Indeed we will confess more: we have never learnt the abacus at all. If we recommend others to learn it, it is because we hope that, for their own sake, they will do as we tell them and not do as we do. Personally we have found one method of ciphering enough, and a great deal more than enough, to poison the happiness of one life-time.

Book recommended. "The Abacus, in its Historic and Scientific Aspects," by Dr. C. G. Knott, F. R. S. E, printed in Vol. XIV, Part I, of the "Asiatic Transactions."

**Abdication.** -The abdication of monarchs, which is exceptional in Europe, has for many ages been the rule in Japan. It came into vogue in the seventh century together

with Buddhism, whose doctrines led men to retire from
worldly cares and pleasures into solitude and contempla-
tion.   But it was made use of by unscrupulous ministers,
who placed infant puppets on the throne, and caused them
to abdicate on attaining to maturity.   Thus it was a common thing during the Middle Ages for three Mikados to be
alive at the same time,—a boy on the throne, his father
or brother who had abdicated, and his grandfather or
other relative who had abdicated also.   From A.D. 987
to 991, there were as many as four Mikados all alive
together—Reizei Tennō, who had ascended the throne at
the age of eighteen, and who abdicated at twenty; En-yū
Tennō, emperor at eleven and abdicated at twenty-six;
Kwazan Tennō, emperor at seventeen and abdicated at
nineteen; and Ichijō Tennō, who had just ascended the
throne as a little boy of seven.   Under the Mikado Go-
Nijō (A.D. 1302—8) there were actually *five* Mikados all
alive together, namely Go-Nijō Tennō himself, made
emperor at seventeen, and his four abdicated predecessors,
Go-Fukakusa Tennō, emperor at four and abdicated at
seventeen;  Kameyama Tennō, emperor at eleven and
abdicated at twenty-six; Go-Uda Tennō, emperor at eight
and abdicated at twenty-one; and Fushimi Tennō, emperor
at twenty-three and abdicated the same year.   Sometimes
it was arranged that the children of two rival branches
of the Imperial family should succeed each other alternately.   This it was, in part at least, which led to the
civil war in the fourteenth century between what were
known as "the Northern and Southern Courts;" for it
was of course impossible that so extraordinary an arrangement should long be adhered to without producing violent
dissensions.

After a time, it became so completely customary that the monarch in name must not be monarch in fact, and *vice versâ*, that abdication, or rather deposition (for that is what it practically amounted to) was almost a *sine quâ non* of the inheritance of such scanty shreds of authority as imperious ministers still deigned to leave to their so-called lords and masters. A reigning Mikado was said to *ascend* to the rank of abdicated Mikado. It was no longer necessary, as at an earlier period, to sham asceticism. The abdicated Mikado surrounded himself with wives and a whole court, and sometimes really helped to direct public affairs. Nor was abdication confined to sovereigns. Heads of noble houses abdicated too. In later times the middle and lower classes began to imitate their betters. Until the period of the late revolution, it was an almost universal custom for a man to become what is termed an *inkyo* after passing middle age. *Inkyo* means literally "dwelling in retirement." He who enters on this state gives over his property to his heirs, generally resigns all office, and lives on the bounty of his children, free to devote himself henceforth to pleasure or to study. Old age being so extraordinarily honoured in Japan, the *inkyo* has no reason to dread Lear's fate. He knows that he will always be dutifully tended by sons who are not waiting to find out "how the old man will cut up." The new government of Japan is endeavouring to put a stop to the practice of *inkyo*, as being barbarous because not European. But to the people at large it appears, on the contrary, barbarous that a man should go on toiling and striving, when past the time of life at which he is fitted to do good work.

Book recommended. "The Gakushikuhin," by Walter Dening, printed in Vol. XV, Part 1, of the "Asiatic Transactions," p. 72. *et seq.*

**Acupuncture.** Acupuncture, one of the three great nostrums of the practitioners of the Far East (the other two being massage and the moxa), was brought over from China to Japan before the dawn of history. Dr. W. N. Whitney describes it as follows in his " Notes on the History of Medical Progress in Japan," published in Vol. XII, Part IV, of the " Asiatic Transactions," p. 354 :—

" As practised by the Japanese acupuncturists, the operation consists in perforating the skin and underlying tissues to a depth, as a rule, not exceeding one-half to three-quarters of an inch, with fine needles of gold, silver, or steel. The form and construction of these needles vary, but, generally speaking, they are several inches long, and of an average diameter of one forty-eighth of an inch. Each needle is usually fastened into a handle, which is spirally grooved from end to end.

" To perform the operation, the handle of the needle is held lightly between the thumb and first finger of the left hand, the point resting upon the spot to be punctured. A slight blow is then given upon the head of the instrument with a small mallet held in the right hand ; and the needle is gently twisted until its point has penetrated to the desired depth, where it is left for a few seconds and then slowly withdrawn, and the skin in the vicinity of the puncture rubbed for a few moments. The number of perforations range from one to twenty, and they are usually made in the skin of the abdomen, although other portions of the body are not unfrequently punctured."

**Adams (Will).** Will Adams, the first Englishman that ever resided in Japan, was a native of Gillingham, near

Chatham, in the county of Kent. Having followed the sea from his youth up, he took service, in the year 1598, as " Pilot Maior of a fleete of five-sayle," which had been equipped by the Dutch East India Company for the purpose of trading to Spanish America. From " Perow," a portion of the storm-tossed fleet came on to " Iapon," arriving at a port in the province of Bungo, not far from " Langasacke" (Nagasaki), on the 19th April, 1600. From that time until his death, in May 1620, Adams remained in an exile, which, though gilded, was none the less bitterly deplored. The English pilot, brought first as a captive into the presence of Ieyasu, who was then practically what Adams calls him, " Emperour" of Japan, had immediately been recognised by that shrewd judge of character as an able and an honest man. That he and his nation were privately slandered to Ieyasu by " the Iesuites and the Portingalls," who were at that time the only other Europeans in the country, probably did him more good than harm in the Japanese ruler's eyes. He was retained at the Japanese court, and employed as a shipbuilder, and also as a kind of diplomatic agent when other English and Dutch traders began to arrive. In fact, it was by his good offices that the foundations were laid both of English trade in Japan and also of the more permanent Dutch settlement. During his latter years he for a time exchanged the Japanese service for that of the English factory established by Captain John Saris at Firando (Hirado) near Nagasaki; and he made two voyages, one to the Loochoo Islands and another to Siam. His constantly reiterated desire to see his native land again, and his wife and children, was to the last frustrated by adverse circumstances. So far as the wife was concerned, he partially comforted himself, sailor fashion,

by taking another—a Japanese with whom he lived at ease
for many years on the estate granted him by Ieyasu at Hemi,
near the modern town of Yokosuka, where their two graves
are shown to this day. Another adventurer, who visited him
there, describes Will Adams's place thus : "This Phebe*
is a Lordshipp geuen to Capt. Adames pr. the ould Em-
perour†, to hym- and his for euer, and confermed to his
sonne, called Joseph. There is above 100 farms, or how-
sholds, vppon it, besides others vnder them, all which are
his vassalls, and he hath power of lyfe and death ouer them
they being his slaues ; and he hauing as absolute authoritie
over them as any tono (or king) in Japan hath over his
vassales." From further details it would seem that he
used his authority kindly, so that the neighbours "reioiced
(as it should seeme) of Captain Adames retorne."

Will Adams's letters have been published by the Hak-
luyt Society in their "Memorials of Japon" (sic), and
republished in a cheaper form at the office of the "Japan
Gazette," Yokohama. They are well-worth reading, both
for the life-like silhouette of the writer which stands out
from their quaintly spelt pages, and for the picture given
by him of Japan as it then was, when the land swarmed
with Catholic friars and Catholic converts, when no em-
bargo had yet been laid on foreign commerce, and when
the native energy of the Japanese people had not yet been
emasculated by two centuries and a half of bureaucracy
and timid seclusion.

**Adoption.** · It is strange, but true, that you may often
go into a Japanese family, and find half a dozen persons

* Our author means Hemi!
† Ieyasu was then dead.

calling each other parent and child, brother and sister, uncle and nephew, and yet being really either no blood relations at all, or else relations in quite different degrees from those conventionally assumed. Galton's books could never have been written in Japan; for though genealogies are carefully kept, they mean nothing—at least from a scientific point of view—so universal is the practice of adoption, from the top of society to the bottom. This it is which explains such apparent anomalies as a distinguished painter, potter, actor, or what not, almost always having a son distinguished in the same line: he has simply adopted his best pupil. It also explains the fact of Japanese families not dying out.

So completely has adoption become part and parcel of the national life that Mr. Shigeno An-eki, the chief recent Japanese authority on the subject, enumerates no less than ten different categories of adopted persons. Adoption is resorted to, not only to prevent the extinction of families and the consequent neglect of the spirits of the departed, but also in order to regulate the size of families. Thus, a man with too many children hands over one or more of them to his friends who have none. To adopt a person is also the simplest way to leave him money, it not being usual in Japan to nominate strangers as one's heirs. Formerly, too, it was sometimes a means of money-making, not to the adopted, but to the adopter. "It was customary"—so writes the authority whom we quote below—"for the sons of the court-nobles when they reached the age of majority to receive an income from the Government. It often happened that when an officer had a son who was, say, only two or three years old, he would adopt a lad who was about fifteen (the age of majority), and then apply for a grant of land or rice for him; after he had secured this, he would make his own son the *yōshi* [adopted son] of the newly adopted youth, and thus, when the former came of age, the officer was entitled to apply for another grant of land."—With this may be compared the plan often followed by business people at the present day. A merchant adopts his head clerk, in order to give him a personal interest in the firm. The clerk then adopts his patron's son, with the understanding that he himself is to retire in the latter's favour when the latter shall be of a suitable age. If the clerk has a son, then perhaps that son will be adopted by the patron's son. Thus a sort of alternate headship is kept up, the surname always remaining the same.

Since the late revolution, adoption has been a favourite method of evading the conscription, as single sons are (or were till recently) exempted from serving. Fond parents, anxious to assist a favourite son to this exemption, would cause him to be adopted by some childless friend. After a few years, it might perhaps be possible to arrange for the lad's return to his former family and resumption of his original surname.

We recommend, as a good occupation for a rainy day, the endeavour to trace out the real relationships (in our European sense of the word) of some of the reader's Japanese servants and friends. Unless we are much mistaken, this will prove to be a puzzle of the highest order of difficulty.

Book recommended. "The Gakushūkai," by Walter Dening, printed in Vol. XV, Part I, of the "Asiatic Transactions," p. ??, et seq

**Ainos.** The Ainos, called by themselves *Aina*, that is

"men," are a very peculiar race, now inhabiting only the northern island of Yezo, but formerly widely spread all over the Japanese archipelago. The Japanese proper, arriving from the south-west, gradually pressed the Ainos back towards the east and north. In retreating, the aborigines left the country strewed with place-names belonging to their own language. Such are, for instance, *Noto*, the name of the big promontory stretching out into the Sea of Japan (*notsu* means "promontory" in Aino), the *Tonegawa*, or River *Tone*, at Tōkyō (*tanne* is Aino for "long"), and hundreds of others. So far as blood, however, is concerned, the Japanese have been little, if at all, affected by Aino influence. The simple reason is that the half-breeds die out. The Ainos are the hairiest race in the whole world, their luxuriantly thick black beards and hairy limbs giving them an appearance which contrasts strangely with the smoothness of their Japanese lords and masters. They are of sturdy build, and distinguished by a flattening of certain bones of the arm and leg (the *tibia* and *humerus*), which has been observed nowhere else except in the remains of some of the cave-men of Europe. The women tattoo mustaches on their upper lip and geometrical patterns on their hands. Both sexes are of a mild and amiable disposition, but are terribly addicted to drunkenness. They are filthily dirty, the practice of bathing being altogether unknown.

The Ainos were till recently accustomed to live on the produce of the chase and the sea fisheries; but both these sources of subsistence have diminished since the settling of the island by the Japanese. Consequently they no longer hold up their heads as in former days, and, notwithstanding the well-intentioned efforts of a paternal

government, they are disappearing more rapidly under
the influence of civilisation than they did during their long
and bloody wars with the Japanese and with each other,
which only terminated in the last century.    At the present
day they number about 15,000 souls, chiefly scattered along
the coast.    Their religion is a simple nature-worship.
The sun, wind, ocean, bear, etc., are deified under the title
of *kamui*, "god," and whittled sticks are set up in their
honour.    The bear, though worshipped, is also sacrificed
and eaten with solemnities that form the most original
and picturesque feature of Aino life.    Some of the Aino
tales are quaint.    Most of them embody an attempt to
account for some natural phenomenon.    The following may
serve as a specimen :—

### WHY DOGS CANNOT SPEAK.

*Formerly dogs could speak.  Now they cannot.  The rea-
son is that a dog, belonging to a certain man a long time
ago, inveigled his master into the forest under the pretext of
showing him game, and there caused him to be devoured by
a bear.  Then the dog went home to his master's widow,
and lied to her, saying: "My master has been killed by
a bear.  But when he was dying, he commanded me to tell
you to marry me in his stead."  The widow knew that the
dog was lying.  But he kept on urging her to marry him.
So at last, in her grief and rage, she threw a handful of
dust into his open mouth.  This made him unable to speak
any more, and therefore no dogs can speak even to this very
day.*

The Aino language is simple and harmonious.    Its
structure in great measure resembles that of Japanese;
but there are some few fundamental divergences, such,

for instance, as the possession of true pronouns. The
vocabulary, too, is quite distinct. The system of counting is extraordinarily cumbrous. Thus, if a man wants
to say that he is thirty-nine years old, he must express
himself thus: "I am nine, plus ten taken from two
score." In Mr. Batchelor's translation of Matthew XII,
40, the phrase "forty days and forty nights" is thus
rendered: *iokap rere ko tu hotne rere ko, kunne rere ko
tu hotne rere ko*, that is "days three days two score three
days, black three days two score three days." The Ainos
know nothing of the use of letters. Tales like the one
we have quoted, and rude songs which are handed down
orally from generation to generation, form their only literature.

Books recommended. Miss Bird's "Unbeaten Tracks in Japan," Vol. II
gives the best popular account of the Ainos.—Students are referred to the "First Me-
morie of the Literature College of the Imperial University of Japan," by Chamberlain
and Batchelor, for full details concerning Aino mythology, grammar, place-names,
etc.; to Chamberlain's "Aino Folk-Lore," in Vol. VI. Part I, of the "Folk-Lore Journal," to numerous papers by Batchelor, scattered through the "Asiatic Transactions,"
to others by Penhallow in "The Canadian Record of Science," and to "Studien über
die Aino," by the younger Siebold. The Memoir above quoted gives a fairly complete
bibliography of Yezo and the Ainos.—The best Japanese work on the subject is the
*Ezo Fuzoku Isan*, published by the Kaitakushi in 1886. It is in twenty volumes.


**Amusements.** The chief amusements of the Japanese
are the ordinary theatre (*shibai*); the Nō theatre, (but this
is attended only by the aristocracy); wrestling matches,—
witnessing, not taking part in them; dinners enlivened
by the performances of singing and dancing-girls; visits
to temples, as much for purposes of pleasure as of devotion; picnics to places noted for their scenery, and especially to places noted for some particular blossom, such as
the plum, cherry, or wistaria. The Japanese also divert
themselves by composing verses in their own language

and in Chinese, and by playing chess, checkers, and
various games of the "Mother Goose" description, of
which *sugoroku* is the chief. Ever since the early days
of foreign intercourse they have likewise had certain kinds
of cards, of which the *kana-garuta*, or "flower-cards," are
the most popular kind,—so popular, indeed, and seductive
that there is an official veto on playing the game for
money. The cards are forty-eight in number, four for
each month of the year, the months being distinguished
by the flowers proper to them, and an extra value being
attached to one out of each set of four, which is further
distinguished by a bird or butterfly, and to a second which
is inscribed with a line of poetry. Three people take part
in the game, and there is a pool. The system of counting
is rather complicated, but the ideas involved are graceful.

Some of the above diversions are shared in by the
ladies; but take it all together, their mode of life is much
duller than that of their European sisters. Confucian
ideas concerning the subjection of women still obtain to
a great extent. Women are not, it is true, actually shut
up, as in India; but it is considered that their true voca-
tion is to sit at home. Hence visiting is much less practised in Japan than with us. It is further to be observed,
to the credit of the Japanese, that amusement, though
permitted, is never exalted by them to the rank of the
great and serious business of life. In England, at least
among the upper classes, a man's shooting, fishing, and
tennis, a girl's dances, garden-parties, and country-house
visitings, appear to be the centre round which all the family
plans revolve. In Japan, on the contrary, amusements
are merely picked up by the way, and are all the more
appreciated.

The above outline sketch, correct for the old days, nearly correct for the present day, will probably require considerable alteration in the near future. Poker, *vingt-et-un*, horse-racing, circuses, quadrilles, polkas, etc., etc., have begun to establish their claims. Even shooting and lawn-tennis have their Japanese devotees ; but for the most part, the interest taken in field sports is languid and not likely to endure. Dancing parties in European style did not come into prominence till the early eighties. For some time, the Japanese ladies went to them in their own charming costume, and merely to look on. They now incase themselves in corsets, and don frills and furbelows ordered from Paris—we beg pardon, from Berlin—and join boldly in the fray. Connoisseurs in such matters aver, however, that their waltzing is not yet quite up to the mark. The aspect of a modern Tōkyō ball-room has been amusingly described both by Pierre Loti in his " Japoneries d'Automne " (chapter entitled " Un Bal à Yeddo "), and by Netto in his " Papierschmetterlinge aus Japan." We have only room for one epigram of Netto's :  " At these festivities Japanese ladies and gentlemen are to be seen taking part in the dancing, especially in the square dances ; but most of them show by the expression of their faces that they are making a sacrifice on the altar of civilisation."

The sports of Japanese children include kite-flying, top-spinning, snow-balling, battledoor and shuttlecock, playing with dolls, etc., etc.,—in fact, most of our old nursery friends, but modified by the *genius loci*.

Books recommended. "Child-Life in Japan," by Mrs. Chaplin-Ayrton.— "The Games and Sports of Japanese Children," by W. E. Griffis, in Vol. II of the " Asiatic Transactions."

**Architecture.** The Japanese genius touches perfection

in small things. No other nation ever understood half
so well how to twist a spray of flowers into artistic line,
how to transform a little knob of ivory into a micro-
cosm of quaint humour, how to express a fugitive thought
in half-a-dozen dashes of the pencil. The massive, the
spacious, the grand, is less congenial to their mental
attitude. Hence they achieve less success in architecture
than in the other arts. The prospect of a Japanese city
from a height is monotonous. Not a tower, not a dome,
not a minaret, nothing aspiring heavenward, save in rare
cases a painted pagoda half-hidden amidst the trees which
it barely tops,—nothing but long, low lines of thatch and
tiles, even the Buddhist temple roofs being but moderately
raised above the rest, and even their curves being only
quaint and graceful, nowise imposing. It was a true
instinct that led Professor Morse to give to his charming
monograph on Japanese architecture the title of "Japanese *Homes*," the interest of Japanese buildings lying less
in the buildings themselves than in the odd domestic
ways of their denizens, and in the delightful little bits of
ornamentation that meet one at every turn—the elaborate
metal fastenings, the carved friezes (*ramma*), the screens
both sliding and folding, the curiously ornamented tiles,
the dainty gardens with their dwarfed trees. What is
true of the dwelling-houses is true of the temples also.
Nikkō and Shiba are glorious, not as architecture (in the
sense in which we Europeans, the inheritors of the Par-
thenon, of the Doges' Palace, and of Lincoln Cathedral,
understand the word architecture), but for the elaborate
geometrical figures, the bright flowers and birds and
fabulous beasts, with which the sculptor and painter of
wood has so lavishly adorned them.

The ordinary Japanese house is a light frame-work structure, whose thatched, shingled, or tiled, roof, very heavy in
proportion, is supported on stones with slightly hollowed
tops, resting on the surface of the soil.   There is no foundation, as that word is understood by our architects.   The
house stands on the ground, not partly in it.  Singularity
number two: there are no walls—at least no continuous
walls.   The side of the house, composed at night of wooden
sliding doors, called *amado*, is stowed away in boxes during
the day-time.   In summer, everything is thus open to the
outside air.   In winter, semi-transparent paper slides,
called *shōji*, replace the wooden sliding doors during the
day-time.   The rooms are divided from each other by
opaque paper screens, called *fusuma* or *karakami*, which
run in grooves at the top and bottom.   By taking out these
sliding screens, several rooms can be turned into one.   The
floor of all the living-rooms is covered with thick mats,
made of rushes and perfectly fitted together, so as to leave
no interstices.   As these mats are always of the same
size—6 feet by 3—it is usual to compute the area of a
room by the number of its mats.   Thus you speak of a
six mat room, a ten mat room, etc.   In the dwellings of
the middle classes, rooms of eight, of six, and of four and
a half mats are those oftenest met with.   The kitchen and
passages are not matted, but have a wooden floor, which
is kept brightly polished.   But the passages are few in a
Japanese house, each room opening as a rule into the others
on either side.

When a house has a second storey, this generally covers
but a portion of the ground floor.   The steps leading up
to it resemble a ladder rather than a staircase.   The best
rooms in a Japanese house are almost invariably at the

back, where also is the garden; and they face south, so as
to escape the northern blast in winter and to get the benefit
of the breeze in summer, which then always blows from
the south. They generally have a recess or alcove, ornamented with a painted or written scroll (*kakemono*) and a
vase of flowers. Furniture is conspicuous by its absence.
There are no tables, no chairs, no wash-hand-stands, no
pianoforte,—none of all those thousand and one things
which we cannot do without. The necessity for bedsteads
is obviated by quilts, which are brought in at night and
laid down wherever may happen to be most convenient.
No mahogany dining-table is required in a family where
each member is served separately on a little lacquer tray.
Cupboards are, for the most part, openings in the wall,
screened in by small paper slides—not separate, movable
entities. Whatever treasures the family may possess are
mostly stowed away in an adjacent building, known in the
local English dialect as a "godown," that is, a fire-proof
storehouse with walls of mud or clay.[*]

These details will probably suggest a very uncomfortable
sum total: and Japanese houses *are* supremely uncomfortable to ninety-nine Europeans out of a hundred. Nothing
to sit on, no fire but a brazier to warm oneself by and yet
abundant danger of fire to be burnt out by, no solidity, no
privacy, the deafening clatter twice daily of the opening
and shutting of the outer wooden slides, draughts insidious-
ly pouring in through innumerable chinks and crannies,
darkness whenever heavy rain makes it necessary to shut
up one or more sides of the house—to these and to various
other enormities Japanese houses must plead guilty. Two

---

[*] "Godown" (pronounced go-down, not god-own) is derived from the Malay word *gdong*, "a warehouse."

things, chiefly, are to be said on the other side.  First,
these houses are cheap—an essential point in a poor country.  Secondly, the people who live in them do not share
our European ideas with regard to comfort and discom-
fort.  They do not miss fire-places or stoves, never having
realised the possibility of such elaborate arrangements
for heating.  They do not mind draughts, having been
inured to them from infancy.  In fact an elderly diplomat,
who, during his sojourn in a Japanese hotel, spent well-
nigh his whole time in the vain endeavour to keep doors
shut and chinks patched up, used to exclaim to us, "*Mais
les japonais* ADORENT *les courants d'air !*"  Futhermore,
the physicians who have studied Japanese dwelling-houses
from the point of view of hygiene give them a clean bill of
health.

Leaving this portion of the subject, which is a matter
of taste, not of argument, let us enquire into the origin
of Japanese architecture, which is a matter of research.
Its origin is twofold.  The Japanese Buddhist temple
comes from India, being a modification of a Chinese
modification of the Indian original.  The other Japanese
styles are of native growth.  Shintō temples, Imperial
palaces, and commoners' dwelling-houses are alike devel-
opments of the simple hut of prehistoric times.  Persons
interested in archæological research may like to hear what
Mr. Satow has to say on the little-known subject of
primeval Japanese architecture.  He says* :—

"Japanese antiquarians tell us that in early times,
before carpenter's tools had been invented, the dwellings
of the people who inhabited these islands were con-

---

* We quote from a paper entitled "The Shintō Temples of Izu," printed in
Vol. II of the "Asiatic Transactions."

structed of young trees with the bark on, fastened
together with ropes made of the rush *Suge* (*scirpus
maritimus*), or perhaps with the tough shoots of the
wistaria (*fuji*), and thatched with the grass called *kaya.*
In modern buildings the uprights of a house stand upon
large stones laid on the surface of the earth, but this
precaution against decay had not occurred to the ancients,
who planted the uprights in holes dug in the ground.

"The ground plan of the hut was oblong, with four
corner uprights, and one in the middle of each of the four
sides, those in the sides which formed the ends being long
enough to support the ridge-pole. Other trees were
fastened horizontally from corner to corner, one set near
the ground, one near the top and one set on the top,
the latter of which formed what we call the wall-plates.
Two large rafters whose upper ends crossed each other,
were laid from the wall-plates to the heads of the taller
uprights. The ridge-pole rested in the fork formed by
the upper ends of the rafters crossing each other.
Horizontal poles were then laid along each slope of the
roof, one pair being fastened close up to the exterior
angles of the fork. The rafters were slender poles or
bamboos passed over the ridge-pole and fastened down
on each end to the wall-plates. Next followed the process of putting on the thatch. In order to keep this in
its place two trees were laid along the top, resting in the
forks, and across these two trees were placed short logs at
equal distances, which being fastened to the poles in the
exterior angle of the forks by ropes passed through the
thatch, bound the ridge of the roof firmly together.

"The walls and doors were constructed of rough
matting. It is evident that some tool must have been

used to cut the trees to the required length, and for this purpose a sharpened stone was probably employed. Such stone implements have been found imbedded in the earth in various parts of Japan in company with stone arrow-heads and clubs. Specimens of the ancient style of building may even yet be seen in remote parts of the country, not perhaps so much in the habitations of the peasantry, as in sheds erected to serve a temporary purpose.

" The architecture of the Shintō temples is derived from the primeval hut, with more or less modification in proportion to the influence of Buddhism in each particular case. Those of the purest style retain the thatched roof, others are covered with the thick shingling called *Hiwada-buki*, while others have tiled and even coppered roofs. The projecting ends of the rafters (called *Chigi*) have been somewhat lengthened, and carved more or less elaborately. At the new temple at Kudanzaka, in Yedo, they are shown in the proper position, projecting from the inside of the shingling, but in the majority of cases they merely consist of two pieces of wood in the form of the letter X, which rest on the ridge of the roof like a pack-saddle on a horse's back, to make use of a Japanese writer's comparison. The logs which kept the two trees laid on the ridge in their place have taken the form of short cylindrical pieces of timber tapering towards each extremity, which have been compared by foreigners to cigars. In Japanese they are called *Katsuo-gi*, from their resemblance to the pieces of dried bonito sold under the name of *Katsuo-bushi*. The two trees laid along the roof over the thatch are represented by a single beam, called *Muna-osar*, or 'roof-presser.' Planking has taken the place of the mats with which the sides of the building were originally closed, and the entrance is closed by a pair of folding doors turning, not on hinges, but on what are, I believe, technically called 'journals.' The primeval hut had no flooring, but we find that the shrine has a wooden floor raised some feet above the ground, which arrangement necessitates a sort of balcony all round, and a flight of steps up to the entrance. The transformation is completed in some cases by the addition of a quantity of ornamental metal-work in brass."

Mr. Satow's account of the palaces of early days is as follows* : "The palace of the Japanese sovereign was a wooden hut, with its pillars planted in the ground, instead of being erected upon broad flat stones as in modern buildings. The whole frame-work, consisting of posts, beams, rafters, door-posts and window-frames, was tied together with cords made by twisting the long fibrous stems of climbing plants, such as *Puraria thunbergiana* (*kuzu*) and *Wistaria sinensis* (*fuji*.) The floor must have been low down, so that the occupants of the building, as they squatted or lay on their mats, were exposed to the stealthy attacks of venomous snakes, which were probably far more numerous in the earliest ages when the country was for the most part uncultivated, than at the present day............ There seems some reason to think that the *yuka*, here translated floor, was originally nothing but a couch which ran round the sides of the hut, the rest of the space being simply a mud-floor, and that the size of the couch was gradually increased until it occupied the whole interior. The rafters projected upward beyond the ridge-pole, crossing each other, as is seen in the roofs of modern Shintō

* See an elaborate paper on "Ancient Japanese Rituals," in Vol. IX, Part II, of the "Asiatic Transactions."

temples, whether their architecture be in conformity with early traditions (in which case all the rafters are so crossed) or modified in accordance with more advanced principles of construction, and the crossed rafters retained only as ornaments at the two ends of the ridge. The roof was thatched, and perhaps had a gable at each end, with a hole to allow the smoke of the wood-fire to escape, so that it was possible for birds flying in and perching on the beams overhead, to defile the food, or the fire with which it was cooked."

To this description of Mr. Satow's, it should be added that fences were in use, and that the wooden doors, sometimes fastened by means of hooks, resembled those with which we are familiar in Europe rather than the sliding, screen-like doors of modern Japan. The windows seem to have been mere holes. Rush-matting and rugs consisting of skins were occasionally brought in to sit upon, and we even hear once or twice of " silk rugs " being used for the same purpose by the noble and wealthy.

Since 1870, the Japanese have begun to exchange their own methods of building for what is locally termed "foreign style," doubtless, as a former resident[*] has wittily observed, because foreign to all known styles of architecture. This "foreign style " is, indeed, not one, but multiform. There is the rabbit-warren style, exemplified in the streets at the back of the Ginza in Tōkyō. There is the wooden shanty or bathing-machine style, of which the new Houses of Parliament promise us a specimen on a large scale. There is the cruet-stand style, so strikingly exemplified in the Yokohama Custom-House. The Brobdingnaggian pigeon-house style is re-

[*] Mr. R. G. Holtham, in his " Eight Years in Japan."

presented here and there both in wood and stone. Its
chief feature is having no windows, at least, none to
speak of. After all, these things are Japan's misfortune,
not her fault. She has discovered Europe, architecturally
speaking, at the wrong moment. We cannot with any
grace blame a nation whom we have ourselves misled.
If Japan's contemporary efforts in architecture are worse
even than ours, it is chiefly because her people have
less money to dispose of. (See also Article on SHINTŌ).

*Books recommended.* "Japanese Homes," by Prof. E. S. Morse.—"Domestic Architecture in Japan," and "Further Notes on Japanese Architecture," by Josiah Conder, F.R.I.B.A., printed in the "Transactions of the Royal Institute of British Architects," 1886-p. Both the above authors have illustrated their works profusely, Prof. Morse giving representations, not only of architectural details proper, but of all the fittings and domestic articles of a middle-class Japanese household. Mr. Conder gives drawings of temples and palaces.—"The Feudal Mansions of Yedo," by T. R. H. McClatchie, in Vol. VII. Part III. of the "Asiatic Transactions." This is a full description of the *yashiki* or *daimyō's* residences.—For what the doctors have to say about Japanese houses from a sanitary point of view, see Drs. Seymour and Beale, in Vol. XVII. Part II. pp. 17—21, of the "Asiatic Transactions."—There are other papers by Messrs. McClatchie, Brunton, and Cawley, more or less concerned with Japanese architecture, scattered through the "Asiatic Transactions."—See also Prof. Milne's paper "On Construction in Earthquake Countries," in Vol. XI of the "Transactions of the Seismological Society of Japan," and the still more elaborate paper bearing the same title and forming the whole of Vol. XIV.

**Armour.** Japanese armour might serve as a text for
those authors who love to discourse on the unchanging
character of the East. Our own Middle Ages witnessed
revolutions in the style of armour as complete as any that
have taken place in the Paris fashions during the last three
hundred years. In Japan, on the contrary, from the beginning of true feudalism in the twelfth century down to
its extinction in 1871, there was scarcely any change.
The older specimens are rather the better, rather the more
complete; the newer are often rather heavier, owing to the
use of a greater number of plates and scales; that is all.

It is true that in quite old times Japanese armour was still
imperfect.  Cloth and the hides of animals seem to have
been the materials then employed.  But metal armour had
already established itself in general use by the eighth century of our era.  The weapons, too, then known were
the same as a millennium later, with the exception of fire-
arms, which began to creep in during the sixteenth century
in the wake of intercourse with the early Portuguese adventurers.  Those who are interested in the subject, either
theoretically or as purchasers of suits of armour brought to
them by curio-vendors, will find a full description in the
second part of Conder's " History of Japanese Costume,"
printed in Vol. IX, Part III, of the " Asiatic Transactions."
They can there read to their hearts' content about corse-
lets, taces, greaves, mamellières, brassarts, and many other
deep matters not known to the vulgar.

**Army.**  For many centuries—say from A.D. 1200 to
1867—" soldier " and " gentleman " (*samurai*) were con-
vertible terms.  To fight was not only a duty but a pleasure,
in a state of society where the security of feudal possessions
depended on the strong arm of the baron himself and of his
trusty lieges.  This was the order of things down to A.D.
1600.  Thenceforward, though peace reigned for two and a
half centuries under the vigorous administration of the
Tokugawa Shōguns, all the military forms of an elder day
were kept up.  They were suddenly shivered into atoms at
the beginning of the present Mikado's reign (A.D. 1868).
Military advisers were then called in, first from France and
then from Germany, the Continental system of universal
conscription was introduced, uniforms of European cut
replaced the picturesque but cumbersome trappings of the

old Japanese knight, and in a word, Japan—possessing, as she has ever done, that military spirit which is the *sine qud non* of all military excellence—Japan stands forth to-day with an army, which, though small, would do no discredit to many a country in Europe. According to the latest published statistics, the Japanese army comprises 196,620 men, all told. Of these, 107,673 form the reserve, and 32,717 the territorial army. It is further necessary to deduct 1,422 for the gensdarmes, 1,186 for the military colony in Yezo, and 3,920 for the military schools. The actual fighting strength of the army in ordinary times is thus a little under 50,000, or was so on the 31st December, 1886, the date to which the statistics refer. Tōkyō, Sendai, Nagoya, Ōsaka, Hiroshima, and Kumamoto are the chief military stations in the Empire, with garrisons varying from 8000 to 6000 men each. The Imperial Guard contains between 4000 and 5000 men. The commander-in-chief is His Imperial Highness Prince Arisugawa Taruhito, a near kinsman of the Mikado's.

**Art.** The beginnings of Japanese art, as of almost all things Japanese excepting cleanliness, are to be sought in China. Even after Japanese art had started on its independent career, it refreshed its inspiration from time to time by a careful study and imitation of Chinese models; and Chinese masterpieces still occupy in the estimation of Japanese connoisseurs a place only hesitatingly allowed to the best native works. Even Chinese subjects preponderate in the classical schools of Japan. Speaking of the productions of the classical Japanese painters, Dr. Anderson says : "It may safely be asserted that not one in twenty of the productions of these painters, who to the present day are

considered to represent the true genius of Japanese art, was
inspired by the works of nature as seen in their own beautiful country."

The first native painter of eminence was Kose-no-Kana-
oka, a court noble who flourished in the ninth century after
Christ, but scarcely any of whose works remain. That the
art of painting, especially on screens, was assiduously cultivated at the Japanese court during the ninth and tenth
centuries is proved by numerous references in literature.
But it was not till about the year 1000 that the *Yamato Ryū*
(lit. "Japanese School"), the first concerning which we
have much positive knowledge, was established by an artist
named Motomitsu. This school contained within itself the
seed of most of the peculiarities that have characterised
Japanese art ever since, with its neglect of perspective, its
impossible mountains, its quaint dissection of roofless in-
teriors, its spirited burlesques of solemn processions, wherein frogs, insects, or hobgoblins take the place of men. In
the thirteenth century this school assumed the name of the
*Tosa Ryū*, and confined itself thenceforward more and more
to classical subjects. Its former humourous strain had been
caught as early as the twelfth century by Toba Sōjō, a
rollicking priest, who, about A.D. 1140, distinguished himself by drawings coarse in both senses of the word, but full
of verve and drollery. These are the so-called *Toba-e*.
Toba Sōjō founded a school. To found a school was
*de rigueur* in Old Japan, where originality was so little
understood that it was supposed that any eminent man's
descendants or pupils, to the twentieth generation, ought
to be able to do the same sort of work as their ancestor
had done. But none of the jovial abbot's followers are
worthy of mention alongside of him.

The fifteenth century was the most glorious period of
Japanese painting. It is a strange coincidence that Italian
painting should then also have been at its zenith. But it
is apparently a coincidence only, there being no facts to
warrant us in assuming any influence of the one on the
other. The greatest names are Chō-Densu and Jōsetsu,
painters of Buddhist subjects. Both of these died early in
the century. They were succeeded by Mitsunobu, the
greatest painter of the Tosa School, and by Sesshū, Shūbun,
and Kanō Masanobu, all of whom were founders of independent schools. The first Kanō's son, Kanō Motonobu,
was more eminent than his father. He handed down the
tradition to his own sons and grandsons, and the Kanō
School continues to be, even at the present day, the chief
stronghold of classicism in Japan. By "classicism" we
mean partly a peculiar technique, partly an adherence to
Chinese methods, models, and subjects, such as portraits
of Chinese sages and delineations of Chinese landscapes,
which are represented of course not from nature but at
second-hand.

The quiet harmonious colouring and the bold calligraphic
drawing of these Japanese "old masters" have justly excited the admiration of succeeding generations of their
countrymen. But the circle of ideas within which the
Kanōs, the Sesshūs, the Shūbuns, and the other classical
Japanese painters move, is too narrow and peculiar for their
productions to be ever likely to gain much hold on the
esteem of Europe. European collectors—such men as
Gonse, for instance—have been looked down on by certain
enthusiasts in Japan for the preference which they evince
for Hokusai and the modern popular school (Ukiyo-e Ryū)
generally. It is very bold of us to venture to express an

opinion on such a matter; but we think that the instinct
which led Gonse and others, to Hokusai led them right,—
that Japanese art was itself led to Hokusai by a legitimate
and most fortunate process of development, that it was led
out of the close atmosphere of academical conventionality
into the fresh air of heaven.

The beginning of the popular movement may be traced
as far back as the end of the sixteenth century in the person of Iwasa Matahei, the originator of the droll sketches
known as *Ôtsu-é*.  But a whole century elapsed before
Hishigawa Moronobu and Hanabusa Itchô began to devote
themselves to the illustration of books in colours and in
popular realistic style.  Then, in the eighteenth century,
came Ôkyo, the founder of the style known as the *Shijô
Ryû*, from the street in Kyôto where the master resided.
Ôkyo made a genuine effort to copy nature, instead of
only talking about doing so, as had been the habit of
the older schools.  His astonishingly correct representations of fishes, his pupil Sosen's portraitures of monkeys,
and other striking triumphs of detail were the result.  But
none of the members of Ôkyo's school succeeded in dis-
embarrassing themselves altogether from the immemorial
conventionalities of their nation when combining various
details into a large composition.  Their naturalism, however, gave an immense impulse, to the popularisation of
art.  A whole cloud of artisan-artists arose,—no longer
the representatives of privileged ancient families, but commoners who drew pictures of the life around them to
suit the genuine taste of the public of their own time
and class.  Art was released from its mediæval Chinese
swaddling-clothes, and allowed to mix in the society of
living men and women.  And what a quaint, picturesque

society it was—that of the time, say, between 1750 and
1850—the "Old Japan" which all now know and appreciate, because the works of the Artisan School have
carried its fame round the world!

The chief of the artisan workers was he whom we call
Hokusai, though his real original name was Nakajima
Tetsujirō, and his *noms de pinceau* were legion. During
the course of an unusually long life (1760—1849), this man,
whose only possessions were his brush and his palette,
poured forth a continuous stream of novel and vigorous
creations in the form of illustrations to books and of
separate coloured sheets—illustrations and sheets which
included, as Dr. Anderson justly says, "the whole range
of Japanese art motives, scenes of history, drama, and
novel, incidents in the daily life of his own class, realis-
ations of familiar objects of animal and vegetable life,
wonderful suggestions of the scenery of his beloved Yedo
and its surroundings, and a hundred other inspirations
that would require a volume to describe." Contemporary
workers in the art of colour-printing were Toyokuni, Kuni-
sada, Shigenobu, Hiroshige, and others in plenty. Then,
in 1853, four years after Hokusai's death, came Commodore Perry, the mere threat of whose cannon shivered
the old civilisation of Japan into fragments. Japanese
art perished. Kyōsai, who survived till 1889, was its
last genuine representative in an uncongenial age. His
favourite subjects had a certain grim appropriateness:
they were ghosts and skeletons. Charity compels us to
draw a veil over the productions of many so-called painters, which, during the last few years, have encumbered
the shop-windows of Tōkyō and disfigured the walls of
exhibitions got up in imitation of European usage. They

seem to be manufactured by the gross. If not worth
much, there are at least plenty of them.

Japanese art is distinguished by directness, facility, and
strength of line, a sort of bold dash due probably to the
habit of writing and drawing from the elbow, not from the
wrist. This, so to say, *calligraphic* quality is what gives a
charm to the merest rough Japanese sketch. It has been
well remarked that if a Japanese artist's work be carried no
further even than the outlines, you will still have something
worthy to be hung on your wall or inserted in your album.
Japanese art disregards the laws of perspective and of light
and shadow. Though sometimes faultlessly accurate in
natural details, it scorns to be tied down to such accuracy
as to an ever-binding rule. Even in the same picture—say,
one of a bird perched on a tree—you may have the bird
exact in every detail, the tree a sort of conventional short-
hand symbol. Or you may have a bamboo which is perfection, but part of it blurred by an artificial atmosphere
which no meteorological eccentricity could place where
the painter has placed it; or else two sea-coasts one above
another—each beautiful and poetical, only how in the world
could they have got into such a relative position? The
Japanese artist does not trouble his head about such matters. He is, in his limited way, a poet, not a photographer.
Our painters of the impressionist school undertake less to
paint actual scenes than to render their own feelings in
presence of such scenes. The Japanese artist goes a step
further: he paints the feelings evoked by the *memory* of
the scenes, the feelings when one is between waking and
dreaming. He is altogether an idealist, and this at both
ends of the scale, the beautiful and the grotesque. Were
he able to work on a large canvas, a very great ideal art

might have been the result. But in art, as in literature,
his nation seems lacking in the genius, the breadth of view,
necessary for making grand combinations. It stops at the
small, the pretty, the isolated, the vignette. Hence the
admirable adaptability of Japanese art to decorative purposes. In decoration, too, some of its more obvious defects retire into the background. Who would look on the
side of a tea-pot for a rigid observance of perspective?
Still less in miniature ivory carvings, such as the *netsukes*,
in the ornaments of sword-guards, the bas-reliefs on bronze
vases, and the patterns in pieces (and many of them are
masterpieces) of embroidery. As decoration for small sur-
faces, Japanese art has already begun to conquer the world.
In the days before Japanese ideas became known to Europe, people there used to consider it essential to have the
patterns on plates, cushions, and what not, arranged with
geometrical accuracy. If on the right hand there was a
cupid looking to the left, then on the left hand there must
be a cupid of exactly the same size looking to the right,
and the chief feature of the design was invariably in the
exact centre. The Japanese artisan-artists have shown us
that this mechanical symmetry does not make for beauty.
They have taught us the charm of irregularity; and if the
world owe them but this one lesson, Japan may yet be
proud of what she has accomplished.

There exists, it is true, nowadays a small band of foreign
enthusiasts, who deny that the art of Japan is thus limited
in its scope and decorative rather than representative.
Having studied it with greater zeal and profit than they
have studied European art, they go so far as to put Japanese art on a pinnacle high above that of Greece and Italy.
These enthusiasts have performed and are still performing

a useful function.  They are disseminating a knowledge of
Japanese art abroad, disseminating it, too, in Japan itself,
where it had been suffered to fall into neglect.  But their
cult of Japanese art partakes of the nature of a religious
faith, and, like other religionists, they are apt to be deficient
in the sense of humour.  They are much too much in earnest ever to smile about such serious matters.  The other
side has to do that for them.  For instance, one of these
apostles of japonism in art recently told the public that the
late painter Kyōsai "was perhaps the greatest limner of
crows that Japan, nay the whole world, has produced."
Does this not remind you of the artist in whose epitaph it
was recorded that he was "the Raphael of cats?"  The
Japanese are undoubtedly Raphaels of fishes, and insects,
and flowers, and bamboo-stems swaying in the breeze ; and
they have given us charming fragments of idealised scenery.
But they have never succeeded in adequately transferring
to canvas "the human form divine," they have never made
grand historical scenes live again before the eyes of posterity, they have never, like the early Italian masters, drawn
away men's hearts from earth to heaven in an ecstasy of
adoration.  In a word, Japanese art, as Mr. Alfred East
tersely said, when lecturing on the subject in Tōkyō, is
"great in small things, but small in great things."  (See
also Articles on ARCHITECTURE, CARVING, METAL-WORK,
MUSIC, and PORCELAIN.)

N.B.  A curious fact, to which we have never seen
attention drawn, is that the Japanese language has no
genuine native word for "art."  To translate the European term "fine art," there has recently been invented
the compound bi-jutsu, by putting together the two Chinese characters bi 美, "beautiful," and jutsu 術, "craft,"

"device," "leger-de-main." But this compound is only understood by the educated. The Japanese language is similarly devoid of any satisfactory word for "nature." The nearest equivalents are *seishitsu*, "characteristic qualities;" *banbutsu*, "all things;" *tennen*, "spontane-ously." This curious philological fact makes it difficult, with the best will and skill in the world, to reproduce most of our discussions on art and nature in a manner that shall be intelligible to those Japanese who know no European language.

*Books recommended.* The above article is founded chiefly on Dr. Wm. Anderson's essay on Japanese Pictorial Art, forming Section 23 of the Introduction to Satow and Hawes' "Handbook for Japan." See also the same author's "History of Japanese Art," in Vol. VII. Part IV, of the "Asiatic Transactions," and especially his admirable engraved opus, "The Pictorial Arts of Japan," with its companion work, the "Catalogue of Japanese and Chinese Paintings in the British Museum."—From among a crowd of recent works bearing on the same subject, we may select "L'Art Japonais," by A. Gonse, and Huish's handy little volume entitled "Japan and Its Art." Great things are expected by Professor Fenollosa's numerous friends from the exhaustive treatise on the subject which that learned connoisseur is believed to be preparing.

**Asiatic Society of Japan.** This society was founded in October, 1872, for "the collection of information and the investigation of subjects relating to Japan or other Asiatic countries." The two seats of the Society are Tōkyō and Yokohama. The entrance fee is $5, and the yearly fee like-wise $5 to residents, but $3 to non-residents. It is also optional to non-residents to become life-members by paying the entrance fee and an additional sum of $16. Members are elected by the council of the society. Persons desirous of becoming members should, therefore, apply to the secre-tary or to some other member of the council. Members receive the "Transactions of the Asiatic Society of Japan" free, from the date of their election, and have the privilege

of purchasing back numbers at half-price. These are the
"Asiatic Transactions," so often referred to in the course
of the present work. Scarcely a subject connected with
Japan but is to be found learnedly discussed in the pages
of the "Asiatic Transactions." A "General Index to
the Asiatic Transactions," recently published by Messrs.
Kelly and Walsh, of Yokohama, is invaluable for reference.

Besides the Asiatic Society, there is in Tōkyō a German
Society, entitled *Deutsche Gesellschaft für Natur- und Völkerkunde Ostasiens*, the scope of whose labours is closely
similar, and whose valuable *Mittheilungen*, or "German
Asiatic Transactions," as we have ventured to call them
when quoting them, are strongly recommended to readers
familiar with the German language. This Society was
founded in 1873.

**Bandai-San.** Bandai-San is a volcano in the province
of Iwashiro and on the borders of Lake Inawashiro, lat.
37' 36' N., long. 140' 6' E. It is 6000 feet in height.
Tradition tells us that devils inhabited it in ancient days,
and that, by their infernal agency, terrible convulsions of
nature and consequent loss of life took place somewhere
about A. D. 806. From that time the mountain remained
comparatively quiet until 7. 45 A. M. on the 15th July,
1888, when a tremendous eruption took place, blowing
out one whole side of the mountain, and precipitating
fifteen hundred and eighty-seven million cubic yards of
mud, rock, and ashes over the surrounding country.
Among the villages destroyed, were three much frequented by the people of the neighbourhood on account of
their mineral waters. The total number of lives lost was

four hundred and sixty-one, and seventy persons were wounded.

**Books recommended.** A detailed scientific account has been published, under the title of "The Eruption of Bandai-San," by S. Sekiya, professor of seismology of the Imperial University. This forms Vol. III, Pt. II, of the "Journal of the College of Science of the Imperial University of Japan."—A more popular account has been republished from the "Japan Mail" newspaper, under the same title.

**Bathing.** Cleanliness is one of the few original items of Japanese civilisation. Almost all other things Japanese have their root in China, but not tubs. We read in the Japanese mythology that the god Izanagi, on returning from a visit to his dead wife in Hades, purified himself in the waters of a stream. Ceremonial purifications continue to form part of the Shintō ritual. But viewed generally, the cleanliness in which the Japanese excel the rest of mankind has nothing to do with godliness. They are clean for the personal satisfaction of being clean. Their hot baths—for they almost all bathe in very hot water of about 110° Fahrenheit—also help to keep them warm in winter. For, though moderately hot water gives a chilly reaction, this is not the case when the water is extremely hot, neither is there then any fear of catching cold. There are some eight hundred public baths in the city of Tōkyō, in which it is calculated that three hundred thousand persons bathe daily, at a cost of 1 *sen* 3 *rin* (about a halfpenny of English money) per head. A reduction of 3 *rin* is made for children. In addition to this, every respectable private house has its own bath-room. Other cities and even villages are similarly provided. Where there are neither bathing establishments nor private bath-rooms, the people take their tubs out-of-doors, unless indeed a policeman, charged with carrying out the new regulations, happens to be prowling about the neighbourhood: for cleanliness is more esteemed by the Japanese than our artificial Western prudery.

Some Europeans have tried to pick holes in the Japanese system, saying that the bathers put on their dirty clothes when they have dried themselves. True, the Japanese of the old school have nothing so perfect as our system of daily renovated linen. But as the bodies even of the men of the lowest class are washed and scrubbed daily, it is hardly to be supposed that their garments, though perhaps dusty outside, can be very dirty within. A Japanese crowd is the sweetest in the world. The charm of the Japanese system of hot bathing is proved by the fact that almost all the foreigners resident in the country abandon their cold tubs in its favour. There seems, too, to be something in the climate which renders hot baths healthier than cold. By persisting in the use of cold water one man gets rheumatism, a second gets fever, a third a never-ending continuance of colds and coughs. So nearly all end by coming round to the Japanese plan.

The Japanese passion for bathing leads all classes to make extensive use of the hot mineral springs in which their volcano-studded land abounds. Sometimes they carry their enjoyment of this natural luxury to an almost incredible extreme. At Kawanaka, a tiny spa not far from Ikao in the province of Jōshū—one of those places, of which there are many in Japan, which look as if they were at the very end of the world, so steep are the mountains shutting them in on every side—the bathers stay in the water for a month on end, with a stone on their lap to prevent them from floating in their sleep. The care-taker of the establishment, a hale old man of seventy, stays in the bath during the entire winter. To be sure, the water is, in this particular case, one or two degrees below blood heat. Thus alone is so strange a life rendered possible. In another case, some of the inhabitants of a certain village famed for its hot springs excused themselves to the present writer for their dirtiness during the busy summer months: "For," said they, "we have only time to bathe twice a day." "How often, then, do you bathe in winter?" "Oh! about four or five times daily. The children get into the bath whenever they feel cold."

**Bibliography.** Léon Pagès' "*Bibliographie Japonaise*" is excellent, so far as it goes, for European books on Japan; but it only goes down to the year 1859. It gives seven hundred and fifteen titles. Though not a regular bibliography, Mr. Satow's admirable article on Japanese Literature in the "American Cyclopædia" gives the titles of a considerable number of native Japanese books. The *Gunsho Ichiran*, published in 1801, is the standard Japanese authority on the subject; but it is very imperfect, the severely classical tastes of the compiler not having permitted him to take any notice of novels and other modern popular works.

**Blackening the Teeth.** This ugly custom is at least as old as A. D. 920; but the reason for it is unknown. It was finally prohibited in the case of men in the year 1870. A black-toothed woman of the old school may, however, still be seen from time to time even at the present day. Every married woman in the land had her teeth blackened, until the present Empress set the example of discontinuing the practice. Fortunately the efficacy of the preparation used wears out after a few days, so that the ladies of Japan experienced no difficulty in getting their mouths white again. Mr. Mitford, in his amusing "Tales of Old Japan," gives the following recipe for tooth-blacking, as having been supplied to him by a fashionable Yedo druggist :—"Take three pints of water, and, having warmed it, add half a teacupful of wine.* Put into this mixture a quantity of red-hot iron ; allow it to stand for five or six days, when there will be a scum on the top of the mixture, which should then be poured into a small teacup and placed near a fire. When it is warm, powdered gall-nuts and iron filings should be added to it, and the whole should be warmed again. The liquid is then painted on to the teeth by means of a soft feather brush, with more powdered gall-nuts and iron, and, after several applications, the desired colour will be obtained."

**Bonin Islands.** This little archipelago, called by the Japanese *Muninlō* (lit. "the Uninhabited Islands") or *Ogasawara-jima*, is situated some five hundred miles to the south of Yokohama, whence it may be reached by steamers which take about three weeks to do the round tour of the Bonins and the Seven Isles of Idzu. A stay of about a week is generally made at Port Lloyd, the chief harbour in the archipelago. The dates of sailing are irregular. Apparently discovered in A. D. 1593 by a *daimyō* named Ogasawara Sadayori, the Bonins were never properly colonised. In A. D. 1827, Captain Beechey, R. N., hoisted the flag of Great Britain at Port Lloyd. Later, in 1853, Perry, the celebrated American commodore, endeavoured to establish a republican government among the English-

---

* By "wine" must of course be meant Japanese saké.

speaking waifs and strays who then formed the population
of the islands—shipwrecked whalers, disorderly seamen
left behind by their skippers, *Kanakas* from the South Sea
Islands, etc. But nothing came of either of these acts of
well-meant interference, and since the seventies the sovereign right of Japan to the archipelago has been no more
disputed. In October, 1880, the administration was placed
under the control of the Governor of Tōkyō, and the resident foreigners were naturalised as Japanese subjects.
From 1886 to 1888 the Bonins attracted a certain amount
of public attention, because they were fixed on by the
Japanese as the place of exile for the unsuccessful Korean
patriot, Kim Ok-Kyūn. The chief products are turtles,
goats, poultry, lemons, and bananas.

**Books recommended.** "The Bonin Islands," by Russell Robertson, printed in
Vol. IV of the "Asiatic Transactions."—"Narrative of a Voyage to the Pacific," by
Captain Beechey. But this is an old book (1831), and probably out of print.

**Books on Japan.** Léon Pagès, in his "*Bibliographie
Japonaise*," enumerates seven hundred and fifteen works
in European languages bearing more or less directly on
Japan. Yet this list was published as far back as 1859,
that is, broadly speaking, before the world had turned its
attention to Japan at all. If there were seven hundred
then, there must be seventy times seven hundred now.
In fact, *not* to have written a book about Japan is fast
becoming a title to distinction. The art of Japan, the
history of Japan, the language, folk-lore, botany, even the
earthquakes and the diseases of Japan—each of these, with,
many other subjects, has a little library to itself. Then
there are the works of an encyclopedic character, and
there are the books of travel. Some of the latter possess
great value, as photographing Japanese manners for us

at certain periods.  Others are at the rodinary low level
of globe-trotting literature—twaddle enlivened by statistics
at second-hand.

We give references at the end of most of the articles of
this work to the chief authorities on each special subject.
At the risk of offending innumerable authors, we now
venture to pick out the following ten works (ten is the
Japanese dozen), as probably the best in a general way that
are accessible to English readers.  Of course it is more
than possible that some of the really best have escaped our
notice or our memory.  Anyhow, an imperfect list will perhaps be deemed better than none at all :—

1. Dr. Rein's "JAPAN," with its sequel, "THE IN-
DUSTRIES OF JAPAN."*  No person wishing to study Japan
seriously can dispense with these admirable volumes.  Of
the two, that on the "Industries" is the better :—agriculture, cattle-raising, forestry, mines, lacquer-work, metal-
work, commerce, etc., etc.,—everything, in fact, has been
studied with a truly German patience, and is set forth
with a truly German thoroughness.  The other volume
is occupied with the physiography of the country, that
is, its geography, fauna, flora, etc., and with an account of
the people both historical and ethnographical, and with
the topography of the various provinces.

2. "THE MIKADO'S EMPIRE," by the Rev. W. E. Griffis.
This is the book best calculated to give the general reader
just what he requires, and to give it to him in a manner
less technical than Rein's.  The first part is devoted to
the history, the second to the author's personal experiences

* Though Dr. Rein is a German and his work was first published in the German
language, the English edition is to be preferred.  For, writes the author in his preface,
"the English translation is based on a careful revision of the original, and may be
considered a new and improved edition of it."

and to Japanese life in modern days. The fifth edition
brings the story down to 1886. More than one reader
of cultivated taste has, indeed, complained of the author's
tendency to "gush," and of the occasional tawdriness of
his style.† But these faults are on the surface, and do
not touch the genuine value of the book.

3. Murray's "HANDBOOK TO CENTRAL AND NORTHERN
JAPAN," by Ernest Satow and A.G.S. Hawes. (See Article
on GUIDE-BOOKS.)

4. The "TRANSACTIONS OF THE ASIATIC SOCIETY OF
JAPAN." There is scarcely a subject connected with Japan
that is not treated of in the pages of these "Transactions." Of course they are not light reading. They
appeal rather to the serious student, who will have nearly
all that he requires if he joins to a perusal of them that
of Rein's work; for the "Asiatic Transactions" are
strongest exactly where Rein is weakest, namely, in
questions of literature and history. Thus the two supplement each other.

5. "JAPAN AS IT WAS AND IS," by Richard Hildreth, an
excellent book, in which the gist of what the various early
travellers have left us concerning Japan is woven together
into one continuous narrative, the exact text of the originals being adhered to as much as possible.

6. "YOUNG JAPAN," by J. R. Black. Mr. Black was one
of the earliest foreign residents of Yokohama, and editor
of various newspapers both in English and in Japanese.
His book is, so to say, the diary of the foreign settlement
at Yokohama from 1858 to 1879, that is, during the two
most eventful decades of modern Japanese history. It

† Thus the name is spoken of as the "nasal ornament," a volcano is a state of eruption is said to "ulcer its crater jaws," laughing is called an "explosion of risibilities,"
etc., etc

records events and impressions, not indeed with any great
literary skill, but with that particular vividness which
contemporary memoirs, jotted down from day to day, as
the events they describe are unfolding themselves, can
alone possess. A perusal of "Young Japan" will help
fair-minded persons to rate at their true value many of
the generalisations of authors of a later time or who have
written at a distance.

7. "THE CAPITAL OF THE TYCOON," by Sir Rutherford
Alcock. Though published more than a quarter of a century ago, and though, as a narrative, it covers only the
brief space of three years (1859-1862), this book is still
delightful and profitable reading. In its pages we live with
the fathers of the men who rule Japan to-day. True, these
men may reject the application to their case of the proverb
which says "like father, like son." But we foreign lookers-
on, who perhaps after all see something of the game, must
be permitted to hold a different opinion, and to believe
that even in cases, so exceptional as Japan's, the political
and social questions of a country can only then be fairly
comprehended when its past is constantly borne in mind.
Sir Rutherford's book combines the light touch of the
skilled diplomat and man of the world with the careful
research of the genuine student.

8. "DESCRIPTIVE AND HISTORICAL CATALOGUE OF JAP-
ANESE AND CHINESE PAINTINGS IN THE BRITISH MUSEUM,"
by Dr. Wm. Anderson. Such a title does an injustice
to what is really an original and valuable book. Who
would think of spending $7.50 on a catalogue? But
this so-called catalogue is really a mine of information
on numberless things Japanese. To begin with, it gives
a complete history of Japanese pictorial art. Then the

author's painstaking research, with the assistance of Mr. Satow, into the "motives" of this art—drawn, as they are, from the history of the country, from its religions, its superstitions, its literature, its famous sites—has shed a flood of light on these and many kindred subjects. Not that the book is easy reading, or meant to be read at all continuously. Still, the store of anecdotes which it contains will interest every person, who, when confronted by a Japanese picture or other *objet d'art*, prefers knowing what it is about to gaping at it ignorantly.

9. "TALES OF OLD JAPAN," by A. B. Mitford. Love, revenge, "the happy despatch," adventure by land and sea, quaint fairy-tales, Buddhist sermons quainter still—in a word, the whole picturesque life of Old Japan—these are the things which Mr. Mitford gives us; and he gives them in a style that renders them doubly attractive.

10. "UNBEATEN TRACKS IN JAPAN," by Miss Bird. Though now ten years old, this remains, to our thinking, the best English book of Japanese travel. The account of the Ainos in the second volume is specially interesting.

Where one has hundreds of books to choose from, such a list as the above might of course be indefinitely extended. Mr. Percival Lowell's "*Soul of the Far East*," for instance, starts to our recollection at once, with its brilliant battle-array of metaphysical epigrams to prove that the Japanese have no soul or at least no individuality. So also do Adams' "*History of Japan*," Mounsey's "*Satsuma Rebellion*," Dickins' multifarious writings on Japanese subjects, Pearson's amusing "*Flights Inside and Outside Paradise*," which is the book of all others to while away a wet day at a tea-house, Dening's "*Life of Hideyoshi*"

17005

and "*Japan in Days of Yore,*" and ever so many more which we cannot enumerate. Then, too, there are the books in foreign languages—such, for instance, as Aimé Humbert's "*Le Japon et les Japonais,*" and Appert's excellent little book of reference, entitled "*Ancien Japon.*" Of Pierre Loti's books, the opinion of the resident French community seems to be but little favourable. Nevertheless, the illustrations to his "*Madame Chrysanthème*" are very pretty, and the letter-press seems to us well-worth skimming through, though the volume is in no-wise to be recommended either to misses or missionaries. What has struck us as the liveliest and best of all popular books on Japan is in German. We mean Netto's "*Papierschmetterlinge aus Japan,*" with its delightful illustrations and its epigrammatic text. With more serious works, too, the Germans are naturally to the front. The "*Mittheilungen*" of the German Asiatic Society (*Deutsche Gesellschaft für Natur und Völkerkunde Ostasiens*) are a mine of information on matters scientific, legal, etc., etc.

Not content with the reality of Japan as it is or as it was, some imaginative writers have begun to found novels on Japanese subjects. We thus have books such as "*Arimas,*" which is whimsical and clever, "*A Captive of Love,*" "*A Muramasa Blade,*" "*Mito Yashiki,*" and others that we have never been able to make up our mind to read. As for books of travel, there is literally no end to the making of them. Almost every possible space of time, from "*Seven Weeks in Japan*" to "*Eight Years in Japan*" and "*Nine Years in Nipon,*" has furnished the title for a volume. There are "*Expeditions to Japan,*" "*Sketches of Japan,*" "*Runs in Japan,*" "*Journeys,*"

"*Travels,*" "*Trips,*" "*Excursions,*" "*Impressions,*" etc., etc., *ad infinitum*—some, no doubt, of considerable value, many not worth the paper they are printed on. The most entertaining specimen, perhaps, of globe-trotting literature is Miss Margaretha Weppner's "*North Star and Southern Cross.*" We do not wish to make any statement which cannot be verified, and therefore we will *not* say that the author is as mad as a March hare; but the book is as funny *as if* it had been written by a March hare. Her *idée fixe* seems to have been that every foreign man in Yokohama and "Jeddo" meditated an assault on her. As for the Japanese, she dismisses them as "disgusting creatures."*

More edifying, if less amusing, than such works are the various monographs on special subjects, particularly those on art. Such are Gonse's "*L'Art Japonais,*" Audsley

---

* Here is a portion of this authoress's description of Yokohama and its foreign residents.—

"It will be well understood that the life of the European in Japan is, after all, a wretched one. The senses and the animal appetite are abundantly provided for; but the mind, the heart, and the soul are left totally destitute. There are clubs, it is true, but at the time of my stay in Yokohama, they were mere gastronomical resorts. The pure-minded men of the island live at home, where they can enjoy just as much comfort as in the clubs, and are rarely seen in them, except when dramatic companies, comedians, whistlers, or such people visit this land. A few of the better Europeans visit the club in full time.

"I had occasion to remark during my stay in Yokohama that the perennial monotony of the place, and the sensual life led there, have reduced many of them to a state bordering on imbecility. It was difficult to believe that the drivelling trash which they talked could have its origin in the head at all. The eyes of such men are dull, and they have a blank of idiotic stare. They see and hear only what directly attracts the stomach and senses. It is useless moralising further on this subject, but I cannot refrain from adding that the impression produced upon a healthy mind by this continuous amusement is very disheartening. Often when contemplating the superb scenery among which these depraved creatures live, I have involuntarily exclaimed in the words of the poet

'Though every prospect pleases,
And only man is vile.'"

and Bowes' various publications on "*Keramic Art*,"
"*Seals*," and "*Enamels*," Huish's handy little "*Japan and
Its Art*," Franks' and Dresser's books, and, above all,
Anderson's "*Pictorial Art of Japan*," which is a magnificent work, conceived in a critical spirit, written with
competent knowledge, and beautifully illustrated. Morse's
"*Japanese Homes*" is a fascinating account, not only of
Japanese architecture, but of every tiny detail of Japanese
domestic life, even down to the water-bucket and the kitchen
tongs. The only drawback is the author's *parti pris* of
viewing everything through rose-coloured spectacles, which
makes those who would fain be instructed by him feel
that they are listening to a special pleader rather than to a
judge.

Among books of reference on special subjects, may be
mentioned the younger Siebold's "*Notes on Japanese
Archæology*," the collection of "*Treaties and Conventions*"
concluded between the Japanese and various foreign Governments, Bramsen's "*Chronological Tables*," by which the
exact equivalent of any Japanese date can be ascertained,
the "*China Sea Directory, Vol. IV*," giving information to
mariners concerning the Japanese coast, the "*Transactions
of the Seismological Society*," the English translations of
the various Codes, the British Consular Trade Reports,
and the yearly reports of the various Departments of the
Imperial Government on such matters as education, railways, posts, etc., etc. Of books by early travellers, the
copious letters of the Jesuit missionaries, the "*Letters of
the English Pilot Will Adams*," Kaempfer's "*History of
Japan*," and the elder Siebold's encyclopedic productions
are the chief. But with the exception of Will Adams's
"*Letters*," these are now all out of print, besides being

out of date.   For the collector and the specialist they undoubtedly possess great value, but they are scarcely to be recommended to the general reader.

**Botany.**  We have not the necessary space, even had we the necessary ability, to enter into a particular description of that rich and wonderful Japanese flora, which excites the imagination of the man of science as much as ever Japanese works of art in porcelain, bronze, and lacquer excited the imagination of the man of taste.   We can only draw attention to a few striking facts and theoretical considerations, referring the reader for all details to Dr. Rein's masterly *résumé* of the subject, and to the works of Maximowicz, Savatier, Asa Gray, Sir Joseph Hooker, Itô Keisuke, and the other specialists whom Rein quotes.

The first impression made on any fairly observant person landing in Japan is the extraordinary variety of the vegetation.   He sees the pine of the north flourishing by the side of the tropical bamboo.   A rice-field, as in India, stretches to his right.   To his left will be a wheat or barley-field, reminding him of Europe.   And the same strange juxtapositions occur wherever he travels throughout the archipelago.   No wonder that the number of known species of trees and plants (exclusive of mosses and other low organisms) rises to the enormous figure of two thousand seven hundred and forty-three, distributed over an unusually large number of genera, while it is almost certain that further investigations will raise the figure considerably, the northern portion of the country  having been as yet but imperfectly explored.   Of forest-trees alone, Japan—or, to be strictly accurate, the Japanese region, which includes also Korea, Manchuria, and a portion of Northern China—

has a hundred and sixty-eight species divided among sixty-six genera, as against the eight-five species in thirty-three genera of Europe. The Atlantic forest region of North America is nearly as rich as Japan, having a hundred and fifty-five species in sixty-six genera. The Pacific forest region of North America is poorer even than Europe, having but seventy-eight species in thirty-one genera. A further very curious fact is that Eastern America and Japan possess sixty-five genera in common. Evidently there must be some powerful underlying cause connecting phenomena apparently so capricious. Rein lays great stress on the similarity of climatic conditions obtaining in Eastern Asia and Eastern America, on the abundant rainfall of Japan, and on the convenient stepping-stones for vegetable immigrants formed by the Kurile Islands, Saghalien, Oki, Iki, the Loochoos, and other islands both to the west and south. May we not also accept Mr. Wallace's theory, as propounded in his charming book, "Island Life," to the effect that the Glacial Epoch had great influence in bringing about the present state of things? When the climate of the north temperate regions grew arctic, some of the trees and plants whose habitat was there must have perished, but others doubtless migrated in a southerly direction, where they could still find sufficient warmth to sustain their existence. In Europe, however, they were stopped—first by the barrier of the Alps, and then by the still more effectual barrier of the Mediterranean. On the Pacific slope of America, they mostly perished owing to the extreme narrowness of their habitat, which allowed of no free emigration in any direction. The conditions of Eastern America and of Eastern Asia were altogether different. Here were

neither mountain ranges nor oceans to obstruct the southward march of the vegetation as it retreated before the
ice; and when the ice had disappeared, all the heat-lov-
ing forms, safely preserved in the south, were able to
return northward again, a considerable remnant of the
richer vegetation of an earlier geological age being thus
handed down to our own days in these two favoured
regions.

A consideration to which little attention has hitherto been
paid is the general identity of the Japanese flora with that
of the adjacent coast of Asia. It is probable that when
Korea shall have been thoroughly explored, not a few
species now designated as *japonica* will be found to be
really continental forms. It is already known that some
of the plants now most common in Japan have been
introduced in historical times through human agency.
Such are, to name but two, the tea-plant and the orange-
tree. The introduction of the latter is mentioned by the
Japanese poets of the eighth century. The tea-plant came
in with Buddhism. We were ourselves, we believe, the
first to point out, some eight years ago, the help which
philology may give to natural science in this field, by
proving that plants and also animals, now inhabiting
Japan but originally imported from China or Korea, may
often be detected in the Japanese language by their slightly
disfigured Chinese or Korean names.[*]

What we have for shortness' sake termed the Japanese
region, is named by Rein "the north-eastern monsoon
region," and is furthermore described by him as the "kingdom of magnolias, camellias, and aralias." It coincides

---

[*] "Asiatic Transactions" Vol. X. Supplement. p. lxx of "Introduction to the Kushi."

very nearly in latitude with the region of the Mediterranean ;
but the character of the two is as different as can well be
imagined. The Japanese region is the delight of the
botanist. The Mediterranean region, with its severer forms
and more sparing growth, better pleases the artist, who
loves vegetation less for its own sake than as a setting for
the works of man.

Books recommended. Rein's "Japan," pp. 135-374, is the best for the general
reader. The following are recommended only to specialists :—"Flora Japonica," by
C. E. Thunberg.—"Flora Japonica," by Siebold and Zuccarini, and other works by
Siebold.—"Prolusio Floræ Japonicæ," by F. A. G. Miquel.—"Mélanges Biologiques,"
published in the "Bulletin de l'Académie Impériale des Sciences de St. Petersburg," by
Maximowicz and others.—"Enumeratio Plantarum," by Franchet and Savatier.—All
the above, except Rein, are in Latin.—"On the Botany of Japan" by Asa Gray.—
"A Catalogue of Plants in the Botanic Garden, Tôkyô, 1887."—Murray has written on
the Pines and Firs, Gerrits on the Timber-trees "(Asiatic Transactions," Vol IV.),
Dickins on the Ferns (Satow and Hawes' "Handbook for Japan." p. 37 of "Introduction," etc, etc. Perhaps the most beautiful of these botanical monographs is that
on the Algæ, by P. K. Kjellman and J. V. Petersen, entitled "Om Japans Laminari-
aceer," and published by the University of Upsala.


**Buddhism.** Superficial writers have often drawn attention to the resemblances between the Buddhistic and the
Roman Catholic ceremonial—the flowers on the altar, the
candles, the incense, the shaven heads of the priests, the
images, the processions. In point of dogma, a whole
world of thought separates Buddhism from every form of
Christianity. Knowledge, enlightenment, is the condition
of Buddhistic grace—not faith. Self-perfectionment is
the means of salvation, not the vicarious sufferings of a
Redeemer. Not eternal life is the end, and active participation in unceasing prayer and praise, but absorption into
Nirvâna (Jap. *Nehan*), practical annihilation. For Buddhism teaches that existence is itself an evil, springing
from the double root of ignorance and the passions. In
logical conformity with this tenet, it ignores the existence

of a supreme God and creator of worlds. There are, it is true, gods in the cosmogony which Buddhism inherited from Brahminism; but they are less important than the *Hotoke* or Buddhas—men, that is, who have toiled upward through successive stages of existence to the calm of perfect holiness.

These few remarks are designed merely to point the reader along the true path of enquiry. It does not, of course, fall within the scope of a manual devoted to things Japanese to analyse the doctrines and practice of the great and complicated Indian religion, which, commencing with the birth of the Buddha Shaka Muni in the year B. C. 1027 (so say the Chinese and Japanese Buddhists, but European scholars prefer the date B. C. 653), gradually became the chief factor in the religious life of all Eastern Asia.

Japan received Buddhism from Korea, which country had obtained it from China. The account which the native history books give of the introduction of Buddhism into Japan, is that a golden image of Buddha and some scrolls of the scriptures were presented to the Mikado Kimmei by the King of Hakusai, one of the Korean states, in A. D. 552. The Mikado inclined to the acceptance of the new religion; but the majority of his council, conservative Shintoists, persuaded him to reject the image from his court. The golden Buddha was accordingly conferred upon one Soga-no-Iname, who turned his country-house into the first Buddhist temple existing on the soil of Japan. A pestilence which shortly broke out was attributed by the partisans of the old religion to this foreign innovation. The temple was razed to the ground; but such dire calamities followed on this act of sacrilege that it was soon allowed to be rebuilt. Buddhist monks and nuns then flocked over from Korea in ever-increasing numbers. Shôtoku Taishi, who was prince regent under the Empress Suiko from A. D. 593 to A. D. 621, himself attained almost to the rank of Buddhist saintship, and from this time forward the new religion became established as the chief religion of the land, though Shintō was never entirely suppressed.

Chinese and Korean Buddhism was already broken up into numerous sects and sub-sects when it reached Japan—sects, too, all of which had come to differ very widely in their teaching from that of the purer, simpler Southern Buddhism of Ceylon and Siam. Japanese Buddhism follows what is termed the "Great Vehicle" (Sansk. *Mahâyâna*, Jap. *Daijô*), which contains many unwarranted accretions to the original teaching of the Buddha. The chief sects now existing in Japan are the Tendai, Shingon, Jôdo, and Zen, which are of Chinese origin, and the Shin (also called Ikkô or Monto) and the Nichiren or Hokke, both native Japanese sects dating from the thirteenth century.

Japanese Buddhism has never yet been thoroughly studied, but should, one would think, be worthy the attention of some competent investigator. It is a fact, curious but true, that the Japanese have never been at the trouble to translate the Buddhist canon into their own language. The priests use a Chinese version, the laity no version at all nowadays, though, to judge from the allusions scattered up and down Japanese literature, they would seem to have been more given to searching the scriptures a few hundred years ago. The Buddhist religion was disestablished and disendowed during the years 1871—4, a step taken in consequence of the momentary ascendency of Shintō. At the present time

(1890), a faint struggle is being made by the Buddhist priesthood against rivals in comparison with whom Shintō is insignificant: we mean the two great streams of European thought—Christianity and science. A notable reception was accorded in 1889 to Colonel Olcott, of esoteric and theosophical fame. But it seems a foregone conclusion that Japanese Buddhism is bound to perish in the encounter with its younger and more energetic foes.

**Books recommended.** Perhaps the best short account of Buddhism for the general reader is that entitled " Buddhism," by Rhys Davids. This work, though published by the Society for Promoting Christian Knowledge, is quite free from Christian prejudice. The legendary life of Buddha and a good outline of Japanese Buddhism are given in the Introduction to Satow and Hawes' " Handbook for Japan."—Students should consult Bunyiu Nanjio's " Short History of the Twelve Japanese Buddhist Sects," and Eitel's invaluable " Sanskrit-Chinese Dictionary," also entitled " Handbook for the Student of Chinese Buddhism."—Interesting specimens of Japanese sermons may be found in Mitford's " Tales of Old Japan," Vol. II, and in J. M. James' " Discourse on Infinite Vision," printed in the "Asiatic Transactions," Vol. VII, Part IV.—The tenets and the devotional literature of the Shin sect have been treated of by James Troup in Vols. XIV and XVII of the " Asiatic Transactions " (the paper in the latter being entitled " The Gobunsho"). This sect curiously illustrates the fact that a religion may, with the lapse of time and by passing from nation to nation, end by becoming almost the exact contrary of what it was at starting. At first sight, one would imagine the Shin sect to be a travesty of Christianity rather than a development of Buddhism.


**Capital Cities.** If Japanese history is to be trusted, Japan has had no less than sixty capitals. This is to be traced to the fact that in ancient days there was a superstitious dread of any place in which a person had died. The sons of a dead man built themselves a new house. Hence, too, the successor of a dead Mikado built himself a new capital. Consequently the provinces of Yamato, Yamashiro, Kawachi, and Setsu, which were the home and centre of the early Japanese monarchy, are dotted with places, now mere villages, sometimes indeed empty

names, but once in the proud position of capitals of the
Empire.

In process of time, such perpetual changes proving in-
compatible with the needs of the more advanced civilisation
introduced from China and Korea, a tendency to keep the
court settled in one place made itself felt during the eighth
century of our era. Nara in Yamato remained the capital
for seven reigns, between the years 709 and 784. After
further wanderings, the court fixed itself at Kyōto in 794;
and this city continued, with few interruptions, to be the
residence of successive generations of Mikados till the year
1868, when it was abandoned in favour of Yedo (Tōkyō),
which had been the capital of the Shōguns ever since the
year 1590. Kyōto, however, still nominally retains the
rank of a metropolis, as is indicated by its new name
of *Sai-kyō* or "western capital," in contradistinction to
*Tō-kyō*, the "eastern capital." The new name, though
little known to foreigners, is in general use among the
Japanese themselves.

The chief sights in and near Kyōto are the Mikado's
palace, the temples named Nishi Hongwanji, Chion-in,
Kiyomizu-dera, Gion, Ginkakuji, Kinkakuji, Higashi Hongwanji, San-jū-san-gen-dō, Inari-no-Jinja, Hieizan, Lake
Biwa, Arashi-yama famous for its cherry blossoms in
spring, and the rapids of the Katsura-gawa. Brocades
and embroidery generally are the products for which Kyōto
is chiefly noted. In the second rank come pottery,
porcelain, and bronze.

Nara, whose charms have been sung by many a Japanese
poet from the eighth century onwards, is distinguished by
the almost English appearance of the park which surrounds
the ancient Shintō temple of Kasuga, where the tame deer

crowd around the visitor to feed out of his hand. In Nara, likewise, stands the great Buddhist temple of Tōdaiji, with the colossal bronze image known as the *Daibutsu*, or " great Buddha," dating from the year 749.

Another of the old capitals, Kamakura, is distant only a few miles from Yokohama. It was never the seat of the Mikados. It was the seat of the Shōguns from 1189 onwards, and of the so-called " Regents" of the Hōjō family duing the troublous Middle Ages. Kamakura, taken by storm and burnt to the ground in 1455 and again in 1526, gradually lost its importance. Woods and rice-fields now stretch over the area that once afforded a home to more than a million inhabitants, and little now remains to tell of its ancient splendour, save the great temple of Hachiman and the magnificent bronze image of Buddha, perhaps the grandest of all Japanese works of art.

**Book recommended.** Messrs. Satow and Hawes' "Handbook for Central and Northern Japan," especially pp. 319-304.

**Carving.** The earliest specimens of Japanese carving, if we may so call objects more probably moulded by the hand, are the clay figures occasionally found in the tumuli of Central and Eastern Japan. Drawings of some of these are given in Mr. Satow's paper on "Ancient Sepulchral Mounds in Kōzuke," printed in Vol. VIII. Part III. of the "Asiatic Transactions." But the art made no progress till the advent of Buddhism in the sixth century. A stone image of the god Miroku was among the earliest gifts of the court of Korea to that of Japan. Wooden images came also. The Japanese themselves soon learnt to carve in both materials. The huge figure of Buddha, hewn in relief on a block of andesite on the way between Ashinoyu and Hakone, is a grand example.   Like so many other celebrated Japanese works of unknown antiquity, it is referred by popular tradition to the Buddhist saint, Kōbō Daishi (ninth century), who is fabled to have finished it in a single night.   The art of wood-carving has always been chiefly in Buddhist hands.   Among the finest examples may be mentioned the powerful "temple guardians" (*Ni-ō*) in the Snikondō at Nara, attributed to the beginning of the seventh century, and the charming painted carvings of flowers and birds in the Nikko temples and in those at Shiba and Ueno in Tōkyō, belonging to the seventeenth and eighteenth centuries.

The Japanese sculptors have occasionally attempted portraiture.   The seated figure of Ieyasu at Shiba is a good example.   But in sculpture, even more than in pictorial art, the strength of the Japanese talent lies rather in decoration and in small things than in representation and in great things.   The *netsukes*—a kind of ornament for the tobacco-pouch, carved out of wood or ivory—are often marvels of minuteness, and alive with a keen sense of humour and the grotesque.

The Japanese Phidias (if we may compare small people with great) was Hidari Jingorō, born in A. D. 1594. The two elephants and the sleeping cat in the mortuary chapel of Ieyasu at Nikkō are among the most celebrated productions of his chisel.   He died in 1634, leaving a flourishing school and a reputation around which legend soon began to busy itself.   A horse which he had carved as an ex-voto, used, it is averred, to leave its wooden tablet at night, and go down to the meadow to graze. On another occasion the artist, having seen a frail beauty

in the street, became so enamoured that on getting home
he set about carving her statue; and between the folds
of the statue's robe he placed a mirror, which the girl
had let drop and which he had picked up. Thereupon
the statue, Galatea-like, came to life, and the two lovers
were made supremely happy. Now for the characteristically Japanese turn given to the tale. The times were
stormy, and it fell out that the life of the daughter of the
artist's lord had to be sacrificed. The artist instantly
cut off his living statue's head and sent it to the enemy,
who were taken in by the ruse which his loyalty had
prompted. But a servant of his lord's, also deceived,
and believing that Hidari Jingorō had really killed their
lord's daughter, took his sword and cut off the sculptor's
right hand. Hence the name of Hidari Jingorō, that is,
"left-handed Jingorō." Probably Jingorō's left-handedness,
which undoubtedly gave him his nickname of *Hidari*, also
suggested the legend.

*Books recommended.* Satow and Hawes' "Handbook for Japan," p. 100 of
" Introduction," *et seq.*—Huish's " Japan and its Art," Chap. XIII.

**Cha-no-yu.** See TEA CEREMONIES.

**Cherry-Blossom.** Properly speaking, the celebrated
cherry-trees of Japan are not cherry-trees at all. Botanists
refuse to admit them to the cherry tribe, and brand them
with the appellation of *Prunus pseudo-cerasus*, that is,
"the plum falsely called cherry." It must be admitted
that the execrable quality of the fruit fully bears out the
severest sentence that science may decree.

Be this as it may, cherry-tree or no cherry-tree, the
*sakura*, as the Japanese call it, has always been to Japan

what the rose is to Western nations.　Poets have sung
it since the earliest ages, crowds still pour forth every
year, as spring comes round, to the chief places where
plantations of it are to be seen.　Even patriotism has
adopted it, in contradistinction to the plum-blossom (*ume*),
which is believed to be of Chinese origin—not, like the
cherry-tree, a true native of Japan.　The poet Motoori
exclaims:

> *Shikishima no*
> *Yamato-gokoro wo*
> *Hito towaba,*
> *Asa-hi ni niou*
> *Yama-sakura-bana !*

which, being interpreted, signifies " If one should enquire
of you concerning the spirit of a true Japanese, point to
the wild cherry-blossom shining in the sun."—Again a
Japanese proverb says:　" The cherry is first among flowers, as the warrior is first among men."

The cherry-blossoms are generally at their finest in
Tōkyō about the 10th April.　The places then best worth
visiting are Ueno Park, Shiba Park, the long avenue of
Mukōjima and, in the neighbouring country, Asuka-yama
and Koganei.　But the most famous spots for cherry-
blossoms in all Japan are Yoshino amid the mountains of
Yamato, and Arashi-yama near Kyōto.

The Japanese are fond of preserving cherry-blossoms in
salt, and making a kind of tea out of them.　The fragrance of this infusion is delicious, but its taste is a
bitter deception.

**Chess.**　Japanese chess (*shōgi*) ‘was introduced from
China centuries ago ; and though it has diverged to some

extent from its Chinese prototype, the two games still have a feature in common which distinguishes them from all other varieties. It is this. The rank on which the pawns are usually posted is occupied by only two pieces, called *pao* by the Chinese, and *hisha* and *kaku* by the Japanese. Also, on either side of the king are two pieces, called *sen* in the Chinese, and *kin* in the Japanese game. These perform the duty imposed on the *fers* or *visir* of the Persian *Shatranj*, which was the equivalent of the modern queen. There is, of course, no queen or piece of similar attributes in either Chinese or Japanese Chess. There are eighty-one squares on the Japanese board, and the game is played with twenty pieces on each side, distinguished not by a difference of colour, but principally by the ideographs upon them. Though the movements of the pieces resemble in most respects those followed in the Western game, there are ramifications unknown to the latter, introducing elements that would puzzle even a native Morphy to trace the move which cost him a defeat. The most important of these are the employment of the pieces captured from the adversary to strengthen one's own game, and the comparative facility with which the minor pieces can attain to higher rank.

Chess is understood by nearly every one in Japan. The very coolies at the corners of the streets improvise out of almost anything around them materials with which to play, and thus while away the tedium of waiting for employment. But it is comparatively little patronised by the educated classes, who hold its rival Go in much higher estimation. Ô is the king, *keima* the knight, *hisha* the rook, and *kaku* the bishop—or pieces having movements like them. *Fu* is the pawn. The movements of the *yari* also resemble those of the rook, but are confined to the single rank on which it stands. *Gin* and *kin* are not found in Western chess. *Gin* moves one square diagonally at a time, also one square forward. If removed from its original position, it can retreat one square diagonally only. The *kin*, besides having similar movements, has also the power of moving one square on each side of itself, but it cannot return diagonally. The object of the game is, as with us, to checkmate the king.

The following is a diagram of the board :—

| Yui Keima Gin | Kaku | Fu | | | | Fu | | Yari |
|---|---|---|---|---|---|---|---|---|
| | | Fu | | | | Fu | Hisha | Keima Yari |
| Gin | | Fu | | | | Fu | | Gin |
| Kin | | Fu | | | | Fu | | Kin |
| O | | Fu | | | | Fu | | O |
| Kin | | Fu | | | | Fu | | Kin |
| Gin Keima Yari | Hisha | Fu | | | | Fu | Kaku | Keima Gin |
| | | Fu | | | | Fu | | Yari |

Books recommended. "Japanese Chess," by W. G. Mason, in the " Westminster Papers" for 1875.—" Das Japanische Schachspiel," by V. Holtz, and " Das Schachspiel der Chinesen," by O. von Möllendorff in the "German Asiatic Transactions."

**Children.** Japan has been called "a paradise of babies." The babies are indeed generally so good as to help to make it a paradise for adults. The late Mrs. Chaplin-Ayrton tried to explain the goodness of Japanese children by the fact of the furnitureless condition of Japanese houses. There is nothing, she said, for them to wish to break, nothing for them to be told not to touch. This is ingenious. But may we not more simply attribute the pleasing fact partly to the less robust health of the Japanese, which results in a scantier supply of animal spirits? In any case, children's pretty ways and children's games add much to the picturesqueness of Japanese life. On the 3rd March every doll-shop in Tôkyo, Kyôto, and the other large cities is gaily decked with what are called *O Hina Sama*—tiny models both of people and of things, the whole Japanese Court in miniature. This is the great yearly holiday of all the little girls. The boys' holiday takes place on the 5th May, which is the festival of Hachiman, the God of War. The cities are then adorned with gigantic paper carps, floating in the air from poles, after the manner of flags—one carp for every son that has been born in the house during the last twelvemonth. The idea is that as the carp swims up the river against the current, so will the sturdy boy, overcoming all obstacles, rise to fame and fortune.

The unpleasant appearance of so many Japanese children's heads is simply due to a form of eczema. The form is one by no means unknown in Europe, and is easily curable in a week. But as popular superstition invests these scabby heads with a health-giving influence in later life, no attempt is made to cure them. Probably shaving with unclean razors has something to do with the disease; for it generally ceases when shaving stops, and has noticeably diminished since the foreign custom of allowing children's hair to grow has begun to gain ground. The Japanese custom is to shave an infant's head on the seventh day after birth, only a tiny tuft on the nape of the neck being left. During the next five or six years, the mother may give rein to her fancy in the matter of shaving her little one's head. Hence the various styles which we see around us. Shaving is left off when a child goes to school, instead of, as among Europeans, generally commencing when he quits it. The Japanese lad's chin does not begin to sport a few hairs for several years later. Japanese infants are not weaned till they are two or three, sometimes not till they are five years old. This is doubtless one cause of the rapid aging of the mothers.

European parents may feel quite at ease about their little ones' chance of health in this country. The highest medical authority declares the mortality among children of European race in Japan to be exceptionally low.

**Chrysanthemums.** See Flowers.

**Clans.** This is the usual English translation of the Japanese word *han* (藩), which may also be rendered "daimiate," that is, the territory and people subject to a *daimyō*, or territorial noble, in feudal Japan. The Japanese clans differed from the Highland clans by the fact that all the members of a clan did not claim a common origin or use the same surname. But they were equally bound to their lord by ties of love and implicit obedience, and to each other by a feeling of brotherhood. This feeling has survived the abolition of feudalism in 1871. Ever since that time, the members of three or four great clans have practically "run" the government of Japan. These are Satsuma, Chōshū, Tosa, and Hizen. Thus, in the cabinet formed on Christmas Day, 1889, and now (April, 1890) governing the country, the ten seats are distributed as follows : three to Satsuma (Counts Saigô, Ôyama, and Matsukata), three to Chôshû (Counts Yamagata, and Yamada, and Viscount Aoki), two to Tosa (Count Gotô and Mr. Iwamura). one to Hizen (Count Itô), and only one to an outsider, formerly a personal retainer of the Shôgun's (Viscount Enomoto). The Minister of the Household (Viscount Hijikata), who does not sit in the Cabinet, is also of Tosa extraction. The President of the Privy Council (Count Ôki) is from Hizen. Nor is this state of things the result of accident. The officially inspired "Japan Mail," in its leader on the subject (26th December, 1889), says straight out : " The organization has evidently been directed by a desire to distribute these important posts as equally as possible among the leading clans."

The student of Japanese politics who will keep the existence of the clans in mind, will find many things become clear to him which before seemed complicated and illogical. Political questions are not necessarily questions of principle. They may simply be questions of personal and clan interest. The present paramount influence of the four clans of Satsuma, Chôshû, Tosa, and Hizen is partly an inheritance from olden times, partly the result of the share which they took in restoring the Mikado to his position as autocrat of the Empire in the revolution of 1868. The two strongest of the four are Satsuma and Chôshû, whence the term *Sat-Chô*, used to denote their combination ; for in Japanese there is no vulgarity in cutting off the tails of words. On the contrary, to do so is considered an elegant imitation of the Chinese style, which is nothing if not brief. The Satsuma men are credited with courage, the Chôshû men with sagacity. The

former are soldiers, men of dash and daring; the latter
are diplomats and able administrators.

**Climate.** The exaggerated estimation in which the
climate of Japan is held by many of those who have
had no experience of it often prepares a great disappoint-
ment for visitors, who find a climate far wetter than that
of England and subject to greater extremes of temperature.
It should be added that it also has more fine days.[*]
    The best season is the autumn. From about the middle
of October to the end of the year, the sky is generally
clear and the atmosphere still, while during a portion of
that time (November), the forests display glorious tints
of red and gold, surpassed only in Canada and the United
States. During January, February and March snow occasionally falls, but it rarely lies longer than a day or
two. The spring is trying, on account of the frequent high
winds, which often seriously interfere with the enjoyment
of the cherry, wistaria, peony, and other flowers, in which
the Japanese take such pride. June and the first half of
July are mostly very rainy. So penetrating is then the
damp that it is impossible to keep books from mildew.
Boots, cigarettes, even glasses, if put away for a day, appear
next morning covered with an incipient forest of whitish,
greenish matter. Meantime the thermometer stands at
about 75°, with but little alteration at night, and the
frequent heavy down-pour makes exercise wearisome, if not
impossible. The second half of July and all August are
hotter but drier, and varied by an occasional heavy storm
lasting from one to three days. The heat generally

---

[*] Tōkiō has 58.11 inches of yearly rainfall, as against 24.76 at Greenwich, but only
158.7 rainy days as against 166.

vanishes suddenly about the second week in September when the second rainy season sets in, and lasts about a month.

One striking peculiarity of the Japanese climate is the constant prevalence of northerly winds in winter and of southerly winds in summer. Rooms facing south are, therefore, the best all the year round, escaping, as they do, the icy blasts of January and February, and profiting by every summer breeze. Another peculiarity is the lateness of all the seasons, as compared with Europe. The grass, for instance, which dies down during the cold, dry winter months, does not become really fit for tennis-playing much before the middle of May. On the other hand, winter is robbed of the gloom of short afternoons by the beautiful clearness of the sky down to the end of the year, and even throughout January whenever it is not actually raining or snowing. Travellers are recommended to choose the late autumn, especially if they intend to content themselves with the beaten tracks of Kyōto, Tōkyō, Miyanoshita, Nikkō, etc., where the Europeanisation of hotels has brought stoves in its train; for stoveless Japanese tea-houses are wofully chilly places. April and May, notwithstanding a greater chance of wet weather, will be better for the wilds and for mountain climbing. There is then, too, neither cold nor heat to fear.

The foregoing description of the Japanese climate applies to the Pacific seaboard of Central Japan, of which Tōkyō is fairly representative. But need we remind the reader that Japan is a large country? The northernmost Kuriles, now Japanese territory, touch Kamchatka. The most southern of the Loochoo Islands is scarcely a degree from the tropic of Cancer. The climate at

the extreme points of the empire therefore differs widely from that of temperate Central Japan. Speaking
generally, the south-eastern slope of the great central
range of the Main Island—the slope facing the Pacific
Ocean and washed by the Kuroshio, or Gulf-Stream
of Eastern Asia—has a much more moderate climate than
the north-western slope, which faces the Sea of Japan,
with Siberia beyond. In Tōkyō, on the Pacific side,
what little snow falls melts almost immediately. In the
towns near the Sea of Japan it lies three or four feet
deep for weeks, and drifts to a depth of fifteen to
eighteen feet in the valleys. But the summer in these
same towns is, like the Tōkyō summer oppressively hot.
Thunder-storms and unexpected showers are rare in Japan,
excepting in the mountainous districts. Fogs, too, are
rare south of Kinkwazan, about 38° 20′ North. From
Kinkwazan right up the eastern coast of the Main Island, all along Eastern Yezo, the Kuriles, and up as far
as Behring's Strait, thick fogs prevail during the calm
summer months—fogs which are relieved only by furious
storms in autumn, and a wintry sea charged with
ice.

The climate of Japan is stated by the highest medical
authority to be excellent for children, less so for adults,
the enormous amount of moisture rendering it depressing,
especially to persons of a nervous temperament and to
consumptive persons. Various causes, physical and social,
contribute to make Japan a less healthy country for female
residents of European race than for the men.

The following table gives the average of thirteen years'
observations (1876-1888), taken by Mr. E. Knipping at the
Central Imperial Meteorological Observatory, Tōkyō :

**TOKYO OBSERVATORY. 35° 41' N. L. 139° 46' E. L. HEIGHT 69 FEET. 13 YEARS 1876-1888. (INCHES AND FAHRENHEIT DEGREES.)**

| | Jan. | Feb. | March | April | May | June | July | Aug. | Sept. | Oct. | Nov. | Dec. | Year. |
|---|---|---|---|---|---|---|---|---|---|---|---|---|---|
| Mean Temperature | 36.7 | 37.9 | 43.9 | 53.8 | 61.5 | 68.3 | 73.9 | 77.0 | 72.1 | 60.3 | 49.6 | 41.0 | 56.5 |
| Mean Maxima | 46.8 | 47.3 | 53.6 | 63.6 | 70.0 | 75.6 | 83.1 | 85.6 | 78.8 | 69.1 | 59.9 | 52.0 | 65.3 |
| Mean Minima | 28.4 | 29.8 | 34.3 | 44.6 | 53.1 | 61.5 | 69.6 | 70.9 | 64.8 | 50.7 | 41.0 | 31.8 | 48.5 |
| Absolute Maximum Temperature | On 14th July, 1886, | | | | | 97.9 | | | | | | | |
| Absolute Minimum Temperature | On 13th January, 1876, | | | | | 15.4 | | | | | | | |
| Mean Rainfall | 3.30 | 3.79 | 4.48 | 4.47 | 5.49 | 7.39 | 4.89 | 3.86 | 8.49 | 7.86 | 4.14 | 1.91 | 58.13 |
| Number of Rainy Days | 7.1 | 9.8 | 10.8 | 14.3 | 13.5 | 14.9 | 13.9 | 11.0 | 14.8 | 13.1 | 8.9 | 6.4 | 138.7 |
| Days with Snow | 2.6 | 3.5 | 1.5 | 0.1 | — | — | — | — | — | — | 0.1 | 0.7 | 8.5 |
| Mean Barometer (reduced to freezing point) | 29.97 | 29.98 | 29.93 | 29.94 | 29.84 | 29.70 | 29.78 | 29.83 | 29.87 | 29.98 | 29.97 | 29.00 | 29.90 |
| Mean Direction of Wind (degrees) | 1 22 W | N 14 W | N 9 W | 76 E | N 47 | 41 NE | 19 E | 23 E | W 63 | N 14 W | W 15 W | W 28 W | |

The "number of rainy days" includes all days on which more than a millimetre of rain fell, and also those on which any snow or hail fell. The "days with snow" are those on which snow fell, regardless of the question whether rain also did or did not fall. Few days are uninterruptedly stormy in Tokyo, perhaps only two or three in the year. The average number of typhoons passing over Japan yearly is three, four or five, of which Tokyo receives about one. The number liable to typhoons are (in a decreasing order of severity) September, August, October, and July. Typhoons have, it is true, been experienced as early as the end of March; but this is a very rare exception.

**Books recommended.** Mr. E. Knipping's various papers in the "German Asiatic Transactions" and in the "*Annalen der Hydrographie und Maritimen Meteorologie*," published at Berlin by the Imperial German Admiralty.—" The China Sea Directory," Vol. IV.

**Confucianism.** To describe in detail this Chinese system of philosophy does not belong to a work dealing with things Japanese. Suffice it to say that Confucius, called by the Japanese *Kōshi*, abstained from all metaphysical flights and devotional ecstasies. He confined himself to practical details of morals and government, and took submission to parents and political rulers as the corner-stone of his system. The result is a set of moral truths—some would say truisms—of a very narrow scope, and of dry ceremonial observances, political rather than personal. This Confucian code of ethics has for ages satisfied the Far-Easterns of China, Korea, and Japan, but would not have been endured for a moment by the more eager, more speculative, more tender European mind. The Confucian Classics consist of what are called, in the Japanese pronunciation, the *Shi-sho Go-kyō*, that is "the Four Books and the Five Canons." The Four Books are "the Great Learning," "The Doctrine of the Mean," "The Confucian Analects," and "The Sayings of Mencius." Mencius, let it be noted, is much the most attractive of the Chinese sages. He had an epigrammatic way about him and a certain sense of humour, which give to many of his utterances a strangely Western and modern ring. He was also the first democrat of the ancient East—a democrat so outspoken as to have at one time suffered exclusion from the libraries of absolutistic Japan. The Five Canons consist of "The Book of Changes," "The Book of Poetry," "The Book of History," "The Canon of Rites," and "Spring and Autumn" (annals of the state of Lu by Confucius).

Originally introduced into Japan early in the Christian era, together with the other products of Chinese civilisation, the Confucian philosophy lay dormant during the Middle Ages, the period of the supremacy of Buddhism. It awoke with a start in the early part of the seventeenth century, when Ieyasu, the great warrior, ruler, and patron of learning, caused the Confucian Classics to be printed in Japan for the first time. During the two hundred and fifty years that followed, the whole intellect of the country was moulded by Confucian ideas. Confucius himself had, it is true, laboured for the establishment of a centralised monarchy. But his main doctrine of unquestioning submission to rulers and parents fitted in perfectly with the feudal ideas of Old Japan; and the conviction of the paramount importance of such subordination lingers on as an element of stability, in spite of the recent social cataclysm which has involved Japanese Confucianism properly so-called in the ruin of all other Japanese institutions.

The most eminent Japanese names among the Confucianists are Itō Jinsai and his son, Itō Tōgai, at Kyōto; Arai Hakuseki, and Ogyū Sorai at Yedo. All four flourished about the end of the seventeenth and the beginning of the eighteenth century. They were merely expositors. No Japanese had the originality—it would have been hooted down as impious audacity—to develop the Confucian system further, to alter or amend it. There are not even any Japanese translations or commentaries worth reading. The Japanese have, for the most part, contented themselves with reprinting the

text of the Classics. themselves, and also the text of the
principal Chinese commentators (especially that of Shushi,
朱子), pointed with diacritical marks to facilitate their
perusal by Japanese students. The Chinese Classics thus
edited formed the chief vehicle of every boy's education
from the seventeenth century until the remodelling of the
system of public instruction on European lines after the
revolution of 1868. At present they have fallen into almost total neglect, though phrases and allusions borrowed
from them still pass current in literature, and even to
some extent in the language of every-day life. Seidō, the
great temple of Confucius in Tōkyō, is now about to be
utilised as an Educational Museum.

**Books recommended.** Dr. Legge's elaborate edition of "The Chinese
Classics," in six larger volumes, and Vol. XVI of the "Sacred Books of the East,"
containing the same writer's translation of the "Book of Changes" (*Yi King*).—
"Confucianism," published by the Society for Promoting Christian Knowledge, is a
much briefer manual of the subject, in popular form.—So far as we know, no study
has been made of the Japanese Confucianists.

**Cormorant-Fishing.** This strange method of fishing
is mentioned in a poem found in the "*Kojiki*," a work
compiled in A. D. 712, while the poem itself probably
dates from a far earlier age. The custom is kept up at
the present day in various districts of Japan, notably on
the River Nagara, near Gifu, in the province of Owari.

First catch your cormorant. "This," we are told by
Mr. G. E. Gregory in Vol. X, Part I, of the "Asiatic
Transactions,"—"This the people do by placing wooden
images of the birds in spots frequented by them and
covering the surrounding branches and twigs with bird-
lime, on settling upon which they stick fast. After
having in this manner caught one cormorant, they place
it among the bushes, instead of the image, and thus

catch more." Mr. Gregory further says that the fisher-
men take such care of the birds that they provide them
with mosquito-nets during the summer, in order to minister to their comfort! Cormorant-fishing always takes
place at night and by torch-light. The method pursued
is thus described by Major-General Palmer, R. E., in a
letter to the "Times," dated 17th July, 1889 :—

"There are, to begin with, four men in each of the
seven boats, one of whom, at the stern, has no duty but
that of managing his craft. In the bow stands the master,
distinguished by the peculiar hat of his rank, and handling
no fewer than 12 trained birds with the surpassing skill
and coolness that have earned for the sportsmen of Gifu
their unrivalled pre-eminence. Amidships is another fisher,
of the second grade, who handles four birds only. Between
them is the fourth man, called *kako*, from the bamboo
striking instrument of that name, with which he makes
the clatter necessary for keeping the birds up to their
work; he also encourages them by shouts and cries, looks
after spare apparatus, &c., and is ready to give aid if
required. Each cormorant wears at the base of its neck
a metal ring, drawn tight enough to prevent marketable
fish from passing below it, but at the same time loose
enough—for it is never removed—to admit the smaller
prey, which serves as food. Round the body is a cord,
having attched to it at the middle of the back a short
strip of stiffish whalebone, by which the great awkward
bird may be conveniently lowered into the water or lifted
out when at work; and to this whalebone is looped a
thin rein of spruce fibre, 12 feet long, and so far wanting
in pliancy as to minimize the chance of entanglement.
When the fishing ground is reached, the master lowers

his 12 birds one by one into the stream and gathers their reins into his left hand, manipulating the latter thereafter with his right as occasion requires. No. 2 does the same with his four birds; the *kako* starts in with his volleys of noise; and forthwith the cormorants set to at their work in the heartiest and jolliest way, diving and ducking with wonderful swiftness as the astonished fish come flocking towards the blaze of light. The master is now the busiest of men. He must handle his 12 strings so deftly that, let the birds dash hither and thither as they will, there shall be no impediment or fouling. He must have his eyes everywhere and his hands following his eyes. Specially must he watch for the moment when any of his flock is gorged—a fact generally made known by the bird itself, which then swims about in a foolish, helpless way, with its head and swollen neck erect. Thereupon the master, shortening in on that bird, lifts it aboard, forces its bill open with his left hand, which still holds the rest of the lines, squeezes out the fish with his right and starts the creature off on a fresh foray—all this with such admirable dexterity and quickness that the 11 birds still bustling about have scarce time to get things into a tangle, and in another moment the whole team is again perfectly in hand.

"As for the cormorants, they are trained when quite young, being caught in winter with bird-lime on the coasts of the neighbouring Owari Gulf, at their first emigration southward from the summer haunts of the species on the northern seaboard of Japan. Once trained, they work well up to 15, often up to 19 or 20, years of age; and, though their keep in winter bears hardly on the masters, they are very precious and profitable hunters during the

five-months' season and well deserve the great care that
is lavished upon them. From four to eight good-sized
fish, for example, is the fair result of a single excursion
for one bird, which corresponds with an average of about
150 fish per cormorant per hour, or 450 for the three
hours occupied in drifting down the whole course. Every
bird in a flock has and knows its number; and one of
the funniest things about them is the quick-witted jealousy
with which they invariably insist, by all that cormorant
language and pantomimic protest can do, on due observance of the recognised rights belonging to their individual
numbers. No. 1, or ' Ichi,' is the doyen of the corps, the
senior in years as well as rank. His colleagues, according
to their age, come after him in numerical order. Ichi is
the last to be put into the water and the first to be taken
out, the first to be fed, and the last to enter the baskets
in which, when work is over, the birds are carried from
the boats to their domicile. Ichi, when aboard, has the
post of honour at the eyes of the boat. He is a solemn,
grizzled old fellow, with a pompous, *noli me tangere* air
that is almost worthy of a Lord Mayor. The rest have
place after him, in succession of rank, alternately on either
side of the gunwale. If, haply, the lawful order of precedence be at any time violated—if, for instance, No. 5
be put into the water before No. 6, or No. 4 be placed above
No. 2—the rumpus that forthwith arises in that family is
a sight to see and a sound to hear.

"But all this while we have been drifting down, with
the boats about us, to the lower end of the course, and
are again abreast of Gifu, where the whole squadron is
beached. As each cormorant is now taken out of the
water, the master can tell by its weight whether it has

secured enough supper while engaged in the hunt; failing
which, he makes the deficiency good by feeding it with
the inferior fish of the catch. At length all are ranged
in their due order, facing outwards, on the gunwale of
each boat. And the sight of that array of great ungainly
sea-birds—shaking themselves, flapping their wings, gaw-
gawing, making their toilets, clearing their throats, looking
about them with a stare of stupid solemnity, and now
and then indulging in old-maidish tiffs with their neighbours—is quite the strangest of its little class I have ever
seen, except perhaps the wonderful penguinry of the
Falkland Islands, whereat a certain French philosopher is
said to have even wept. Finally, the cormorants are sent
off to bed, and we ourselves follow suit."

**Cremation.** Cremation followed Buddhism into Japan
about A. D. 700, but never entirely superseded the older
Shintō custom of disposing of the dead by interment.
Ludicrous as it may appear, cremation was first discontinued in the case of the Mikados on the representations
of a fishmonger named Hachibei, who clamoured for the
interment of the Emperor Go-Kōmei in 1644. On the
18th July, 1873, cremation was totally prohibited by the
government, whose members seem to have had some
confused notion as to the practice being un-European
and therefore barbarous. Having discovered that far from
being un-European, cremation was the goal of European
reformers in such matters, they rescinded their prohibition
only twenty-two months later (23rd May, 1875). There
are now five cremation-grounds in Tōkyō, namely Kiri-
gaya, Higurashi, Kameido, Ōgi-Shinden, and Kami-Ochi-
ai. The usual charges for cremation according to the old

native style are: 1st class, $7; 2nd class, $2.50; 3rd class, $1.50. But the good priest of whom we caused enquiry to be made on this point, said that if we would keep the matter quiet, perhaps a slight reduction might be effected for a friend. The charges for cremation according to the improved European methods which have begun to come into vogue during the last two or three years, are: 1st class, $7; 2nd class, $4.50; 3rd class, $3.

It should be added that on the 19th June, 1874, a law was passed against intramural interment, except in certain special cases. It is still prohibited, unless when the body has been cremated before burial.

**Currency.** The Japanese currency consists of gold, silver, nickel, copper, and paper; but the gold is rarely seen. The system is decimal. The nomenclature is as follows :

| | |
|---|---|
| 1 *yen* (dollar) | = 100 *sen*. |
| 1 *sen* (cent) | = 10 *rin*. |
| 1 *rin* | = 10 *mo* (or *mon*). |
| 1 *mo* | = 10 *shu* |
| 1 *shu* | = 10 *kotsu*. |

Government accounts do not take notice of any value smaller than the *rin*. But estimates by private tradesmen often descend to *mo* and *shu*, which are incredibly minute fractions of a farthing, as will be realised when it is remembered that the *yen*, or Japanese silver dollar itself, having shared in the universal depreciation of silver, is not now worth much more than 3 shillings sterling, or 76 cents American gold. No coins exist, however, to represent these Lilliputian sums. There are silver pieces

of 1 *yen* and under, nickel pieces of 5 *sen*, copper pieces
for lesser values, and paper for various values great and
small, from 20 *sen* upward.  The large oblong copper
pieces with a hole in the middle, enabling them to be strung
on a string are called *tenpō*, because coined during the
period styled *Tenpō* (A. D. 1830—1844).  They are worth
eight *rin*.  The smaller round coins, also having a hole
in the middle, and commonly known to foreigners as
"cash," are worth, some 10 *mō*, some 15, some 20.
The Mexican silver dollar circulates at par with the *yen*
in the Treaty Ports, but is not current at Tōkyō or in the
interior.

The Imperial mint is situated at Ōsaka.  It was started
under British auspices, but the last of the British employés left in 1889.  The manufactory of paper money
is at Tōkyō.  This paper money, which at one time fell
to eighty per cent discount, has stood at par ever since
1884.

**Cycle.** "Better fifty years of Europe than a cycle of
Cathay," sings the laureate.  But it has been pointed out
that after all, there is little difference between the two
terms of his comparison.  The Chinese cycle, which the
Japanese have adopted for historical purposes, has but
sixty years.  (See Article on Time.)

**Daimyō.** The *daimyōs* were the territorial lords or
barons of feudal Japan.  The word means literally "great
name."  Accordingly, during the Middle Ages, warrior
chiefs of lesser degree, corresponding, as one might say,
to our knights or baronets, were known by the correlative
title of *shōmyō*, that is, "small name."  But this latter

fell into disuse.    Perhaps it did not sound grand enough
to be welcome to those who bore it.    Under the Tokugawa
dynasty, which ruled Japan from A.D. 1603 to 1867, the
lowest *daimyōs* owned land assessed at ten thousand bales
of rice per annum, while the richest fief of all, that of
Kaga, was worth over a million bales.    The total number
of the *daimyōs* in modern times was about three hundred.

It should be borne in mind that the *daimyōs* were not
the only aristocracy in the land, though they were incomparably the richest and the most important.    In the
shadow of the Mikado's palace at Kyoto, poor but very
proud of their descent from gods and emperors, looking
down on the feudal *daimyō* aristocracy as on a mere set
of military adventurers and *parvenus*, lived, or rather
vegetated through centuries, the *kuge*, the legitimist
aristocracy of Japan.    The revolution of 1868, in bringing
about the fall of the *daimyōs*, gave the *kuge* an opportunity at last.    With the restoration of the Mikado to
absolute power, they too emerged from obscurity; and on
the creation of a new system of ranks and titles in 1884,
they were not forgotten.    The old *kuge* took rank as new
dukes, marquises, and counts, and, what is more, they
were given pensions.

**Decorations.**    The heraldry of feudal Japan did not
include orders of knighthood, or decorations for military
and other service.    Modern Japan adopted these things

from Europe in the year 1875. There are now six orders
of knighthood, namely, the Order of the Chrysanthemum,
the Order of the Paulownia, the Order of the Rising Sun,
the Order of the Sacred Treasure, the Order of the Crown,
and the Order of the Golden Falcon. The Order of the
Crown is for ladies only. All the Orders are divided into
various classes. The Grand Cordon of the Order of the
Chrysanthemum is the highest honour which the Japanese
Court can bestow. It is, therefore, rarely bestowed on any
but Royal personages. The Order of the Rising Sun is
the distinction most frequently conferred on the foreign
employés of the Government for long and meritorious service, the class given being usually the third, fourth, fifth,
or sixth, according to circumstances—rarely the second.
The holder of such a decoration, down to the sixth class
inclusive, is, even though he be a civilian, granted a
military funeral—posthumous honours which most decorated persons, we imagine, would gladly exchange for
a permanent passport ennbling them to travel and reside
wherever they pleased in Japan while living.

We next come to the War Medal, of which there is but
one class. Conformably with the usage of European
countries, it is given only for foreign service, not for service
in a civil war. Those who took part in the Formosan
expedition gained it, not those who helped to put down
the Satsuma rebellion. After it ranks the Civil Medal,
with three classes distinguished by a red, blue, and green
ribbon respectively. Then there is the Yellow Ribbon
Medal, conferred on those who gave proof of patriotism
by subscribing to the Coast Defence Fund in 1887. It
is divided into two classes, called respectively Gold and
Silver. More recent still is the Commemorative Medal

struck in 1889 for distribution to those who were present at the proclamation of the Constitution on the 11th February of that year. There are two classes of it—Gold for princes, Silver for lesser folk.

The Order of the Falcon, conferred for military merit only, is the newest of all the Japanese decorations. It was established on the 11th February, 1890, in commemoration of Jimmu Tennō, the Romulus of Japan.

**Demoniacal Possession.** Chinese notions concerning the superhuman powers of the fox, and in a lesser degree of the badger and the dog, entered Japan during the early Middle Ages. One or two mentions of magic foxes occur in the "Uji Jūi," a story-book of the eleventh century; and since that time the belief has spread and grown till there is not an old woman in the land—or, for the matter of that, scarcely a man either—who has not some circumstantial fox story to relate as having happened to some one who is at least the acquaintance of an acquaintance. As recently as 1889, a tale was widely circulated and believed of a fox having taken the shape of a railway train on the Tōkyō-Yokohama line. The phantom train seemed to be coming towards a real train which happened to be running in the opposite direction, but yet never got any nearer to it. The engine-driver of the real train, seeing all his signals to be useless, put on a tremendous speed. The result was that the phantom was at last caught up, when, lo and behold! nothing but a crushed fox was found beneath the engine-wheels.

The name of such tales is legion. More curious and interesting is the power with which these demon foxes are credited of taking up their abode in human beings in a

manner similar to the phenomena of possession by evil
spirits, so often referred to in the New Testament.  Dr.
Baelz, of the Imperial University of Japan, who has had
special opportunities of studying such cases in the hospital
under his charge, has kindly communicated to us some
remarks, of which the following is a *résumé* :—

" Possession by foxes (*kitsune-tsuki*) is a form of nervous
disorder or delusion, not uncommonly observed in Japan.
Having entered a human being, sometimes through the
breast, more often through the space between the finger-
nails and the flesh, the fox lives a life of his own, apart
from the proper self of the person who is harbouring him.
There thus results a sort of double entity or double consciousness.  The person possessed hears and understands
everything that the fox inside says or thinks, and the two
often engage in a loud and violent dispute, the fox speaking
in a voice altogether different from that which is natural to
the individual.  The only difference between the cases of
possession mentioned in the Bible and those observed in
Japan is that here it is almost exclusively women that are
attacked—mostly women of the lower classes.  Among
the predisposing conditions may be mentioned a weak intellect, a superstitious turn of mind, and such debilitating
diseases as, for instance, typhoid fever.  Possession never
occurs except in such subjects as have heard of it already,
and believe in the reality of its existence.

" The explanation of the disorder is not so far to seek as
might be supposed.  Possession is evidently related to
hysteria and to the hypnotic phenomena which physiologists
have recently studied with so much care, the cause of all
alike being the fact that, whereas in healthy persons one
half of the brain alone is actively engaged—in right handed

persons the left half of the brain, and in left-handed persons
the right—leaving the other half to contribute only in a
general manner to the function of thought, nervous excitement arouses this other half, and the two—one the organ
of the usual self, the other the organ of the new pathologi-
cally affected self—are set over against each other. The
rationale of possession is an auto-suggestion, an idea arising either with apparent spontaneity or else from the subject-matter of it being talked about by others in the patient's
presence, and then overmastering her weak mind exactly
as happens in hypnosis. In the same manner, the *idea* of
the possibility of cure will often actually effect the core.
The cure-worker must be a person of strong mind and
power of will, and must enjoy the patient's full confidence.
For this reason the priests of the Nichiren sect, which is
the most superstitious and bigoted of Japanese Buddhist
sects, are the most successful expellers of foxes. Occasionally fits and screams accompany the exit of the fox. In
all cases—even when the fox leaves quietly—great pros-
tration remains for a day or two, and sometimes the
patient is unconscious of what has happened.

"To mention but one among several cases, I was once
called in to a girl with typhoid fever. She recovered; but
during her convalescence, she heard the women around her
talk of another woman who had a fox, and who would
doubtless do her best to pass it on to some one else, in
order to be rid of it. At that moment the girl experienced
an extraordinary sensation. The fox had taken possession
of her. All her efforts to get rid of him were vain. 'He is
coming! he is coming!' she would cry, as a fit of the fox
drew near. 'Oh! what shall I do? Here he is!' And
then, in a strange, dry, cracked voice, the fox would speak.

and mock his unfortunate hostess. Thus matters continued for three weeks, till a priest of the Nichiren sect was sent for. The priest upbraided the fox sternly. The fox (always, of course, speaking through the girl's mouth) argued on the other side. At last he said : 'I am tired of her. I ask no better than to leave her. What will you give me for doing so?' The priest asked what he would take. The fox replied, naming certain cakes and other things, which, said he, must be placed before the altar of such and such a temple, at 4 P.M. on such and such a day. The girl was conscious of the words her lips were made to frame, but was powerless to say anything in her own person. When the day and hour arrived, the offerings bargained for were taken by her relations to the place indicated, and the fox quitted the girl at that very hour.

"A curious scene of a somewhat similar nature may occasionally be witnessed at Minobu, the romantically situated chief temple of the Nichiren sect, some three days' journey from Tōkyō into the interior. There the people sit praying for hours before the gigantic statues of the ferocious-looking gods called Ni-ō, which are fabled to have been carried thither from Kamakura in a single night on the back of the hero Asaina in the thirteenth century. The devotees sway their bodies backwards and forwards, and ceaselessly repeat the same invocation, *Namu myōhō renge kyō! Namu myōhō renge kyō!* At last, to some of the more nervous among them, wearied and excited as they are, the statues' eyes seem suddenly to start into life, and they themselves rise wildly, feeling a snake, or maybe a tiger, inside their body, this unclean animal being regarded as the physical incarnation of their sins. Then, with a

cry, the snake or serpent goes out of them, and they themselves are left fainting on the ground."—

So far Dr. Baelz. Oddly enough, we ourselves once
had to submit to exorcism at the hands of Shintō priests.
It was in the summer of 1879, the great cholera year, and
we were accused by the authorities of a certain village at
which we desired to halt of having brought the demon of
cholera with us. For, true to human nature, each town,
each village, at that sad season, always proclaimed itself
spotless, while loudly accusing all its neighbours of
harbouring the contagion. Accordingly, after much parley,
which took place in the drenching rain, with night
approaching and with the impossibility of finding another
shelter for many miles, some Shintō priests were sent
for. They arrived in their white vestments and curiously
curved hats, and bearing branches of trees in their hands.
They formed in two lines on either side of the way, and
between them our little party of two Europeans and one
Japanese servant had to walk. As we passed, the priests
waved the dripping branches over our heads, and struck us
on the back with naked swords. After that, we were
sullenly accorded a lodging for the night. To the honour
of the Japanese government, let it be added that when we
returned to Tōkyō and reported the affair, the village
authorities were at once deposed and another mayor and
corporation set to reign in their stead.

Perhaps we ought to apologise for thus obtruding our
own personal adventures on the reader. We have only hesitatingly done so, because it seems to us that the exorcism
of two Englishmen near the end of the nineteenth century
is a little incident sufficiently-strange to merit being put
on record.

**Divorce.** Divorce, extremely common among the lower classes in Japan, is rare among the upper classes. Why, indeed, should a man take the trouble to get divorced from an uncongenial wife, when any wife occupies too inferior a position to be able to make herself a serious nuisance, and when society has no objection to his keeping any number of mistresses? As for the actual law on the subject, we have not been able to ascertain it, and are under the impression that it is not well-defined. Until the time of the late revolution, Confucian ideas on the subject modelled the law. Now, according to Confucius, there are seven grounds on which a man may divorce his wife. They are: disobedience, barrenness, lewd conduct, jealousy, leprosy or any other foul and incurable disease, talking too much, and thievishness;—in plain English, a man may send away his wife whenever he gets tired of her. But her rights as against him are less extensive. Confucian ideas being now obsolete in Japan, or at least obsolescent, it may be taken for granted that new divorce laws will soon be passed.

In the year 1888, the latest for which statistics have been published, the proportion of divorces to marriages throughout Japan was as follows:

Marriages: 8.55 per thousand of the entire population.

Divorces: 2.84 per thousand.

In other words, one marriage out of every three ended in a divorce. (See also Article on MARRIAGE.)

*Books recommended. ,"Japanisches Familien-und Erbrecht," by Dr. H. Weipert, in Heft 43 of the "German Asiatic Transactions," pp. 104—7.*

**Docks.** See SHIPPING.

**Dress.** It would take a folio volume elaborately illustrated to do justice to all the peculiarities of all the varieties of Japanese costume.

Speaking generally, it may be said that the men are dressed as follows. First comes a loin-cloth (*fundoshi*) of bleached muslin. Next to this a shirt (*juban*) of silk or cotton, to which is added in winter an under-jacket (*dōgi*) of like material. Outside comes the gown (*kimono*), or in winter two wadded gowns (*shitagi* and *uwagi*), kept in place by a narrow sash (*obi*). On occasions of ceremony, there is worn furthermore a sort of broad pair of trowsers, or perhaps we should rather say a divided skirt, called *hakama*, and a stiff coat called *haori*. The *hakama* and *haori* are invariably of silk, and the *haori* is adorned with the wearer's crest in three places. The head is mostly bare, but is sometimes covered by a very large straw hat, while on the feet is a kind of sock, named *tabi*, reaching only to the ankle, and having a separate compartment for the big toe. Of straw sandals there are two kinds, the movable *zōri* used for light work, and the *waraji* which are bound tightly round the feet and used for hard walking only. People of means wear only the *tabi* indoors, and a pair of wooden clogs, called *geta*, out-of-doors. The native costume of a Japanese gentleman is completed by a fan, a parasol, and in his belt a pipe and tobacco-pouch. Merchants also wear at their belt what is called a *yatate*—a kind of portable ink-stand with a pen inside.

Take it altogether, the Japanese gentleman's costume, and that of the ladies as well, is a highly elegant and sanitary one. The only disadvantage is that the flopping of the *kimono* hinders a free gait. Formerly the Japanese gentleman wore two swords, and his back hair was drawn forward in a cue over the carefully shaven middle of the

skull; but both these fashions are obsolete. The wearing
of swords in public was interdicted by law in 1876, and
the whole gentry submitted without a blow.

Besides the loin-cloth, which is universal, the men of the
lower classes, such as coolies and navvies, wear a sort of
dark-coloured pinafore (*hara-gake*) over the bust, crossed
with bands behind the back. They cover their legs with
tight-fitting drawers (*momo-hiki*) and a sort of gaiters
(*kyahan*). Their coat, called *shirushi-banten*, is marked
on the back with a Chinese character or other sign to
show by whom they are employed. But *jinrikisha*-men
wear the *happi*, which is not thus marked—that is, when
they wear anything; for in the country districts and in
the hot weather, the loin-cloth is often the sole garment of the common people, except when they espy a
policeman coming round the corner to enforce the modern
law against nudity. It is not unusual to see a kerchief
(*hachimaki*) tied over the brow, to prevent the perspira-
tion from running into the eyes. Travellers of the middle
and lower classes are often to be distinguished by their
*kimono* being lifted up and shoved into the sash behind,
by a kind of silk drawers called *patchi*, by a sort of
mitten or hand-protector called *tekkō*, and by a cape (*kap-
pa*—the word is a corruption of the Spanish *capa*). The
peasants wear a straw overcoat (*mino*) in rainy or snowy
weather.

The Japanese costume for women is less different from
that of the men than is the case with us. Beneath all,
come two little aprons-round the loins (*koshi-maki* and
*suso-yoke*), then the shirt, and then the *kimono* or *kimonos*
kept in place by a thin belt (*shita-jime*). Over this is
bound the large sash (*obi*), which is the chief article of

feminine adornment. In order to hold it up, a sort of panier or "Improver" (*obi-age*) is provided underneath, while a handsome string (*obi-dome*) keeps it in position above. Japanese women bestow lavish care on the dressing of their hair. Their combs and hair-pins of tortoise-shell, coral, and other costly materials often represent many months of their husband's salaries. Fortunately all these things, and even dresses themselves, can be handed down from mother to daughter, as jewels and lace may be in European lands, Japanese ladies' fashions not changing quickly.

A Japanese lady's dress will often represent a value of $200, without counting the ornaments for her hair. A woman of the smaller shop-keeping class may have on her, when she goes out holiday-making, some $40 or $50 worth. A gentleman will rarely spend on his clothes as much as he lets his wife spend on hers. Perhaps he may not have on more than $60 worth. Thence, through a gradual decline in price, we come to the coolie's poor trappings, which may represent as little as $5, or even $2, as he stands.

Children's dress is more or less a repetition in miniature of that of their elders. Long swaddling-clothes are not in use. Young children have, however, a bib. They wear a little cap on their heads, and at their side hangs a charm-bag (*kinchaku*), made out of a bit of some bright-coloured damask, containing a charm (*mamori-fuda*) supposed to protect them from being run over, washed away, etc. There is also generally fastened somewhere about their little person a metal ticket (*maigo-fuda*) with their name and address, as a precaution against their getting lost.

Those having any acquaintance with Japan, either personal or by hearsay, will understand that when we say that the Japanese *wear* such and such things (in the present tense), we speak of the native costume, which is still in fairly common use, though unfortunately no longer in universal use. The undignified billycocks and pantaloons of the West are slowly but surely supplanting the picturesque, aristocratic-looking native garb—among the men more especially, as almost all officials are now obliged to wear European dress when on duty, but also among the women. It seems scarcely credible, but it is true, that the Japanese imagine their appearance to be improved when they exchange their own costume for ours; and they are angry with people who tell them the contrary. In this, as in many other matters, their former exquisite taste has died a sudden death.

It was a charming sight to see the Japanese ladies, so short a time ago as the seventies and the early eighties dressed in their own costume—*dressed*, mind you, not merely having clothes on. A bevy of them at a party—for they had begun to come out and mix with Europeans in society—was a symphony of greys and browns and other delicate hues of silk and brocade, the faultless costume being matched by the coy and at the same time perfectly natural and simple manner and musical voice of the wearers. In 1886 the Court ordered gowns from Berlin—likewise corsets, and those European shoes in which a Japanese lady finds it so hard to walk without looking as if she had taken just a little drop too much. Of course the Court speedily found imitators. Indeed, as a spur to the recalcitrant, a sort of notification was issued, "recommending" the adoption of European costume by the ladies of Japan.

In vain the local European press cried out against the barbarism, in vain every foreigner of taste endeavoured privately to persuade his Japanese friends not to let their wives make guys of themselves, in vain Mrs. Cleveland and the ladies of America wrote publicly to point out the dangers with which the corset, and European fashions generally, threaten the health of those who adopt them. The die was cast when, on the 1st November, 1886, the Empress and her ladies appeared in their new German dresses at Chiarini's Circus. The Empress herself would indeed look charming in any garb. Would one could say as much for all those with her and for those that have followed since! The very highest society of Tōkyō contains, it is true, a few—a very few—women of whose dress Pierre Loti can say without flattery, "*toilette en somme qui serait de mise à Paris et qui est vraiment bien portée.*" But the majority! No caricature could do justice to the bad figures, the ill-fitting garments, the screeching colours, that have run riot during the last four years.

A curious contention is, however, raised on the opposite side; and perhaps it is a true one. The contention is that a Japanese lady is treated more respectfully by her husband when she is in European dress than when, by retaining her national costume, she seems to say to him and to the world: "I belong to the old school, and acknowledge the subjection of women as inferior creatures." We have ourselves noticed the same lady walk into the room after her husband when dressed *à la japonaise*, but before him when *à l'européenne*. This means a great deal. If one has to endure the spectacle of Berlin wool tippets worked in stripes of blue, yellow, purple, brick-red, and bottle-green, and of stays worn upside down, it is at least some

comfort to know that these grim-looking garments have it
in their power to produce such mighty moral effects.

**Earthquakes and Volcanoes.** "Oh! how I wish I
could feel an earthquake!" is generally among the first
exclamations of the newly-landed European. "What a
paltry sort of thing it is, considering the fuss people
make about it!" is generally his remark on his *second*
earthquake (for the *first* one he invariably sleeps through).
But after the fifth or sixth he never wants to feel another; and his terror of earthquakes grows with length of
residence in an earthquake-shaken land, such as Japan has
been from time immemorial.   Indeed, geologists tell us that
much of Japan would never have existed but for the seismic
and volcanic agency which has elevated whole districts
above the ocean by means of repeated eruptions.

The cause of earthquakes is still obscure.   The learned
incline at present to the opinion that the causes may be
many and various; but the general connection between
earthquakes and volcanoes is not contested.   The "fault-
ing" which results from elevations and depressions of the
earth's surface, the infiltration of water to great depths
and the consequent generation of steam, the caving in
of subterranean hollows—hollows themselves produced in
all probability by chemical degradation—these and other
causes have been appealed to as the most probable.

One highly remarkable fact is that volcanic and earthquake-shaken regions are almost always adjacent to areas
of depression.   The greatest area of depression in the
world is the Pacific basin; and accordingly round its
borders, from Kamchatka through the Kuriles to Japan,
thence through a line of small islands to the Philippines

and to Java, then eastward to New Zealand, and right up the Western coast of South America, is grouped the mightiest array of volcanoes that the world contains. Another fact of interest is the greater occurrence of earthquakes during the winter months. This has been explained by Dr. Knott as the result of "the annual periodicity of two well-known meteorological phenomena—namely, snow accumulations over continental areas, and barometric gradients."*

The Japanese, like most other nations, had perforce submitted to the ravages of earthquakes, without attempting to investigate the causes of earthquakes scientifically. All they had done was to collect anecdotes and superstitions connected with the subject, one of the most popular of which latter (popular indeed in many parts of the world besides Japan) is that earthquakes are due to a large subterranean fish which wriggles about whenever it wakes up. As for Japanese history, it is a concatenation of earthquake disasters, exceeded only by those which have desolated South America.

With the advent of the theoretically minded European, a new era was inaugurated. A society named the Seismological Society of Japan was started in the spring of 1880, chiefly through the efforts of Professor John Milne, F. R. S., who has ever since devoted all his energies to wrestling with the problems which earthquakes, earth oscillations, earth currents, and seismic and volcanic phenomena generally, supply in such perplexing quantity. Latterly, too, the Japanese government has lent a helping hand by the establishment of a chair of seismology

---

* See his learned paper on the subject in Vol. IX. Part 1, of the "Transactions of a Seismological Society of Japan."

in the Imperial University, and of several hundreds of
observing stations all over the empire—an empire remember, dotted with no less than fifty one active volcanoes,
and experiencing about five hundred shocks yearly.

Can earthquakes be prevented? If they cannot be prevented, can they at least be foretold? Both these questions must unfortunately be answered in the negative.
Still, certain practical results have been arrived at by Mr.
Milne and his fellow-workers, which are by no means
to be despised. It is now possible to make what is
called a "seismic survey" of any given plot of ground,
and to indicate which localities will be least liable to
shocks. It has also been shown that the complete
isolation of the foundations of a building from the surface
of the soil obtains for the building comparative immunity
from damage. The reason is that the surface shakes
more than the adjacent lower layers of the soil, just as,
if several billiard-balls be placed in a row, an impulse
given to the first one will make only the last one fly off,
while those in the middle remain nearly motionless. For
the same reason, it is dangerous to build near the edge
of a cliff. To architects, again, various hints have been
given, both from experience accumulated on the spot,
and also from that of Manila and other earthquake-shaken
localities. The passage from natural to artificial vibrations being obvious, Professor Milne has been led on to
the invention of a machine which records, after the manner of a seismograph, the vibrations of railway trains.
This machine keeps an automatic record of all the motions
of a train, and serves to detect irregularities occurring at
crossings and points, as also those due to want of ballast,
defects in bridges, and so on.

Thus, imperfect as it still is, imperfect as the nature of the case may perhaps condemn it always to remain, the science of seismology has already borne practical fruit in effecting a saving of tens of thousands of dollars. To those who are interested in seismometers and seismographs, in earthquake maps and earthquake catalogues, in seismic surveys, in microseisms, earth tremors, earth pulsations, and generally in earth physics, we recommend a perusal of the "Transactions of the Seismological Society of Japan," of which fourteen volumes have been published, and of the volume entitled " Earthquakes," by Professor Milne in the "International Scientific Series." Volume IX, Part II, of the "Seismological Transactions" is specially devoted to the volcanoes of Japan, and contains a mass of statistics, anecdotes, historical details, and illustrations—each individual volcano, from the northernmost of the Kuriles down to Asó-San in Kyûshû, which is the largest crater in the world, being treated of in detail. The "*Ansei Kembun Roku*" and the "*Ansei Kembun Shi*" are capitally illustrated Japanese accounts of the great earthquake which wrecked Yedo in 1855. Lovers of the ghastly will search long before they find anything more to their taste than the delineations there given of men and women precipitated out of windows, cut in two by falling beams, bruised, smashed, imprisoned in cellars, overtaken by tidal waves, or worse still, burnt alive in one of the great fires caused by the sudden overturning of thousands of candles and braziers all over the city. Truly these are gruesome books.

**Education.** During the Middle Ages, education was in the hands of the Buddhist priesthood. The temples

were the schools, the subject most insisted on was the
Buddhist Sûtras. The accession of the Tokugawa family
to the Shôgunate (A. D. 1603-1867) brought with it a
change. The educated classes became Confucianist. Accordingly the Confucian Classics—the " Four Books "
and the " Five Canons"—were installed in the place of
honour, learnt by heart, commented on as carefully as
in China itself. Besides the Chinese Classics, instruction was given in the native history and literature. Some
few ardent students picked their way through Dutch
books that had been begged, borrowed, or stolen from the
Hollanders at Nagasaki, or bought, for their weight in
gold, for the sake of the priceless treasures of medical and
other scientific knowledge known to be concealed in them.
But such devotees of European learning were forced to
maintain the greatest secrecy, and were hampered by almost
incredible difficulties. For the government of the day
frowned on all things foreign, and more than one zealous
student expiated by his death the crime of striving to
increase knowledge.

With the revolution of 1868, the old system of education crumbled away. Indeed, even before 1868 the learning of foreign languages, especially English, had been
tacitly connived at. A complete reform was initiated—a
reform on Western lines—and it was carried out at first
chiefly under American advice. The present Imperial
University of Japan is the representative and heir of
several colleges which were formed in Tôkyô some twenty
years ago—a Language College, a Medical College, a
College of Engineering. At the same time, primary instruction was being placed on a new basis, and specially
promising lads were sent across seas to acquire Western

learning at its source. When not allowed to go abroad, even well-born young men were happy to black the shoes of some foreign family, in the hope of being able to pick up scraps of foreign languages and foreign manners. Some of the more enterprising took French leave, and smuggled themselves on board homeward-bound ships. This was how—to mention but two well-known instances— the adventurous youths, Itō and Inoue, entered on the career which has led them at last to become ministers of state.

The following statistics concerning the present condition of education in Japan are taken from the official report for 1888, which is about to be published :—

| | | | | | | |
|---|---|---|---|---|---|---|
| School Districts | | | | | | 10,933 |
| Population of the Empire | ...(Male | 21,258,418 | Female | 19,023,165) | | 41,131,583 |
| School Population | ...( | 3,618,726 | „ | 5,301,629) | | 6,920,345 |
| Number of Children of School Age receiving Instruction | ( „ | 2,379,072 | „ | 897,517 ) | | 3,277,489 |
| Number of Children of School Age not receiving Instruction | ( „ | 1,538,751 | „ | 2,104,106 ) | | 3,642,857 |
| Number of Pupils receiving Instruction per cent of School Population | | | | | | 47½ |
| Elementary Schools { Public | , (Simple 11,730, Ordinary 12,190, Higher 1,405) | | | | | 13,295 |
| { Private | „ | 65 | „ | 800 „ | 114) | 958 |
| Teachers in Public Elementary Schools | (Male | 23,884 | Female | 894) ... | | 24,758 |
| Pupils in Public Elementary Schools | ( „ | 2,072,049 | „ | 841,710 ... | | 2,873,758 |
| Pupils in Private Elementary Schools | ( „ | 29,304 | „ | 24,891 ... | | 54,195 |
| Average Number of Daily Attendance in Public Elementary Schools | | | | | | 1,942,848 |
| Average Number of Daily Attendance in Private Elementary Schools | | | | | | 45,718 |
| No. of Higher Middle Schools . (Gov.) | | | | | | 7 |
| „ „ Pupils of | ...(Male) | | | | | 3,830 |
| „ „ Ordinary Middle Schools .. (Public 41 Private 5) .. | | | | | | 46 |

| | | |
|---|---|---|
| No. of Pupils in Public Ordinary Middle Schools | (Male) | 8,903 |
| No. of Pupils in Private Ordinary Middle Schools | ( „ ) | 1,331 |
| No. of Instructors in University | | 128 |
| „ „ Students | | 738 |
| Higher Normal School (Gov.) | | 1 |
| No. of Pupils in Higher Normal Schools | (Male 87 Female 67) | 154 |
| No. of Ordinary Normal Schools (Public) | | 46 |
| „ „ Pupils in Ordinary Normal Schools | (Male 1,416 Female 662) | 3,078 |
| No. of Special Schools (Gov. 4 Public 23 Private 41) | | 66 |
| „ „ Pupils in Gov. Special Schools | (Male 612 Female 26) | 638 |
| No. of Pupils in Public Special Schools | ( „ 2,733 „ 2 ) | 2,735 |
| No. of Pupils in Private Special Schools | ( „ 8,180 „ 70 ) | 8,250 |
| No. of Higher Female Schools (Gov. 1 Public 6 Private 12) | | 19 |
| „ „ Pupils in Gov. Higher Schools | | 755 |
| No. of Pupils in Public Higher Female Schools | | 1,567 |
| No. of Pupils in Private Higher Female Schools | | 2,583 |
| No. of Miscellaneous Schools (Gov. 1 Public 34 Private 1,344) | | 1,379 |
| „ „ Pupils in Gov. Miscellaneous Schools | (Male 46 Female 73) | 81 |
| No. of Pupils in Public Miscellaneous Schools | ( „ 2,477 „ 576 ) | 2,053 |
| No. of Pupils in Private Miscellaneous Schools | ( „ 70,979 „ 13,643 ) | 83,960 |
| Total Number of Schools (Gov. 15 Public 25,449 Private 2,123) | | 27,003 |
| „ „ Teachers „ Instructors and | (Male 65,297 Female 3,743) | 69,039 |
| Total number of Students and Pupils | ( „ 2,164,663 „ 884,372 ) | 3,094,351 |
| No. of Pupils per cent of Population | | 7.54 |
| No. of Kindergartens (Gov. 1 Public 73 Private 18) | | 92 |
| „ „ Infants in Gov. Kindergartens | (Male 112 Female 79) | 191 |
| No. of Infants in Public Kindergartens | ( „ 2,890 „ 8,336 ) | 3,846 |
| No. of Infants in Private Kindergartens | ( „ 505 „ 470 ) | 900 |
| No. of Foreign Instructors (180 Male, 67 Female)* | | 247 |

---

* Of this total, 126 were American, and 77 British. The highest number attained by any other nationality (the Germans) was 19.

Table showing the Sources of Income of Public Schools.

| | Yen. | Increase for the year | Decrease for the year. |
|---|---|---|---|
| Balance from the Preceding Year | 912,005, 151 | 199,037. 443 | ... |
| School Fees .. | 1,594,268. 177 | 548,901. 173 | .. |
| Voluntary Contributions . | 718,719. 303 | 261,796. 338 | ... |
| Interest on Various Funds . | 471,165, 663 | 1,318. 723 | ... ... |
| District, Town, and Village Rates | 5,870,916. 330 | ... .. | 173 114. 253 |
| Local Taxes... ... .. | 1,197,354. 137 | ... .. | 70,725. 764 |
| Miscellaneous .. ... ... | 815,738. 443 | 48,819. 663 | ... .. |
| Total ... ... ... | 9,330,167. 683 | 784,364. 434 | ... .. |

The University includes five faculties, namely, Law,
Literature, Science, Engineering, and Medicine. The
College of Medicine is under exclusively German influence,
though there are also Japanese professors. The other
colleges have professors of various nationalities, chiefly
Japanese, German, and English. The students number
over seven hundred. Other important educational establishments started and supported by the government are
the Higher Normal School, the Higher Commercial School,
the Technological School, the Nobles' School, the Naval
and Military Academies in Tōkyō, and six Higher Middle
Schools in the provinces. There are also numerous large
private colleges, of which the best-known is the Keiō
Gijiku. Its director, Mr. Fukuzawa, is a real power in the
land. Writing with admirable clearness, publishing a
popular newspaper, not keeping too far ahead of the times,
in favour of Christianity to-day because its adoption might
gain for Japan the good will of Western nations, all eager-
ness for Buddhism to-morrow because Buddhist doctrines
can be better reconciled with those of evolution and development, pro and anti-foreign by turns, inquisitive, clever, not

overballasted with judicial calmness, this eminent private
schoolmaster, who might be minister of education, but
who has consistently refused all office, is the intellectual
father of half the young men who now fill the middle
and lower posts in the government of Japan.

From Mr. Fukuzawa, who leads Young Japan in ostenta-
tiously denying the importance of all religious dogmas, is
a long step to the missionaries, with whom school-teaching
is of course ancillary to proselytism. Among their scho-
lastic establishments, the Meiji Gakuin at Tôkyô and the
Dôshisha at Kyôto, both founded under American auspices,
may be selected for notice. The latter has recently been
raised to the status of a Christian University.

Female education is officially provided for by the High
School for Girls, the Peeresses' School, the female section
of the Higher Normal School, etc., etc. Nor in even the
most cursory enumeration of the educational institutions of
the country, is it possible to omit a reference to the Educational Society of Japan, which, as perhaps the most
successful of all the many Japanese learned societies,
does honour to the judgment and management of its
originator, Mr. Tsuji Shinji, now and for many years past
Vice-Minister of Education.

The leading idea of the Japanese Government in all its
educational improvements, is the desire to assimilate the
national ways of thinking to those of European countries.
How great a measure of success has already been attained,
can be best gauged by comparing one of the surviving old-
fashioned literati of the Tempô period (A. D. 1830—1844)
with an intelligent young man of the new school, brought-
up at the University or at Mr. Fukuzawa's. The two seem
to belong to different worlds. At the same time it is clear

that no efforts, however arduous, can make the Europeanisation complete. In effect, what is the situation? All
the nations of the West have, broadly speaking, a common
past, a common fund of ideas, from which everything
that they have and everything that they are springs
naturally, as part of a correlated whole—one Roman
Empire in the background, one Christian religion at the
centre, one gradual emancipation, first from feudalism
and next from absolutism, worked out or now in process
of being worked out together, one art, one music, one
kind of idiom, even though the words expressing it vary
from land to land. Japan stands beyond this pale, because her past has been lived through under conditions
altogether different. China is her Greece and Rome.
Her language is not Aryan, as even Russia's is. Allusions familiar from one end of Christendom to the other
require a whole chapter of commentary to make them at
all intelligible to a Japanese student, who often has not,
even then, any words corresponding to those which it is
sought to translate. So well is this fact understood by
Japanese educators that it has been customary of late
years to impart most of the higher branches of knowledge through the medium of the English language. This,
however, is an enormous additional weight hung round
the student's neck. For a Japanese to be taught through
the medium of English is infinitely harder than it would
be for English lads to be taught through the medium of
Latin, as Latin does not, after all, differ so very widely
in spirit from English. It is, so to say, English in other
words. But between English and Japanese the gulf fixed
is so wide and gaping that the student's mind must be
for ever on the stretch. The simpler and more idiomatic

the English, the more it taxes his powers of comprehension.

It is difficult to see any way out of this *cul-de-sac*.   All the greater, therefore, is the praise due to a body of educators who fight on so bravely, and on the whole so successfully.   As for the typical Japanese student, he belongs to that class of youths which is the schoolmaster's delight—compliant, intelligent, deferential, studious almost to excess.   His only marked fault is a tendency common to all subordinates in Japan—a tendency to wish to steer the ship himself.   "Please, Sir, we don't want to read American history any more.   We want to read how balloons are made."   Such is a specimen of the requests which every teacher in Japan must have had to listen to over and over again.   No country has hitherto been so little democratic as Japan in government.   No country has been so democratic in everything else.

*Books recommended.*   The annual "Report of the Minister of State for Education," and the "Calendars" of the University and the various other educational institutions.

**EE—EE.**  These letters, which appear over the door of many a forwarding agency in modern Japan, stand for the English word "express."

**Esotericism.**  When an Englishman or American hears the word "esoteric" mentioned, the first thing, probably, that comes into his head is Buddhism, the second the name of Mr. Sinnett or of Madame Blavatsky.  Matters stand somewhat differently in Japan.  Not religion only, but every art here is or has been esoteric—poetry, music, porcelain-making, fencing, even bone-setting, and cookery itself.  Esotericism is not a unique mystery shrouding a special class of subjects. It is a general attitude of the mind at a certain stage, and a very natural attitude too, if one takes the trouble to look into it. Ordinary men do not wear their hearts on their sleeves for daws to peck at. Why should an artist do so with his art ? Why should he desecrate his art by initiating unworthy persons into its principles ? Nor is it merely a question of advisability, or of delicacy and good taste. It is a question of possibility and impossibility. Only sympathetic pupils are fitted by nature to understand certain things; and certain things can only be taught by word of mouth, and when the spirit moves one. Moreover, there comes the question of money. Esoteric teaching of the lower arts may be said to have performed, in old days, the functions of our modern system of patents.

Such are, it would seem, the chief headings of the subject, considered in the abstract. Fill them out, if you please, by further reflection and further research; and if you wish to talk to your Japanese friends about esotericism, remember the fascinating words *hiden*, " secret tradition ; " *hijutsu*, " secret art ; " and *okugi*, " inner mysteries," which play a notable part in Japanese history and literature.

Many are the stories told of the faithful constancy with which initiation into hidden mysteries has been sought. Early in the tenth century there lived a great musician, a nobleman named Hakuga-no-Sammi. But one Semi-Maro was a greater musician still. He dwelt in retirement, with no other companion but his lute, and there was a melody of which he alone had the secret. Hakuga —as he may be styled for shortness' sake—went every evening for three years to listen at Semi's gate, but in vain. At last, one autumn night, when the wind was soughing

through the sedges, and the moon was half-hidden by a
cloud. Hâkuga heard the magic strains begin, and, when
they ceased, he heard the player exclaim, "Alas! that
there should be none to whom I might hand on this
precious possession!" Thereupon Hakuga took courage.
He entered the hermitage, prostrated himself, declared his
name and rank, and humbly implored to be received by
Semi as his disciple. This Semi consented to, and gradually revealed to him all the innermost recesses of his art.
The story, whether true or not, is a favourite one with
Japanese painters.

Undoubtedly authentic, and very different in its tenor,
is the tale of Katô Tamikichi, a manufacturer of porcelain
at the beginning of the eighteenth century. His master,
Tsugane Bunzaemon, who owned a kiln in the province of
Owari, envied the skill of the Karatsu porcelain-makers in
the use of blue and white, and was determined to penetrate
their secret. Accordingly he succeeded in arranging a
marriage between one of his pupils, Katô Tamikichi, and
the daughter of the chief of the Karatsu people. Katô,
thus taken into the family in so distant a province, was
regarded as one of themselves and admitted into their fullest confidence. Things went on quietly for years, during
which he became the father of several children. At last, one
day, Katô expressed a longing desire to revisit the scenes of
his childhood and to enquire after his old master. Nothing
doubting, the Karatsu people let him go. But when he
reached Owari, he disclosed to his former master all
that he had learnt at Karatsu, the consequence of which
was that the Owari porcelain was greatly improved, and
obtained an immense sale in the neighbouring market of
Ôsaka, the richest in the empire. When this came to the

ears of the Karatsu people, they were so much enraged that they caused Katō's wife and children to be crucified. He himself died a raving lunatic.

Since the latter part of the Middle Ages, the general prevalence among the upper classes of luxury, idleness, and a superstitious veneration for the past, even in trivial matters, together with a love of mystery, produced the most puerile whims. For instance, the court nobles at Kyōto kept to themselves, with all the apparatus of esotericism, the interpretation of the names of three birds and of three plants mentioned in an ancient book of poetry called the *Kokinshū.* No sacrament could have been more jealously guarded from impious hands, or rather lips. But when the great scholar, Motoori, disdaining all mumbo-jumbo, brought the light of true philological criticism to bear on the texts in question, lo and behold! one of the mysterious birds proved to be none other than the familiar wagtail, the second remained difficult to fix accurately, and the third name was not that of any particular species, but merely a general expression signifying the myriad little birds that twitter in spring. The three mysterious trees were equally common-place.

Foolish as the three bird secret was (and it was but one among a hundred such), it had the power to save the life of a brave general, Hosokawa Yūsai, who, being besieged in A. D. 1600 by a son of the famous ruler Hideyoshi, was on the point of seeing his garrison starved into a surrender. This came to the ears of the Mikado; and His Majesty, knowing that Hosokawa was not only a warrior, but a learned man, well-versed in the mysteries of the *Kokinshū*—three birds and all—and fearing that this inestimable store of erudition might perish with him and

be lost to the world for ever, exerted his personal influence
to such good effect that an edict was issued commanding
the attacking army to retire.

Viewed from a critical standpoint, Chinese and Japanese
esoterics well deserve thorough investigation by some
competent hand. We ourselves do not think that much
would be added thereby to the world's store of wisdom.
But we do think that a flood of light would be shed upon
some of the most curious nooks and crannies of the human
mind.

**Eta.** The origin of the *eta*, or Japanese pariahs, is
altogether obscure. Some see in them the descendants of
Korean captives, brought to Japan during the wars of the
latter part of the sixteenth century. By others they are
considered to be the illegitimate descendants of the celebrated generalissimo Yoritomo, who lived as far back as
the twelfth century. Even the etymology of the name
is a subject of dispute among the learned, some of whom
believe it to be the Chinese compound *e-ta* 穢多, "defilement abundant," while others derive it from *e-tori* 餌取,
"food-catchers," in allusion to the slaughtering of cattle
and other animals, which, together with skinning such
animals, digging criminals' graves, and similar degrading
occupations, constituted their means of livelihood. We
ourselves incline to date back the first gradual organisation
of the *eta* as a separate class to a very early period indeed—
say the seventh or eighth century—when the introduction
of Buddhism had caused all those who were connected in
any way with the taking of life to be looked on with horror
and disdain.

The legal distinction between the *eta* and other persons

of the lower orders was abolished on the 12th October,
1871, at which time the official census gave 287,111 as
the number of *eta* properly so called, and 982,800 as
the total number of outcasts of all descriptions.   Scorn
of the *eta* has naturally survived the abolition of their
legal disabilities.   It is a favourite theme of contemporary
novelists, one of whom, Enchō, has excellently adapted
the plot of Wilkie Collins' "New Magdalen" to the
Japanese life of our day, by substituting for the courtesan
of the English original a girl who had degraded herself by
marrying an *eta*.

*Book recommended.* "The Eta Maiden and the Hatamoto," in Vol. I of
Mitford's "Tales of Old Japan."


**Eurasians.**   Half-castes are often called Eurasians, from
their being half-*Eu*ropeans and half-Asiatics or *Asians*.
They are as a rule delicate, and the girls are often pretty,
though always betraying in their eyes the secret of their
mixed origin.   Eurasians usually resemble the Japanese
mother rather than the European father, in accordance
with the general physiological law whereby the fair parent
gives way to the dark.   The time that has elapsed since
Japanese Eurasians began to become numerous is not long
enough to inform us whether this mixed race will endure,
or whether, as so often happens in such cases, it will die
out in the third or fourth generation.


**Exterritoriality.**   Exterritoriality, or extra-territoriality,
as it is called by extra-particular speakers, is the exemption
of the foreigners residing in a country from the action of the
laws of that country.   This exemption exists both in China
and Japan.   Thus, if an Englishman commits a murder, he

is tried, not by any Japanese judge, but by the nearest
British consular court. In civil cases where one party is a
Japanese and the other a foreigner, the suit is carried into
the court of the defendant's nationality. If I want to sue
a Japanese, I must sue him in a Japanese court; but a
Japanese sues me in the British court.

Exterritoriality, claimed thirty years ago as the only
*modus vivendi* which could render the existence of civilised
Christian beings endurable in the Japan of those days, has
since then been violently assailed by some as unjust to
Japan, whose independent sovereign rights it is held to
infringe. Thus, the partisans of exterritoriality found
their arguments on alleged practical utility, whereas its
opponents argue deductively from considerations of abstract
right. For a long time most foreigners were in favour
of exterritoriality, and almost all Japanese against it. But
since 1889 not a few Japanese of the educated classes have
gone over to the exterritorial camp, because they fear that
if the more pushing European race be allowed free access to
every part of the country, the mines, the industries, and
finally the land itself will pass into foreign hands. We do
not purpose to discuss this thorny question. It has already
been discussed to satiety in the local press—wrangled
about, preached about, raved about. The new-comer who
wishes to make himself agreeable is advised not to touch
upon the exterritoriality controversy. All residents are
utterly sick and weary of it.

**Fairy-Tales.** The Japanese have plenty of fairy-tales;
but the greater number can be traced to a Chinese, and
several of these again to a Buddhist, that is, to an Indian,
source. Among the most popular are " Urashima," " Mo-

motarō," "The Battle of the Monkey and the Crab,"
"The Tongue-Cut Sparrow," "The Mouse's Wedding,"
"The Old Man who Made the Trees to Blossom," "The
Crackling Mountain," and "The Lucky Tea-Kettle."

Though it is convenient to speak of these stories as
"fairy-tales," fairies properly so-called do not appear in
them. Instead of fairies, there are goblins and devils,
together with foxes, cats, and badgers, possessed of superhuman powers for working evil. We feel that we are in
a fairy-land altogether foreign to that which gave Europe
"Cinderella" and "Puss in Boots"—no less foreign to
that which produced the gorgeously complicated marvels of
the "Arabian Nights."

Books. "The Japanese Fairy-Tale Series," published by the Kōbunsha, Tōkyō.—
Mitford's "Tales of Old Japan," latter part of Vol. I.—Griffis' "Japanese Fairy
World."—"Olden-Time Tales for Little People."

**Fashionable Crazes.** Japan stood still so long that she
has to move quickly and often now, to make up for lost
time. Every year or two there is a new craze, over which
the nation, or at least that part of the nation which resides
in Tōkyō, goes wild for a season. The chief crazes
witnessed during the last seventeen years are as follows :—

1873. This was the rabbit year. There are none of
these little quadrupeds in Japan. Hence, when imported
as curiosities, they fetched incredible prices. As much as
$1000 was sometimes paid for a single specimen. Specu-
lations in $400 and $500 rabbits were of daily occurrence. In the following year, 1874, the government put a
capitation tax on rabbits, the price fell in consequence from
dollars to cents, and the luckless rabbit-gamblers were
ruined in a moment.

1874-5. Cock-fighting.

1876-7. The *omoto* (*Rhodea japonica*), a plant with bright red berries.

1882-3. Printing dictionaries and other works by subscription. Many of these literary enterprises turned out to be fraudulent, and had to be dealt with by the police. About 1883 was also the great time for founding societies, learned and otherwise.

1884. Boating on the River Sumida.

1885. Velocipedes, and the *Rhodea japonica* again; also whist, which the Japanese call *torompu*, a corruption of our word "trump."

1885-7. Waltzing and gigantic funerals. During these years there was also, in official circles, an epidemic of what was locally known as "the German measles."

1887. Mesmerism, table-turning, and planchette.

1888. Wrestling, in which the then prime minister, Count Kuroda, led the fashion.

1889. Joint stock companies. A general revival of all native Japanese amusements, Japanese costume, anti-foreign agitation, etc. This was the great year of reaction.

**Filial Piety.**[*]  Filial piety is the virtue *par excellence* of China and Japan. From it springs loyalty[†] which is but the childlike obedience of a subject to the Emperor, who is regarded, in Chinese phrase, as "the father and mother of his people." On these two fundamental virtues the whole fabric of society is reared. Accordingly, one of the gravest dangers to Japan at the present time arises from the sudden importation of our less patriarchal Western ideas on these points. The traditional basis of morality is sapped.

---

[*] In Japanese, *kō*, or more popularly *oya-kōkō*.

[†] In Japanese, *chū*, or *chūshin*.

There are no greater favourites with the people of Japan than the "Four-and-Twenty Paragons of Filial Piety" (*Ni-jū-shi Kō*), whose quaint acts of virtue Chinese legend relates. For instance, one of the Paragons had a cruel stepmother who was very fond of fish. Never repining at her harsh treatment of him, he lay down naked on the frozen surface of a lake. The warmth of his body melted a hole in the ice, at which two carp came up to breathe. These he caught and set before his stepmother. Another Paragon, though of tender years and having a delicate skin, insisted on sleeping uncovered at night, in order that the mosquitoes should fasten on him alone, and allow his parents to slumber undisturbed. A third, who was very poor, determined to bury his own child alive, in order to have more food wherewith to support his aged mother, but was rewarded by heaven with the discovery of a vessel filled with gold, on which the whole family lived happily ever after. A fourth, who was of the female sex, enabled her father to escape, while she clung to the jaws of the tiger which was about to devour him. But the drollest of all is the story of Rōraishi. This Paragon, though seventy years old, used to dress in baby's clothes and sprawl about upon the floor. His object was piously to delude his parents, who were really over ninety years of age, into the idea that they could not be so very old after all, seeing that they still had such a puerile son.

Those readers who wish to learn all about the remaining nineteen Paragons should consult Anderson's "Catalogue of Japanese and Chinese Paintings," page 171, where also an illustration of each is given. The Japanese have established a set of "Four-and-Twenty Native Paragons" (*Honchō Ni-jū-shi Kō*) of their own, but these are less popular.

The first question a European will probably ask or. being told of the lengths to which filial piety is carried in the Far-East is: how can the parents be so stony-hearted as to think of allowing their children thus to sacrifice themselves? But such a consideration never occurs to a Chinese or Japanese mind. That children should sacrifice themselves to their parents is, in the Far-Eastern view of things, a principle as indisputable as the duty of men to cede the best of everything to women is with us. Far-Eastern parents accept their children's sacrifices much as our women accept the front seat—with thanks perhaps, but as a matter of course. No text in the Bible raises so much prejudice here against Christianity as that which commands a man to leave his father and mother and cleave to his wife: "There! you see it," exclaims the anti-Christian Japanese, pointing to the passage, "I always said that it was an immoral religion."

**Flowers.** An enemy has said that Japanese flowers have no scent. The assertion is incorrect: witness the plum-blossom, the wild rose, and the many sweet-smelling lilies and orchids. But granting even—for the sake of argument, if for nothing more—that the fragrance of flowers greets one less often in Japan than at home, it must be allowed on the other side that the Japanese show a more genuine appreciation of flowers than we do. The whole population turns out several times in the year for no other purpose than to visit places which are noted for certain kinds of blossoms. It is round these that the national holiday-makings of the most holiday-loving of nations revolve, and no visitor to Japan should fail to see one or other—all, if possible—of these charming

flower festivals. The principal flowers cultivated in Tōkyō
are :—

The plum-blossom, which comes into flower about
the end of January, and lasts on into March;

| | |
|---|---|
| the cherry-blossom, | first half of April; |
| the tree-peony, end of April or beginning of May; |
| the wistaria, | first week in May; |
| the iris, | first week in June; |
| the lotus, | early in August; |
| the chrysanthemum, | first three weeks of |

November;

the maple (for the Japanese include bright leaves under
the general designation of flowers), all November.

The Japanese care but little for some flowers which
to Europeans commend themselves as the most beautiful,
and they make much of others which we should scarcely
notice. All sorts of considerations come into play besides
mere "look-see" (if we may for once be allowed to use a
convenient Pidjin-English term). The insignificant blossom of the straggling lespedeza shrub is a favourite, on
account of ancient poetic fables touching the amours of the
lespedeza as a fair maiden, and of the stag her lover. The
camellia is neglected, because it is considered unlucky. It
is considered unlucky, because its red blossoms fall off whole
in a way which reminds people—at least it reminds Japanese people—of decapitated heads. And so on in other
cases. It is impossible to enumerate all.

A very curious sight is to be seen at Dangozaka in
Tōkyō at the proper season. It consists of chrysanthemums worked into all sorts of shapes—men and gods,
boats, bridges, castles, etc., etc. Generally some historical
or mythological scene is portrayed, or else some tableau

from a popular drama. There, too, may be seen very fine chrysanthemums *au naturel*, though not quite such fine ones as the *élite* of Tokyo society is admitted to gaze on once a year in the old palace at Akasaka, and after having once seen which no one will again speak of the chrysanthemums at the Temple in London. The mere variety is amazing. There is not only every colour, but every shape. Some of the blossoms are immense—larger across than a man's hand can stretch. Some are like large snow-balls— the petals all smooth, and turned in one on the top of the other. Others resemble the tousled head of a Scotch terrier. Some have long filaments stretched out like star-fish, and some, as if to counterbalance the giants, have their petals atrophied into mere drooping hairs. But the strangest thing of all is to see five or six kinds, of various colours and sizes, growing together on the same plant—a nosegay with only , one stem—the result of judicious grafting. Of the same kind of blossoms, as many as six hundred odd have been known to be produced on one plant. Last November, though there was no plant quite so phenomenal, there were several with over two hundred and over three hundred blossoms. One had four hundred and seventeen. In other cases the triumph is just the opposite way. The whole energies of a plant are made to concentrate on the production of a single blossom. But then what a blossom! A tawny, dishevelled monster, perhaps, called "Sleepy Head" (for each variety has some quaint name), or else the "Golden Dew," or the "White Dragon," or the "Fisher's Lantern"—a dark russet this— or the "Robe of Feathers," a richly clustering pink and white, or loveliest of all, the "Starlit Night"—a delicately fretted creature, looking like Iceland moss covered with

hoar-frost. Such results are obtained only by the accumulated toil of years, and especially by care, repeated
many times daily, during the seven months that precede the
period of blossoming. Such care is amply rewarded; for
the chrysanthemum is a flower which will last several
weeks if duly sheltered from the early frosts.

Bouquèt-making is not left in Japan as it is in Europe,
to individual caprice. Europeans are, in this respect,
wild children of nature. The Japanese have made an art
of it, not to say a science. Indeed, they invoke the aid of
Confucianism itself, and arrange flowers philosophically,
with due regard to the active and passive principles of
nature, and in obedience to certain traditional rules which
have been jealously handed down in the various flower-
schools ever since Sen-no-Rikyū first taught the art in
the sixteenth century of our era. It is well-worth any
one's while to read Mr. Conder's summary of the subject,
given in Vol. XVII, Part II, of the "Asiatic Transactions," and carefully to study the numerous illustrations
with which it is adorned. Whatever the reader may think
of the so-called flower *philosophy*, he will at least have
gained acquaintance with a graceful and intricate art, and
with a curious chapter in the history of the human mind.
Linear effect, and a certain proportion achieved by means of
irregularity, are the key-note and the dominant of Japanese
floral compositions. The guiding principle is not contrast
of colour.

An enthusiastic local critic, who is up to the ears in love
with all things Japanese, opines that the Japanese linear
arrangement of stems and leaves stands "at an onmeasura-
ble height above the barbaric massing of colours that
constitutes the whole of the corresponding art in the West."

Such a verdict will scarcely find acceptance with those who
esteem colour to be nature's most glorious gift to man, and
the grouping of colours (unless we set above it the
grouping of sounds in music) to be the most divine of
human arts.   Still, Japanese floral arrangements offer a
subject as charming as it curious; and we are greatly mistaken if it and Japanese gardening will not make many
a European convert when once they shall have been set
before the home public in an intelligible and attractive
manner, without too many hard Japanese words.   We
believe that Mr. Conder is now engaged on a work of this
kind.

**Food.**  Like most other nations, the Japanese take
three meals a day—one on rising in the morning, one
at noon, and one at about sunset.  Much the same sort
of food is partaken of at all these meals, but breakfast
is lighter than the other two.  The staple is rice—which
is replaced by millet or some other cheaper grain in the
poorer country districts—rice with fish and eggs, and
vegetables either fresh or pickled.  Beans, in particular,
are in constant requisition.

Buddhism has left its impress here, as on everything in
Japan.   To Buddhism was due the abandonment of a meat
diet, now over a thousand years ago.  The permission to
eat fish, though that too entailed the taking of life, which
is contrary to strict Buddhist tenets, seems to have been
a concession to human frailty.  Pious frauds, moreover,
came to the rescue.  One may even now see the term
"mountain whale" (*yama-kujira*) written up over certain
eating-houses, which means that venison is there for sale.
The logical process is this:—A whale is a fish.  Fish may

be eaten. Therefore, if you call venison "mountain whale," you may eat venison. Of course no actual prohibition against eating flesh, such as existed under the old régime, exists now. But the custom of abstaining from it remains pretty general; and though beef and pork were introduced at the time of the late revolution, along with Herbert Spencer's philosophy and French *chassepots*, recent statistics show that meat-eating is again on the wane.

Of beverages the chief are tea, which is taken without sugar or milk, and *sake*, an alcoholic liquor prepared from rice and resembling the Chinese *sam-shu*. It is generally taken hot, and at the *beginning* of dinner. Only when the drinking-bout is over, is the rice brought in.

Japanese dishes fail to satisfy European cravings. After a Japanese dinner, you have simultaneously a feeling of fulness and a feeling of having eaten nothing that will do you any good. The food is clean, admirably free from grease, often pretty to look at. But try to live on it—no! The Japanese, doubtless, being to the manner born, prefer their own rice and other dishes for a continuance. At the same time, they do not object to an occasional dinner in European style. Experts say that Japanese food, though poor in nitrogen and especially in fat, is rich in carbon, and amply sufficient to support life, provided the muscles be kept in action, but that it is indigestible and even deleterious to those who spend their time squatting on the mats at home. This accounts for the healthy looks of the coolies, and for the too often dyspeptic and feeble bodily habit of the upper classes, who take little or no exercise.

The following is a specimen of the bill of fare at a Japanese banquet. The reader must understand that

everything is served in small portions, as each guest has
a little table to himself, in front of which he squats on
the floor :—

PRELIMINARY COURSE, served with *saki* :—*suimono*, that
is, a kind of bean-curd soup ; *kuchi-tori*, a relish, such as
an omelette, or chestnuts boiled soft and sweet, or *kama-
boko*, which is fish pounded and then rolled into little
balls and baked ; *sashimi*, minced raw fish ; *hachi-sakana*,
a fine, large fish, either broiled with salt or boiled with
soy ; *uma-ni*, bits of fish or sometimes fowl, boiled with
lotus-roots or potatoes in soy and in a sort of liqueur
called *mirin* ; *su-no-mono*, sea-ears or sea-slugs served with
vinegar ; *chawan*, a thin fish soup with mushrooms, or
else *chawan-mushi*, a thick custardy soup.

FIRST COURSE (*Zembu*) :—*Shiru*, soup which may be
made of bean-curd, of fish, of sea-weed or of some other
material ; *o hira*, boiled fish, either alone or floating in
soup ; *tsubo*, sea-weed or some other appetiser, boiled
in a small deep bowl or cup ; *namasu*, raw fish cut in
slices, and served with vinegar and cold stewed vegetables ;
*aemono*, a sort of salad made with bean sauce or pounded
sesamum seeds ; *yakimono*, raw fish (although the name
means " broiled "), served in a little bamboo basket, but
generally only looked at and not eaten ; *kō-no-mono*,
pickled vegetables, such as egg-plant, cabbage-leaves, or
the strong-smelling raddish (*daikon*), which is as great
a terror to the noses of most foreigners as European
cheese is to the noses of most Japanese.

SECOND COURSE (*Ni no zen*) :—soup, raw fish (but only
if none has been served in the first course), and rice.

Such banquets as the above are of course not given
every day. At smaller dinners not more than half such

a *menu* would be represented. Quiet well-to-do people, living at home, may have a couple of dishes at each meal—a broiled fish perhaps, and some soup, or else an omelette, besides pickles to help the rice down with. The Oriental abstemiousness which figures so largely in travellers' tales, is no part of real Japanese manners. To make up for the comparative lightness and monotony of their food, the Japanese take plenty of it. It is the custom, too, to set food before a guest, at whatever time of day he calls. On such occasions *soba* is in request—a sort of buckwheat vermicelli, served with soy and the sweet liqueur called *mirin*; or else *shiruko*, that is, rice-cakes with a sauce made of red beans and sugar; or *sushi*, rice-cakes plastered over with fish or with seaweed on which vinegar has been sprinkled. Even when these things are not given—and among the Europeanised upper classes they are a good deal abandoned—tea and cakes are always set before every guest. Many of the Japanese cakes and sugar-plums are pleasant eating. They atone to some extent for the absence of puddings and for the singular poorness of Japanese fruit.

The latest thing in Tōkyō is a bread diet for the *jinrikisha*-men, resorted to on account of the excessive dearness of rice. Since the winter of 1889—90, piles of loaves have been displayed at every little cook-stall. The bread, which is of poor quality, is made palatable by means of molasses.

**Forfeits.** The Japanese play various games of forfeits, which they call *Ken*, sitting in a little circle and flinging out their fingers, after the manner of the Italian *mora*. The most popular kind of *Ken* is the *Kitsune-Ken*, or "fox

forfeit," in which various positions of the fingers represent
a fox, a man, and a gun.   The man can use the gun, the
gun can kill the fox, the fox can deceive the man; but
the man cannot kill the fox without the gun, nor the fox
use the gun against the man.   Hence a number of
combinations.   Another variety of the game of forfeits
is the Tomo-se, or "Follow me" in which the beaten
player has to walk round the room after the conqueror,
with something on his back, as if he were the conqueror's
baggage coolie.   The dance called by foreigners "John
Kino" is a less reputable member of the same family
of games.°

**Forty-Seven Rōnins.**    Asano, Lord of Akō, while at
Yedo in attendance on the Shōgun, was entrusted with the
carrying out of one of the greatest state ceremonies of those
times—nothing less than the reception and entertainment
of an envoy from the Mikado.   Now Asano was not so
well-versed in such matters as in the duties of a warrior.
Accordingly he took counsel with another nobleman, named
Kira, whose vast knowledge of ceremonies and court etiquette was equalled only by the meanness of his disposition.   Resenting honest Asano's neglect to fee him for the
information which he had grudgingly imparted, he twitted
and jeered at him for a country lout unworthy the name
of daimyō.   At last, he actually went so far as to order
Asano to bend down and fasten up his foot-gear for him.
Asano, long-suffering though he was, could not brook such
an insult.   Drawing his sword, he slashed the insolent
wretch in the face, and would have made an end of him,
had he not sought safety in flight.   The palace—for this

---

° "John Kino" seems to be a corruption of chon ki-na or chot ki-na, "just come here!"

scene took place within the precincts of the palace—was of course soon in an uproar. Thus to degrade its majesty by a private brawl was a crime punishable with death and confiscation. Asano was condemned to perform *harakiri* that very evening, his castle was forfeited, his family declared extinct, and all the members of his clan disbanded :—in Japanese parlance they became *rōnins*, literally " wavemen," that is, wanderers, fellows without a lord and without a home. This was in the month of April, 1701.

So far the first act. Act two is the vengeance. Ōishi Kuranosuke, the senior retainer of the dead *daimiyō*, determines to revenge him, and consults with forty-six others of his most trusty fellow-lieges as to the ways and means. All are willing to lay down their lives in the attempt. The difficulty is to elude the vigilance of the government. For mark one curious point: the vendetta, though imperatively prescribed by custom, was forbidden by law, somewhat as duelling now is in certain Western countries. Not to take vengeance on an enemy involved social ostracism. On the other hand, to take it involved capital punishment. But not to take it was an idea which never entered the head of any chivalrous Japanese.

After many secret consultations, it was determined among the Rōnins that they should separate and dissemble. Several of them took to plying trades. They became carpenters, smiths, and merchants in various cities, by which means some of their number gained access to Kira's mansion, and learnt many of the intricacies of its corridors and gardens. Ōishi himself, the head of the faithful band, went to Kyōto, where he plunged into a course of drunkenness and debauchery. He even discarded his wife and children, and took a harlot to live with him. Thus was their enemy, to whom full reports of all these doings were brought by spies, lulled at last into complete security. Then suddenly, on the night of the 30th January, 1703, during a violent snow-storm, the attack was made. The Forty-Seven Rōnins forced the gate of Kira's mansion, slew his retainers, and dragged forth the high-born but chicken-hearted wretch from an outhouse in which he had sought to hide himself behind a lot of firewood and charcoal. Respectfully, as befits a mere gentleman when addressing a great noble, the leader of the band requested Kira to perform *harakiri*, thus giving him the chance of dying by his own hand and so saving his honour. But Kira was afraid, and there was nothing for it but to kill him like the scoundrel that he was.

That done, the little band formed in order, and marched (day having now dawned) to the temple of Sengakuji at the other end of the city. On their way thither, the people all flocked out to praise their doughty deed, a great *daimyō* whose palace they passed sent out refreshments to them with messages of sympathy, and at the temple they were received by the abbot in person. There they laid on their lord's grave, which stood in the temple-grounds, the head of the enemy by whom he had been so grievously wronged. Then came the official sentence, condemning them all to commit *harakiri*. This they did separately, in the mansions of the various *daimyōs* to whose care they had been entrusted for the last few days of their lives, and then they also were buried in the same temple grounds, where their tombs can be seen to this day. Two centuries of the enthusiastic admiration of a whole people has been the reward of their obedience to the ethical code of their time and country.

# Gardens.

**Books recommended.** "The Forty-Seven Rōnin," the first story in Mitford's "Tales of Old Japan." Mr. Mitford gives, in his charming style, various picturesque details which want of space forces us to omit.—Dickins' "Chiushingura or the Loyal League," is a translation of the popular play founded on the story of the Rōnin.—There is a whole literature on the subject, both native and European. Of native books, the *I-ro-ha Bunko* is the one best worth reading. It is easy, graphic, and obtainable everywhere. In it and its sequel, the *Ushi ne Ahebono*, the adventures of each of the Forty-Seven Rōnin are traced out separately, the result being a complete picture of Japanese life a hundred and ninety years ago. It should, however, be remembered that these works belong rather to the catalogue of historical novels than to that of history proper.

**Gardens.** A garden without flowers may sound like a contradiction in terms. But it is a fact that many Japanese gardens are of that kind, the object which Japanese landscape gardeners set before them being to produce something park-like, to suggest some famous natural scene, in which flowers may or may not appear, according to the circumstances of the case. When they do, they are generally grouped together in beds or under shelter, and removed as soon as their season of bloom is over, more after the manner of a European flower-show. In this way are obtained horticultural triumphs, such as are described in the Article on FLOWERS. Triumphs of another kind are achieved by dwarfing. Thus you may see a pine-tree or a maple, sixty years old and perfect in every part, but not more than a foot high. Japanese gardeners are also very skilful in transplanting large trees. A judicious treatment of the accessory roots during a couple of years enables massive, aged trees to be removed from place to place, so that the money of the Japanese *nouveau riche* can raise up everything—even an ancestral park—on whatever spot he chooses.

Japanese landscape gardening is one of the fine arts. Ever since the middle of the fifteenth century, generations

of artists have been busy perfecting it, elaborating and
refining over and over again the principles handed down
by their predecessors, until it has come to be considered
a mystery as well as an art, and is furnished—not to say
encumbered—with a vocabulary more complicated and
recondite than any one who has not perused some of the
native treatises on the subject can well imagine. There is
a whole set of names for different sorts of garden lanterns,
another for water-basins, another for fences (one authority
enumerates nineteen kinds of screen fences alone), another
—and this is a very important subject—for those large
stones, which, according to Japanese ideas, constitute the
skeleton of the whole composition.

Then, too, there are rules for every detail; and different
schools of the art or science of gardening have rules
diametrically opposed to each other. For instance, larger
trees are planted and larger hills made by one school in the
front portion of a garden, and smaller ones in the further
portions, with the object of exaggerating the perspective and
thus making the garden look bigger than it really is. Another school teaches the direct contrary. Suggestion is
largely used, as when part of a small lake is so adroitly
hidden as to give the idea of greater size in the part
unseen, or as when a meander of pebbles is made to
represent a river-bed. Everything, in fact, has a reason—
generally an abstruse reason.

Gardens are supposed to be capable of symbolising
abstract ideas, such as peace, chastity, old age, etc.
The following passage from the authority quoted below
will show how the garden of a certain Buddhist abbot is
made to convey the idea of the power of divine truth:—
" This garden consists almost entirely of stones arranged

in a fanciful and irregular manner in a small enclosure,
the sentiment expressed depending for its value upon
acquaintance with the following Buddhist legend, somewhat reminding us of the story of Saint Francis and the
birds.   A certain monk Daita, ascending a hillock and
collecting stones, began to preach to them the secret precepts of Buddha, and so miraculous was the effect of the
wondrous truths which he told that even the lifeless stones
bowed in reverent assent.   Thereupon the Saint placed
them upon the ground around him, and consecrated them
as the ' Nodding Stones.' "

Book recommended.   " The Art of Landscape Gardening in Japan," by Josiah
Conder. printed in Vol. XIV, Part II, of the " Asiatic Transactions."

Geography.  The boundaries of Japan have expanded
greatly in the course of ages.   The central and western
portions of the Main Island, together with Shikoku, Kyūshū, and the lesser islands of Iki, Tsushima, Oki, Awaji,
and perhaps Sado, formed the Japan of early historic days,
say of the eighth century after Christ.   At that time the
Ainos, though already in full retreat northwards, still held
the Main Island as far as the 38th or 39th parallel of
latitude.   They were soon driven across the Strait of Tsugaru into Yezo, which island was itself gradually conquered during the period extending from the twelfth to the
seventeenth century.   In the eighteenth century a portion
of Saghalien was added to the Japanese territory.   But a
discussion having arisen on this subject between Japan
and Russia, the weaker of the two powers naturally went to
the wall.   Saghalien, with its valuable coal-fields and fisheries, was ceded to Russia by the treaty of St Petersburg
in 1875, and the barren, storm-swept Kurile Islands were
obtained in exchange.   Meanwhile, the Loochoo and Bonin

Islands had been added to the Japanese possessions, which thus, in their present and furthest extent, stretch from Kamchatka on the North, (lat. 50° 56') to Formosa on the South (lat. 24° 6'), and from 122° 45' to 156° 32' of longitude East of Greenwich.

Japan proper—that is, omitting Yeso, the Kuriles, the Loochoos, and the Bonins—consists of three large islands, of which one, the largest, has no name in popular use, while the other two are called respectively Shikoku and Kyûshû, together with the small islands of Sado, Oki, Tsushima, and a multitude of smaller ones still. The largest island is separated from the two next in size by the celebrated Inland Sea, for which latter also there is no generally current Japanese name. The area of the entire Japanese Empire is between 146,000 and 147,000 square miles. Hardly twelve per cent of this total area is cultivated, or indeed cultivable. By far the greater portion of it is covered by mountains, many of which are volcanoes, either active or extinct. Fusiyama itself was in eruption as lately as January, A.D. 1708. Of recently active volcanoes, we may mention Asama, Shirane-San, and Bandai-San in Eastern Japan, Vries Island (Ōshima) not far from the entrance to Yokohama harbour, Asō-San in Kyûshû, which has the largest crater in the world, and the beautifully shaped Komagatake, near Hakodate. Others, extinct or quiescent, are Ontake, Hakusan, Tateyama, Nantai-zan, Chōkai-zan, Iide-san, Ganju-san, and Iwaki-yama on the Main Island, and Sakura-jima, Kirishima-yama, and Unzen-ga-take in Kyûshû. The grandest mountain mass in Japan is the Shinano-Hida range—granite giants of from 8000 to 9000 feet in height.

Owing to the narrowness of the country, most Japanese

streams are rather torrents than rivers. The rivers best worth mentioning are the Kitakami, the Abukuma, the Tone, the Tenryū, and the Kiso, flowing into the Pacific Ocean, the Shinano-gawa flowing into the Sea of Japan, and the Ishikari in Yezo. Most of the smaller streams have no general name, but change their name every few miles on passing from village to village.

Lake Biwa near Kyōto is the largest lake, the next being Lake Inawashiro, on whose northern shore rises the ill-omened volcano, Bandai-San. The so-called lakes to the north-east of Tōkyō are but shallow lagoons formed by the retreating sea. The most important straits are the Strait of La Pérouse between Yezo and Saghalien, the Strait of Tsugaru between Yezo and the Main Island, the Kii Channel (Linschoten Strait) between the Main Island and Eastern Shikoku, the Bungo Channel between Western Shikoku and Kyūshū, and the Strait of Shimonoseki between the south-western extremity of the Main Island and Kyūshū. The most noteworthy gulfs or bays are Volcano Bay in Southern Yezo, Aomori Bay at the northern extremity of the Main Island, Sendai Bay in the north-east, the Gulfs of Tōkyō, Sagami, Suruga, Owari, and Kagoshima facing south, and the Bay of Toyama between the peninsula of Noto and the mainland.

Of peninsulas the chief are Noto, jutting out into the Sea of Japan, and Kazusa-Bōshū and Izu, not far from Tōkyō on the Pacific Ocean side. It is an interesting fact that both Noto and Izu, words meaningless in Japanese—mere place-names—can be traced back to terms still used by the Ainos to designate the idea of a "promontory" or "peninsula." Finally, even so rapid a sketch as this cannot pass over the waterfalls of Nikkō, of Nachi in

Kishū, and of Kōbe. Still less must we forget the mighty river in the sea—the Kuroshio, or " Black Current"—which, flowing northwards from the direction of Formosa and the Philippine Islands, warms the southern and south-eastern coasts of Japan much as the Gulf Stream warms the coasts of western Europe.

There are two current divisions of the soil of the Empire— an older and more popular one into provinces (*kuni*), of which there are eighty-four in all, and a recent, purely administrative one into prefectures (*ken*), of which at the present moment, April, 1890 (for the number has suffered numerous changes), there are forty-three. Groups of provinces also receive special names in popular and historical parlance. Such are, for instance, the Go-Kinai, or " Five Home Provinces," consisting of the Kyōto-Nara-Ōsaka district, and the Kwantō which includes all the provinces of the East. The three chief cities (*san-fu*) of Japan are Tōkyō, Kyōto, and Ōsaka. Other important towns are Nagoya in the province of Owari, Kanazawa in Kaga, Hiroshima in Aki, Sendai in Rikuzen, Tokushima in Awa (Island of Shikoku), Wakayama in Kishū, Toyama in Etchū, Kagoshima in Satsuma, Kumamoto in Higo, Sakai in Izumi, and Fukuoka in Chikuzen—all with a population of over 40,000 souls. The "open ports" of Yokohama, Kōbe, Nagasaki, Niigata, and Hakodate all have over 40,000 inhabitants, excepting Nagasaki which has over 30,000.

Books recommended. Rein's "Japan."—"The Geography of Japan." by Ernest Satow, printed in Vol. I of the "Asiatic Transactions."—" The China Sea Directory." Vol IV.—" Whitney's Dictionary of Roads, Towns, and Villages in Japan."


**Geology.** It is popularly supposed that Japan entirely consists, or at' least nearly entirely consists, of volcanic rocks. Such a supposition is true for the Kurile Islands, partially true for the northern half of the Main Island and for Kyûshû. But for the remainder of the country, that is, the southern half of the Main Island and Shikoku, the supposition is quite without support.

The backbone of the country consists of primitive gneiss and schists. Amongst the latter, in Shikoku, there is an extremely interesting rock consisting largely of piedmontite. Overlying these amongst the Palæozoic rocks, we meet in many parts of Japan with slates and other rocks possibly of Cambrian or Silurian age. Trilobites have been discovered in Rikuzen. Carboniferous rocks are represented by mountain masses of *Fusulina* and other limestones. There is also amongst the Palæozoic group an interesting series of red slates containing *Radiolaria*.

Mesozoic Rocks are represented by slates containing *Ammonites* and *Monotis*, evidently of Triassic age, rocks containing *Ammonites Bucklandi* of Liassic age, a series of beds rich in plants of Jurassic age, and beds of Cretaceous age containing *Trigonia* and many other fossils.

The Cainozoic or Tertiary system forms a fringe round the coasts of many portions of Japan. It chiefly consists of stratified volcanic tuffs rich in coal, lignite, fossilised plants, and an invertebrate fauna. Diatomaceous earth exists at several places in Yezo. In the alluvium which covers all, have been discovered the remains of several species of elephants, which, according to Dr Edmund Naumann, are of Indian origin.

The most common eruptive rock is andesite. Such rocks as basalt, diorite, and trachyte are comparatively rare. Quartz porphyry, quartzless porphyry, and granite are largely developed.

The most extensively worked mineral in Japan is coal,
large deposits of which exist near Nagasaki in the south,
and at Poronai and other places in Yezo at the northern
extremity of the Empire. Not only is the output sufficient
to supply Japan, but considerable quantities are shipped to
Hongkong and other ports in China. Copper is largely
found and the antimony production is among the most
notable in the world. From one of the mines in Shikoku
come the wonderful crystals of antimonite which are such
conspicuous objects in the mineralogical cabinets of Europe
and America. Silver is extensively mined; but the production of other metals, for instance, gold and tin, is relatively
small.

Books recommended. "Die Kaiserlich Geologische Reichsanstalt von Japan," by T. Wada.—"Ueber den Bau und die Entstehung der Japanischen Inseln,"
by E. Naumann.—"Catalogue of Japanese Minerals contained in the Imperial
College of Engineering, Tōkyō," by J. Milne.—"Les Produits de la Nature Japonaise
et Chinoise," by A. J. C. Geerts.—"Kaitakushi Reports," by Benjamin S. Lyman.—
"Bulletin of the Geological Survey of Japan."

**Go.** Go, sometimes, but with little appropriateness,
termed " checkers " by European writers, is the most popular
of the in-door pastimes of the Japanese,—a very different
affair from the simple game known to Europeans as goban
or gobang. It is the great resource of most of the visitors
to the hot springs and other health-resorts, being often
played from morning till night, save for the intervals devoted to eating and bathing. Go clubs and professors of
the art are found in all the larger cities. Go may with
justice be considered more difficult than chess. There is
in it more scope for sustained effort, and one false move
does not put a player hors-de-combat, as is so often the case
in our Western games of skill.

Go was introduced into Japan from China by Shimo-

michi-no-Mabi, commonly known as Kibi Daijin, who
flourished during the reign of the Emperor Shōmu (A. D.
724-756). In the middle of the seventeenth century, a
noted player, called Honnimbō, was summoned from Kyōto
to entertain the Chinese ambassador then at the court of
the Shōgun, from which time forward special *Go* players
were always retained by the Shōguns of the Tokugawa
dynasty.

*Go* is played on a square wooden board. Nineteen
straight lines crossing each other at right angles make
three-hundred and sixty-one *me*, or crosses, at the points of
intersection. These may be occupied by a hundred and
eighty white and a hundred and eighty-one black men
("stones," as they are termed in Japanese). The object
of the game is to enclose these crosses, and to capture as
many of the adversary's men as possible. There are nine
spots on the board, called *seimoku*, supposed to represent
the chief celestial bodies, while the white and black men
represent day and night, and the number of crosses the
three hundred and sixty degrees of latitude, exclusive of the
central one, which is called *taikyoku*, that is, the Primor-
dial Principle of the Universe.

In playing, if the combatants are equally matched,
they take the white stones alternately; if unequal, the
weaker always takes the black, and odds are also given
by allowing him to occupy the spots—that is, to place
stones upon them at the outset. A description of how
the game proceeds would be of little utility here, it
being so complicated as to make the personal instruction
of a teacher indispensable. Very few foreigners have
succeeded in getting beyond a rudimentary knowledge
of this interesting game. We know only of one, a Ger-

man named Korschelt, who has taken out a diploma of proficiency.

**Book recommended.** Elaborate details will be found in O. Korschelt's essay on "Das Go-Spiel," published in Parts 11—24 of the "German Asiatic Transactions."

**Gobang.** A simple Japanese game, which was introduced into England a few years ago. It is played on the *Go* board and with the *Go-ishi* or round black and white "men." The object of the game is to be first in getting five men in a row in any direction.

**Government.** In theory the Mikado,—heaven-descended, absolute, infallible,—has always been the head and fountain of all power. It belongs to him by a divine right, which none have ever dreamt of disputing. The single and sufficient rule of life for subjects is implicit, unquestioning obedience, as to the mandates of a god. The comparatively democratic doctrines of the Chinese sages, according to whom "the people are the most important element in a nation, and the sovereign is the lightest," have ever been viewed with horror by the Japanese, to whom the antiquity and the absolute power of their Imperial line are badges of perfection on which they never weary of descanting. A study of Japanese history shows, however, that the Mikado has rarely exercised much of his power in practice. Almost always it has been wielded in his name, often sorely against his will, by the members of some ambitious family, which has managed to possess itself of supreme influence over the affairs of state. Thus, the Fujiwara family soon after the civilisation of the country by Buddhism, then the Taira, the Minamoto, and the Hôjô during the Middle Ages, and the Tokugawa, in modern times, held the reins of state in succession. Even

since the revolution of 1868, whose avowed object was
to restore the Mikado to his pristine absolutism, it seems
to be allowed on all hands that at least a large share of
the reality of power has lain with the two great clans of
Satsuma and Chôshū, while the aim of the two clans
next in influence—Tosa and Hizen—has been to put
themselves in Satsuma and Chôshū's place.  In February,
1889, there was granted a Constitution, which establishes
a Diet consisting of two houses, and lays the foundation
of a new order of things.  The first elections for the Diet
are to take place in July, 1890.  A certain measure of
control over public affairs will thenceforth be vested in the
nobility, and in those gentlemen and commoners whose
property qualification entitles them to vote or to be voted
for.  A certain measure of popular control over local affairs
was also granted in 1889.

The administration is at present divided into ten departments, namely, the Imperial Household, the Army,
the Navy, the Interior, Foreign Affairs, Justice, Finance,
Education, Commerce-Agriculture, and Communications
(that is, Posts, Telegraphs, etc.), each presided over by
a minister of state.  These, with the exception of the
minister of the Household Department, constitute the
Cabinet.  The Cabinet is responsible only to the Mikado,
by whom also each minister is appointed and dismissed at will.  Besides the Cabinet, there is a Privy Council and a Senate; but in view of probable impending
changes, it would be useless to enter into a description of
the present functions of those bodies.  There are three
capital cities, Tôkyô, Kyôto, and Ôsaka, each, with its
strip of adjacent country, administered by a governor.
The rest of the Empire is divided into prefectures.  A

very large proportion of the revenue is raised by taxation on the land.

Viewed from an English or American point of view, the
Japanese are a much-governed people, the number of officials being large, their authority great, and all sorts of
things which with us are left to private enterprise being
here in the hands of government. But possibly there may
be no such contrast between Japan and the nations of Continental Europe. It is not either half of Anglo-Saxondom
that attracts the eyes of the governing class of contemporary Japan. Their cynosure is Imperial Germany.

**Guide-books.** By far the fullest and best is Murray's
" Handbook for Central and Northern Japan," by Satow and
Hawes, 2nd edit., London, and Yokohama, 1884. Unfortunately this work, which is a mine of information, not
only on the topography, but on the history, traditions, art,
etc., of Japan, is now out of print, and second-hand copies
command high prices. There is a smaller "Tourists'
Guide" by W. E. L. Keeling; a "Handy Guide Book to
the Japan Island," by W. H. Seton Karr, and an "Official
Railway and Steamboat Traveller's Guide," of which new
editions appear every few months. All these smaller guide-
books are more or less compilations from Messrs. Satow
and Hawes' work.

**Harakiri.** Need we say that *hara-kiri* was for centuries
the Japanese method *par excellence* of committing suicide?
Indeed the time-honoured custom can hardly yet be said to
be quite extinct, when there still lives fresh in our memory
the case of the young Japanese midshipman on board the
British man-of-war, who, discouraged by a reprimand from

the authorities at Tôkyô, which the incoming mail had just brought him, went and committed *harakiri* that night in his——portmanteau !

*Harakiri* has sometimes been translated "the happy dispatch." But the original Japanese is less euphemistic. It means "belly-cutting;" and that is what the operation actually consists in, neither more no less. Or rather, no: there *is* more. In modern times, at least, people not having always succeeded in making away with themselves expeditiously by this method, it became usual for a friend— a "best man," as one might say—to stand behind the chief actor in the tragedy. When the latter thrust his dirk into himself, the friend at once chopped off his head.

*Harakiri* is not an aboriginal Japanese custom. It was evolved gradually during the Middle Ages. The cause of it is probably to be sought in the desire, on the part of vanquished warriors, to avoid the humiliation of falling into their enemies' hands alive. Thus the custom would come to be characteristic of the military class, in other words, of the feudal nobility and gentry. From being a custom, it next developed into a privilege. At a date difficult to fix, but which was probably not later than A. D. 1500, noblemen and gentlemen (that is, *daimyôs* and *samurai*) began to be exempted from the indignity of being put to death by the common executioner, like malefactors of the baser sort. They were allowed to commit *harakiri* instead, the time and place being notified to them officially, and officials being sent to witness the ceremony.

It is an odd fact that the Japanese word *harakiri*, so well-known all over the world, is but little used by the Japanese themselves. The Japanese almost always prefer to employ the synonym *seppuku*, which they consider more

elegant because it is derived from the Chinese. After all,
they are not singular in this matter. Do not we ourselves
say "abdomen," when what we mean is plain Saxon?—well,
we will not shock ears polite by mentioning the word
again. Latinisms in English, "Chinesisms" in Japanese,
cover a multitude of sins.

Books recommended. The whole subject is elaborately described, in Appendix
A to the "Tales of old Japan," by A. B. Mitford, who himself had the rare, the gruesome, opportunity of seeing *harakiri* performed.—Chamberlain's " Romanised Japanese Reader," Extract No. 63, gives a literal translation of a native account of the *harakiri* of Asano, Lord of Akô, whose death was so dramatically revenged by the famous
" Forty-Seven Rônins."

**Heraldry.** In Japan, as in Europe, feudalism produced
the "nobyl and gentyl sciaunce" of heraldly, though the
absence of such powerful stimuli as tournaments and the
crusades prevented Japanese heraldry from developing to
the same high degree of complication as the heraldry of the
West. Most of the great *daimyôs* possessed three crests
or badges (*mon*), the lesser *daimyôs* had two, ordinary
*samurai* one. These served in time of war to adorn the
breastplate, the helmet, and the flag. In time of peace
the crest was worn, as indeed it still is by those who retain
the native garb, in five places on the upper garment,
namely, at the back of the neck, on each sleeve, and on
each breast. Various other articles were marked with it,
such as lanterns, travelling-cases (what modern curio-
dealers call "*daimyô* boxes"), etc., etc. The Imperial
family has two crests, the sixteen-petalled chrysanthemum
(*kiku no go mon*), and the leaves and flowers of the paulownia (*kiri no go mon*). The crest of the Tokugawa
dynasty of *Shôguns* was three hollyhock leaves, whose
points met in the centre. The bamboo, the rose, the
peony, even the radish (*daikon*), furnished crests for noble

families. Other favourite " motives " are birds, butterflies, running water, fans, feathers, ladders, bridle-bits, Chinese characters, and geometrical designs. One small *daimyō*, named Aoki, had for his crest the summit of Fujiyama, with its trifurcated peak issuing from the clouds. The great Shimazu family of Satsuma has the cross within a circle. Flags and banners of various shapes and sizes have been in use from the earliest ages. The present national flag—a red ball on a white ground— was only formally adopted in the year 1859. But it is a very ancient badge, intended to represent the rising sun, and therefore highly appropriate to Japan, as the most eastern of all lands.

*Books recommended.* "Japanese Heraldry" by T. R. H. McClatchie, printed in Vol. V of the "Asiatic Transactions." Our account is a *précis* of McClatchie's essay.—Appert's "*Ancien Japon,*" in which all the daimyōs' crests are beautifully figured.

**History and Mythology.** To the eye of the critical investigator, Japanese history, properly so-called, opens only in the latter part of the fifth or the beginning of the sixth century after Christ, when the gradual spread of Chinese culture, filtering in through Korea, had sufficiently dispelled the gloom of original barbarism to allow of the keeping of records.

The whole question of the credibility of the early history of Japan has been carefully gone into during the last ten years by Aston and others, with the result that the first date pronounced trustworthy is A. D. 461, and it is discovered that even the annals of the sixth century are to be received with caution. We have ourselves no doubt of the justice of this negative criticism, and can only stand in amazement at the simplicity of most European writers, who have accepted without sifting them the uncritical statements of the Japanese annalists. One German professor, the late Dr. Hoffmann, actually discusses the *hour* of Jimmu Tennō's accession in the year 660 B. C., which is much as if one should gravely compute in cubic inches the size of the pumpkin which Cinderella's fairy godmother turned into a coach and six. How comes it that profound erudition so often lacks the salt of humour and the guidance of common sense?

Be this as it may, criticism is not at all a "Japanesey" thing; and as Japanese art and literature contain frequent allusions to the early history (so-called) of the country, the chief outlines of this history, as preserved in the works entitled *Kojiki* and *Nihongi*, both dating from the eighth century after Christ, may here be given. We include the mythology under the same heading, for the reason that it is absolutely impossible to separate the two. Why, indeed, attempt to do so, where both are equally fabulous?

Before, then, the beginning of the world of men, there existed numerous generations of gods. The last of these "divine generations," as they are termed, were a brother and sister, named respectively Izanagi and Izanami, who, uniting in marriage, gave birth to the various islands of the Japanese archipelago and to a great number of additional gods and goddesses. The birth of the God of Fire caused Izanami's death, and the most striking episode of the whole Japanese mythology ensues, when her husband, Orpheus-like, visits her at the gate of the under-world to implore her to return to him. She would fain do so, and bids him wait while she takes counsel with the deities of the place. But he, impatient at her long tarrying, breaks off one of the teeth of the comb in his hair, lights it and goes in, only to find her a hideous mass of putrefaction, in the midst of which are seated the eight Gods of

Thunder. Eight, be it observed, is the mystic number of the Japanese, as six is the mystic number of the Ainos whom their ancestors drove out.

Returning to south-western Japan, Izanagi purifies himself by bathing in a stream, and as he does so, fresh deities are born from each article of clothing that he throws down on the river-bank, and from each part of his person. One of these deities was the Sun-Goddess Ama-terasu, who was born from his left eye, while the Moon-God sprang from his right eye, and the last born of all, Susanoo, whose name means "the Impetuous Male," was born from his nose. Between these three children their father divides the inheritance of the universe.

At this point the story loses its unity. The Moon-God is no more heard of, and the traditions concerning the Sun-Goddess diverge from those concerning the Impetuous Male Deity in a manner which is productive of inconsistencies in the rest of the mythology. The Sun-Goddess and the Impetuous Male Deity have a violent quarrel, and at last the latter breaks a hole in the roof of the hall in Heaven where his sister is sitting at work with her "celestial weaving-maidens," and through it lets fall "a heavenly piebald horse which he had flayed with a backward flaying." The consequences of this impious act were so disastrous that the Sun-Goddess withdrew for a season into a cave, from which the rest of the eight hundred myriad deities with difficulty allured her. The Impetuous Male Deity was thereupon banished, and the Sun-Goddess remained mistress of the field. Yet, strange to say, she thenceforward retires into the background, and the most bulky section of the mythology consists of stories concerning the Impetuous Male Deity and his descendants,

who are represented as the monarchs of Japan, or rather
of the province of Izumo. The Impetuous Male Deity
himself, whom his father had charged with the dominion
of the sea, never assumes that rule, but first has a curiously told amorous adventure and an encounter with an
eight-forked serpent in Izumo, and afterwards reappears
as the capricious and filthy deity of Hades, who, however,
seems to retain some authority over the land of the living,
as he invests his descendant of the sixth generation with
the sovereignty of Japan.

Of this latter personage a whole cycle of stories is told,
all centring in the province of Izumo. We learn of his
conversations with a hare and with a mouse, of the
prowess and cleverness which he displayed on the occasion of a visit to his ancestor in Hades, which is in this
cycle of traditions a much less mysterious place than the
Hades visited by Izanagi, of his amours, of his triumph
over his eighty brethren, of his reconciliation with his
jealous consort, and of his numerous descendants. We
hear too of a Lilliputian deity, who comes across the sea
to request this monarch of Izumo to share the kingdom
with him.

This last-mentioned legend repeats itself in the sequel.
The Sun-Goddess resolves to bestow the sovereignty of
Japan on a child of whom it is doubtful whether he were
born of her or of her brother, the Impetuous Male Deity.
Three embassies are sent from Heaven to Izumo to arrange matters; but it is only a fourth that is successful,
the final ambassadors obtaining the submission of the
monarch or deity of Izumo, who surrenders his throne and
promises to serve the new dynasty (apparently in the under-
world) if a palace or temple be built for him and he be

appropriately worshipped. Thereupon the child of the deity whom the Sun-Goddess had originally chosen descends to earth—not to Izumo in the north-west, as the logical sequence of the story would lead one to expect—but to the peak of a mountain in the south-western island of Kyūshū.

Here follows a quaint tale accounting for the odd appearance of the *bêche-de-mer*, and another to account for the shortness of the lives of mortals, after which we are told of the birth under peculiar circumstances of the heaven-descended deity's three sons. Two of these, Hoderi and Hoori, whose names may be Englished as " Fire-Shine " and " Fire-Fade," are the heroes of a very curious legend, which includes an elaborate account of a visit paid by the latter to the palace of the God of Ocean, and of a curse or spell which gained for him the victory over his elder brother, and enabled him to dwell peacefully in his palace at Takachiho for the space of five hundred and eighty years—the first statement resembling a date which the Japanese historians vouchsafe. Fire-Fade's son married his own aunt, and was the father of four children, one of whom, " treading on the crest of the waves, crossed over to the Eternal Land," while a second "went into the sea-plain," and the two others moved eastward, fighting with the chiefs of Kibi and Yamato, having adventures with gods both with and without tails, being assisted by a miraculous sword and a gigantic crow, and naming the various places they passed through after incidents in their own career. One of these brothers was Kamu-Yamato-Iware-Biko, who (the other having died before him) is accounted the first human Emperor of Japan—the first Mikado. The posthumous name of of Jimmu Tennō was

given to him more than fourteen centuries after the date
which the historians assign for his decease.

Henceforth Yamato, which had scarcely been mentioned
before, and the provinces adjacent to it, become the centre
of the story, and Izumo again emerges into importance.
A very indecent love-tale forms a bridge which unites the
various fragments of the mythology ; and the "Great Deity
of Miwa," who is identified with the deposed monarch
of Izumo, appears on the scene. Indeed, during the rest of
the story, this "Great Deity of Miwa" and his colleague
the "Small August Deity" (Sukuna-Mi-Kami), the deity
Izasa-Wake, the three Water-Gods of Sumi, and the
"Great Deity of Kazuraki," form, with the Sun-Goddess
and with a certain divine sword preserved at the temple of
Isonokami in Yamato, the only objects of worship specially
named, the other gods and goddesses being no more heard
of. This portion of the story is closed by an account of
the troubles which inaugurated the reign of Jimmu's successor, Suisei Tennō, and then occurs a blank of (according to the accepted chronology) five hundred years, during
which absolutely nothing is related excepting dreary genealogies, the place where each sovereign dwelt and where
he was buried, and the age to which he lived—this after
the minute details which had been given concerning the
previous gods or monarchs down to Suisei inclusive. It
should likewise be noted that the average age of the first
seventeen monarchs (counting Jimmu Tennō as the first), is
nearly ninety-six years if we follow the *Kojiki*, and over a
hundred if we follow the accepted chronology which is
based chiefly on the divergent statements contained in the
*Nihongi*. The age of several of the monarchs exceeds a
hundred and twenty years.

The above-mentioned lapse of a blank period of five centuries brings us to the reign of the Emperor known to history by the name of Sūjin Tennō, whose life of one hundred and sixty-eight years (one hundred and twenty according to the *Nihongi*) is supposed to have immediately preceded the Christian era. In this reign, the former monarch of Izumo or god of Miwa again appears and produces a pestilence, of the manner of staying which Sūjin is warned in a dream.

In the ensuing reign an elaborate legend, involving a variety of circumstances as miraculous as any in the earlier portion of the mythology, again centres in the necessity of pacifying the great god of Izumo; and this, with details of internecine strife in the Imperial family, of the sovereign's amours, and of the importation of the orange from the "Eternal Land," brings us to the cycle of traditions of which Yamato-Take, a son of the Emperor Keikō, is the hero. This prince, after assassinating one of his brothers, accomplishes the task of subduing both western and eastern Japan; and notwithstanding certain details which are unsavoury to the European taste, his story, taken as a whole, is one of the most striking in Japanese legend. He performs marvels of valour, disguises himself as a woman in order to slay the brigands, is the possessor of a magic sword and fire-striker, has a devoted wife who stills the fury of the sea by sitting down upon its surface, has encounters with a deer and with a boar who are really gods in disguise, and finally dies on his way westward before he can reach his home in Yamato. His death is followed by a highly mythological account of the laying to rest of the white bird into which he ended by being transformed.

The succeeding reign is a blank, and the next transports us without a word of warning to quite another scene. The sovereign's home is now in Kyūshū—the south-western most island of the Japanese archipelago—and four of the gods, through the medium of the sovereign's consort, who is known to posterity as the Empress Jingō, reveal the existence of the land of Korea, of which, however, this is not the first mention in the histories.    The Mikado disbelieves the divine message, and is punished by death for his incredulity.    But the Empress, after a special consultation between her prime minister and the gods and the performance of various religious ceremonies, marshals her fleet, and, with the assistance of the fishes both great and small and of a miraculous wave, reaches Shiragi (one of the ancient divisions of Korea), and subdues it.    She then returns to Japan, the legend ending with a curiously naïve tale of how she sat a-fishing one day on a shoal in the River Ogawa in Kyūshū, with threads picked out of her skirt for lines.    The date of the conquest of Korea, according to the orthodox chronology, is A. D. 200.

The next episode is the warrior empress's voyage up to Yamato—another joint in the story, by means of which the Yamato cycle of legends and the Kyūshū cycle are brought into apparent unity.    The *Nihongi* has even improved upon this by making Jingō's husband dwell in Yamato at the beginning of his reign and only remove to Kyūshū later, so that if the less skilfully elaborated *Kojiki* had not been preserved, the tangled skein of the tradition would have been still more difficult to unravel. The Empress's army defeats the troops raised by the native kings or princes, who are represented as her stepsons, and from that time forward the story runs on in a single channel, with Yamato as its scene of action.

China likewise is now first mentioned, books are said to have been brought over from the mainland, and we hear of the gradual introduction of various useful arts. Even the annals of the reign of Jingō's son, Ōjin Tennō, however, during which this civilising impulse from abroad is said to have commenced, are not free from details as miraculous as any in the earlier portions of the history. The monarch himself is said to have lived a hundred and thirty years, while his successor lived eighty-three (according to the *Nihongi*, Ōjin lived a hundred and ten, and his successor Nintoku reigned eighty-seven years). It is not till the next reign that the miraculous ceases, a fact which significantly coincides with the time at which, says the *Nihongi*, "historiographers were first appointed to all the provinces to record words and events, and forward archives from all directions."

This brings us to the beginning of the fifth century of our era, just three centuries before the compilation of the annals that have come down to us, but only two centuries before the compilation of the first history of which mention has been preserved. From that time the story in the *Kojiki*, though not well told, gives us some very curious pictures, and reads as if it were trustworthy. It is tolerably full for a few reigns, after which it again dwindles into mere genealogies, ending with the death of the Empress Suiko in A. D. 628. The *Nihongi*, on the contrary, gives full details as far as A.D. 701, that is, to within nineteen years of the date of its compilation.

The reader who has followed this summary, or who will take the trouble to study the original Japanese texts for himself, will perceive that there is no break in the story—at least no chronological break—and no break between the fabulous and the real, unless it be in the fifth century of our era, or more than a thousand years later than the date usually assumed as the starting-point of authentic Japanese history. The only breaks are—not chronological—but topographical.

This fact of the continuity of the Japanese mythology and history has been fully recognised by the leading native commentators, whose opinions are those considered orthodox by modern Shintoists, and they draw from it the conclusion that everything in the standard national histories must be accepted as literal truth—the supernatural equally with the natural. But the general habit of the more sceptical Japanese of the present day, that is to say, of ninety-nine out of every hundred of the educated, is to reject or rather to ignore the legends of the gods, while implicitly believing the legends of the emperors, from Jimmu Tennô, in B. C. 660, downwards. For so arbitrary a distinction there is not the shadow of justification. The so-called history of Jimmu, the first earthly Mikado, of Jingô, the conqueress of Korea, of Yamato-take, and of the rest, stands or falls by exactly the same criterion as the legends of the creator and creatress Izanagi and Izanami. Both sets of tales are told in the same books, in the same style, and with an almost equal amount of supernatural detail. The so-called historical part is as devoid as the other of all contemporary evidence. It is contradicted by the more trustworthy, because contemporary, Chinese and Korean records, and—to turn from negative to positive testimony—can be proved in some

particulars to rest on actual forgery. For instance, the
fictitious nature of the calendars employed to calculate
all the early dates for about thirteen centuries (from B. C.
660 onward) has been exposed by that careful investigator,
Mr. Wm. Bramsen, who says, with reference to them, " It
is hardly too severe to style this one of the greatest
literary frauds ever perpetrated."

But a truce to this discussion. We have only entered
into it because the subject, though perhaps dry, is at
least new, and because one's patience is worn out by seeing
book after book glibly quote the so-called dates of early
Japanese history as if they were solid truth, instead of
being the merest haphazard guesses and baseless imagin-
ings of a later age. Arrived at A. D. 600, we stand on
*terra firma*, and can afford to push on more quickly.

About that time occurred the greatest event of Japanese
history, the conversion of the nation to Buddhism (approximately A. D. 552—621). So far as can be gathered
from the accounts of the early Chinese travellers, Chinese
civilisation had slowly—very slowly—been gaining ground
in the archipelago ever since the third century after Christ.
But when the Buddhist missionaries crossed the water,
all Chinese institutions followed them and came in with
a rush. Mathematical instruments and calendars were
introduced; books began to be written (the earliest that
has survived, and indeed nearly the earliest of all, is the
already mentioned *Kojiki*, dating from A. D. 712); the
custom of abdicating the throne in order to spend old age
in prayer was adopted—a custom which, more than anything else, led to the effacement of the Mikado's authority
during the Middle Ages.

Sweeping changes in political arrangements began to be

made in the year 645, and before the end of the eighth century, the government had been entirely remodelled on the Chinese centralised bureaucratic plan, with a regular system of ministers responsible to the sovereign, who, as "Son of Heaven," was theoretically absolute. In practice this absolutism lasted but a short time, because the entourage and mode of life of the Mikados were not such as to make of them able rulers. They passed their time surrounded only by women and priests, oscillating between indolence and debauchery, between poetastering and gorgeous temple services. This was the brilliant age of Japanese classical literature, which lived and moved and had its being in the atmosphere of an effeminate court. The Fujiwara family engrossed the power of the state during this early epoch (A. D. 670—1050). While their sons held all the great posts of government, the daughters were married to puppet emperors.

The next change resulted from the impatience of the always manly and warlike Japanese gentry at the sight of this sort of petticoat government. The great clans of Taira and Minamoto arose, and struggled for and alternately held the reins of power during the second half of the eleventh and the whole of the twelfth century. Japan was now converted into a camp. The real master of the empire was he who, strongest with his sword and bow and heading the most numerous host, could partition out the land among the chief barons, his retainers. By the final overthrow of the Taira family at the sea fight of Dan-no-Ura in A. D. 1185, Yoritomo, the chief of the Minamotos, rose to supreme power, and obtained from the Court at Kyōto the title of *Shōgun*, literally "Generalissimo," which had till then been applied in its proper meaning to those generals who were sent from time to time to subdue the Ainos or rebellious provincials, but which thenceforth took to itself a special sense, somewhat as the word *Imperator* (also meaning originally "general") did in Rome. The coincidence is striking. So is the contrast. For, as Imperial Rome never ceased to be theoretically a republic, Japan contrariwise, though practically and indeed avowedly ruled by the Shōguns from A. D. 1190 to 1867, always retained the Mikado as theoretical head of the state, descendant of the Sun-Goddess, fountain of all honour. There never were two emperors, acknowledged as such, one spiritual and one secular, as has been so often asserted by European writers. There never was but one emperor —an emperor powerless it is true, seen only by the women who attended him, often a mere infant in arms, who was discarded on reaching adolescence for another infant in arms. Still, he was the theoretical head of the state, whose authority was merely delegated to the Shōgun as, so to say, Mayor of the Palace.

By a curious parallelism of destiny, the Shōgunate itself more than once showed signs of fading away from substance into shadow. Yoritomo's descendants did not prove worthy of him, and for more than a century (A. D. 1205 — 1333) the real authority was wielded by the so-called "Regents" of the Hōjō family, while their liege-lords, the Shōguns, though keeping a nominal court at Kamakura, were for all that period little better than empty names. So completely were the Hōjōs masters of the whole country that they actually had their deputy governors at Kyōto and in Kyūshū in the South-West, and thought nothing of banishing Mikados to distant islands. Their rule was made memorable by the repulse of the Mongol fleet sent by

Kublai Khan with the purpose of adding Japan to his
gigantic dominions. This was at the end of the thirteenth
century, since which time Japan has never been attacked
from without.

During the fourteenth century, even the dowager-like
calm of the Court of Kyōto was broken by internecine
strife. Two branches of the Imperial house, supported
each by different feudal chiefs, disputed the crown. One
was called the *Hokuchō*, or "Northern Court," the other
the *Nanchō*, or "Southern Court." After lasting some
sixty years, this contest terminated in A. D. 1392 by the
triumph of the Northern dynasty, whose cause the powerful
Ashikaga family had espoused. From 1338 to 1565, the
Ashikagas ruled Japan as Shōguns. Their Court was a
centre of elegance, at which painting flourished, and the
lyric drama, and the tea ceremonies, and the highly intricate
arts of gardening and flower arrangement. But they
allowed themselves to sink into effeminacy and sloth, as
the Mikados had done before them; and political authority,
after being for some time administered less by them than
in their name, fell from them altogether in 1597.

Meanwhile Japan had been discovered by the Portuguese
(A. D. 1542); and the imprudent conduct of the Portuguese
and Spanish friars (*bateren*, as they were called—a corruption of the word *padre*) made of the Christian religion an
additional source of discord. Japan fell into utter anarchy.
Each baron in his fastness was a law unto himself. Then,
in the latter half of the sixteenth century, there arose
successively three great men—Ota Nobunaga, the Taikō*
Hideyoshi, and Tokugawa Ieyasu. The first of these con-

---

\* The word *taikō* (太閤) means "great councillor." But being rarely applied to any
except Hideyoshi, it has almost come to form part of his name.

ceived the idea of centralising all the authority of the state in a single person; the second, Hideyoshi, who has been called the Napoleon of Japan, actually put the idea into practice, and joined the conquest of Korea (A. D. 1592—1598) to his domestic triumphs. Death overtook him in 1598, while he was revolving no less a scheme than the conquest of China. Ieyasu, setting Hideyoshi's youthful son aside, stepped into the vacant place. An able general, unsurpassed as a diplomat and administrator, he first quelled all the turbulent barons, then bestowed a considerable portion of their lands on his own kinsmen and dependents, and either broke or balanced, by a judicious distribution of other fiefs over different provinces of the Empire, the might of those greater feudal lords, such as Satsuma and Chōshū, whom it was impossible to put altogether out of the way. The Court of Kyōto was treated by him respectfully, and investiture as Shōgun for himself and his heirs duly obtained from the Mikado.

In order further to break the might of the *daimyōs*, Ieyasu compelled them to live at Yedo, which he had chosen for his capital in 1590, during six months of the year, and to leave their wives and families there as hostages during the other half. What Ieyasu sketched out, the third Shōgun of his line, Iemitsu, perfected. From that time forward, " Old Japan," as we know it from the Dutch accounts, from art, from the stage, was crystallised for two hundred and fifty years—the Old Japan of isolation (for Iemitsu shut the country up to prevent complications with the Spaniards and Portuguese), the Old Japan of picturesque feudalism, of *harakiri*, of a society ranged in castes and orders and officered by spies, the Old Japan of an ever-

increasing skill in lacquer and porcelain, of aristocratic
punctilio, of supremely exquisite taste.

Unchangeable to the outward eye of contemporaries,
Japan had not passed a hundred years under the Tokugawa
*régime* before the seeds of the disease which finally killed
that *régime* were sown.    Strangely enough, the instrument of destruction was historical research.    Ieyasu
himself had been a great patron of literature.    His
grandson, the second Prince of Mito, inherited his taste.
Under the auspices of this Japanese Mæcenas, a school of
literati arose to whom the antiquities of their country
were all in all—Japanese poetry and romance as against
the Chinese Classics ; the native religion, Shintō, as
against the foreign religion, Buddhism ;    hence, by an
inevitable extension, the ancient legitimate dynasty of the
Mikados, as against the upstart Shōguns.    Of course this
political portion of the doctrine of the literary party was
kept in the background at first ; for those were not days
when opposition to the existing government could be
expressed or even hinted at without danger.    But nevertheless it gradually grew in importance, so that, when
Commodore Perry came with his big guns (A. D. 1853—4),
he found a government already tottering to its fall, many
who cared little for the Mikado's abstract rights, caring
a great deal for the chance of aggrandising their own
families at the Shōgun's expense.

The Shōgun yielded to the demands of Perry and of the
representatives of the other foreign powers—England,
France, Russia—who followed in Perry's train, and consented to open Yokohama, Hakodate, and certain other
ports to foreign trade and residence (1857—9).    He even
sent embassies to the United States and to Europe in 1860

and 1861. The knowledge of the outer world possessed by the Court of Yedo, though not extensive, was sufficient to assure the Shōgun and his advisers that it was vain to refuse what the Western powers claimed. The Court of Kyōto had had no means of acquiring even this modicum of worldly wisdom. According to its view, Japan, "the land of the gods," should never be polluted by outsiders, the ports should be closed again, and the "barbarians" expelled at any hazard.

What specially tended to complicate matters at this crisis was the independent action of certain *daimyōs*. One of them, the Prince of Chōshū, acting, as is believed, under secret instructions from the Court of Kyōto, fired on ships belonging to Great Britain, France, Holland, and the United States—this, too, at the very moment (1863) when the Shōgun's government, placed between foreign aggression and home tumult, as between hammer and anvil, was doing its utmost to effect by diplomacy the departure of the foreigners whom it had been driven to admit a few years before. The consequence of this act was what is called "the Shimonoseki Affair," namely, the bombardment of Shimonoseki, Chōshū's chief sea-port, by the combined fleets of the powers that had been insulted, and the exaction of an indemnity of $3,000,000. Though doubtless no feather, this broke the Shōgunate's back. The Shōgun Iemochi attempted to punish Chōshū for the humiliation which he had brought on Japan, but failed, was himself defeated by the latter's troops, and died. Hitotsubashi, the last of his line, succeeded him. But the Court of Kyōto, prompted by the great *daimyōs* of Chōshū and Satsuma, suddenly decided on the abolition of the Shōgunate. The Shōgun submitted to the decree, and those of his followers who did not were routed—first at Fushimi near Kyōto (17th January, 1868), then at Ueno in Yedo (4th July, 1868), then in Aizu (6th November, 1868), and lastly at Hakodate (27th June, 1869), where some of them had endeavoured to set up an independent republic.

The government of the country was reorganised during 1867—8, nominally on the basis of a pure absolutism, with the Mikado as sole wielder of all authority both legislative and executive. Thus the literary party had triumphed. All their dreams were realised. They were henceforth to have Japan for the Japanese. The Shōgunate, which had admitted the hated barbarian, was no more. Even their hope of supplanting Buddhism by the old national religion, Shintō, was in great measure accomplished. They believed that not only European innovations, but everything—even Japanese—that was newer than A. D. 500, would be for ever swept away. Things were to go back to what they had been in the primitive ages, when Japan was really " the land of the gods."

From this dream they were soon roughly wakened. The shrewd clansmen of Satsuma and Chōshū, who had humoured the ignorance of the Court and the fads of the scholars only as long as their common enemy, the Shōgunate, remained in existence, now turned round, and declared in favour, not merely of foreign intercourse, but of the Europeanisation of their own country. History has never witnessed a more. sudden *volte-face*. History has never witnessed a wiser one. We foreigners, being mere lookers-on, may no doubt sometimes regret the substitution of common-place European ways for the glitter, the glamour of picturesque Orientalism. But can it be doubtful which of the two civilisations is the higher, both materially and

intellectually? And does not the whole experience of the
last three hundred years go to prove that no Oriental
state which retains distinctively Oriental Institutions can
hope to keep its territory free from Western aggression?
What of India? What of China? And what was
Commodore Perry's visit but a threat to the effect that if
Japan chose to remain Oriental, she should not be allowed
to remain her own mistress? From the moment when the
intelligent *samurai* of the leading clans realised that the
Europeanisation of their country was a question of life and
death, they (for to this day the government has continued
practically in their hands) have never ceased carrying on
the work of reform and progress.

The following are some of the chief measures and events
of the last twenty years :—

1871. The *daimyates* abolished and prefectures established in their stead—in other words, a centralised bureaucracy substituted for feudalism. The disestablishment
of Buddhism begun. The social disabilities of the pariah
class (the so-called *eta* and *hinin*) removed. Posts and
telegraphs introduced. Mint opened at Ōsaka.

1872. First railway. Conscription law. Law against
nudity in cities.

1873. This year was specially fruitful in pro-foreign
measures. The European calendar was introduced; the
persecuted Catholics were released; vaccination, photography, European dress for officials, meat-eating, etc., etc.,
came into vogue.

1874. Saga rebellion. Formosan expedition.

1875. Establishment of the Mitsubishi Steam Ship Company. Provincial governors first summoned to Tōkyō for
consultation. Saghalien ceded to Russia in exchange for

the Kurile Islands. Establishment of orders of knighthood.

1876. Treaty with Korea. Higo rebellion. Commutation of the *samurai's* pensions. Edict against the wearing
of swords by the *samurai* (took effect from 1st January,
1877).

1877. Satsuma rebellion. Reduction of land-tax from
3 to 2½ per cent. First National Industrial Exhibition at
Ueno in Tōkyō.

1878. Murder of Minister Ōkubo. Military mutiny at
the Takebashi Barracks, Tōkyō. Development of commercial enterprise by the establishment of the Bourse and
the Tōkyō Chamber of Commerce. '

1879. Dispute with China concerning Loochoo. Loochooan King brought captive to Tōkyō, and his kingdom
annexed. Various distinguished foreigners visit Japan,
notably ex-President Grant.

1880. Penal Code and Code of Criminal Procedure
published. Prefectural assemblies established. Stringent
regulations concerning public meetings.

1881. Discontent of the liberals at the Imperial Rescript
deferring the adoption of constitutional government till
1890. Trouble in Yezo arising from the winding up of the
Kaitakushi (Colonisation Department).

1882. Political excitement. Organisation of the present
Liberal and Radical parties (*Kaishintō* and *Jiyūtō*).
Trouble with Korea.

1883. Establishment of the Supreme Court of Justice.

1884. Insurrection prompted by the radicals of the prefecture of Saitama. Creation of orders of nobility on the
European pattern. English introduced into the curriculum
of the common schools.

1885. Reforms in the method of administration, reduction in the number of officials, highest offices filled by
new men, such as Itô, Inoue, etc. These changes are
locally known as the *Ö-jishin*, that is, "the Great Earthquake."—Formation of the Japan Steam Ship Company
(*Nippon Yüsen Kaisha*).

1885—7. The second most violent attack of the "foreign
fever." European music, dancing, athletics, card-playing,
velocipede-riding, etc., etc., all came in with a rush, as did
European dress for Japanese ladies. Predominance of
German influence.

1886. Dissatisfaction of the radicals. Trouble with
China arising from a sailors' brawl at Nagasaki.

1887. Count Inoue's negotiations for Treaty Revision
fall through. Passing of the " Peace Preservation Act,"
whereby many radicals, especially those of the Tosa clan,
were banished from the capital.

1888. Eruption of the volcano, Bandai-San.

1889. A constitution promulgated whereby Japan, hitherto
an absolute monarchy, becomes a constitutional monarchy
after the pattern of Prussia and other continental European
states. Establishment of local self-government. Treaty
ratified with Mexico. Treaties concluded with other western powers, but not ratified.

1890. This year is to witness the opening of the first
" Diet," in accordance with the terms of the Constitution.

＊　　＊　　＊　　＊　　＊　　＊　　＊　　＊　　＊　　＊

It is not possible to conclude this sketch of Japanese
history by the usual formula, " Books Recommended "—
for the reason that there are none to recommend. The
chapters devoted to history in the works of Griffis, Rein,
etc., hold, it is true, a respectable position as embodying

the usual traditional account of the subject. Adams' work, too, is good in its way, though the title, "A History of Japan," is a misnomer. The book is, in fact, an account of the foreign relations of the Japanese government in modern times. But a critical history of Japan remains to be written —a work which should do for every century what Mr. Aston has done for the earliest centuries only.[*] Here more than anywhere else is it necessary to listen at back-doors, to peep through conventional fences, and to sift native evidence by the light of foreign testimony. We should know next to nothing of what may be termed the Catholic episode of the sixteenth and seventeenth centuries, had we access to none but the official Japanese sources. How can we trust those same sources when they deal with times yet more remote? There seems little doubt that the ruling powers at any given time manipulated both the more ancient records and the records of their own age, in order to suit their own private ends. Sometimes, indeed, the process may have been almost unconscious. The Japanese themselves are beginning to awake to these considerations. Mr. Shigeno An-eki, for instance, the eminent head of the Historiographical Bureau, has undertaken to prove how certain historical episodes were "cooked" under the Tokugawa dynasty of Shōguns. A little reflection will show that such manipulations of history are likely to be the rule rather than the exception in Asiatic countries. The love of truth for truth's sake is not a general human characteristic, but one of the exceptional traits of the modern European mind, developed slowly by many causes, chiefly by those habits of accuracy which physical science does so much to foster.

---

[*] See his essay entitled "Early Japanese History," printed in Vol. XXI, Part I, of the "Asiatic Transactions."

Outside Europe and her colonies it is easy to manipulate
records, because such manipulation shocks no one deeply,
because the people are told nothing about the matter, and
because, even if they were told, they have neither the means
nor the inclination to be critical.

**Interviewing.** Interviewing in Japan, and by Japanese
journalists! Yes, it has come even to that in these latter
days, and no book on Japanese things and manners which
omits the interviewer can be deemed complete. The
following account of the way in which two Canadian ladies
connected with the press were interviewed on their arrival
at Yokohama appeared in one of the home papers.* The
account is not only cleverly written. It is true to the
life.

\*  \*  \*  \*  \*  \*  \*  \*  \*  \*  \*

" 'Perhaps,' said I, ' it is the bill.'

" 'This is a European hotel,' remarked Orthodocia, scorn-
fully. We stood in an apartment of the 'Grand' of Yokohama half-an-hour after we had landed. 'They wouldn't
send their bills in Japanese. Besides, it's a little prema-
ture, I think. We haven't been in the country twenty
minutes yet. But it may possibly be a form of extortion
practised by that bobbing person with a full moon on his
head that pulled us from the wharf in his perambulator.
So far as I am concerned'—emphatically—'he shall not
have another penny. I am under the impression now that
go-jis-sen go-rin† was altogether too much to give him.

* We should like to be able to give credit to the proper quarter. Unfortunately we
have seen nothing but the reprint in one of the Yokohama papers, which did not mention either the original source or the name of the writer.

† Japanese for 57½ cents.

It sounds like the price of land in Lombard-street. You can do as you like.'

"Thus privileged, I turned the bit of pasteboard over, and read on the other side a legend in English to the effect that the gentleman downstairs represented a certain *Shimbun* in Tokio. Now *Shimbun*, being interpreted, means newspaper.

"'Orthodocia,' said I, solemnly, 'this is no overcharge! It's something much worse. It's a reporter. We are about to be interviewed—in Japanese. If he succeeds in getting anything out of us, however, it will be extortion indeed.'

"Orthodocia turned pale. 'He will demand impressions,' she said. 'They always do. Have you got any convenient? Could you lend me one?'

"We do not know to this day to what circumstance we owed the honour of appearing in print in Japan—whether we were mistaken for individuals of distinction, or whether we were considered remarkable on our own merits on account of being by ourselves, but we went downstairs fully believing it to be a custom of the country, a rather flattering custom, to which we were much pleased to conform; and this is a true chronicle of what happened.

"It was a slender, round-faced youth who made his deprecating bow to us in the drawing-room. His shoulders sloped, his gray-blue *kimono* lay in narrow folds across his chest like what the old-fashioned people at home used to call a sontag. American boots were visible under the skirt of the garment, and an American stiff felt hat reposed on the sofa beside him. His thick short black hair stood crisply on end, and out of his dark eyes slanted a look of modest inquiry. He was the most unaggressive reporter

I have ever seen. His boots and his hat were the only things about him that I could connect with journalism, as I had previously been acquainted with it.

"'How do you do?' I said, seeing that the silence must be broken and the preliminaries gone through with by somebody.

"'Yes,' he responded, with an amiability that induced Orthodocia to get up hurriedly and look out of the window. "Did the ladies arrive to the *Duke of West-minster?*' looking from one to the other of us.

"'We believe they did,' gasped Orthodocia, and immediately looked out of the window again. I edged my chair toward the other window. Then the cloven hoof appeared in the shape of a note-book. He produced it with gentle ostentation, as one would a trump card. The simile is complete when I add that he took it from his sleeve.

"'How old is lady?' calmly, deliberately.

"'I—I forget,' stammered this historian; 'forty-five, I believe.'

"The reporter put it down.

"'Other lady, your friend—not so old? Older? More old?'

"'I am twenty-two years of age,' adds Orthodocia, gravely, with a reproachful glance at me, 'and I weigh ten stone. Height, five feet eight inches. I am in the habit of wearing fives; in gloves, six and a-half.'

"The reporter scribbled convulsively.

"'Ladies will study Japanese porrytick please say.'

"'I beg pardon?'

"'Yes.' Fills another page.

"Orthodocia, suavely: 'Are they produced here to any extent?'

"'We have here many porrytick—ribarer, conservative, monarchist.'

"'Oh!'—More recourse to the window.

"'Orthodocia,' I said, severely, 'you may not be aware of it, but your conduct is throwing discredit upon a person hitherto fairly entitled to the world's good opinion—which is me. Continue to be absorbingly interested in that brick wall, and allow me to talk to the gentleman.'

"'We have come,' I said it distinctly—'to see Japan as far as Japan will permit. Her politics, system of education, customs, and arts will be of—ahem—interest to us. We cannot truthfully say that we expect to penetrate more deeply into the national life than other travellers have done. In repressing this expectation we claim to be original. We confess that our impressions will naturally be super-ficial, but we hope to represent the crust so charmingly that nobody will ask for any of the—interior—of the—well of the pie.'

"'That's equivocal,' said Orthodocia, 'and ridiculous.'

"'Notwithstanding the well-known reticence of the Jap-anese,' I continued, 'we hope to meet some of them who will show us something more of their domesticity than we can see through the windows.'

"'You will acquire language of Japan?'

"'Not all of it, I think. It seems a little difficult, but musical—much more musical than our ugly English,' interposed Orthodocia.

"'Yes. Will you the story of your journey please say?'

"'Certainly. We came from Montreal to Vancouver by the C. P. R.—that is the best Western railroad on the continent. Some people say that you never would have

heard of Canada in Japan but for the C. P. R., but they
are mostly jealous Republican Americans.'

" The reporter bowed.

"' We travelled three thousand nine hundred miles by
this railway across the North-West and through the Rocky
Mountains.' Here Orthodocia dwelt upon the remarkable
snow-sheds for protection against avalanches. She went
on with confidence to speak of the opening up of trade
between Canada and Japan by the C. P. R. and its steam-
ship line, and I added a few remarks about the interest in
Japanese establishing firms of their own there; while the
reporter flattered our eloquence by taking down notes
enough to fill a quarto volume. We had never been
interviewed before—we might never be again—and were
determined to make the occasion an illustrious one. We
were quite pleased with ourselves as the nice little creature
bowed himself out, promising to send us the fortunate
*Shimbun* which would publish the interview, with a translation of the same, a day or two later.

" I suppose it was Orthodocia's effect upon him—the effect
I had begun to find usual—but he didn't send the *Shimbun*; he brought it next morning with much apology and
many bows. I have before me a pencilled document in
the handwriting of three persons. The document contains
the interview as it was set down in the language of the
translator, who sat with an expression of unruffled repose,
and spake aloud from the *Shimbun* which he held in his
hand. Sometimes Orthodocia took it down, sometimes
he took it down himself, sometimes I took it down
while Orthodocia left the room. The reason for this will
perhaps be self-evident. Orthodocia and I possess the
document in turns, to ward off low spirits. We have

only to look at it to bring on an attack of the wildest hilarity.

"The reporter came entirely in Japanese costume the second time, and left his wooden sandals outside on the stairs. He left most of his English there, too, apparently, but he bowed all the way from the door to the middle of the apartment in a manner that stood for a great deal of polite conversation. Then he sat down and we sat down, and Orthodocia prepared to transcribe the interview which had introduced us to the Japanese nation from his lips. It was a proud, happy moment.

"The reporter took the journal with which he was connected out of one of the long, graceful, flowing sleeves which make life worth living for masculine Japan. He told us that it was the * * *Shimbun*, and he carefully pointed out the title, date, beginning and end of the articles which we marked, intending to buy several copies of the *Shimbun* and send them home. We were anxious that the people there should be kept fully enlightened as to our movements, and there seemed to be a great deal of detail in the article. Its appearance was a little sensational, Orthodocia thought, but she silently concluded, with her usual charity, not to blame the reporter for that, since he couldn't possibly be considered responsible for the exaggerations of the Chinese alphabet.

"'Yesterday,' translated the reporter solemnly —I must copy the document which does not give his indescribable pronunciation—'by Canada steamer ladies arrived. The correspondent who is me, went to Grand Hotel, which the ladies is. Ladies is of Canada and in-the-time-before of England. They have a beautiful countenance.'

"Here the reporter bowed, and Orthodocia left the room

for the first time. I think she said she must go and get her pencil sharpened. She left it with me, however, and I took up the thread of the interview.

"'Object of ladies' locomotion, to make beautiful their minds.' Miss Elder-Lady answered, 'Our object is to observe habits, makings, and beings of the Japanese nation, and to examine how civilisation of America prevails among the nation. And other objects is to examine the art and drawing and education from the exterior of the confectionery. In order to observe customs of Japan we intend to learn a private house.'

"We were getting on swimmingly when Orthodocia reappeared, having recovered in the interval, and told the reporter that he must think foreigners very abrupt and rude, and that he really spoke English extremely well. To both of which remarks he responded—with a polite suavity that induced me to turn my back upon her in an agony of suppressed feeling—'Yes.'

"'Miss Younger-Lady-measuring-ten-stone-and-wearing-six-shoes-and-a-half,-continue,-' The railroad between the Montreal and Canada is passing.'——

"'I beg pardon,' said the unhappy Orthodocia, with an awful galvanism about the corners of her mouth. 'I didn't quite catch what you said—I mean what I said.'

"The reporter translated it over again.

"'Perhaps,' said I, nervously, 'it's a misprint.'

"'No,' the reporter replied gravely, 'Miss Younger Lady.'

"'Gracious!' said Orthodocia.

"'And if by the railroad we employ the steamer, the commerce of Montreal and Japan will prevail. Correspondent asked to Miss Younger-Lady, may I heard the story your caravansery?'

"Orthodocia retired. It was a little trying for me, but when he continued, 'From Montreal to Canada the distance is three thousand miles,' I was glad she had gone. I am afraid I choked a little at this point, for just here he decided to wrestle with the pencil himself. When he handed the paper back again I read: 'While we are passing the distance between Mount Rocky I had a great danger, for the snow over the mountain is falling down, and the railroad shall be cut off. Therefore, by the snow shade, which is made by the tree, its falling was defend. Speaking finish. The ladies is to took their caravansery attending among a few days. Ladies has the liability of many news.'

"'That last item,' said Orthodocia, who had come in with the excuse of some tea, 'is frightfully correct.'

"Having dispatched the business of the hour and a-half, the reporter began to enjoy himself, while Orthodocia and I tried to seat ourselves where we couldn't see each other's faces in the mirror over the mantel-piece. He drank his tea with his head on a level with the table, and if suction can express approval it was expressed. He said that there were fourteen editorial writers on his *Shimbun*, and that its circulation was one million. Which shows that for the soul of a newspaper man Shintoism has no obvious advantages. He dwelt upon the weather for quarters of an hour at a time. The Japanese are such a leisurely people. He took more tea, by this time stone-cold. He said he would bring a Japanese 'gentleman and rady' to see us, and in response to our inquiry as to whether the lady was the wife or the sister of the gentleman, he said with gravity, 'I do not know the rady's wife.' He asked us for our photographs, and when Orthodocia retired for the fifth time

he thought she had gone to get them, and staid until I
was compelled to go and pray her to return. It was the
ringing of the two o'clock lunch bell that suggested to him
that the day was waning, and that perhaps he had better
wane too.''

**Ise.** Ise has been termed the Mecca of Japan, because
it is the site of the two chief temples (*daijingū*) of Shintō,
the aboriginal Japanese religion. Properly speaking, Ise
is the name, not of a town or of a temple, but of a province.
The name of the town nearest to the temples is Yamada.
The name of the nearest port is Kami-Yashiro. Ise may
be easily reached from Tōkyō either by land or by sea.
The land route follows the Tōkaidō railway as far as
Nagoya, whence it is a *jinrikisha* ride of some twelve *ri*
to Yokkaichi and thence of eighteen more to the shrines.
The sea route, by Nippon Yūsen Kaisha steamer, takes
the traveller direct from Yokohama to Yokkaichi in twenty
hours, thence by small steamer to Kami-Yashiro, close to
the shrines, in about five hours.

To the student of Japanese history and religion, the word
Ise is in itself a magnet. But it may be a question
whether the ordinary tourist would be repaid by going
out of his way to visit the temples of a creed which binds
itself to the severest architectural simplicity—white pine-
wood and a thatch of rushes, no carvings, no paintings,
no images, nothing but an immense antiquity, and even
that only in the sense of historic continuity; for immemorial custom decrees that the two shrines shall be
razed to the ground and rebuilt once every twenty years
in precisely the same style. The wood of the old temples
is, on such occasions, hewn into a myriad pieces, and

distributed as relics to the faithful. The temples were last rebuilt in 1889. The deities chiefly worshipped at Ise are the Sun-Goddess *Ama-terasu*, and *Toyauke-hime* the Goddess of Food. Viscount Mori, once Japanese representative at Washington and later at the Court of St. James, perished by the hand of a Shintō fanatic on the 11th February, 1889, for the crime of having lifted with his walking-stick the curtain which hides the chief shrine from vulgar gaze.

Books recommended. "The Shintō Temples of Ise," by Ernest Satow, in Vol. II of the "Asiatic Transactions," and the same author's "Handbook for Japan," p. 167.—Miss Bird's "Unbeaten Tracks in Japan," Vol. II. p. 278, *et seq*.—The "Japan Daily Mail" of the 23rd and 24th October, 1889, contained an elaborate account of the consecration of the new temples, from the pen of Major-General Palmer. R. E.

**Japan.** Our word "Japan," and the Japanese *Nihon* or *Nippon*, are alike corruptions of *Jih-pĕn*, the Chinese pronunciation of the characters 日 本, literally "sun-origin," that is, "the place the sun comes from"—a name given to Japan by the Chinese on account of the position of the archipelago to the east of their own country. Marco Polo's *Zipangu* and the poets' *Cipango* are from the same Chinese compound, with the addition of the word *Kwo* 國, which means "country."

The name *Nihon* ("Japan") seems to have been first officially used by the Japanese government in A. D. 670. Before that time, the usual native designation of the country was *Yamato*, properly the name of one of the central provinces. *Yamato* and *O-mi-kuni*, that is, "the great august country," are the names still preferred in poetry and *belles-lettres*. Japan has other ancient names, some of which are of learned length and thundering sound, for instance, *Toyo-ashi-wara-no-chi-aki-no-naga-i-ho-aki-no-*

*misn-ko-no-kuni*, that is, "the-Luxuriant-Reed-Plains-the-Land-of-Fresh-Rice-Ears-of-a-Thousand-Autumns—of-Long-Five-Hundred-Autumns." But we shall not detain the reader with an enumeration of them. Any further curiosity on this head may be satisfied by consulting the pages of the *Kojiki*. (See "Asiatic Trasactions," Vol. X, Supplement.)

**Japanese People (Characteristics of the).** Any account of the characteristics of a people must deal with two main points, namely, physical characteristics and mental characteristics. We will first say a few words about the physical characteristics, referring those who desire exhaustive information to Dr. Baelz's admirable monograph entitled "*Die Körperlichen Eigenschaften der Japaner*," printed in Parts 28 and 32 of the "German Asiatic Transactions."

I. PHYSICAL CHARACTERISTICS. As stated in the Article entitled RACE, the Japanese are Mongols, that is, they are distinguished by a yellowish skin, straight black hair, scanty beard, almost total absence of hair on the arms, legs, and chest, broadish prominent cheek-bones, and more or less obliquely set eyes. These, with the other characteristics to be mentioned presently, are common both to the more slenderly built, oval-faced aristocracy, and to pudding-faced Gombei, the "Hodge" of Japanese Arcadia. Compared with people of European race, the average Japanese has a long body and short legs, a large skull with a tendency to prognathism (projecting jaws), a flat nose, coarse hair, scanty eye-lashes, puffy eyelids, a sallow complexion, and a low stature. The average stature of Japanese men is about the same as the average stature of European women. The women are proportionately smaller. The lower classes are mostly strong, with well-developed arms, legs, and chests. The upper classes are too often weakly.

The above description will perhaps not be considered flattering. But it is not ours; it is the doctors'. Then, too, ideas of beauty differ from land to land. We Anglo-Saxons consider ourselves a handsome race. But what are we still, in the eyes of the majority of the Japanese people, but a set of big, red, hairy barbarians with green eyes?

The Japanese women are, on the whole, handsomer than the men, and have, besides, pretty manners and charming voices. Village beauties are rare, most girls of the lower class with any pretentions to good looks being, as it would seem, sent out to service at tea-houses in the towns, or else early obtaining husbands. Japanese children, with their dainty little ways and old-fashioned appearance, always insinuate themselves into the affections of foreign visitors.

The Japanese age earlier than we do. It has also been asserted that they are less long-lived. But this is doubtful. If statistics may be trusted, the number of octogenarians, nonagenarians, and even centenarians is fairly high. In Japan, as in other countries, the number of very old women considerably exceeds that of the very old men. The diseases which make most havoc are consumption, diseases of the digestive organs, and the peculiar affection called *Kakke* of which mention will be found in a separate article. The Japanese have less high-strung nerves than we Europeans. Hence they endure pain more calmly, and meet death with comparative indifference.*

---

* We have classed indifference to death among the physical characteristics, because none can doubt that a less sensitive nervous system must at least tend in that

II. MENTAL CHARACTERISTICS. The tape-line, the weighing-machine, the craniometer, and the hospital returns give means of ascertaining a nation's physical characteristics which almost any one can apply and which none may dispute. Far different is it when we try to gauge the phenomena of mind. Does a new-comer venture on the task? He is set down as a sciolist, a man without experience—the one thing declared needful. Does an old resident hold forth, expecting his experience to command attention? The *Globe-trotter journalisticus* from London, or maybe the cultured Bostonian literary critic, jumps upon him, tells him that living too long in one place has given him mental myopia, in other words has rendered his judgment prejudiced and worthless. The late Mr. Gifford Palgrave said in the present writer's hearing that an eight weeks' residence was the exact time qualifying an intelligent man to write about Japan. A briefer period (such was his ruling) was sure to produce superficiality, while a longer period induced a wrong mental focus. By a curious coincidence, eight weeks was the exact space of time during which Mr. Palgrave had been in Japan when he delivered himself of this oracle.

Again, are you in the Japanese service, and do you praise Japan? Then you must be a sycophant. Do you find fault with it? " Ah! don't you know?" it will be said, "when they renewed his engagement the other day, they

direction. It is possible, however, that opinions and beliefs have had some influence in the matter Buddhism is a tolerant, hopeful creed, and promises rest at last to all, even though it may have to be purchased by the withal at the price of numerous transmigrations. Christianity, on the other hand, with its terrible doctrine of the final and hopeless perdition of the immense majority of the human race, may have steeped in a still more sombre hue the naturally excitable and self-questioning European mind. The Greeks and Romans appear to have braved death with an indifference to which few moderns can attain.

cut his salary down $50 a month." Worst of all is it
if you are a Yokohama merchant. Then you are informed
flatly that you are an ignoramus, a "dollar-grinder," and
that, as you never see any Japanese of the better class, but
only coolies and hucksters, what you are pleased to call your
opinion is a mere impertinence worth less than nothing.

All things considered, the would-be critic of Japanese
mind, manners, and morals has a thankless task before him.
The present writer feels that he cannot hope to escape
being classed in some one or other of the above-named
categories of pariahs not fit to have an opinion of their
own. He has, therefore, decided to express none at all,
but simply to quote the opinions of others. Perhaps he
may thus avoid blame and unpleasantness. He has chosen
the opinions impartially, or rather he has not chosen
them, but taken them anyhow, as they happened to come
uppermost in his box of scraps. He has not, it is
true, thought fit to include all or any of the absurdities of
the casual passer-by—one French count, for instance,
a stripling of twenty, who spent just three months in the
country and then wrote a book about it, sums up his acquired wisdom in the tremendous assertion, "*Le Japonais
n'est pas intelligent*." Of recent trash of this kind there
is enough to fill many volumes. But who would care to
read it ? The opinions which we quote will be seen to be
in some cases judgments of the people, in others judgments of the country. But it is impossible to separate
one class from the other :—

"This nation is the delight of my soul." (St. Francis
Xavier, middle of sixteenth century.)

"The people of this Iland of *Iapon* are good of nature,

curteous aboue measure and valiant in warre : their iustice is seuerely excecuted without any partialitie vpon transgressors of the law. They are gouerned in great ciuilitie. I meane, not a land better gouerned in the world by ciuill policie. The people be verie superstitious in their religion, and are of diuers opinions."—This last sentence does not fit the present day. No one now accuses the Japanese of superstitious religionism. Our author is again in touch with modern times when he speaks of " the peopell veri subiect to thear gouvernours and superiores." (WILL ADAMS, early in the seventeenth century.)

" Bold,......... heroic,......... revengeful,.........desirous of fame,.........very industrious and enured to hardships,... ......great lovers of civility and good manners, and very nice in keeping themselves, their cloaths and houses, clean and neat..........As to all sorts of handicrafts, either curious or useful, they are wanting neither proper materials, nor industry and application, and so far is it, that they should have any occasion to send for masters from abroad, that they rather exceed all other nations in ingenuity and neatness of workmanship, particularly in brass, gold, silver and copper..........Now if we proceed farther to consider the Japanese, with regard to sciences and the embellishments of our mind, Philosophy perhaps will be found wanting. The Japanese indeed are not so far enemies to this Science, as to banish the Country those who cultivate it, but they think it an amusement proper for monasteries, where the monks leading an idle lazy life, have little else to trouble their heads about. However, this relates chiefly to the speculative part, for as to the moral part, they hold it in great esteem, as being of a higher and divine origin...

......I confess indeed, that they are wholly ignorant of musick, so far as it is a science built upon certain precepts of harmony. They likewise know nothing of mathematicks, more especially of its deeper and speculative parts. No body ever cultivated these sciences but we Europeans, nor did any other nations endeavour to embellish the mind with the clear light of mathematical and demonstrative reasoning. ........They profess a great respect and veneration for their Gods, and worship them in various ways: And I think I may affirm, that in the practice of virtue, in purity of life, and outward devotion, they far out-do the Christians: Careful for the Salvation of their Souls, scrupulous to excess in the expiation of their crimes, and extremely desirous of future happiness.........Their Laws and Constitutions are excellent, and strictly observed, severe penalties being put upon the least transgression of any."
(ENGELBERT KAEMPFER, end of seventeenth century.)

SIR RUTHERFORD ALCOCK, one of the most acute writers on Japan, is also one of the most difficult to quote from, as his whole book, "The Capital of the Tycoon," is one continued criticism of the Japan of his time (about 1860), and one would like to quote it all. Here are a couple of his witty sayings:

"(Japan) is a very paradise of babies."

"There is a mistake somewhere, and the result is that in one of the most beautiful and fertile countries in the whole world the flowers have no scent, the birds no song, and the fruit and vegetables no flavour. One of my colleagues gave the characteristics of the country in another triology, which I am bound to say was not inferior in accuracy, if less poetical. 'Women wearing no crinoline, houses har-

bouring no bugs, and the country no lawyers.'   The last is
perhaps the most astonishing of the whole."

Sir Rutherford speaks in his preface of "the incorrigi-
ble tendency of the Japanese to withhold from foreigners
or disguise the truth on all matters great and small."
Yet he allows that they are "a nation of thirty millions
of as industrious, kindly, and well-disposed people as
any in the world."—Their art, too, rouses his admiration, though he makes a reservation to the effect that
there are some departments in which they have failed
to produce anything to be named in the same day with
the works of the great artists of Europe.  "Perhaps in
nothing," says he, "are the Japanese to be more admired than for the wonderful genius they display in arriving at the greatest possible results with the simplest
means, and the smallest possible expenditure of time
and labour or material.  The tools by which they produce their finest works are the simplest, and often the
rudest that can be conceived.  Wherever in the fields or
the workshops nature supplies a force, the Japanese is
sure to lay it under contribution, and make it do his
work with the least expense to himself of time, money,
and labour.  To such a pitch of perfection is this carried, that it strikes every observer as one of the moral
characteristics of the race, indicating no mean degree of
intellectual capacity and cultivation."                  .

"In moral character, the *average* Japanese is frank,
honest, faithful, kind, gentle, courteous, confiding, affec-
tionate, filial, loyal.  Love of truth for its own sake, chastity, temperance, are not characteristic virtues."  (Rev.
W. E. Griffis, in "The Mikado's Empire.")

" Surely, for happiness, gentleness, and sobriety, for soft-
voiced and always smiling chatter, for the blessed faculty
of inhaling healthful enjoyment from the simplest things...
......no other country can even profess to show the match
of a festival crowd in Japan......... Police in such a throng,
it seems to us, can have no more to do than the lilies of the
valley." (MAJOR-GENERAL PALMER, R. E., in the " Japan
Daily Mail.")

Here are a few shorter dicta on the land and its peo-
ple :—
"Calm and imperturbably polite." (JOHN R. BLACK, in
" Young Japan.")

" The land of disappointments." (An OLD RESIDENT in
Japanese service.)

" The land of gentle manners and fantastic arts." (SIR
EDWIN ARNOLD, in a letter to the " Daily Telegraph.")—
The same author says of the Japanese people : " They have
the nature rather of birds or butterflies than of ordinary
human beings."

" The land indeed of the sunrise, but also the land of
the sunset of romance." (CURT NETTO, in " Papierschmetterlinge aus Japan.")

" Le Japon, voyez-vous, c'est une traduction mal
faite." (A resident diplomat, quoted in one of MR.
HENRY NORMAN's letters on Japan to the " Pall-Mall
Gazette.")

" Japan is a Capua." (A GLOBE-TROTTER.)

"A pocket-country, compact and complete in its neat smallness." (Hon. Lewis Wingfield, in "The Wanderings of a Globe-Trotter.")

Pierre Loti, in his "*Madame Chrysanthème*" and "*Japoneries d'Automne*," emphasises over and over again one particular aspect of Japanese life—its smallness, its quaintness, its comicality. Here are just a few samples of the adjectives which he sows broad-cast over his pages, almost exhausting the resources of the French language in that particular line: *petit, bizarre, disparate, hétérogène, invraisemblable, mignon, bariolé, extravagant, inimaginable, frêle, monstrueux, grotesque, misère, exotique, lilliputien, minuscule, maniéré*, etc., etc., *ad infinitum*. The houses are all *maisonnettes*; each garden is, not a *jardin*, but a *jardinet*; each meal a *dinette*, each inscription a *grifonnage*. The Kōbe-Kyōto railway is, "*un drôle de petit chemin de fer, qui n'a pas l'air sérieux, qui fait l'effet d'une chose pour rire, comme toutes les choses japonaises.*"—Of course there is an element of truth in all this. Query: is it the whole truth?

People are fond of drawing comparisons between the Chinese and the Japanese. Almost all seem agreed that the Japanese are much the pleasanter race to live with— clean, kindly, artistic. On the other hand, the Chinese are universally allowed to be far more trustworthy. "I know," says the late Manager of the Hongkong and Shanghai Bank in Shanghai, "of no people in the world I would sooner trust than the Chinese merchant or banker............ For the last twenty-five years the bank has been doing a very large business with Chinese in Shanghai, amounting,

I should say, to hundreds of millions of taels, and we have never met with a defaulting Chinaman."—Wofully different from this is the tale told by the European bankers and merchants in Japan. They complain, it is true, not so much of actual wilful dishonesty—though of that, too, they affirm there is plenty—as of pettiness, constant shilly-shallying, unbusinesslikeness almost passing belief. One dictum, which we caught the other day from the lips of a thoroughly practical Briton, puts the thing in a nut-shell : " Good-natured, artistic, and all that, but muddle-pated folk when it comes to matters of business."

The average judgment formed by those who have lived some time in the country, seems to resolve itself into three principal items on the credit side, which are cleanliness, kindliness, and a refined artistic taste, and three items on the debit side, namely, vanity, unbusinesslike habits, and an incapacity for appreciating abstract ideas. A whole book, and a very clever one too—Mr. Percival Lowell's " Soul of the Far East"—has been written to prove that they have no soul.

MR. WALTER DENING, whose acquaintance with modern Japanese literature and with the men who produce it is probably unrivalled, writes as follows :

" It is well-known that one of the most marked characteristics of the Japanese mind is its lack of interest in metaphysical, psychological, and ethical controversy of all kinds. It is seldom you can get them to pay sufficient attention to such questions to admit of their understanding even their main outlines." And again :—

" Neither their past history nor their prevailing tastes show any tendency to idealism. They are lovers of the practical and the real: neither the fancies of Goethe nor the reveries of Hegel are to their liking. Our poetry and our philosophy and the mind that appreciates them are alike the result of a network of subtle influences to which the Japanese are comparative strangers. It is maintained by some, and we think justly, that the lack of idealism in the Japanese mind renders the life of even the most cultivated a mechanical, humdrum affair when compared with that of Westerns. The Japanese cannot understand why our controversialists should wax so fervent over psychological, ethical, religious, and philosophical questions, failing to perceive that this fervency is the result of the intense interest taken in such subjects. The charms that the cultured Western mind finds in the world of fancy and romance, in questions themselves, irrespective of their practical bearings, is for the most part unintelligible to the Japanese."

One more quotation only. It is from the REV. G. M. MEACHAM, a missionary of many years standing, and resumes what hundreds of residents have thought and said :—

"A few months do not suffice to give a correct understanding of the situation, though the visitor should enjoy the kind attention and guidance of high officials. There are perhaps no people under heaven who know better the happy art of entertaining their guests, and none perhaps who succeed better in preoccupying them with their views. Indeed the universal experience of those who remain long enough in this country to see beneath the surface is that first impressions are very deceitful."

So far this little symposium (that is the fashionable word, is it not?) on the mental characteristics of the Jap-

anese. Any one who thinks it not full enough or not representative enough, is earnestly requested to contribute to it,
either from his personal experience or from his reading.

**Jinrikisha.** The origin of the *jinrikisha* is, to use a
grandiloquent phrase, shrouded in obscurity. One native
account attributes the spark of invention to a paralytic old
gentleman of Kyōto, who, some time before 1868, finding
his palanquin uncomfortable, took to a little cart instead.
According to another version, one Akiha Daisuke, of
Tōkyō, was the inventor, about 1870, but the first official
application to be allowed to manufacture *jinrikishas* was
made about the same time by a man called Takayama
Kōsaku. The usual foreign version is that an American
named Goble, half-cobbler and half-missionary, was the
person to suggest the idea of a modified perambulator
somewhere about 1867 ; and this has the support of Mr.
Black, the author of "Young Japan." In any case, the
invention, once made, found wide-spread favour. There
are now over 33,000 *jinrikishas* in Tōkyō alone ; and the
ports of China and of the Malay peninsula, as well as
Japan, owe to the *jinrikisha* a fruitful source of employment
for their teeming coolie population and of comfort for the
well-to-do residents.

The compound word *jin-riki-sha* (人力車) means literally "man-power-vehicle," that is, a vehicle pulled by a
man. Some have imagined *sha* to be a corruption of
the English "car." This is quite erroneous. *Sha* is a
good old Chinese word. The poor word *jinrikisha* itself
suffers many things at the hands of Japanese and foreigners alike. The Japanese generally cut off its tail and
call it *jinriki*, or else they translate the Chinese syllable

*ska* into their own language, and call it *kuruma*. The English cut off its head and maltreat the vowels, pronouncing it *rickshaw*.

The total cost of the outfit of a *jinrikiska*-man—coat, drawers, hat, and lantern all complete, as per the [Tōkyō police regulations of October, 1889—is estimated at $4.

**Kaempfer.** If Marco Polo was the first to bring the existence of such a country as Japan to the knowledge of Europeans, and Mendez Pinto the first to tread its shores, Engelbert Kaempfer (1651—1716) may truly be called its *scientific* discoverer. A native of Lemgow in Westphalia, he travelled while a youth in North Germany, Holland, and Poland. At the age of thirty-two he joined the Swedish diplomatic service as a secretary of legation, in which capacity he proceeded through Russia and Tartary to the court of Ispahan. Insatiable for a sight of yet more distant lands, he then entered the service of the Dutch East India Company as a surgeon, sailed from Ormuz to Batavia in 1688, and thence viâ Siam to Japan, where he arrived in the month of September, 1690. At that time, the Dutch were the only Christian nation permitted to trade with Japan, and even they were confined to Deshima, a quarter of Nagasaki, where jealous care was taken by the authorities to keep them in ignorance of all Japanese matters. A yearly journey to Yedo to make obeisance before the Shōgun was the only change in their monotonous existence.

Kaempfer remained in Japan but two years and two months. Yet, in this short period and under these disadvantageous circumstances, he compiled a work which for the first time gave the world fairly accurate information concerning the history, geography, religious beliefs, man-

ners and customs, and natural productions of the mysterious
Island Empire. Returning to Europe in 1694, Kaempfer
settled, first at Leyden and then in his native town, where
he employed himself in writing his two celebrated works,
the "History of Japan" and the "*Amænitates Exoticæ*,"
in practising as a physician, and in quarrelling with the
odious wife whose bad temper is said to have aggravated
the fits of colic which ended in his death.

The "History of Japan" appeared, strange to say, first in
an English translation in 1727—8; then in Latin (1728),
Dutch (1729), and French (1729). All these were translated from the English version. Lastly, in 1777, came a
German edition—not exactly the German original, because
Kaempfer's style was so terribly dry and involved as to
make the booksellers fear that it would disgust even the
German public, long-suffering as the German public is in
that respect. The diction was accordingly modernised and
touched up. Hence Kaempfer's work has never appeared
in Kaempfer's words. Copies of all the editions are now
rare, and fetch high prices at auction.

**Kakke.** *Kakke* is the same disease as that known in
India and the Malay peninsula under the name of *beri-beri*,
and may be defined in popular language as a sort of
paralysis, as it is characterised by loss of motive power
and by numbness, especially in the extremities. It is often
accompanied by dropsy. In severe cases it affects the
heart, and may then become fatal. *Kakke* is the national
scourge of Japan, and attacks with special frequency and
virulence young and otherwise healthy men—women much
less often. It springs, in the opinion of the best authorities, not from actual malaria, as has been sometimes

thought, but from a climatic influence resembling malaria. That it is more or less contagious would appear from the frequency with which it attacks soldiers in barracks and seamen crowded together on board ship. It should, however, be stated that others have sought the origin of the disease in the national diet—some in rice, some in fish. In favour of this latter view is to be set the consideration that the peasantry, who often cannot afford either rice or fish, and have to eat barley or millet instead, suffer much less than the towns-folk, and the further fact that great improvement in this respect has been observed in the health of the Japanese navy ever since Dr. Takaki, I.J.N., introduced a meat diet for the seamen. But the subject remains mysterious, notwithstanding the labours of the authors mentioned below.

**Books recommended.** "Kak'ke," by Dr. Wm. Anderson, printed in Vol. VI. Part I, of the "Asiatic Transactions" (also published in pamphlet form). "*Infectionskrankheiten in Japan,*" by Dr. E. Baelz, in the "German Asiatic Transactions," Vol. III, p. 371.—"*Die Japanische Kak-ke,*" by Dr. B. Scheube.—"*Geographisch-medicinische Studien,*" by Dr. Wernich; and others in European languages, besides reports in Japanese by Drs. Takaki and Miura.

**Kana.** See WRITING.

**Kurile Islands.** The Kuriles are a long chain of islands, rocky and useless for the most part, stretching for some ten degrees of latitude between Kamchatka and Yezo. Their name is of Russian origin, and means "the smokers," in allusion to the many active volcanoes which they contain. Originally inhabited by a shifting population of Ainos and perhaps men of some other native race, the Kuriles attracted the cupidity of the Cossacks who conquered Kamchatka at the end of the seventeenth century. At that time the islands swarmed with fur-bearing animals, now ruthlessly hunted to the verge of extinction. Gradually the whole group passed under Russian sway, though the government of Yedo always asserted its right to the southernmost portion of the chain. At last, by the treaty of St. Petersburg, concluded in 1875, the Kuriles were formally ceded by Russia to Japan, in exchange for the far more valuable territory of southern Saghalien, which had till then been claimed as a Japanese possession.

**Books recommended.** Unfortunately, the best work on the history of the Kuriles is buried in the Russian language. It is a paper by A. Polonsky, in Vol. IV of the Memoirs of the Ethnographical Section of the Geographical Society of St. Petersburg, entitled "Kurilui."—The Kuriles have been exhaustively discussed from a geographical and geological point of view by Professor Milne, in Vol. IX, Part II, pp. 115—130, of the "Transactions of the Seismological Society of Japan."

**Kyōto.** See CAPITAL CITIES.

**Laoquer.** It is acknowledged by all connoisseurs that in the art of lacquer the Japanese far surpass their teachers, the Chinese. This may be partly because the lacquer-tree, though also apparently introduced from China, finds in Japan a more congenial climate. But we shall scarcely err in attributing the superiority chiefly to the finer esthetic instincts of the Japanese. So exactly did lacquer-work suit their taste and talent that they were already producing triumphs in this branch of art at an epoch when England was still rent by the barbarous struggles of the Heptarchy.

Appreciation of lacquer is a thing which has to be acquired, but which, when acquired, grows upon one, and places the best lacquer in the category of almost sacred things. To show a really fine piece casually to a newcomer, or to send it home as a gift to one of the uncultivated natives of Europe or America, is, as the Japanese proverb says, "like giving guineas to a cat." He will take it up for an instant, just glance at it, say "What a pretty little thing!" and put it down again, imagining it to be worth at most a couple of dollars. Not improbably it cost a hundred, and was the outcome of years of patient toil and marvellous art.

The chapter on lacquer in Rein's "Industries of Japan" is one of the fullest in that painstaking work. Rein spent five months in acquiring a knowledge of the art himself. Mr. J. J. Quin, too, of the British Consular Service in Japan, qualified himself by study under a practical teacher, and was able to send to the Royal Museum at Kew an exhaustive collection illustrative of every process employed, from the knives and gloves used by the lacquer-tappers to the most perfect specimens of the gold lacquerer's art. His researches are embodied, partly in a paper printed in Vol. IX of the "Asiatic Transactions," partly in a "Report by Her Majesty's Acting Consul at Hakodate." Most of the facts in the following short account are taken from one or other of these two authorities.

The material employed is the sap which exudes from the lacquer-tree (*Rhus vernicifera*) when incised. This tapping for lacquer, as it may perhaps be called, affords a livelihood to a special class of men, who, on the approach of mild weather in April, spread all over the northern provinces of the Empire, where the best lacquer-trees grow, and continue their operations on into the autumn. The age of the tree, the season when the tree is tapped, and the treatment to which the sap is afterwards subjected—as, for instance, by being mixed with iron filings, turpentine, or charred wood—produce widely different kinds of lacquer, which are accordingly appropriated to different uses. Every species of lacquer turns black on exposure to the light;

and it is a fact, curious but undoubtedly authentic, that lacquer dries most quickly in a damp atmosphere. The damper the atmosphere and the darker the room, so much the more quickly will the lacquer dry.

Many kinds of material admit of being lacquered. On metal, in particular, very pleasing results have been obtained. But the favourite material is wood, and the best kinds of wood for the purpose are the *hinoki* (Chamæcyparis obtusa) and *kiri* (Paulownia imperialis). The woods of the Cryptomeria japonica (*sugi*) and Planera japonica (*keyaki*) are those most used for general purposes, such as common bowls, trays, etc. The Japanese constantly employ lacquer utensils for holding boiling soups, alcoholic drinks, and even burning cigar-ashes. But so strong is the substance that it suffers little if any damage from such apparently rough treatment.

The process of lacquering is complicated and tedious. To begin with, the surface of the wood is covered with triturated hemp and glue, and then the first coating of lacquer is applied, only to be itself covered with the very finest hempen cloth. Numerous coatings of various qualities of lacquer are laid on this as a foundation. A careful drying intervenes between each coating, and a partial rubbing off with a whetstone follows each drying. A powder formed of calcined deer's horn serves in most cases to give the final polish. But all this process, of which we have merely indicated the bare outlines, is itself but a preparatory one if the object is to produce one of those beautiful gold lacquered boxes which the word "lacquer" generally calls up in the mind of the European collector. We give Quin's account of gold lacquer nearly in full:

"When it is desired to apply flat gold lacquer to an article that has received the plain coats, as related, the process is as follows :—

"A thin species of paper, prepared with sizing made of glue and alum, is used. On this paper the design required to be transmitted to the lacquered article is drawn. On the reverse of this paper, the outline is lightly traced in lacquer—previously roasted over live charcoal to prevent its drying—with a very fine brush made of rat's hair. This paper is then laid on the article to be lacquered and is rubbed with a spatula made of Hinoki or whalebone, where the lacquer has been applied, and on removing the paper the design is observed lightly traced in lacquer.

"To make it perfectly plain, this is rubbed over very lightly with a piece of cotton wool, charged with finely powdered whetstone, or tin; this brings the pattern out white. From one tracing, upwards of twenty impressions can be taken off, and when that is no longer possible, from the lacquer having become used up, it only requires a fresh tracing over the same paper to reproduce the design *ad infinitum.* This tracing does not dry, owing to the lacquer used for the purpose having been roasted, as previously mentioned, and can be wiped off at any time.

"The pattern thus traced out is then filled in with groundwork lacquer, with a brush made of hare's hair, great care being taken not to touch or paint out the original tracing line. This is then powdered over with fine gold dust, silver dust, or tin dust, according to the quality of the ware. This dust is applied with a piece of cotton wool, charged with the material to be used, and the article is then gently dusted with a very soft brush made from the long winter coat of a white horse to remove any loose metal dust that might adhere to the article, and to slightly smoothen the surface. If the article under manufacture is large, only a small portion is done at a time, and it is at once enclosed in an air-tight press, so as to prevent any dust or outside matter adhering to the freshly lacquered surface. At the proper time, when the lacquer has sufficiently hardened, the article is taken out, and the part over which the gold dust has been sprinkled, receives a coat of transparent varnish (*Suki urushi*), laid on with a hare's hair brush, and a further portion is prepared with a coating of gold dust, as on the previous day: the article is again closed up in the air-tight damp press as before, till dry. When the portion which has received the second coat of lacquer over the gold dust is quite hard, it is rubbed smooth with a piece of hard charcoal made from camellia wood, or *Hōnoki* until the whole is level with the surrounding parts. Then it is rubbed with the finger and some finely powdered whetstone and deer's horn, with the smallest quantity of oil, till it attains a fine polish. If upon this surface any further work takes place, such as the veining of leaves, or the painting of stamens, etc., of flowers, these are traced in lacquer and covered with gold dust, and when dry the final polish is given with the finger and powdered deer's horn. The above is the usual mode of making flat gold lacquer.

" TOGI-DASHI (BRINGING OUT BY POLISHING).

" This style consists in applying to the plain lacquered article the design required, in the same manner as in *Hira-makiye*. The whole surface of the article then receives a coat either of black lacquer or transparent lacquer, which, when dry, is ground down with *Hōnoki* charcoal till the pattern shows out. It is then polished off in the same manner with deer's horn and oil, on the point of the finger.

For making *Togi-dashi*, gold dust of a slightly coarser quality is used than for ordinary *Hira-makiye*.

" TAKA-MAKIYE (RAISED GOLD LACQUER).

" The first and second processes are the same as when making flat lacquer, but instead of gold dust, finely powdered camellia charcoal is shaken over the freshly lacquered surface. After drying, the article is carefully dusted with a soft rag to remove any loose charcoal powder, and the parts are further washed with a brush and water, to bring out the fine lines, etc. Some Yoshino lacquer is then rubbed on the charcoal surface with a piece of cotton wool, a coating of *Sabiko* applied, and the article set to dry in the damp press. Afterwards the surface is ground smooth with *Hōnoki* charcoal, and a further rubbing is given with camellia charcoal powdered, on a piece of cotton cloth. A coating of *Taka-maki* lacquer is then given, and the article is put again in the press to dry: on removing it, the process of grinding with *Hōnoki* and powdered camellia charcoal is repeated. Yoshino lacquer is then rubbed on with a piece of cotton wool as before, and the article is again set to dry. When taken out, it is polished smooth with powdered whetstone on the point of the finger, a coat of *Shita-maki* or groundwork lacquer, given, and then the gold powder is applied,—for small work with a fine brush, and for large work, shaken through a quill with muslin over one end. The article is then again set to dry, and the remainder of the process is the same as for flat lacquer.

" According as the lacquer is to be more or less raised, two or more coats of *Taka-maki* lacquer have to be given, till the required height is obtained, and it is at this period of the process that the shape of the hills, rocks, trees, or flowers is worked out."

So far Mr Quin. It should be added that much of the
so-called gold or silver lacquer is really manufactured with
the aid of bronze and tin, especially at the present time,
when cheapness and quantity are insisted on by a public
whose taste is imperfectly educated. The lacquer poison,
of which so much has been said by travellers, is never
fatal, though it is extremely painful in some cases. Blood
to the head, swelling, violent itching and burning, and
occasionally small festering boils are the symtoms. Lacquer in any stage, except when perfectly dry, is capable of
producing it.

The tallow-tree, or vegetable wax-tree, as it is sometimes called, is closely allied to the lacquer-tree, both belonging to the same genus, *Rhus*. The berries of the tallow-
tree are crushed in a press, and the exuding fat is warmed,
purified, and made into candles. The berries of the lacquer-
tree are often treated in the same manner.

**Language.** It is still doubtful under what family of
languages Japanese should be classed. In structure, though
not to any appreciable extent in vocabulary, it closely resembles Korean; and both it and Korean may possibly be related to Mongol and to Manchu, and may therefore lay claim
to be included in the so-called "Altaic" group. In any
case, Japanese is what philologists term an agglutina-
tive language, that is to say, it builds up its words and
grammatical forms by means of suffixes loosely soldered to
the root or stem, which is invariable. Though not originally related to Chinese, Japanese has adopted an enormous
number of Chinese words, such words having naturally followed Chinese civilisation into the archipelago. Even at
the present day, the Japanese language has recourse to

Chinese for terms to indicate all such new things and ideas as "telegram," "velocipede," "photography," "democracy," "limited liability," etc., etc., much as we ourselves have recourse to Latin and Greek.

The fundamental rule of Japanese syntax is that qualifying words precede the word they qualify. Thus the adjective or genitive precedes the noun which it defines, the adverb precedes the verb, and explanatory or dependent clauses precede the principal clause. The object likewise precedes the verb. The predicative verb or adjective of each clause is placed at the end of that clause, the predicative verb or adjective of the main clause rounding off the entire sentence, which is often, even in familiar conversation, extremely long and complicated. The following is an example of Japanese construction :—

| | |
|---|---|
| *Kono goro ni itarimashite,*<br>**This period at having-arrived,**<br>*Bukkyō to mōsu mono*<br>**Buddhism that (they) say thing**<br>*wa, tada katō-jimmin no*<br>**as-for, merely low-class-people 's**<br>*shinjiru tokoro to naite,*<br>**believing place that having-become,**<br>*chūtō ijō de*<br>**middle-class thence-upwards as**<br>*wa sono dōri wo wakimae-*<br>**as-for, the reason (accus.) discern-**<br>*teru hito ga sukunaku; shūmon*<br>**ing people are (num.) being-few. religion**<br>*to ieba, sōshiki no toki*<br>**that if-one-says, funeral-rite 's time**<br>*bakari ni mochiiru koto no*<br>**only (to employ thing 's**<br>*yō ni omoimasu.*<br>**manner as (they) think.** | "At the present day Buddhism has sunk into being the belief of the lower classes only. Few persons in the middle and upper classes understand its *raison d'être*, most of them fancying that religion is a thing which comes into play only at funeral services." |

This one example may suffice to show how widely different (compared with Europe) are the channels in which Japanese thought flows. Nor is it merely that the idioms differ, but that the same circumstances do not draw from Japanese speakers remarks similar to those which they would draw from European speakers. In accidence, also, the dissimilarity is remarkable. Japanese nouns have no gender or number, Japanese adjectives no degrees of comparison, Japanese verbs no persons. On the other hand, the verbs have peculiar complications of their own. They have a negative voice, and forms to indicate causation and potentiality. There is also an elaborate system of honorifics, which replaces to a certain extent the use of persons in the verb and makes good the absence of personal pronouns.

Japanese—with its exotic grammar, its still uncertain affinities, its ancient literature—is a language worthy of more attention than it has yet received. We say language, but languages would be more strictly correct, the modern colloquial speech having diverged from the old classical tongue almost to the same extent as Italian has diverged from Latin. The Japanese still employ in their books, and even in correspondence and advertisements, a dialect which is partly classical and partly artificial. This is what is termed the "Written Language." The student is therefore confronted by a double task. (See also Articles on LITERATURE and WRITING.)

Books recommended. The foregoing article is condensed from the present writer's "Handbook of Colloquial Japanese." See also Imbrie's "English-Japanese Etymology."—The best book on the classical language is Aston's "Grammar of the Japanese Written Language."—The best Japanese-English dictionary is that compiled by Dr. Hepburn. It is published in two forms—a larger giving the Chinese characters and numerous examples, and a smaller for the pocket. Satow and Ishibashi's small dictionary is to be preferred for English-Japanese. Gubbins' "Dictionary of Chinese-Japanese Words," now in course of publication, is specially valuable to students of the modern literary style.

**Law.** Dutifully obedient to authority and not naturally litigious, the Japanese are nevertheless becoming a nation of lawyers. No branch of study is more popular than law with the young men of the new generation. It seems to have for them a sort of abstract and theoretical interest ; for (and more's the pity) Japanese law has at no time been the genuine outcome of the national life, as English law, for instance, is the outcome of English national life—a historical development fitting itself to the needs of the nation as a well-made glove fits the hand. Twelve hundred years ago Japan borrowed Chinese law wholesale. She is borrowing French and German law wholesale to-day. There are now two parties—a pro-codification party and an anti-codification party. The former is the party in power, being backed by the statesmen who see in European codes for Japan a prerequisite of fair treatment of Japan by European nations. The point of view of the anti-codification party is : "Japan for the Japanese. Our laws must suit our people. They must not be mere handles for obtaining treaty revision. Wait to codify until the national courts, interpreting national needs, shall have evolved precedents of their own. French and German codes are alien things, mechanically superimposed on our Japanese ways of thought and modes of life, which are not in touch with foreign civilisations and the laws that have sprung from them."

Which of these parties is in the right? The anti-codification party founds itself on history, on natural development. On the other hand, might it not be plausibly argued that, wholesale imitation and the adoption of foreign ways having always been Japan's method of proceeding, and being therefore a sort of inverted originality of her own, the pro-codificationists are, in effect, more truly inheritors

of the national tradition than the so-called nationalists? It
is of course out of the question that any opinion we, as
ignorant laymen, may hold on such a subject can be worth
anything. Our only object is to present both sides, and to
present them briefly.

The new codes resulting from the legislative activity
of the present reign are: (1) the Criminal Code and the
Code of Criminal Procedure, drafted by M. Boissonnade
de Fontarabie on the basis of the Code Napoleon, with
modifications suggested by the old Japanese Criminal Law;
these were published in 1880, and came into force in 1882;
(2) the Civil Code, the Code of Civil Procedure, and the
Commercial Code, which are on the eve of publication.
Though not actually entitled codes, we may also include:
(3) the Constitution, with its attendant laws regarding the
Imperial House, the Diet, and Finance; (4) the Laws for
the Exercise of Local Self-Government; and (5) divers sta-
tutes on miscellaneous subjects, one of the most important
of which is banking.

Crimes, as classified in the Japanese Criminal Code, are
of three kinds, namely: (1) crimes against the state or the
Imperial Family, and in violation of the public credit,
policy, peace, health, etc.; (2) crimes against person and
property; (3) police offences. There is also a subdivision
of (1) and (2) into major and minor crimes.

The punishments for major crimes are: (1) death by
hanging: (2) deportation with or without hard labour, for
life or for a term of years; (3) imprisonment with or without hard labour, for life or for a term of years. The punishments for minor crimes include confinement with or without hard labour, and fines. The punishments for police
offences are detention for from one to ten days without hard

labour, and fines varying from 5 *sen* to $1.95. The Court which tries persons accused of major crimes consists of three judges, that for minor crimes of one judge, and that for police offences of one *juge de paix*.* Capital punishments are carried out in the presence of a procurator. They are now extremely rare. Criminals condemned to deportation are generally sent to the Island of Yezo, where they sometimes work in the mines. The ordinary prisons are situated in various parts of the Empire, and number one hundred and ninety-three.

A person who has suffered injury by crime lodges his complaint at a police-office or with the procurator of any court having jurisdiction over the crime in question. Policemen can arrest an offender whose crime was committed in their presence, or which the complainant avers to have actually seen committed. In all other cases they can arrest by warrant only. Bail is allowed at the discretion of the judge, but only after reference to the procurator who has taken up the case. Accused persons are often kept in prison for a considerable time before trial, and no lawyer is allowed to be present at the preliminary examination, which also is often long delayed. February, 1890, witnessed the passing of a new law relative to the organisation of judicial courts—a law embodying, indeed, the usage developed since the establishment of the courts in 1872, but introducing certain changes borrowed rather from German than from French sources. It is to come into force in November of the same year.

The history and nature of modern Japanese legal institutions is, very briefly, as follows. Down to 1872, the

* The system being French, it seems advisable to retain the French terms in cases where there is no exact, or no generally current, English equivalent.

judicial department had united in itself the functions of
chief law-court and chief executive office for the transac-
tion of judicial business throughout the land, the same staff
of officials serving for both purposes. In that year, however, a separation took place. Judges, procurators, a
judicial police for the arrest of prisoners, *avoués*, *avocats*,
and notaries were established, as also separate judicial
courts and a law school. The pattern copied was French.
Since that time numerous changes have taken place. At
present the courts are divided into local courts (presided
over by *juges de paix*), district or provincial courts, courts of
appeal, and a supreme court (*cour de cassation*), all of which
have jurisdiction both in criminal and civil suits. Each of
these courts has branch offices established to accommodate
suitors, regard being had to population and to the area of
jurisdiction. The local courts have jurisdiction over police
offences; the district courts over crimes, besides acting as
courts of preliminary investigation; the appeal courts hear
new trials; the supreme court hears criminal appeals on
matters of law. All crimes of whatever sort are subjected
to preliminary examination before actual trial. The con-
ducting of criminal cases, from the very beginning down to
the execution of the criminal, if he be condemned to suffer
death, rests with the procurator, who unites in his own person the functions of public prosecutor and of grand jury.

The present judiciary consists partly of men trained
under the old pre-European *régime*, partly of graduates of
the Law College of the Imperial University and of the
private law colleges, of which there are six in Tōkyō and
eight altogether in the Empire. About a thousand young
men graduate yearly. Lawyers are bound to pass a certain
examination before being admitted to practise at the bar;

but it is of a very theoretical nature, and is likely to be soon
revised. The new law concerning the constitution of courts
requires candidates for judgeships to pass two competitive
examinations, unless they are graduates of the University,
in which case they need only pass the second of the two,
after having served as probationary judges for a term of
three years. Judges are appointed for life. Their salaries
vary from $700 to $4,000 per annum. The presidents of
courts are, however, more highly remunerated. The
president of the supreme court receives $5,500, and is of
*shinnin* rank.* The chief procurator, who is of *chokunin*
rank, receives $4,000.

The system of trial, as well in civil as in criminal cases,
in entirely inquisitorial. It was so in Old Japan, and is so
in France, whence modern Japanese law comes. Formerly
no convictions were made except on confession by the
prisoner. Hence an abundant use of torture, now happily
abolished, and a tendency, even in civil cases, to suspect
guilt in the defendant, although the *theory* is that the
defendant must be presumed innocent until actually proved
to be the contrary. In this characteristic, Japan but con-
forms to her Continental models, and indeed to the universal usage of mankind with the solitary exception of the
English. The judge conducts the trial alone. All questions by counsel must be put through him. Counsel
do not so much defend their clients as represent them.
They even testify for their clients, strange as such a thing
must sound to English ears. Another peculiarity is that
husband and wife, parent and child, master and servant, are
prohibited from appearing as witnesses against each other.

* All officials are classified into four ranks, *shinnin*, *chokunin*, *sōnin*, and *hannin*.
The *shinnin* are the highest of all, receiving their nominations from the Mikado
himself.

At the same time, they are not entirely excluded from the examination. The code of criminal procedure draws a fine distinction, excluding them as witnesses, but admitting them as "referees"—we can think of no better equivalent for the difficult Japanese term *sankônin*, 参考人. A sankônin is a witness and yet not an authoritative witness, a sort of second-rate witness, if one might so phrase it. The idea is, of course, that persons thus related are likely to be prejudiced in each other's favour, and that their testimony should accordingly be allowed little weight in comparison with that of others more probably impartial. Witnesses are sworn, though not exactly in the European manner. The oath is rather a solemn asseveration, and is entirely unconnected with any religious sanction. It is in the form of a written document to which the person sworn affixes his seal. The proceedings at a trial are all committed to writing, but not in the actual words used, as Japanese custom is averse to the employment of the colloquial for literary purposes. The gist of the questions and answers is therefore translated into the book style.

Needless to say that the above is the merest shadowy outline of a vast subject. Transformed, revolutionised as it has been, Japanese law nevertheless retains not a few curious features of its own, which would interest both the legal specialist and the student of history and sociology. In departments of legal activity that are not yet covered by the new codes, the customary law of an earlier date is still followed. Land-tenure and all such family matters as succession, marriage, adoption, etc., in which it is most difficult to effect sudden changes, belong to this category.

**Books recommended.** Ignorant as we are of law, the foregoing article must be considered as proceeding from our informant, Mr. K. Masujima, of the Japanese Bar and of the Middle Temple, London. All that we have done has been to put into shape and abridge the information which he kindly supplied.—Little has yet been written on the new laws of the present day. For an account of the earlier or traditional law may be recommended Weipert's "*Japanisches Familien- und Erbrecht*," published in Part 13 of the "German Asiatic Transactions," and the various other works in English and German which he enumerates on p. 85 of his own elaborate essay. To these may be added Masujima's paper "On the Jōrinin or Japanese Legal Seal," printed in Vol. XVII. Part II, of the "Asiatic Transactions," and Ouldine' "Report on Taxation in Japan, with a Supplementary Paper on Land-tenure."—Those who can read Japanese should refer to the *Saibun Seishi* 裁判 聲誌, a periodical founded by Mr. Masujima in 1886 for the purpose of reporting law-cases, there being no other system of reporting in use. This periodical reports the decisions of the supreme court, the chief business of that court being to see to the uniform administration of the law throughout the Empire, with regard to principle as well as to practice.

**Lighthouses.** The Imperial Japanese Lighthouse Bureau, which is among the best-organised branches of the public service, owed its inception to Sir Harry Parkes, one of whose earliest actions, on the restoration of the Mikado to absolute power in 1868, was to represent to the Japanese government the necessity of properly lighting the dangerous coast of this archipelago, if foreign trade was to be successfully carried on. Indeed he had already approached the Shōgun's advisers on the same subject as far back as 1866, with the result that M. Verny, a French engineer then occupied in building the dockyard at Yokosuka, was charged with the erection of four lighthouses in the neighbourhood of Yedo—one at Kwannonzaki, one at Jōgashima, one at Nojima, and one between the Shinagawa forts. But it was not till 1868 that lighthouse work was taken in hand systematically by men specially trained for the purpose. In that year the Board of Trade, on Sir Harry Parkes' recommendation, sent out both the necessary apparatus and the necessary *personnel*, with Mr. R. H. Brunton as engineer-in-chief. By November, 1875, when Sir Harry was invited to make a tour of inspection along the coast, over thirty lighthouses were already in working order. From that time forward, there has been constant advance, the Japanese coast being now one of the best-lighted in the world.

Japan remained, so to say, at school in this matter for some twelve or thirteen years, after which time the English lighthouse-keepers and most of the other foreign employés were discharged. But though dispensing with the foreign *personnel* about 1880, and though strongly urged in 1884 by patriotic petitioners to cut down all foreign influence root and branch, and to erect lighthouses with regard to the needs of native shipping exclusively, the government has wisely refused to subscribe to such a jingo policy. The instructions for lighthouse-keepers remain, as in the past, those of the Scottish Board of Northern Lights. The catadioptric apparatus which is used in most of the Japanese lighthouses is still imported from France, though the clockwork and other machinery are manufactured in Japan. The chief tangible result of the movement of 1884 was the appointment of a permanent committee of officials of the Naval Department and of the Department of Communications, whose business it is to decide on plans of lighthouse extension. To light the remoter portions of the Island of Yezo was the last care of this committee. Its attention is now about to be turned to the Kuriles and the Loochoos. There are plans for no less than ninety-seven new lighthouses, to be erected at a cost of ten million dollars—some on these outlying islands, some to supplement deficiencies in the lighting of Japan proper. The total number of lighthouses at present in working order is sixty-eight.

In addition to lighthouses, the bureau has established lightships, buoys, and beacons. There is also a system of

fog-signals, chiefly from Kinkwasan northward on the Main
Island, and on the east coast of Yezo, those portions of the
country being specially subject to fogs.

*Books recommended.* "List of the Japanese Lighthouses, Lightships,
Buoys and Beacons," published annually by the Department of Communications, and
containing a map.—The only full account of the progress of lighthouse work in Japan
is, so far as we know, that contained in a history of the Department of Public Works,
composed in the Japanese language and entitled "Kōbushō Enkaku Hōbōku." (工 部 省
沿 革 報 告. More detailed statistics are to be found in the "Kōbu Tōkeishi" (工 部 統
計 誌, but they only go down to 1885. The "Kōbushō Enkaku Hōboku" goes one
year further.

**Literature.** We hear of one or two Japanese books as
having been composed in the seventh century of the Christian era, shortly after the spread of a knowledge of the
Chinese ideographs in Japan had rendered a written literature possible. The earliest work, however, that has come
down to us is the *Kojiki*, or " Record of Ancient Matters,"
dating from the year 712. This work has sometimes been
called the Bible of the Japanese, because it contains the
mythology and earliest history of the nation; but it gives
no moral or religious precepts. It was followed in A. D.
720 by the *Nihongi*, or " Chronicles of Japan," a more pre-
tentious work, written in Chinese, the Latin of that age and
country. In about A. D. 760 came the *Man-yōshū*, or " Collection of a Myriad Leaves." It is an anthology of the
most ancient poems of the language, and is invaluable as
a repertory of facts and allusions interesting to the philologist, the archeologist, and the historian. Its poetical merit
is also rated very high by the orthodox native critics, who
are unacquainted with any literature but their own, unless
it be the Chinese. From that time forward the literary
stream has never ceased. It has flowed in a double channel—that of books in the native language, and that of books

written in Classical Chinese. Chinese has been generally preferred for grave subjects—law, for instance, and history; Japanese for poetry, romance, and other branches of *belles-lettres*. Mr. Satow, following the native authorities, classes Japanese literature under seventeen heads, which are :

I. STANDARD HISTORIES. Besides the *Kojiki* and *Nihongi* already mentioned, the most important standard history is the *Dai Nihonshi*. This huge work in one hundred volumes was compiled at the end of the seventeenth century by a whole company of Japanese and Chinese men of learning, under the general superintendence of the second Prince of Mito, who was a munificent patron of literature.

II. MISCELLANEOUS HISTORICAL WORKS, that is, histories written by private persons and therefore devoid of official sanction. Such are the *Mizu Kagami*, the *Gempei Seisuiki*, the *Heike Monogatari*, the *Taiheiki*, and a host of others, concluding with the *Nihon Gwaishi*, which, a few years ago, was in every educated person's hands, and which, by its strongly imperialist sentiments, contributed in no small measure to bring about the fall of the Shōgunate.—All Japanese histories are written in a style which repels the European reader. They are for the most part annals rather than histories properly so-called. Mr. Satow's translation of the first five books of the *Nihon Gwaishi* should be glanced through by any one who doubts this assertion. He will find it almost impossible to bring himself to believe that a book so intolerably dry could ever have fired a whole nation with enthusiasm. That it did so is one of the curiosities of literature.

III. LAWS. The *Ryō no Gige* and the *Engi-shiki* are the works in this division which are most often quoted.

IV. Biography.

V. Poetry. (See Article on this subject.)

VI. Classical Romances. This is the most curious department of standard Japanese literature, lifting, as it does, the curtain from the long-forgotten life of the Japanese Court of the tenth and eleventh centuries of our era. The lords and ladies of those days step out before us, with all the frivolity but also with all the elegance of their narrow aristocratic existence, which was bounded by the horizon of the old capital Kyôto. We have their poetastering, their amorous intrigues of course, their interminable moon-gazings and performances on the flute, even minute descriptions of their dresses and of the parties they gave—one among many witnesses to the fact that a large proportion of the authors were women. The earliest book commonly classed among the romances is more properly a fairy-tale; for it deals with the adventures of a maiden who was exiled from the moon to this our workaday world. It is entitled *Taketori Monogatari* (*monogatari* means "tale," "romance"). To mention but three or four more out of a hundred, there are the *Utsubo Monogatari* and the *Ise Monogatari*, both attributed to the tenth century, the *Konjaku Monogatari*, with its sequel the *Uji Jūi*, which are collections of shorter tales, and the *Genji Monogatari*, which dates from the year 1004, and is the most celebrated of all, chiefly on account of its ornate style.

VII. Miscellanies. These books are a sort of *olla podrida* of the thoughts of their authors—opinions, verses, anecdotes, scraps of autobiography—jotted down without any attempt at classification, but with a great deal of literary chiselling. The two miscellanies most to be recommended are the *Makura no Sôshi*, by a court lady named Sei

Shônagon who flourished in the eleventh century, and the *Tsurezure-Gusa* by a Buddhist monk who died in the year 1350.

VIII. DIARIES. Of these, the *Hôjôki* is perhaps the one which the student will find most interesting. Like the *Tsurezure-Gusa*, it is the work of a Buddhist monk. The author describes the calamities of his times, and dwells on the superiority of life in a hermit's cell to that which he had previously led amidst worldly vanities. It dates from about the year 1200. The *Murasaki Shikibu Niki*, which is the diary of the most celebrated of Japanese authoresses, is remarkable as being probably the hardest book to construe in the Japanese language. It has cost us personally many a groan.

IX. TRAVELS. Under this heading, the bibliographers class many works which might more advantageously be counted among the DIARIES, as not only are they diaries in effect, but are entitled so by their authors. The easiest and most attractive of the Japanese classics is to be found in this division. It is entitled the *Tosa Niki*, that is, " Diary of [a Voyage Home from] Tosa." It dates from the year 935. Travels are the least voluminous department of Japanese literature. How should it accord with the fitness of things in this stay-at-home country to have a Sir John Maundeville or a Captain Cook?

X. DRAMAS. These are treated of in the Article on the THEATRE.

XI. DICTIONARIES AND WORKS ON PHILOLOGY. The best native dictionaries of Classical Japanese are the *Wa-kun no Shiori* and the *Gagen Shûran*. But both are unfortunately fragmentary. A complete dictionary of Japanese in Japanese is still to be compiled. The fullest native grammar is the *Kotoba no Chikamichi*, by Minamoto-no-Shigetane. The chief writers of the old school on general philological subjects are Mabuchi (died 1769), Motoori (died 1801), and Hirata (died 1843). In Motoori's works the Classical Japanese language reached its acme of perfection. Specially remarkable are, among his greater undertakings, the standard commentary on the *Kojiki*, entitled *Kojiki Den*, and, among his lighter essays, the *Tama-Gatsuma* containing jottings on all sorts of subjects, philological and otherwise.

XII. TOPOGRAPHY. The newer and more popular publications of this class are really the best, though they are less esteemed by the Japanese literati than are other works bearing the stamp of higher antiquity. These popular topographical works are illustrated guide-books to the various provinces of the empire, and are known under the collective name of *Meishô Zue*. They are by various authors of the present century, but are all constructed on a uniform plan, somewhat resembling that of our county histories, though more discursive and better adapted to the practical needs of travellers.

XIII. LITERATURE OF THE SHINTÔ RELIGION. Chief works: the *Kojiki Den*, already mentioned under another heading—for indeed it is one of the corner-stones of Japanese literature—and Hirata's still but half-published *magnum opus*, entitled *Koshi Den*. This latter is remarkable for its extraordinary elaborateness and for the vast erudition of its author. Unfortunately Hirata was very bigoted as well as very learned. Consequently the reader must be always on his guard, so as to distinguish how much really belongs to Shintô and how much to Hirata himself; for Hirata never scrupled to garble a sacred text, if he could thereby

support his own views as to what the sacred writers *ought*
to mean.   Extremely curious to the specialist are the ancient
Shintō rituals termed *Norito*, round which a mass of
modern commentary has gathered.

XIV. BUDDHIST LITERATURE.  This division comprises
singularly few works of merit, Buddhism having found an
uncongenial soil in the Japanese mind.  We do not know
of any Japanese Buddhist book that takes, either in literature
or popularity, a place at all comparable to that taken among
ourselves by the "Imitation of Christ," the English Prayer-
Book, or the "Pilgrim's Progress."  Shintō, though im-
measurably inferior to Buddhism as a religion, must be
admitted to have carried off from its rival all the literary
laurels on Japanese soil.  Besides the Buddhists proper,
there is a school of moralists calling themselves *dōtokusha*,
founded partly on Buddhism, partly on Confucianism, partly
on utilitarian common sense.  Some of their *Dōwa*, or
"Moral Discourses," have a certain interest.  But the best
things in this line are two collections of moral aphorisms
entitled *Jitsu-Go Kyō*, or "Teaching of the Words of
Truth," and *Dōji Kyō*, or "Teaching for Children."

XV. MODERN FICTION.  Japan's greatest modern novel-
ist, in the opinion of the Japanese themselves, is Bakin
(1767—1848), the most widely popular of whose two hundred and ninety works is the *Hakkenden*, or "Tale of Eight
Dogs," itself consisting of no less than a hundred and six
volumes.  Though Japanese volumes are smaller than ours,
the *Hakkenden* is a gigantic production.  Another universally popular novel is the *Hiza-Kurige*, by an author
whose *nom de plume* is Jippensha Ikku.  In our opinion
it is, with some of the lyric dramas (*Nō no Utai*), the
cleverest outcome of the Japanese pen.  In it are relat-

ed, with a Rabelaisian coarseness, but also with a Rabelaisian verve and humour, the adventures of two men called Yajirōbei and Kidahachi as they travel along the Tōkaidō from Yedo to Kyōto. The impecunious heroes walk most of the way. Hence the title of *Hiza-Kurige*, which may be roughly rendered "Shanks's Mare." The author of this work occupies in literature a place akin to that which Hokusai occupies in art. Warmly appreciated by the common people, who have no preconceived theories to "live up to," both Hokusai and Jippensha Ikku are admitted but grudgingly by the local dispensers of fame to a place in the national Walhalla. They must look abroad for the appreciation of critics taking a wider view of the proper functions of literature and art. Gravity, severe classicism, conformity to established rules and methods— such have hitherto constituted the canon of orthodox Japanese literary judgment. Many Japanese novels are of the historical kind. The most interesting of these is the *Iroha Bunko*, by one Tamenaga Shunsui, which, with its sequel, the *Yuki no Akebono*, gives the lives of each of the celebrated Forty-Seven Rōnins. The *Ōoka Meiyo Seidan* is another book of this class much to be recommended to the student for its interest and its easy style. It purports to be an authentic account of numbers of *causes célèbres* tried by Ōoka, the Japanese Solomon, who flourished early in the eighteenth century.

XVI. MISCELLANEOUS LITERATURE. Under this heading come cyclopedias, works on industries, sciences, arts, and inventions, works on Confucianism, works on Japanese and Chinese antiquities, and on a hundred other subjects.

To the foregoing enumeration borrowed from Mr. Satow, we venture to add one item more, namely :—

XVII. EUROPEANISED LITERATURE. The recent opening
of the country was the death-blow to Japanese literature
proper. True, thousands of books and pamphlets still pour
annually from the press—more, probably, than at any previous time. But the greater number are either translations
of European works, or else works conveying European
ideas. It is but natural and right that this should be so.
Immense civilising effects in every department of scientific
activity are being produced by the contemporary school of
Europeanised authors, with Fukuzawa, Nishi Shū, Katō
Hiroyuki, and a dozen other eminent men leading the van.
But of course their translations, adaptations, and imitations
interest Western readers, who are in possession of the
originals, less than do the books written under the old
*régime*. Even Japanese novel-writing proceeds nowadays
*à l'européenne*. Not methods alone are borrowed wholesale,
but even subjects. We would willingly wager ten thousand
to one that not a single reader of these pages could ever
guess the hero of the most popular Japanese novel of recent
years. It is——Epaminondas! The work in question,
entitled *Keikoku Bidan*, takes the whole field of Theban
politics for its subject-matter. That not a few of the allusions may be transferred without much difficulty to the
Japanese politics of the present day, is doubtless one reason
for the immense sale it has had. The author, Yano
Fumio, was able to take a trip to Europe and to build himself a fine house with the proceeds.

And now it may be asked: What is the value of this
Japanese literature—so ancient, so voluminous, locked up
in so recondite a written character? We repeat what we
have already said of the "Collection of a Myriad Leaves"—
that it is invaluable to the philologist, the archeologist, the

historian, the student of curious manners doomed to disappear. We may add that there are some clever and many pretty things in it. The *Tosa Niki*, for instance, is charming—charming in its simplicity, its good taste, its love of scenery and of children. The *Makura no Sōshi* has numerous touches of wit and delicate satire. Some of the lyric dramas are remarkable poems. For Jippensha Ikku, the Rabelais of Japan, we have already expressed our warm admiration. On the other hand, much of that which the Japanese themselves prize most highly in their literature seems intolerably flat and insipid to the European taste. The romances—most of them—are every bit as dull as the histories, though in another way. The histories are too brief, the romances too long-winded. If the authoress of the *Genji Monogatari*, though lauded to the skies by her compatriots, has been branded by Georges Bousquet as *cette ennuyeuse Scudéry japonaise*, she surely richly deserves it. And what shall we say of Bakin, on whom her mantle has fallen in modern times—Bakin and his *Hakkenden*, which every Japanese has read and re-read till he knows it almost by heart? " How inimitable!" cries the enraptured Japanese reader, " how truly excellent!" " Excellent, yes!" the European retorts, " excellent to send one to sleep, with its interminable accounts of the impossible adventures of eight knights, who personify the eight cardinal virtues through the labyrinth of a hundred and six volumes!"

Sum total : what Japanese literature most lacks is genius. It lacks thought, logical grasp, depth of pathos. It is too timorous, too narrow to compass great things. Perhaps the Court atmosphere and predominantly feminine influence in which it was nursed for the first few centuries of its

existence stifled it, or else the fault may have lain with the
Chinese formalism in which it grew up. But we suspect
that there was some original sin of weakness as well.
Otherwise the clash of India and China with old mythological Japan, of Buddhism with Shintō, of imperialism with
feudalism, and of all with Christianity in the sixteenth
century and with Dutch ideas a little later, would have
produced more important results. If Japan has given us
no music, so also has she given us no immortal verse.
But Japanese literature has occasional graces, and is full
of incidental scientific interest. The intrepid searcher for
facts and "curios" will, therefore, be rewarded if he has
the courage to devote to it the study of many years. A
certain writer has said that "It should be left to a few
missionaries to plod their way through the wilderness of
the Chinese language to the deserts of Chinese literature."
This sweeping condemnation is unjust in the case of
Chinese. It would be unjust in that of Japanese also, even
with all deductions made.

Books recommended. An elaborate article on "Japanese Literature," by
Ernest Satow, is Vol. IX of Ripley and Dana's "American Cyclopædia." —"On the
Various Styles used in Japanese Literature," by B. H. Chamberlain, printed in Vol.
XIII, Part 1, of the "Asiatic Transactions."—The following translations or sum-
maries of Japanese works are easily accessible:—"An Ancient Japanese Classic" (the
Tosa Niki) by W. G. Aston, in Vol. III, Part II; "A Literary Lady of Old Japan,"
by the same, in Vol. XVI, Part III; "Ancient Japanese Rituals," by Ernest Satow, in
Vols. VII and IX; the Gobunsho (a Buddhist Book), by James Troup, in Vol. XVII,
Part 1; "The Kojiki," by B. H. Chamberlain, in the Supplement to Vol. X; and other
translations by the same, in other volumes of the "Asiatic Transactions." There are
also some interesting translations by Eby and others in a now extinct magazine, the
"Chrysanthemum." See also the works of Hoffmann, Pfizmaier, de Rosny, Pulsi,
Terrestini, Severini, and Lange, and the Articles on MORAL MAXIMS, POETRY, and
WOMAN in the present work.

**Looahoo.** Loochoo—pronounced *Dūchu* by the natives
and *Ryūkyū* by the Japanese—is, in its widest acceptation,

the general name of several groups of islands stretching
nearly the whole way between the southernmost outlying
islets of the Japanese archipelago and the north-eastern extremity of Formosa. But it is usually restricted in practice
to the central group, the chief members of which are
Amami-Ōshima and Okinawa-Shima. This group is of
coral formation, and lies between 127° and 130° longitude
east of Greenwich, and between 26° and 28° 30' of north
latitude. To this position it owes a mild climate, marred
only by the extreme violence of occasional typhoons during
the summer months. The soil is so fertile as to produce
two crops of rice yearly.

In race and language the Loochooans are closely allied
to the Japanese, but for many centuries the two peoples
seem not to have communicated with each other. The veil
first lifts in A. D. 1187 with the accession of King Shunten,
said to have been a son of Tametomo, the famous Japanese archer. It is recorded that the Loochooans first sent
an ambassador with presents to the Shōgun of Japan in the
year 1451, that they discontinued such presents or tribute
at the beginning of the seventeenth century, and were
chastised for this neglect by the then Prince of Satsuma.
Loochoo continued to be a sub-fief of Satsuma, but with a
ruler bearing the title of king, until the time of the Japanese revolution of 1868. Meanwhile the Loochooans, who
had obtained their civilisation from China, also paid tribute
to the Chinese court, and received investiture for their
kinglets from Peking. The little kingdom thus faced two
ways, so that trouble was bound to ensue. An embassy
was sent to Tōkyō in 1878, to endeavour to arrange matters
in such wise that the double protectorate might be maintained, China being, as the envoys said, honoured by the

Loochooans as their father, and Japan as their mother.
But the Japanese Government refused to admit this claim.
The Loochooan king was brought captive to Tōkyō in
1879, and the archipelago was organised into a Japanese
prefecture under the title of Okinawa-Ken. The change,
though intensely disagreeable to the little insular court and
aristocracy, who forfeited most of their privileges, is said to
have been beneficial to the people at large.

The Loochooans—even the men—are distinguished in
appearance by a top-knot of hair, through which they pass
a large pin or skewer of gold, silver, or copper, according to
their rank. Formerly corpses, instead of being interred at
once, were left to decay either in a provisional grave or in a
stream of water, and it was only after three years that the
final funeral rites were performed. This custom has happily
fallen into disuse. The capital of Loochoo is Shiuri, whose
port is Nafa, called by the Japanese Okinawa. The chief
products are rice and sugar, the latter of which is the main
staple of commerce. The area of the islands has been
roughly estimated at 1000 square miles, and the population
at 170,000. The Loochoos may easily be reached from
Kōbe *via* the Inland Sea and Kagoshima. The steamer
first visits the island of Amami-Ōshima, and then proceeds
to Nafa, where it stops three days. The round trip from
Kōbe and back takes seventeen days.

Books recommended. "A Voyage of Discovery to Corea and Loochoo," by
Captain Basil Hall, R. N., London, 1818.—"Notes regarding the Principality of
Loochoo," by J. H. Gubbins, printed in the "Journal of the Society of Arts" for the
3rd June, 1881.—"Die Liu-kiu Insel Amami-Ōshima," by Dr. L. Doederlein, printed
in Parts 23, 24, and 25 of the "German Asiatic Transactions."

**Luck (Gods of).** The Seven Gods of Luck (*Shichi-Fuku-
Jin*) are : Fukurokuju, distinguished by a preternaturally

long head, and typifying longevity and wisdom; Daikoku, whose rice-bales show him to be the god of wealth; Ebisu, bearing a fish, and serving as the patron of honest work; Hotei, with an enormous naked abdomen, a bag on his back and a fan in his hand, and signifying contentment and good nature; Bishamon, the impersonation of war, clad in armour, and bearing a spear and a toy pagoda; Benten, the goddess of love, distinguished by being the only female in the assemblage; and Jurōjin a sort of repetition of Fukurokuju, both being often accompanied by a stag and a crane.

The Seven Gods of Luck have been swept together from many incongruous sources—Japanese Shintoism, Chinese Taoism, Indian Buddhism and Brahmanism. Their union in one group is the result of nothing more recondite than popular ignorance and confusion of ideas, and can be traced no further back than the time of Ieyasu (about A. D. 1600). The reader will find in Anderson's "Catalogue of Japanese and Chinese Paintings in the British Museum," pages 27—46, a full discussion of the origin and attributes of these divinities, and will be surprised to discover how slender is the basis on which their modern popularity has been reared.

**Maps.** Much the best detailed map of Japan is that now being published in sections by the Imperial Geological Office, and obtainable at the Tōyōdō (東陽堂) in Tōkyō, and of Messrs. Kelly and Walsh in Yokohama. The Yokohama section is particularly useful, including, as it does, many of the localities most frequently visited by pleasure-seekers, such as Kamakura, Enoshima, Miyanoshita, etc. Also to be recommended is Hassenstein's German atlas of eight sectional maps, all completed. Sections III and IV, which take in Central Japan, from the Inland Sea on the West to beyond Tōkyō and Nikkō on the East and North, are the most generally useful. It is, only to be regretted that the author should have considered the usual method of spelling Japanese not good enough for him, and should accordingly have evolved a new one from the depths of his own inner consciousness. Stanford's "Library Map of Japan," compiled by E. Knipping, and Farsari's little map, entitled "The Environs of Yokohama," may also be mentioned.

The "*Fuji-mi Jū-san Shū*," or "Thirteen Provinces round Fusiyama," is the best of the old-fashioned Japanese maps. The distances are given in figures, and the roads are clearly indicated. The father of Japanese cartography was Inō Chūkei (born A. D. 1744), of whose life and labours Dr. Knott has given a short account in Vol. XVI, Part II, of the "Asiatic Transactions."

**Marriage.** In everything relating to marriage, the difference between East and West is still very strongly marked. Marriage among the Japanese is less of a personal and more of a family affair than it is in Western lands. Religion has no say in the matter, and the law regards it from a different point of view. An Englishman chooses his wife himself; but the English law, though perfectly neutral during this initial stage of the proceedings, steps in as soon as the knot is tied, and imperiously forbids its severance except in case of adultery by one of the parties. Japanese marriages, on the contrary, are arranged by the two families, and the step is less solemn and not irrevocable, the Japanese law remaining as neutral at the end as at the beginning. For though marriage is a legal contract while it lasts, it may, like other contracts, be terminated by the joint request and consent of the contracting parties. Divorce, too, at the request of one party—generally the man—is easy to obtain.

The way things are managed is this. When their child—be it boy or girl—has reached a marriageable age, the duty of the parents is to secure a suitable partner. Custom, however, rules that the conduct of the affair must be entrusted to a middleman (*nakōdo*)—some discreet married friend, who not only negotiates the marriage, but remains through life a sort of godfather to the young couple, a referee to whom disputes may be submitted for arbitration. Having fixed on an eligible *parti*, the middleman arranges for what is termed the *mi-ai*, literally, the "mutual seeing"—a meeting at which the lovers (if persons unknown to each other may be so styled) are allowed to see, sometimes even to speak to each other, and thus estimate each other's merits. In strict etiquette, the interview should take place either at the middleman's own residence, or at some other private house designated by the parents on both sides. But among the middle and lower classes, a picnic, a party to the theatre, or a visit to a temple often serves the purpose. If the man objects to the girl or the girl to the man after the "mutual seeing," there is an end of the matter, in theory at least. But in practice the young people are in their parents' hands, to do as their parents may ordain. The girl, in particular, is a nobody in the matter. It is not for girls to have opinions.

If both parties are satisfied with what they have seen of each other, presents consisting of clothes, or of money to purchase clothes, and of certain kinds of fish and edible seaweed, are exchanged between them. This exchange of presents is called *yuinō*. It corresponds to betrothal, and is binding—if not in actual law, at any rate in custom.

The presents once exchanged, neither party can draw back.
A lucky day is then chosen for the wedding. When it
comes, the bride, dressed all in white, the colour of mourning—to signify that she dies to her own family and that she
will never leave her husband's house but as a corpse—is
borne away at nightfall to her new home, escorted by the
middleman and his wife. The parental house is swept out
on her departure, and in former days a bonfire was lighted
at the gate—ceremonies indicative of the purification
necessary after the removal of a dead person.

The wedding, which takes place immediately after the
bride's arrival at the house of her husband's parents, is of
the nature of a dinner-party. The distinguishing feature of
it is what is termed the *san-san ku-do*, that is, literally,
"three three, nine times," because both the bridegroom and
the bride drink three times out of each of three wine-cups
of different sizes, making nine times in all—or rather they
do not drink, but only lift the cup to their lips. Another
intrinsic part of the ceremony is the changing of garments.
The bride, on reaching her new home, changes her white
dress for one given to her by her husband. But immediately after the ceremonial drinking-bout and while the
guests are still assembled at the feast, she retires and
puts on a coloured dress, brought with her from her
parents' house. The bridegroom changes his dress at the
same time in another apartment.* At the conclusion of
the feast, the newly married couple are led into the
bridal chamber by the middleman and his wife, whereupon
they pledge each other in nine more cups of wine. It is
significant that the husband, as lord and master, now

* Some men are now married in European evening dress, in which case no change
takes place.

drinks first. At the earlier stage of the proceedings the bride drank first, in her quality of guest. This ends the wedding ceremony.

A few days later—strictly speaking, it should be on the third day—a visit is paid by the couple to the bride's parents. This is termed her *sato-garri*, or "return home." On this occasion, she wears a dress presented to her by her husband's family. Meantime the necessary notice has been given to the authorities, which is the only legal form to be observed. It consists in a request to the district office by the head of the family to which the girl formerly belonged, that her entry of registration may be transferred to the office within whose jurisdiction her husband, or the head of her husband's family, if the husband himself be not householder, has his domicile. An official intimation of the transfer succeeds this request, and all is then in order.

The above is the most usual form of marriage. In some cases, however, the bridegroom is adopted into the bride's family, instead of the bride into the bridegroom's. This takes place when a parent has only a daughter, or daughters, but no son. In order to preserve the family intact—due regard being had to the circumstance that no female can be its legal head—it is then necessary to adopt a son-in-law, who, literally becoming a son in the eyes of the law, drops his own surname and takes that of his wife. None but poor men are generally willing to place themselves in such a false position.

Amongst the lower classes, ceremonies and considerations of all kinds are often honoured only in the breach. Many of the so-called marriages of plebeians are mere concubinage founded on mutual convenience. This accounts for the "boy" and the cook—to their foreign master's increasing astonishment—being found to bring home a new wife almost as often as they bring home a new saucepan. Such laxity would never be tolerated in well-bred circles.

When it is added that a Japanese bride has no bridesmaids, that the young couple go off on no honey-moon, that a Japanese wife is not only supposed to obey her husband, but actually does so, that the husband, if well enough off, probably has a concubine besides and makes no secret of it, indeed often keeps her in the same house with his wife, and that the mother-in-law, with us a terror to the man, is not only a terror but a daily and hourly cross to the girl—for in nine cases out of ten, the girl has to live with her husband's family and be at the beck and call of his relations—when due consideration is given to all these circumstances, it will be seen that marriage in Japan is a vastly different thing, socially as well as legally, from marriage in England or the United States. The reader will be still more firmly persuaded of this truth, if he will take the trouble to glance at the Articles on DIVORCE and on WOMAN. He will see that in this part of the world it is a case, not of *place aux dames* but *place aux messieurs.*\*

---

\* May the writer be permitted here to record a little experience of his own? In his "Introduction to the Kojiki," he had drawn attention to the inferior place held by women in ancient as in modern Japan. Some two years ago (April, 1886), six of the chief literati of the old school did him the honour to translate this "Introduction" into Japanese, with a running commentary. They patted him on the back for many things; but when they reached the observation anent the subjection of women, their wrath exploded. "The subordination of women to men," so runs this commentary, "is an extremely correct custom. To think the contrary is to harbour European prejudices . . . For the man to take precedence over the woman is the grand law of heaven and earth. To ignore this, and to talk of the contrary as barbarous, is absurd."—It does not fall to every one's lot to be anathematised by half-a-dozen Japanese literary popes—and that, too, merely for taking the part of the ladies!

The men, having everything their own way, naturally marry young. Speaking broadly, there are no bachelors in Japan. For the same reason, there are no old maids. The girls are married off without being consulted, and they accept their fate as a matter of course, because their mothers and grandmothers, ever since the beginning of the world, accepted a like fate before them.

**Maru.** It is often asked: What does the word *Maru* mean in the names of ships—as *Tōkyō Maru, Sagami Maru, Kōryō Maru*, etc.? The answer is that the origin of the term is obscure. *Maru* means "round," but how came ships by so inappropriate a name?

The first thing to note is that in former times ships had not the monopoly of the name. Swords, musical instruments of various kinds, pieces of armour, dogs, hawks, and the concentric sections of castles, were called *Maru* also. The probability is that two distinct words—*Maru* and *Maro*, have flowed into one and so got confused. To name the concentric sections of a castle *Maru*, "round," was but natural. The word *Maro*, on the other hand, is an archaic term of endearment. Hence its use in such ancient proper names as *Tamura-Maro*, a great general who subdued the Ainos; *Abe no Naka-Maro*, an eminent Chinese scholar of the eighth century; *Okina-Maro*, a favourite dog of the Mikado Ichijō, and so on. The warrior's pet sword, the sportsman's favourite dog or hawk, the oarsman's boat, would naturally come to be distinguished by the same half-personal name, much as the English sailor or engineer calls his ship or locomotive "she." When the ancient word *Maro* ceased to be understood, it easily slid into the more familiar *Maru*, by the alteration of the final vowel, *o* and *u* being particularly apt to interchange in Japanese.

Observe that *Maru* is used of merchant-vessels only. Men-of-war take *Kan* instead, as *Maya Kan*, *Asama Kan*. *Kan* is a Chinese word meaning "war-vessel."

**Massage.** Massage is the technical name, in use among doctors, for that process of rubbing the skin and kneading the muscles which in common language is called shampooing. Massage has for centuries played a great rôle in Japanese medicine—it, acupuncture, and the moxa being universally credited with more than all the many virtues which Holloway, among ourselves, claims for his pills, and "Mother Seigel" for her syrup. The sham- pooers, popularly known as *amma san*, also occupy a con- spicuous place in Japanese social life. Immemorial custom limits the profession to the blind, who thus support their families, instead of, as is mostly the case in Western countries, being a burden to them. Such sums are they enabled to accumulate that they often turn money-lenders as well.

Till recently—that is, until about the year 1870—all the shampooers in Japan formed one immense guild under two provosts, one of whom lived at Yedo, the other at Kyōto. This guild possessed various legal privileges, and admittance to it took place on the passing of certain tests and the payment of fees. It was divided into several grades, the rise from grade to grade being conditioned by new tests and higher fees. For the highest grade to which any ordinary blind mortal could aspire—the grade next under that of provost—a fee of $1000 was exacted. This organisation is now fast falling into decay; but the melancholy whistle of the blind shampooer, as he slowly feels his way along the streets at night, staff in hand, is still one of the characteristic sounds of every Japanese village.

Massage is much to be recommended to tired pedestrians and to persons suffering from lumbago, rheumatism, and other pains and aches. The Japanese shampooers, however, make the mistake of shampooing down instead of shampooing up. A portion of the good done is thus neutralised, one object of scientific massage being to help back towards the centre the blood which is lingering in the superficial veins.

**Book recommended.** Dr. W. N. Whitney's " Notes on the History of Medical Progress in Japan," published in Vol. XII. Part IV. of the " Asiatic Transactions," p. 331.

**Metal-Work.** Bronze was introduced into Japan from China, and the Japanese still call it " the Chinese metal " (*Kara-kane*). But it is the metal in which Japanese art over a thousand years ago had already won its brightest laurels. The chief forms are the mirror, the temple bell, the gong, the vase (originally intended for the adornment of Buddhist altars), the lantern, and the colossal representation of divine personages. The grandest example of such colossal bronze-casting is the *Daibutsu* (literally, " great Buddha") at Kamakura, which dates from the thirteenth century. He who has the time should visit the *Daibutsu* repeatedly ; for, like St. Peter's and several other of the greatest works of art and of nature, it fails to produce its full effect on a first or even on a second visit ; but the impression it produces grows on the beholder each time that he gazes afresh at the calm, intellectual, passionless face, which seems to concentrate in itself the whole philosophy of the Buddhist religion—the triumph of mind over sense, of eternity over fleeting time, of the enduring majesty of *Nirwana* over the trivial prattle, the transitory agitations of mundane existence. The chief dimensions are stated as follows in Messrs. Satow and Hawes' "Handbook for Japan":—

|  | Feet. | Inches. |
|---|---|---|
| Height ... ... ... ... ...49. | 49. | 7. |
| Circumference ... ... 97. | 97. | 2.2 |
| Length of face ... ... ... 8. | 8. | 5.15 |
| Width from ear to ear ... 17. | 17. | 9.2 |
| Length of eye ... ... ... 3. | 3. | 11.6 |
| ,, ,, ear ... ... ... 6. | 6. | 6.54 |
| ,, ,, nose ... ... ... 3. | 3. | 9.22 |
| Width of mouth ... ... 3. | 3. | 2.08 |
| Circumference of thumb ... 3. | 3. | 0.0 |

"The eyes are of pure gold," say the same authorities, "and the silver boss [on the forehead] weighs 30 pounds avoirdupois. The image is formed of sheets of bronze cast separately, brazed together, and finished off on the outside with the chisel."

Armour is another use to which metal (iron and steel) was put from the very earliest ages. The best examples of iron and steel armour date from the thirteenth and fourteenth centuries. The best swords date from the same time. The ornamental sword-hilts, guards, etc., date only from the sixteenth century onwards. The eighteenth and nineteenth centuries have been the most fruitful epoch for the production of small bronze objects, whose chief *raison d'être* is ornament, such as clasps, paper-weights, small figures of animals, mouth-pieces for pipes, and vases intended for dwelling-rooms—not for Buddhist altars, as in earlier days. The gold and silver work of the Japanese is less

remarkable than their bronzes; but in enamel—especially in
what is known as *cloisonné* enamel—they are beyond all
praise. This branch forms also a noticeable exception to
the general decay of Japanese art since the opening of the
country. Never was more marvellous *cloisonné* work seen
than is turned out to-day from the shops of Tōkyō and
Kyōto.

**Books recommended.** Rein's "Industries of Japan," pp. 416 and 488.—
"L'Art Japonais," by L. Gonse.—"Ornamental Arts of Japan," by Audsley.—"Japan
and its Art," by Huish.

**Mikado.** Though this is the name by which the whole
outer world knows the sovereign of Japan, it is not that
now used in Japan itself, except in poetry and on great
occasions. The Japanese have got into the habit of calling
their sovereign by such alien Chinese titles as *Tenshi*, "the
Son of Heaven;" *T'en-ō*, or *Tennō*, "the Heavenly Emperor," *Shujō*, "the Supreme Master." His designation in
the official translations of modern public documents into
English is "Emperor." But we do not anticipate that
this is likely to supersede, in literary and colloquial European usage, the traditional title of "Mikado," which is at
once ancient, sonorous, and distinctively Japanese.

The etymology of the word *Mikado* is not quite clear.
Some—and theirs is the current opinion—trace it to
*mi*, "august," and *kado*, a "gate," reminding one of
the "Sublime Porte" of Turkey. Mr. Satow prefers to
derive it from *mika*, an archaic word for "great," and *to*,
"a place." In either case the word is one indicative of
the highest respect, as it is but natural that the name
used by the Japanese of old to designate their heaven-
descended sovereign should be. The word *Mikado* is
often employed to denote the monarch's Court as well as

the monarch himself, such double usage being one of the peculiar features of Japanese grammar.

The antiquity of the Imperial Family of Japan is unparalleled. The Japanese themselves claim that after endless ages passed in higher spheres, it began its earthly career with the first human monarch, Jimmu Tennō, in the year 660 before Christ. From this, historical criticism bids us subtract more than a millennium, as Japanese history does not become a record of solid facts till the fifth or sixth century *after* Christ. It should also be pointed out that the succession has by no means followed those strict rules which Europe considers necessary for legitimacy. Many Mikados, even down to quite recent times, have been the sons of concubines. Others have been merely adopted from some related branch. Still, all deductions made, the family as such stands forth proudly as the oldest reigning family in the world. We know positively that it has reigned ever since the dawn of history in this archipelago, and that even then it was considered of immemorial age. The fact is peculiarly striking if we reflect upon the usually brief life of Oriental dynasties. Little wonder, therefore, all things considered, if a religious reverence for the Imperial line is as axiomatic in Japan, as completely removed beyond all doubt or controversy, as is the doctrine of the equal rights and duties of all men in the democratic societies of the West.

**Mineral Springs.** Japan, the land of volcanoes and earthquakes, is naturally rich in mineral springs; and the Japanese, with their passion for bathing, make the fullest use of them. The most noted of the many hundreds of Japanese spas are: for sulphur baths, Kusatsu, Ashinoyu,

Yumoto, Nikkō, Yumoto near Hakone, and Unzen near
Nagasaki; for iron baths, Ikao and Arima; for salt baths,
Atami and Isobe. Miyanoshita, one of those best-known
to foreigners, has only traces of salt and soda. Its waters
may therefore be used without medical advice, simply for
pleasure's sake. There are powerful iron and sulphur
springs at Ōjigoku (lit. "big hell") some four miles beyond
Miyanoshita, at which it is intended to establish baths on a
large scale. Sulphur, iron, and salt are everywhere the
chief minerals found in the Japanese springs. Very few
contain carbonic acid gas. Very few are cold. There are
none resembling Kreuznach, none efficacious, like Vichy
and Karlsbad, in diseases of the liver and stomach. On
the other hand, Kusatsu stands alone in the world for the
quantity of iron, sulphur, and free mineral acids which it
contains; and the cures which it is capable of working on
lepers, on syphylitic persons, and on those afflicted with
the severer forms of rheumatism are little short of miraculous. The Japanese have a proverb to the effect that love
is the only grave distemper against which Kusatsu can
effect nothing.

In many cases a spring is famous in its own neighbourhood only. But it then almost invariably gains in one
way what it loses in another. The good country folk for
twenty miles around consider it a panacea for all the ills to
which flesh is heir. It is impossible to picture to oneself
anything more grotesquely dissimilar to an Ems or a Hom-
burg than one of these tiny spas, perched—say—amidst
the mountains of Shinshū or Etchū, and visited only by
Japanese of the most old-fashioned type and most limited
means—where, instead of a *table d'hôte*, each guest is
served in his own poor room with a bowl of rice or maybe

millet, a fid of salted egg-plant, and perhaps, on high days
and holidays, a small broiled fish. Even this is luxury to
the state of things existing in some remote districts, where
the peasant invalids come, bringing their own rice and their
own bedding with them on pack-horses, and pay only three
cents a day for lodging, for the use of the mineral spring,
and a titbit or two at each meal to help the rice down.

In opposition to all European sanitary ideas, the mineral
springs of Japan are used at very high temperatures. Invalids enter baths of from 110° to 115° Fahrenheit, and
their healthy friends go in with them for the sake of killing
time agreeably. At Kusatsu the temperature of the baths
is higher still. It ranges from 120° to 130° Fahrenheit.
Imagine, if you can, the agony entailed on those condemned
to enter these baths, covered as their bodies are with the
festering sores that arise from nameless diseases. So ex-
cruciating is this agony that experience has dictated a peculiar device for meeting it: the bathers are subjected to
military discipline. The squad of unfortunates approaches
the bath to the sound of the trumpet, they wet their scalp
and forehead at another trumpet blast, in order to prevent a
rush of blood to the head, and so on throughout the performance, notice being given to them of the passing of the
minutes while they sit boiling, with a view to keeping up
their courage by the knowledge that the ordeal will soon be
over. The whole life at Kusatsu is so strange that he
whose stomach is not easily upset by nasty sights would do
well to go and inspect it. To squeamish persons we say
most emphatically: "Stay away!"

**Mirrors.** Japanese mirrors are circular, and are made
of metal—generally of bronze coated on the front with an

amalgam of tin and quicksilver beautifully polished. The
back is adorned in relief with flowers, birds, or Chinese
characters, and there is a handle on one side, the general
appearance being that of a sort of handsome metal fan.
An extraordinary peculiarity characterises some of these
Japanese mirrors : when bright sunlight is made to fall on
their *face*, the design on their *back* is reflected on the
opposite wall ! So strange a phenomenon has naturally
attracted the attention of men of science. After some
discussion, the verdict seems to be that it arises from the
uneven pressure which the front receives when being
polished, owing to the presence of the pattern in relief on
the back.

Books recommended. "On the Magic Mirrors of Japan." by Professors
Ayrton and Perry, in the "Proceedings of the Royal Society," Vol. XXVII, pp. 127—
142.—Our own remarks are founded on Rein's "Industries of Japan," p. 147.

Missions. (1. ROMAN CATHOLIC.) The Catholic religion
was first preached in Japan about the middle of the sixteenth century. Contemporary documents inform us that
this important event was brought about in the following
manner. While St. Francis Xavier was evangelising India
and the Sunda Islands, a Japanese fugitive named Anjirô,
a native of Kagoshima, was introduced to him. Anjirô met
with a kind reception, and having accompanied Xavier to
Goa, was there baptised together with his two servants.
This was in A. D. 1548. Xavier then formed the design
of evangelising Japan, a design which was confirmed in
the following year, when the Saint, who happened to be
at Malacca, received tidings from some Portuguese merchants of a supernatural occurrence which had brought into
prominence the marvellous virtues of the Cross, and of the
desire expressed by the Prince of Satsuma to send for

Christian preachers and learn from their lips the truths of religion.

Xavier at once embarked for Japan, accompanied by his three Japanese neophytes. He arrived at Kagoshima on the 15th August, 1549, where he was received with distinguished courtesy by the prince, and forthwith began to preach the Gospel. During the two years and a half of his residence in Japan, he visited Hirado, Yamaguchi, and Kyôto. The numerous wonderful cures which he effected gave such weight to his words that he had the consolation of being able to found in various places Christian communities animated with a zeal which led them to constitute themselves missionaries to the households of their friends and kinsmen. The converts were drawn from all classes alike. Noblemen, Buddhist priests, men of learning, embraced the faith with the same alacrity as did the poor and ignorant. By the year 1582 the whole island of Amakusa, and the greater part of the Gotô Islands and of the daimiates of Ômura and Yamaguchi were Christian. Christianity flourished likewise in Kyôto, and the holy name of Jesus was carried into the furthest provinces of the North. The total number of Japanese professing the Faith at that period is estimated at over six hundred thousand souls. The apostolate was exercised by a hundred and thirty-eight European missionaries. They belonged without exception to the Society of Jesus; and their activity, inspired by the loftiest motives, had the most beneficial influence on the people of Japan.

A noteworthy feature of this nascent church is to be found in the embassies sent by the Christian princes to Rome to wait on the head of the Church Catholic. The first of these embassies, organised by the Lords of Bungo, Arima, and Ômura, left Japan early in 1582, and reached

Rome in 1585. It was received with the greatest honours, as well by the Sovereign Pontiff himself as by the other European princes. The Japanese princes, in their letters to the Pope, expressed their heartful gratitude for the happiness vouchsafed to them of knowing Christ, and entreated His Holiness to look with favour on themselves and on all the Christians of their dominions.

Such was the happy situation of the Christian Church in Japan, when peril was suddenly conjured up by the jealousy subsisting between the Portuguese and the Spanish traders, who, in order to compass each other's ruin, began to libel each other to the Japanese authorities. At this juncture Toyotomi Hideyoshi—better known under the name of Taikō Sama—had, after a long series of civil wars, become Mayor of the Palace. Vainglorious to excess, he wished to see himself worshipped after the fashion of one of the ancient Japanese conquerors. The wrath of this ruler was roused, in A. D. 1587, by a tale brought to his ears of the *soi-disant* bravado of a certain Portuguese captain,* whereupon he issued an edict banishing all the missionaries, most of whom were Portuguese by birth. Thanks, however, to the missionaries' own prudence, the storm was stayed. They abstained from appearing in public, and remained shut up in their colleges, busy with the compilation and publication of books both religious and philological, and with the education of a native priesthood. Until the breaking out of the persecution of 1596, the work of evangelisation continued to proceed apace. The new converts numbered about ten thousand yearly, though

---

* "The king, my master," so he is reported to have said, " begins by sending priests who win over the people, and when this is done, he despatches his troops to join the native Christians, and the conquest is easy and complete."

all were fully aware of the risk to which they exposed themselves by embracing the Catholic faith.

At length the persecution came. The cause of it is to be sought, partly in the indiscreet zeal of the newly landed Franciscans and Dominicans, who were mostly Spaniards, and therefore disposed, as well from national as from sectional religious reasons, to look with an unfriendly eye on their predecessors, the Portuguese Jesuits, partly in the slanders circulated against all Christians by the Buddhist priests. The trial was one of fire and blood. History has no more edifying page than that which tells of the courage with which the neophytes met their doom.

Happily for the Church of Japan, the authority of the Mayor of the Palace was not respected equally in all the provinces of the empire. If in those districts which were more specially subject to him, his edicts were carried out with punctuality and rigour, the *daimyōs* of certain other provinces did not fear to connive at the profession of Christianity in their domains. Some even went so far as openly to protect it. An example of this occurred in 1614, the very year in which more than sixty misionaries were expelled from Japan and nine Christian churches were destroyed at Nagasaki. In this year it was that Date Masamune, *daimyō* of Sendai, despatched an embassy to the Pope and to the King of Spain. The embassy consisted of a Franciscan monk, Father Sotelo, of one of Date's vassals named Hasekura Rokuemon, and of some fifty persons of lesser degree, all of whom were baptized during the voyage. Date, in his letter to the Pope, begged that a number of missionaries might be sent to preach the Gospel in his domains.

At the beginning of the seventeenth century, the Japanese

Christians numbered about one million—the fruit of half a century of apostolic labour accomplished in the midst of comparative peace. Another half-century of persecution was about to ruin this flourishing church, to cut off its pastors, more than two hundred of whom suffered martyrdom, and to leave its laity without the offices of religion. In vain did the Christians attempt secrecy and endeavour to conceal a few priests. A price was set on the priests' heads, and their enemies, the more surely to discover both them and their native converts, had recourse to denunciation by spies and to the infamous obligation of trampling on the cross.[*] The edicts ordering these measures remained in force for over two centuries.

Nevertheless the Church of Japan was not forgotten. The Jesuit Father Sidotti and others, nothing daunted, disembarked on the Japanese coast at intervals during the eighteenth century, but were at once thrown into prison. In 1846 the Pope nominated a bishop and several missionaries, who took up their station in the neighbouring Loochoo Islands, and entered Japan on the signing of the treaties of 1858. These men had the joy, in 1865, to discover several Christian communities round about Nagasaki, surviving the ruin of the church of their forefathers over two centuries before. They had preserved certain prayers, the rite of baptism, and a few books. But if these Christian communities survived, the persecuting spirit survived also. In 1867 all those Christians—and they numbered over four thousand—who refused to forswear their faith, were torn from their native villages and distributed over various pro-

---

[*] Specimens of the crosses used for this purpose are preserved in the Museum at Uëno, Tōkyō. They are little plates of yellow copper, on which is represented in relief the Passion of Our Lord.

vinces of the Empire, where they were kept as prisoners by
the respective *daimyôs*. After six years of exile, they were
at length set at liberty in 1873. The Church of Japan,
thus restored, is now slowly but surely developing, thanks
to the toleration enjoyed under the Imperial Government.

The Church of Japan was governed from 1846 to 1877
by a single bishop, from 1877 to 1888 by two bishops, and
since 1888 by three, whose respective residences are at
Tôkyô, Ôsaka, and Nagasaki. The Catholic population of
the empire amounted, on the 15th August, 1889, to 40,538
souls, as against 37,745 in 1888, and 35,886 in 1887.
They are grouped in 217 congregations, spread more or less
all over the country, but most thickly in the island of Kyûshû. The clergy consists—besides the 3 bishops—of 67
European missionaries and 15 Japanese priests. There are
also 8 European priests and 59 nuns (of whom 56 are
European and 3 Japanese), busy in teaching, and having
the management of 4 schools and 18 homes for orphans.
The missionaries are assisted by 309 catechists.

II. PROTESTANT, ETC. The first Protestant missionaries
landed in Japan in 1859. They were American Episcopa-
lians, and the Japan missions have ever since continued to
be chiefly in American, though not in Episcopalian, hands.
The first Protestant baptism took place in 1864, the first
native church was organised at Yokohama in 1872, and the
first church building was dedicated in 1875. In 1872 the
work of Biblical translation, till then hindered by want of
sufficient familiarity with the language, was vigorously
undertaken. It should be added that the existence of
several Chinese versions, which all educated Japanese could
read, rendered the necessity for a version in the vernacular
less urgent than would have been the case in other lands.

A complete version of the New Testament was completed in 1880, of the Old Testament in 1887. Meanwhile the opposition of the government to Christianity faded away, and the number of converts increased—slowly at first, for in 1872 no more than ten persons had been baptized, but afterwards by leaps and bounds. Besides actual evangelising work, much general school work has been engaged in, sometimes with the enlightened object of sapping the secular outposts of Japanese religious error, sometimes rather as a means towards obtaining a passport to enable the bearer to reside in the interior. The venerable Dr. Hepburn and others have also combined the art of healing bodies with that of curing souls.

Perhaps the most important event in the history of Japanese Protestantism is the amalgamation into one body of the scattered forces of the various American and Scottish Presbyterian churches. By this amalgamation was formed, in 1877, "the United Church of Christ in Japan" (*Nihon Kirisuto Itchi Kyōkwai*), which body tends to attract to itself the missions of the other smaller evangelical denominations. The chief Protestant college in Tōkyō, the *Meiji Gakuin*, belongs to this United Church. In December, 1889, the total number of Japanese Protestant converts was 31,181; of foreign missionaries, 527; of ordained native ministers, 135; of organised churches, 274 (more than half of these being self-supporting); and of Sunday schools, 350. The amount of contributions by the native Christians for various religious purposes amounted in 1889 to $53,503. There are several native religious clubs or associations, of which the Young Men's Christian Association (*Seinenkwai*) and the Women's Temperance Association (*Kyōfūkwai*) are the most flourishing.

Among the Protestant bodies above mentioned are included the Episcopal Church of America, presided over for thirty years past by Bishop Williams, and the Church of England, which has been for over twenty years in the field. The first bishop of the English Church in Japan, Dr. Poole, was appointed in 1883. Besides the new bishop, Dr. Bickersteth, there are now two archdeacons, more than twenty European clergy, some half-dozen clergy of Japanese birth, and a number of European lay workers of both sexes. The English and American Episcopal Churches work, as far as possible, in unison. The total Japanese membership of the two in 1889 was 3,422.

In 1885, a German pastor of the liberal school of theology arrived in Japan. He has since then been joined by a second, and they have organised small churches in Tōkyō and Yokohama, both for the Japanese and for their own countrymen, who had till that time dispensed with religious ministrations. The latest arrival of all is Unitarianism, in the person of Professor Knapp and five fellow-workers (1889).

The Orthodox Russian Church, presided over by Bishop Nicolai, has had a mission in Japan ever since the year 1870. It numbers over 1,700 baptised converts, and claims a total following of 17,000. The Russian cathedral, which is about to be opened for worship, is the only ecclesiastical edifice in Tōkyō with any pretensions to magnificence.

III. GENERAL CONSIDERATIONS. To those who can look back thirty years, or even only twenty years, the change in the position of Christianity in Japan is most striking, indeed well-nigh incredible. Then it was perilous for a Japanese to confess Jesus. Now such confession is rather fashionable than otherwise. Then it was hard work for a missionary to obtain a native teacher. Now there are hundreds of ordained and unordained native preachers and teachers of Christianity. The old proclamation, which, since A. D. 1638, had prohibited the religion of Jesus as "a corrupt sect," was still posted on the notice-boards of the public thoroughfares as late as 1873. The government now openly tolerates the building of churches and the perform-ance of Christian funeral rites, though we are not aware of the old anti-Christian laws having ever been formally re-pealed. The danger is now, not from persecution, but from worldly-minded favour. Some of the leaders of Japanese thought, while professing themselves personally indifferent to all religions, have cold-bloodedly advocated the adop-tion of Christianity as a school of morals and music, and as likely to be advantageous in political negotiations with the powers of the West. To make all Japan Christian by edict some fine morning, is not on the programme of the Japanese statesmen of the hour. But that something of the kind should happen within the next twenty years, is not nearly so unlikely as many things that have actually happened in this land of realised improbabilities.

Having begun prophesying, we may as well continue. Our second prophecy is that the Christians of Japan will be occupied with questions of morals and practice—the temper-ance question, for instance, and Sunday observance—rather than with subtle doctrinal theories, the Japanese mind being too essentially unspeculative for the fine distinctions of the theologians to have any charm for it, much less for it to seek to split new hairs for itself. The failure of Buddhist metaphysical abstractions to take any hold of the national sympathies, is a finger-post in history pointing to what may be expected in the future.

Books recommended. (I. Catholic.) "Histoire de la Religion Chrétienne au Japon," by Father Crasset.—"Histoire du Christianisme dans l'Empire du Japon," by Father Charlevoix.—"Histoire de la Religion Chrétienne au Japon," by Léon Pagès.—The above are general accounts, or résumés of the subject. See also Hildreth's "Japan as it Was and Is."—The literature of Catholicism in Japan is very voluminous, beginning with the Jesuits' "Letters" in the sixteenth and seventeenth centuries, and coming down to the special treatises by Léon Pagès (e. g., "Les Vingt-Six Martyrs Japonais" and "La Persécution des Chrétiens au Japon"). Satow, and others. Satow's researches are, for the most part, scattered through the volumes of the "Asiatic Transactions;" but one of his most interesting essays, entitled "The Jesuit Mission Press in Japan from 1591 to 1610," giving extracts and fac-similes, was printed privately as a separate work.

(II. Protestant.) "The Proceedings of the Osaka Conference of 1883.—Rev. H. Loomis' "Statistics of Missions," published yearly.—The "Reports" of the various missionary societies.

Moral Maxims. Few Japanese books are more likely to please the foreign student than two small volumes of practical ethics, entitled respectively *Jitsugo Kyō*, or "Teaching of the Words of Truth," and *Dōji Kyō*, or "Teaching for the Young." They are ascribed to Buddhist abbots of the ninth century; but the doctrine of both has a Confucian no less than a Buddhistic flavour. Both were for many ages as familiar to the youth of Japan as the Sermon on the Mount is to us. The following may serve as specimens:—

"Treasures that are laid up in a garner decay: treasures that are laid up in the mind do not decay.

"Though thou shouldst heap up a thousand pieces of gold: they would not be so precious as one day of study.

"If thou, being poor, enter into the abode of the wealthy: remember that his riches are more fleeting than the flower nipped by the hoarfrost.

" If thou be born in the poor man's hovel, but have wisdom : then shalt thou be like the lotus-flower growing out of the mud.

" Thy father and thy mother are like heaven and earth : thy teacher and thy lord are like the sun and moon.

" Other kinsfolk may be likened unto the rushes : husbands and wives are but as useless stones.

" He that loveth iniquity beckoneth to misfortune : it is, as it were, the echo answering to the voice.

" He that practiseth righteousness receiveth a blessing : it cometh as surely as the shadow followeth after the man.

" Be reverent when thou goest past a grave : alight from thine horse when thou goest past a Shintō shrine.

" When thou art near a Buddhist temple or pagoda, thou shalt not commit any unclean act : when thou readest the sacred writings, thou shalt do nothing unseemly.

" Human ears are listening at the wall : speak no calumny, even in secret.

" Human eyes look down from the heavens : commit no wrong, however hidden.

" When a hasty word hath once been spoken : a team of four horses may pursue, but cannot bring it back.

" The flaw in a mace of white jade may be ground away : but the flaw of an evil word cannot be ground away.

" Calamity and prosperity have no gate : they are there only whither men invite them.

" From the evils sent by heaven there is deliverance : from the evils we bring upon ourselves there is no escape.

" The Gods punish fools, not to slay but to chasten them : the teacher smiteth his disciple, not from hatred but to make him better.

" Though the sins committed by the wise man be great, he shall not fall into hell : though the sins committed by the fool be small, he shall surely fall into hell.

" Life, with birth and death, is not enduring : and ye should haste to yearn after Nirvâna.

" The body, with its passions, is not pure : and ye should swiftly search after intelligence.

" Above all things, men must practise charity : it is by almsgiving that wisdom is fed.

" Less than all things, men must grudge money : it is by riches that wisdom is hindered."

Books recommended. Full translation of the Daji Kyô in Vol. IX, Part III, of the "Asiatic Transactions," and of the Jishago Kyô in the "Cornhill Magazine" for August, 1876.

**Mourning.** The Japanese, like other nations under Chinese influence, are very strict on the subject of mourning. Formerly three mourning codes (*Bukki Ryō*) prevailed simultaneously. Of these one was for Shintō priests, another for the Kyōto nobility, and yet another for the *daimyōs* and *samurai*. The last alone has survived, and its prescriptions are followed by all the well-to-do classes. Mourning, be it remarked, consists of two things—the wearing of mourning garments, and abstinence from animal food. This premised, the following table is self-explanatory :—

| | *Garments.* | *Food.* |
|---|---|---|
| Great-great-grandparents* ... | 30 days | 10 days |
| Great-grandparents* ... | 90 ,, | 20 ,, |
| Grandparents* ... ... ... | 150 ,, | 30 ,, |
| Real parents ... ... ... | 13 months | 50 ,, |
| Adopted parents ... ... ... | 13 ,, | 50 ,, |
| Step-parents ... ... ... | 30 days | 10 ,, |
| Father's legitimate wife† ... | 30 ,, | 10 ,, |
| Divorced mother ... ... | 150 ,, | 30 ,, |
| (Woman's) parents-in-law ... | 50 ,, | 20 ,, |
| Uncle and aunt* ... ... | 90 ,, | 20 ,, |
| Husband ... ... ... ... | 13 months | 50 ,, |
| Wife ... ... ... ... ... | 90 days | 20 ,, |
| Brothers and sisters ... ... | 90 ,, | 20 ,, |
| Half-brothers and sisters* ... | 30 ,, | 10 ,, |

* On the paternal side. The inferior position occupied in the East by women causes a considerable reduction to be made in the period of mourning for corresponding relatives on the maternal side. A maternal grandmother, for instance, is only mourned for during 90 days, a maternal uncle during 30 days.

† A man's legitimate wife is the "legal mother" of his children by concubines. Such children mourn their "legal mother's" death during the period indicated in the text.

|                          | Garments. | Food. |
|--------------------------|-----------|-------|
| Eldest son    ...   ...   ...   ... | 90 days | 20 days |
| Other children   ...   ...   ... | 30  ,, | 10  ,, |
| Eldest son's eldest son ...   ... | 30  ,, | 10  ,, |
| Other grandchildren ...   ... | 10  ,, | 3  ,, |
| Adopted son   ...   ...   ...   ... | 30  ,, | 10  ,, |
| Nephews and nieces ...   ... | 7  ,, | 3  ,, |
| First cousins ...   ...   ...   ... | 7  ,, | 3  ,, |

Infants under three months are not mourned for, and the period of mourning for children is greatly reduced if they are under seven years of age.

Whenever a death occurs in the family of an official, he must at once report it to the department to which he is attached. The theory is that he should remain at home during the whole of the proper period of mourning. But as this would cause inconvenience in practice, he is always absolved from the operation of the rule, and ordered to "attend office though in mourning." Whenever any member of the Imperial Family dies, a notification is issued prohibiting all sound of music throughout the land for the space of three days, and sometimes for a longer period if the deceased personage stood very near the throne.

Periodical visits to the grave of the deceased—*haka-mairi*, as they are termed—form an essential part of the Japanese system of mourning. The days prescribed by custom for these visits are the seventh day after decease, the fourteenth, twenty-first, thirty-fifth, forty-ninth, and hundredth; then the first anniversary, the third anniversary, the seventh, thirteenth, seventeenth, twenty-third, twenty-seventh, thirty-third, thirty-seventh, fiftieth, and hundredth. On the more important of these occasions Buddhist services are performed, for instance, on the first and third anniversaries. By some, especially among the poorer class, the whole of this extensive programme proves to be impossible of fulfilment, and even in the upper classes not a few are now to be found who sensibly imitate Europe by moderating the outward symbols of grief; but the seventh and thirty-fifth days and the first and third anniversaries are never neglected. Observe that all these numbers are calculated according to the old Japanese "inclusive" system of reckoning, which reduces by one every number except one itself. Thus the so-called thirty-fifth day is really the thirty-fourth, the so-called third anniversary is really the second, and so on.

International mourning is observed by New Japan with a punctiliousness bordering on the comical. A few years ago, the chief civic dignitary of the capital had issued invitations for a ball. As the guests were arriving, there simultaneously arrived news of the translation to celestial spheres of some German "Transparency" (to use Thackeray's phrase)—not a crowned head at all. Hush the music, out with the lights! Good people all, retire to mourn. There can be no dancing to-night.—Imagine the Lord Mayor of London or the *Préfet* of the *Département de la Seine* interrupting his festivities every time a vacancy occurs in the "Almanac de Gotha!"

**Moxa.** "Moxa" is one of the few Japanese words that have found their way into the English language. It is properly *mogusa*, a contraction of *mos-kusa*, that is "the burning herb"—a name given to the plant which we call "mugwort," on account of the use to which it is put. It is employed as a cautery, little fragments of it being rolled into a cone, and then applied to the body and set fire to.

In the old Chinese and Japanese system of medicine, burning with the moxa was considered a panacea for almost every human ill.   It was prescribed for fainting fits, nose-bleeding, rheumatism, and a hundred other ailments.   A woman unable to bear the pangs of child-birth was to be relieved by having three places burnt with it on the little toe of her right foot.   In addition to this, the moxa was used as a punishment for children, many being burnt—generally on the back—when more than usually naughty. This practice, which is not yet quite obsolete, accounts for some at least of the cicatrices on the naked backs and legs of *jinrikisha*-men and other coolies.   There is a well-known story of a child, who, having committed arson, and rendered himself thereby liable, under the former severe law of the realm, to be burnt alive, was dragged out with impressive pomp to the place of execution, but let off at the last moment with an unusually severe dose of the moxa.

*Book recommended.* Whitney's "Notes on the History of Medical Progress in Japan," published in Vol. XII, Part IV, of the "Asiatic Transactions," especially p. 289. et seq., from which some of our statements have been taken.


**Music.**   Music, if that beautiful word may be allowed to fall so low as to denote the strummings and squealings of Orientals, is supposed to have existed in Japan ever since mythological times.   But Japanese music as now known—its lutes, flutes, drums, and fiddles of various sorts—came over from China, like most other things good and bad, in the train of Buddhism.   The *samisen*, or banjo, was apparently introduced from Manila as recently as the year 1700.

The perfection of Japanese classical music may be heard at Tōkyō from the Band of Court Musicians attached to the

Bureau of Rites. Having said that it may be heard, we hasten to add that it cannot be heard often by ordinary mortals. The easiest way to get a hearing of it is to attend one of the concerts given by the Musical Society of Japan (an association founded in 1886 for the cultivation of both Japanese and European music), at which the Court Musicians occasionally perform. A more curious ceremony still is the performance by these same musicians, at certain Shintô festivals, of a *silent* concert. Both stringed and wind instruments are used in this concert. But it is held that the sanctity of the occasion would be profaned were any sound to fall on unworthy ears. Therefore, though all the motions of playing are gone through, no strains are actually emitted! This is but one among many instances of the strange vagaries of the Japanese musical art, and of the extreme esoteric secrecy in which the families hereditarily entrusted with the handing down of that art shroud their knowledge.

The chanting of the Buddhist liturgy, also, at certain temple services is considered classical. This chanting has been held by some to resemble the Ambrosian and early Gregorian tones; but local colouring is sufficiently provided for inasmuch as each performer utters the strain in the key that best suits the pitch of his own voice. For all this classical music there exists a notation—a notation which is extremely complicated. There is none for the more popular instruments—for the *samisen* and *kokyu*, and even in many cases for the *koto*. An attempt was made to introduce one about the middle of the last century; but the teachers of those instruments, deeming their means of livelihood threatened, successfully opposed the innovation, much as codification is opposed by English lawyers.

It may seem odd that so fundamental a question as the nature of the Japanese scale should still be a matter of debate. Yet so it is. Mr. Ellis's opinion on the subject will be found in his paper mentioned below. But Mr. Isawa, the greatest Japanese authority on music, says, in a private communication addressed to us, that Mr. Ellis has been misled on some important points by his having given too much weight to the performances of an ignorant woman at the "Japanese Village" in London. As well, says Mr. Isawa, take a *jinrikisha*-man for referee in questions of grammar and diction, as such a woman for an authority on delicate matters of musical intervals. According to Mr. Isawa, the second, fourth, fifth, and sixth in the classical music of Japan, are identical with the same intervals of the modern European scale, but the third (major third) is sharper, and the seventh flatter. The popular or *samisen* scale is different. Like the scale of mediæval Europe, it has for its chief peculiarity a semitone above the tonic. This is one among various reasons for believing the *samisen*, together with its scale, to have found its way here from the Spaniards at Manila, and not from Loochoo according to the current Japanese opinion.

Be the scale what it may, the effect of Japanese music is, not to soothe, but to exasperate beyond all endurance, the European breast. Its only time is common time. Harmony it has none. It knows nothing of our distinction of modes, and therefore, as a writer on the subject has pointed out, it lacks alike the vigour and majesty of the major mode, the plaintive tenderness of the minor, and the marvellous effects of light and shade which arise from the alternations of the two. Perhaps this is the reason why

the Japanese themselves are so indifferent on the subject.
One never hears a party of Japanese talking seriously about
music; musical questions are never discussed in the newspapers; no one goes to a temple service

"Not for the doctrine, but the music there;"
a Japanese Bayreuth is unthinkable. Men "on the spree"
send for singing girls chiefly in order to ogle and chaff
them, and to help along the entertainment by a little noise.
To ask the name of the composer of any tune the girls are
singing, is a thing that would never enter their heads.

Books recommended. "On the Musical Scales of Various Nations," by A. J.
Ellis, F.R.S., printed in the "Journal of the Society of Arts" for the 27th March,
1885.—"Some Japanese Musical Intervals," by Rev. Dr. Veeder, in Vol. VII, Part II,
of the "Asiatic Transactions."—"On Primitive Music, especially that of Japan," by
Rev. Dr. Syle, in Vol. V, Part I, of the same.—For specimens of Japanese music transcribed into the European musical notation and with the words of the songs in Roman
character, see a small book published in 1888 by the Tōkyō Academy of Music, and
entitled "Collection of Japanese Koto Music." The most delicate-minded need not
fear having their morals tainted by strumming through this little volume, as the
editors make a point of telling us in their preface that in this their edition of the old
Koto music, "for those words and tunes occurring therein, which are liable to offend
the public feelings on account of their vulgarity and meanness, pure and elegant ones
have been substituted, thus preventing their hateful effects upon the social character." At the same time, the few entirely new compositions of their own which the
compilers have ventured to add, have all "been prepared with a care not to injure
that virtue which is inherent in our old Koto music." Historical accuracy is thus so
perfectly unfettered as taste and morals.

**Mythology.** See HISTORY.

**Names.** The Japanese have more than one kind of
surname, more than one kind of Christian (or should we
say heathen?) name, besides nicknames, *noms-de-plume*,
and even separate posthumous names. The subject is a
labyrinth. We merely sketch out the following as a clue to
help the student in threading his way through it. He will
find, then, that there are:—

1. The *kabane* or *sei*, a very ancient and aristocratic sort of family name, but now so widely diffused as to include several surnames in the narrower sense of the word. The grand old names of *Minamoto*, *Fujiwara*, *Tachibana*, are *kabane*.

2. The *uji* or *myōji*, our surname, and dating like it only from mediæval times. Most names of this class are originally nothing more than the names of the localities in which the families bearing them resided, as *Yama-moto*, " foot of the mountain ; " *Ta-naka*, " among the rice-fields ; " *Matsu-mura*, " pine-tree village."

3. The *zokumyō* or *tsūshō*, literally, " common name." It corresponds pretty closely to our Christian name. Very often such names end in *tarō* for an eldest son, in *jirō* for a second, in *saburō* for a third, and so on down to *jūrō* for a tenth son, as *Gentarō*, *Tsunejirō*, etc.; or else these distinctive terminations are used alone without any prefix. They mean respectively " big male," " second male," " third male," and so on. Other *zokumyō* end in *emon*, *suke*, *nojō*, *bei*—words originally serving to designate certain offices, but now quite obsolete in that acceptation.

4. The *nanori* or *jitsumyō*, that is, " true name," also corresponding to our Christian name. Examples of it are *Masashige*, *Yoshisada*, *Tamotsu*, *Naka*. Until recently, the *jitsumyō* had a certain importance attached to it and a mystery shrouding it. It was used only on solemn occasions, especially in combination with the *kabane*, as *Fujiwara no Yoritsugu* (*no* = " of "). Since the late revolution, there has been a tendency to let No. 1 retreat into the background, to make No. 2 equivalent to the European surname, and to assimilate Nos. 3 and 4, both being employed indiscriminately as equivalents of the European

Christian name. If a man keeps No. 3, he drops No. 4,
and *vice versâ.*—The classes of names next to be mentioned,
though all existing in full force, are less important than the
first four classes.

5. The *azana*, sometimes—but not happily—translated
"nickname," like *Kunteki, Bunrin, Sotan, Snkitsn.* Chinese scholars specially affect them. They are not vulgar,
like our nicknames, but on the contrary, highly elegant.

6. The *gô. Nom de plume* or *nom de pinceau* is the
nearest European equivalent, but almost every Japanese of
a literary or artistic bent has one. Indeed he may have
several. Some of the Japanese names most familiar to
foreign ears are merely such *noms de plume,* assumed and
dropped at will, for instance, *Hokusai* (who had half-a-
dozen others), *Ôkyo,* and *Bakin.* Authors and painters
are in the habit of giving fanciful names to their residences, and then they themselves are called after their
residences, as *Bashô-an* ("banana hermitage"), *Susunoya-
no-Aruji* ("master of the house with a bell"). Such
names often end in *Dôjin, Sanjin, Koji, Okina,* that
is, "hermit," "mountaineer," "retired scholar," "aged
man."

7. The *haimyô* and *gagô.* These are but varieties of the
*gô,* adopted by comic poets and by painters.

8. The *geimyô,* or "artistic name," adopted by singing
and dancing-girls, actors, story-tellers, and other profess-
ional amusers of the public. Thus, *Ichikawa Danjūrô* is
not the real name, but only the hereditary "artistic name,"
of the most celebrated of living Japanese actors. To his
friends in private life, he is Mr. Horikoshi Shū (Horikoshi
is the *myôji,* No. 2; Shū is the *jitsumyô,* No. 4).

9. The *okuri-na,* or posthumous honorific appellation of

exalted personages. These are the names by which all the Mikados are known in history—names which they never bore during their lives. *Jimmu Tennō* and *Kōmei Tennō* are examples.

10. The *kōmyō* or *kaimyō*, a posthumous appellation chosen by the Buddhist priests for each believer immediately after death, and inscribed on the funeral tablet. Such names end in *in, koji, shinshi, shinjo, dōji,* etc., according to the age, sex, rank, and sect of the deceased.

It is characteristic of Japanese ways that the native friend who assisted in the above classification, never thought of mentioning women's names (*yobi-na*), which we will call No. 11. They are generally taken from the name of some flower or other graceful natural object, and preceded by the word *o*, "honourable." Thus we have *O Kiku*, "Chrysanthemum;" *O Take*, "Bamboo;" *O Gin*, "Silver;" *O Haru*, "Springtime," etc., etc.

It was formerly the custom for a man to change his name at any crisis of his career. It is still unfortunately the custom for places to do so. Hundreds of place-names have been altered since the revolution of 1868, to the great confusion of geographical and historical studies. The change of Yedo to Tōkyō is only the best-known of these. The idea, which is an old Chinese one, is to emphasise by the adoption of a new name some new departure in the fortunes of a city, village, mountain, school, etc. It is as if we should have changed the name of London and other places at the Reformation, or of Eton when the new Latin grammar was introduced. Another peculiarity is what may be termed the transmission of names. A teacher, for instance, hands on his own *nom de plume* to a favourite pupil, in order to help to start him in popular favour. In

this manner a bit of faience may be signed "Kenzan," and
yet not be by the original Kenzan at all. In many cases
only a part of the name is given or adopted. The Shôguns
of the Tokugawa dynasty offer a good example of this
remarkable custom. The name of the founder of the house
being *Iyyasu*, his successors styled themselves *Iemitsu,
Ietsuna, Ienobu*, and so on.

Now were we, or were we not, right in the statement with
which we set out, that Japanese names are a labyrinth?

**Nara.** See Capital Cities.

**Navy.** The foundation of the Japanese navy dates from
the last days of the Shôgunate, when the services of a
small party of British naval officers and men, under the
leadership of Commander Tracey, R. N., were obtained
through the instrumentality of Sir Harry Parkes, then
British minister at Yedo. This was in September, 1867.
Five months later the revolution which precipitated the
Shôgun from his throne broke out, and the naval mission, as it was termed, was withdrawn, first to Yokohama,
and then home to England. During the troublous times
which ensued, some of the greater *daimyôs* devoted all
their energies to military matters. One of them, the Prince
of Hizen, eager to possess a navy of his own, engaged
Lieutenant Hawes, of the Royal Marines, as gunnery in-
structor on board a vessel named the *Ryûjô-Kan*; and this
officer, who had an unusual talent for organisation, and
who occupied himself, both on board the *Ryûjô-Kan* and
later on in other positions, with many things besides
gunnery and the training of the marines, may be considered
the real father of the Japanese navy.

In the year 1873, when all storms were over and the
Mikado had long been restored to absolute power, the
British government lent the services of a second naval
mission, headed by Commander Douglas, R. N., and
consisting of thirty officers and men. A naval college
was built in Tōkyō, and instruction in all the necessary
branches was commenced in earnest, young officers and
seamen being drafted off from time to time to the various
ships, so as to constitute, as it were, a leaven by which a
practical knowledge of naval matters should be spread.
The drill was formed on the model of the English Naval
Gunnery School, and the excellence of the system can
be traced to the present day. The second naval mission
left Japan after six years' service. The Japanese government has, however, generally retained one or two English
officers in its employ, either to help on board the training-
ships, or to superintend the higher education of the officers,
and to keep the Japanese navy abreast of modern improvements. Dockyard work has been until recently in French
hands. M. Bertin, the famous French shipbuilder, spent
several years in Japan.

The navy, as at present constituted, comprises a total
force of 8000, of whom 800 are officers. There are, in
addition, 400 midshipmen and cadets under training. The
*matériel* of the fleet consists of twenty-three vessels, including one iron-clad, a few modern cruisers, several coast-
defence vessels, and cruisers of an older type. The
" mosquito fleet " consists of one or two fast despatch-
vessels and five torpedo-boats. The building programme
includes six modern fast cruisers and seventeen torpedo-
boats.

Besides the above, there are various smaller craft useful

for coast defence. A cruising fleet of nine powerful ships is kept in commission, to show the flag at foreign ports and to serve as a school for naval manœuvres and gunnery practice. Some of these vessels attain a speed of 18 knots, and carry modern high velocity guns. The remainder are of the corvette type of ten years ago, and were built in Japan. The Imperial dockyard is situated at Yokosuka, which may be considered the head-quarters of the Japanese navy. The "territorial system" is, however, now being put in force, and four additional naval stations have been chosen at different points on the coast. These are Kure in the Inland Sea, Sasebo some forty miles from Nagasaki, Maizuru on the west coast, and Mororan in the island of Yezo. The instruction of the senior officers is carried on at the Naval Academy in Tōkyō—corresponding roughly to Greenwich—that of the cadets at the Naval College at Etajima in the Inland Sea, which corresponds to the "Britannia." There are also Naval Medical and Paymasters' Schools in Tōkyō. The Engineer students are for the present provided for in the Naval College.

As for the men, the original intention was to raise them by conscription, as the army is raised; but practical considerations haven resulted in manning the ships chiefly by volunteers. The naval estimates amount, in round numbers, to £1,000,000. But there is also a special naval loan, in the absence of which it would have been impossible to bring the service up to the necessary standard of efficiency. Coast defence, too, has been assisted by the subscriptions of private individuals. Every branch of the Japanese navy is in a state which reflects the greatest credit on the Imperial authorities.

**Newspapers.** The founder of Japanese journalism was an Englishman, Mr. John Black, one of the earliest foreign residents at Yokohama. Before his time there no doubt existed street-criers (*yomi-uri*), who hawked small sheets roughly struck off from wooden blocks whenever some horrid murder or other interesting event took place. Then, in 1871, appeared a small quasi-journalistic venture, entitled the *Shimbun Zasshi*, believed to be inspired by Kido, a then prominent politician. But Mr. Black's *Nisshin Shinjiski*, started in 1872, was the first newspaper worthy of the name—the first to give leading articles and to comment seriously on political affairs. The seed once sown, Japanese journalism grew apace. There are now no less than six hundred and forty-eight newspapers, magazines, journals of societies, etc., published in the empire. The most important newspapers appearing in the capital are the *Kwampō*, or "Official Gazette;" the *Chōya Shimbun* (*shimbun* means "newspaper"), the *Yūbin Hōchi Shimbun*, and the *Mainichi Shimbun*, liberal; the *Kokumin Shimbun*, *Tōkyō Shimpō*, and *Tōkyō Kōron*, radical; the *Kōko Shimbun*, conservative; the *Nippon*, conservative and anti-foreign;. the *Nichi-Nichi Shimbun*, opportunist; and the *Jiji Shimpō*, independent. The tastes of the lower classes are catered for by the *Yomi-uri Shimbun*, the *Kaishin Shimbun*, the *Eiri Chōya*, and several more. Among the magazines, erudition is represented by *Bun* (what a name to English ears, but it means "literature" in Japanese!), Christianity by the *Rikugō Zasshi*, red-hot Chauvinism by the *Nipponjin*, criticism by the *Shuppan Geppyō*, satire and humour by the *Maru-Maru Chimbun*. The names of Yano Fumio, Fukuzawa Yukichi, Seki Naohiko, Shimada Saburō, and

Fukuchi Gen-íchirō may be mentioned as among those of the leading Japanese journalists.

The Japanese press-laws are rigorous, and the censors display much zeal in the execution of their duty. Is it a matter for surprise if the newspaper writers resort to allegory, to *double-entendre*, and to every kind of ingenious device, in the hope—the not always successful hope—of conveying, by hook or by crook, more than meets the ear, without running foul of the police? Is it surprising that they sometimes lament their fate in piteous terms? The following extract from the *Nichi-Nichi Shimbun*, which is by no means a radical sheet, or given to exaggeration, exposes the situation in a simple and truthful manner. It formed part of a leading article published on the 8th September, 1889 :—

"Newspapers and magazines," says the editor, "are confronted by a special danger—the danger, namely, of suspension when their words are held to be prejudicial to public order, and a suspension, too, against which there is no appeal. Article XIX of the Newspaper Regulations now in force says that 'When a newspaper has printed matter *which is considered*\* prejudicial to public order or subversive of public morality, the minister of state for the Interior is empowered to suspend its publication either totally or temporarily.' Nor is there a word said in the Regulations of any standard whereby the prejudicial or non-prejudicial character of a statement or argument is to be determined. It is sufficient that the official in question should determine, in accordance with his own individual opinion, that the statement or argument *is* thus prejudicial to public order, for a newspaper to incur at any moment the

_____

* The italics are in the original.

penalty of suspension either total or temporary.* It is
indisputable that the authorities are empowered by the law
of the land to act thus.  The Constitution itself gives them
this power.  The consequence is that we writers for the
press are ever obliged, on taking our pen in hand, to keep
to ourselves seven or eight out of every ten opinions
which we would fain express."

The most striking commentary on the above extract is
the fact that during the month following the proclamation
of the Constitution, newspapers were suspended at the rate
of two a week.  It appears, from a careful perusal of the
"Official Gazette," wherein all such matters are regularly
chronicled, that the total number of newspaper suspensions
during the year 1889 was forty-three, giving an average of
one every eight or nine days.  The period of suspension
varied from seven days to eighty-nine days, and some of
the newspapers thus punished never appeared again—
whether because totally suppressed, or because long suspension ruined their finances, we are unable to say.  Imprisonment for press offences is very common.  In March,
1890, an offending editor was condemned to captivity for
no less a term than four years and a half.  So completely has newspaper suppression come to count among
the regular features of Japanese political life, that, for
instance, we read one day in the columns of the "Japan
Mail"† that such and such a newspaper has been suspended, "but we are not in a position to define the exact
nature of the misdemeanour."  Another day it is (this as

---

* Another cause for the suspension of a newspaper is disrespect to the Imperial
Family or to officials.
† The "Japan Mail," being a strongly pro-official paper, is irrefragable evidence on
such a point.  We mean that it is sure never to overstate any unpopular action on
the part of the authorities.

late as September, 1889): "At present most of the papers and journals in the capital that are opposed to the treaty programme of the minister of state for Foreign Affairs are under suspension."

But let us be just. There is one consideration which must in fairness be advanced on the other side. It is this: interference with liberty of speech and printing probably galls a Japanese less than it would those to whom such liberty is part of their native air. These restrictive measures are not, historically speaking, retrograde measures, that is, they do not come after better things in the past. Under the old feudal *régime*, not only did liberty of speech not exist in fact: the right to some measure of it was not so much as recognised in theory, nor would the men who made the revolution of 1868 have dallied with the idea for a moment in their then frame of mind. They would have shuddered at it as sacrilege. The idea has entered Japan more recently, in the wake of English and American text-books for schools and of Anglo-Saxon ideas generally. That there should now be a cry for more, only shows that something has already been obtained.

The foreign press at the "Treaty Ports" is entirely in English hands. The "Japan Mail," "Japan Herald," and "Japan Gazette," published at Yokohama, are rendered far more interesting than the majority of non-metropolitan journals by the constant and striking changes in Japanese politics and social life that have to be chronicled. At Kōbe there are the "Hyōgo News" and the "Kōbe Herald," at Nagasaki the "Rising Sun and Nagasaki Express."

**Nikkō.** A rhyming Japanese proverb says, "Do not use the word magnificent until you have seen Nikkō:"

*Nikkō wo minai uchi wa,*
*" Kekkō " to iu-na !*

Nikkō's is a double glory—a glory of nature and a glory of art. Mountains, cascades, monumental forest-trees, had always stood there. To these, in the seventeenth century, were added the mausoleums of the illustrious Shōgun Ieyasu and of his scarcely less famous grandson Iemitsu. Japanese wood-carving and painting on wood being then at their zenith, the result was the most perfect assemblage of shrines in the whole land. But though there is gorgeousness, there is no gaudiness. The sobriety which is the key-note of Japanese taste gives to all these gay designs and bright colours its own chaste character. The actual tombs are of plain bronze—no gold, no ornament of any kind. As Mitford says, " There is no small amount of poetical feeling in this simple ending to so much magnificence ; the sermon may have been preached by design, or it may have been by accident, but the lesson is there."

Book recommended. Satow and Hawes' "Handbook for Japan," pp. 440-460.

**Nō.** See THEATRE.

**Nobility.** The Japanese nobility may be called very old or very new, according to the way one looks at it. In its present form it dates from the 7th July, 1884, when the Chinese titles of *kō*, *kō\**, *haku*, *shi*, and *dan*, corresponding respectively to our duke (or prince), marquis, count, viscount, and baron, were bestowed by Imperial edict on a number of distinguished persons. But there had been an aristocracy before. Properly speaking, there had been two—the *kuge*

---

\* These two *kō*'s, though chancing to sound alike, are different words written with different Chinese characters. The first is 公 (Chinese *kung*), the second is 侯 (Chinese *hou*).

who were descended from the younger sons of ancient Mikados, and the *daimyôs* who were the feudal lords lifted to title and wealth by the sword and by the favour of the Shôguns. When feudalism fell, the *daimyôs* lost their territorial titles, and were amalgamated with the *kuge* under the designation of *kwazoku,* or ",flowery families," which is still the current name for noblemen generally, irrespective of what their particular grade may be.

These aristocrats by birth formed the nucleus of the new nobility of 1884, among' the five grades of which they were distributed according to their historical and other claims to distinction. To them was added a number of new men, eminent for their talents or for services rendered to the Imperial cause. The members of the nobility receive pensions from the civil list. They are also placed under special restrictions. For instance, they may not marry without government permission. On the other hand, the new Constitution grants to a certain number of them the privilege of sitting in the upper house of the Imperial Diet.

**Numerical Categories.** Number has long exercised a peculiar fascination over the Far-Eastern mind. Europeans, no doubt, sometimes use such expressions as "the Four Cardinal Virtues" and "the Seven Deadly Sins;" but it is not part of our mental disposition to divide up and parcel out almost all things visible and invisible into numerical categories fixed by unchanging custom, as is the case among the nations from India eastward. The Chinese speak of their "Three Religions," of "the Three Forms of Obedience," "the Four Classics," "the Five Duties," "the Eight Diagrams," "the Four- and-Twenty Paragons of Filial Piety," whole pages of their books of reference being devoted to lists of expressions of this kind. The Japanese have followed suit. They have adopted all the Chinese numerical categories, and have invented new ones of their own. Here are a dozen of the commonest, chosen from among many scores:—

THE THREE VIEWS (三景), viz. Matsushima near Sendai in the North, Miyajima in the Inland Sea, and Ama-no-Hashidate on the Sea of Japan. These are considered the three most beautiful places in the empire.

THE THREE IMPERIAL INSIGNIA (三種神器), namely, the sword, mirror, and jewel that have been handed down from Mikado to Mikado ever since the beginning of the dynasty.

THE THREE DIVINE POETS (和歌三神), namely Kakino-moto-no-Hitomaro, Sumiyoshi-no-Kami, and Tama-tsu-Shima.

THE FOUR HEAVENLY KINGS (四天王). Originally an Indian Buddhist category, the term is applied in Japan to various sets of four great warriors. For instance, Sakai, Sakakibara, Ii, and Honda were the Four Heavenly Kings, in other words, the four eminent generals, who helped to put the Tokugawa dynasty of Shōguns on the throne.

THE FOUR CLASSES OF SOCIETY (四民), namely, warriors, farmers, artisans, and merchants. Observe that in Old Japan the merchants ranked last.

THE FIVE REGENT HOUSES (五摂家), that is, the five noble families of Konoe, Kujō, Nijō, Ichijō, and Takatsu-kasa, from which alone regents of the empire (*sesshō*) could formerly be chosen to govern during the minority of a Mikado.

THE FIVE FESTIVALS (五節句). They are the 7th January, popularly termed *Nana-Kusa*, or "seven herbs," because seven kinds of herbs are supposed to be then plucked and

eaten; the 3rd March, on which is celebrated the birthday
of all the little girls in Japan; the 5th May, the birthday
festival of the boys; the 7th July, called *Tanabata*, and
serving to commemorate the mythological loves of certain
stars; and the 9th September, which used to be the
chrysanthemum festival, but which the recent adoption of
the Gregorian calendar has placed too early for the appearance of those flowers.

"THE SEVEN HERBS" (七草). Different authorities give
different lists.

"THE EIGHT VIEWS" (八景). Following an old Chinese
precedent, almost every picturesque neighbourhood in Japan
has its eight views. The best-known are "the Eight
Views of Lake Ōmi" (*Ōmi Hakkei*), which are enumerated
as follows:—the autumn moon seen from Ishiyama, the
evening snow on Hirayama, the sunset at Seta, the evening
bell of Miidera, the boats sailing back from Yabase, the
bright sky with a breeze at Awazu, rain by night at Kara-
saki, and the wild geese alighting at Katata. Pretty and
thoroughly Oriental ideas—are they not?

"THE EIGHT GREAT ISLANDS" (大八洲), namely, the
eight largest islands of the Japanese archipelago, hence in
poetry Japan itself.

"THE ONE-AND-TWENTY GREAT ANTHOLOGIES" (二十一
大集). These are the standard collections of Japanese classical poetry, brought together by Imperial command during
the Middle Ages.

"THE SIX-AND-THIRTY POETICAL GENIUSES" (三十六
歌仙). A full list of their names is given in Anderson's
"Catalogue of Japanese and Chinese Paintings," page 145.

**Parkes (Sir Harry S.).** Born at Birchill's Hall, Stafford-

shire, in 1828, Sir Harry Parkes came out to Canton as
a little boy, his widowed mother having married a missionary, named Gutzlaff. He thus acquired at an early age
that intimate knowledge of the Chinese language and of
the Oriental character, which helped to make of him
England's most trusty and able servant in the Far-East
for a period of 43 years, that is, until his death as British
Minister to the Court of Peking, in 1885. Beginning
as interpreter to Sir Henry Pottinger during the first
China War of 1842, he occupied in turn most of the
Chinese consular posts, notably that of Canton, where he
was appointed Commissioner during the occupation of
the city by the British troops. He was also instrumental
in negotiating a treaty with Siam. But the most romantic
episode of his life was his capture by the Chinese during
the war of 1860, when, together with a few companions
who had been sent by Sir Hope Grant to parley with
Prince Tsai, the Chinese Emperor's nephew, he was
treacherously seized, cast into a dungeon, and put to
the torture. Most of his companions perished of agony;
but Sir Harry survived, and in 1865 he was appointed
Minister Plenipotentiary and Envoy Extraordinary to the
Court of Yedo, which post he continued to hold till 1883,
when he was promoted to Peking. His career in Japan
coincided with the most stirring years of modern Japanese
history. He even helped to mould that history. When,
at the beginning of the civil war of 1868, all his diplomatic
colleagues were inclined to support the Shōgun, Sir Harry,
better informed than they as to the historical rights of the
Mikado and the growing national feeling in favour of
supporting those rights, threw the whole weight of British
influence into the loyal side against the rebels.

Sir Harry was always a staunch supporter of his country's commercial interests, and a believer in the "gunboat policy" of his master, Lord Palmerston. His outspoken threats and occasional fits of passion earned for him the dread and dislike of the Japanese during his sojourn in Japan. But no sooner had he quitted Tōkyō than they began to acknowledge that his high-handed policy had been founded in reason. On his death soon after, a long telegram of condolence was sent to London by Count Inoue, then Minister for Foreign Affairs, saying: "His Imperial Majesty's Government cannot but feel great grief at the death of one who has contributed so much to the improvement and progress of this country, and whose long residence has won so many friends among Japanese officials." The respect felt for his talents was more pithily, if less diplomatically, expressed by a high Japanese official who said to a friend of the present writer: "Sir Harry Parkes was the only foreigner in Japan whom we could not twist round our little finger."

*Book recommended. Mr. Demetrius Boulger is said to have been entrusted with the task of preparing a biography of Sir Harry Parkes; but none has yet appeared, so far as we are aware.*

**Perry (Commodore).** Matthew Calbraith Perry, Commodore in the United States Navy, was born at Newport, Rhode Island, in the year 1794, and died at New York in 1858. In the naval circles of his day, Perry's name was well-known as that of an upright and energetic officer; but his title to lasting fame rests on his having been the man who opened Japan to the world. Various attempts, American and other, had been previously made in order to attain an end so desirable on commercial grounds, so necessary for the protection of shipwrecked mariners. Liberalism,

too, was then in the air. Unrestricted international
intercourse was at that time regarded by all Christian
nations as an indisputable right, a sacred duty. Americans
could with some good grace, or at least without breach of
logic, insist on the door of Eastern Asia being flung open
to them; for they had not yet begun to barricade themselves behind a Chinese wall of exclusiveness.

In July, 1853, Commodore Perry's fleet anchored off
Uraga, a port distant one day's journey from Yedo. Setting
aside all the obstacles which Japanese astuteness sought to
place in his way, Perry delivered to the representatives
of the Shōgun the letter of President Fillimore demanding
the establishment of international relations. Then he
steamed away to Loochoo and China. Next spring he
returned for an answer. The answer took the shape of
Japan's first foreign treaty, which was signed at Kanagawa
on the 31st March, 1854. By this treaty the ports of
Shimoda and Hakodate were opened to American trade,
and good treatment promised to shipwrecked American
mariners. Such were the first-fruits of the triumph over
Japan's stubborn refusal to recognise the existence of
the outside world. Treaties with the other nations of
Christendom, and a revolution which, after plunging Japan
into confusion and bloodshed, has regenerated on Western
lines all her institutions, ideas, and aims—this, which it
takes so few words to say, but which implies so much, is
the result of what Perry was instrumental in doing. Many
things precious to the lover of art and antiquity perished in
the process. For Old Japan was like an oyster :—to open
it was to kill it.

Perry being thus a hero, fancy and myth have already
begun to gather round his name. Patriotic writers have

discoursed on "the moral grandeur of his peaceful triumph," and have even gone so far as to try to get people
to believe that the Japanese are proud of having been made
to knuckle under to him. Perry's was a peaceful triumph
only in a catachrestical sense, analogous to that of Napoleon's maxim that "Providence is on the side of the big
battalions." To speak plainly, Perry triumphed by fright-
ening the weak, ignorant, utterly unprepared, and insuf-
ficiently armed Japanese out of their senses. If he did
not use his cannon, it was only because his preparations
for using them and his threats of using them were too
evidently genuine to be safely disregarded by those who
lay at his mercy. His own "Narrative" is explicit on this
point. Nor shall we, at least, blame him. Perry was a
naval officer, and he acted with the vigour of a naval officer,
carrying out the orders of his superiors, and at the same
time bringing to bear on the situation the tact of a born
diplomatist. The event shows that the "gunboat policy,"
so often decried by well-meaning but misinformed persons,
is really and truly a policy well-suited to certain times and
places—to circumstances in which all other methods of
action are liable to be interpreted to mean weakness.
Might is right in many cases. The gunboat policy is the
only one which is understood by a semi-civilised Oriental
power, such as Japan then was and remained for several
years after. We therefore give Perry all honour. As for
the sentimental gloss which has been laid over his actions,
few will probably be found to pay any heed to it.

Books recommended. "Narrative of the Expedition of an American Squadron under Commodore Perry," by Perry and Hawks, Vol. I.—"Matthew Calbraith
Perry," by Rev. W. E. Griffis.

**Philosophy.** The Japanese have never had a philosophy

of their own.   Formerly they bowed down before the shrine
of Confucius.   They now bow down before the shrine of
Herbert Spencer.

**Pidjin-Japanese.**   In China, where the native language
is very difficult to pick up, and the natives themselves have
a decided talent for learning foreign tongues, the speech of
the most numerous body of foreigners—the English—has
come to be the medium of intercourse.   It is not pure
English, but English in that modified form known as
" Pidjin-English."   In Japan, where the conditions are reversed, we have " Pidjin-Japanese " as the *patois* in which
new-comers soon learn to make known their wants to
coolies and tea-house girls, and serving even as the
vehicle for grave commercial transactions at the open ports.
An old Yokohama resident, who modestly hid his name
under the alias of " the Bishop of Homoco," made up a
most entertaining little book on this subject a few years
ago, entitling it " Exercises in the Yokohama Dialect."
But its humour cannot be fully appreciated except by those
to whom real Japanese is familiar.

In the dialect under consideration, a "lawyer" is called
*consul-bobbery-skto,* a "dentist" is *ha-daikusan,* a "lighthouse" is *fune-haiken-sarampan-nai-rōsoku,* a "marine
insurance surveyor" is *sarampan-fune-haiken-danna-san,*
and so on.   We wish it were possible for us to give the
Pidjin-English version of the Lord's prayer, beginning
*Ototlsan nikai arimas;* but reverence forbids.

**Poetry.**   Japanese poetry is more interesting than Japanese prose, for the reason that it is more original, less

---

* " Pidjin " is believed to be a corruption of the word " business."

permeated by adventitious Chinese elements.  Chinese poetry has rhyme, parallelism, and an intricate arrangement
of words according to their "tones."  Of all this, the Japanese know nothing.  From the dawn of history to the present
day, Japanese verse has simply consisted of alternate lines
of five and seven syllables, with generally an additional line
of seven syllables at the end.  Occasionally a Japanese
poem will be half a page or a page in length.  But the immense majority are tiny odes of thirty-one syllables, the
lines being arranged thus : 5,7,5,7,7.  The first three lines
of such an ode, or *uta*, is called the *kami no ku*, or "upper
hemistich;" the second is the *shimo no ku*, or "lower hemistich."  A slight pause is always made between the two
in reciting.  Thus :

| (5) | Hototogisu |
| (7) | Nakitsuru kata wo |
| (5) | Nagamureba— |
| (7) | Tada ari-ake no |
| (7) | Tsuki zo nokoreru.[b] |

That is, literally rendered,

"When I gaze towards the place where the cuckoo has
been singing—nought remains but the moon in the early
dawn."

The chief subjects of the Japanese muse are the flowers,
the birds, the snow, the moon, the falling leaves in autumn,
love—of course—the shortness of life.  Many Japanese
odes are mere exclamations—words outlining a picture for

* Some critic, very wise in everything but Japanese, will perhaps say that the first
and fifth and the second and fourth lines of this little poem do rhyme together, after
all.  We would remind him that rhyme is an intentional likeness of sounds, not
an accidental likeness, and that such accidental concurrences are not to be prevented
in a language which, like Japanese, has but six finals, namely, the five vowels a, e, i,
o, u, and the consonant n.  No rhyme is perceived in any such cases by the Japanese
themselves.

the imagination, not making any assertion for the logical
intellect.  Take, for instance, the following, written by an
anonymous poet a thousand years ago :

> *Shira-kumo ni*
> *Hane uchi-kawashi*
> *Tobu kari no—*
> *Kazu sae miyuru*
> *Aki no yo no tsuki !*

That is,

" The moon on an autumn night, making visible the
very number of the wild-geese flying past with wings inter-
crossed in the white clouds."—Such a manner of expression
may seem strange at first ; but its charm grows upon one.

With the doubtful exception of the *Nô*, or Classical
Dramas, all the genuine poetry of Japan is lyrical.  The
Japanese have also burlesque or comic stanzas.  Even their
serious poetry admits of plays upon words, and of another
ornament named " pillow-words " (*makura-kotoba*).  These
are words devoid of meaning themselves, but serving as
props for other significant words to rest on.  Acrostics,
anagrams, and palindromes are well-known to the Japanese,
all such conceits having come in early in the Middle Ages.
To about the end of the ninth century may be traced the
institution of the poetical tournaments known as *uta-
awase*.  A favourite game at these tournaments called
*renga*, wherein one person composes the second hemistich
of a verse and another person has to provide it with a first
hemistich, seems to date from the eleventh century.  The
*hokku*, an ultra-lilliputian kind of poem having but seventeen syllables (5, 7, 5), is of more modern origin.

The twin stars of early Japanese poetry are Hitomaro
and Akahito, both of whom loved and sang during the

opening years of the eighth century. Perhaps the most illustrious next to them—illustrious not only in verse, but in prose—is Tsurayuki, a great noble of about the year 930, after which time the decline of Japanese poetry set in. There are many other well-known poets, and also poetesses. But the Japanese consider poetry more as the production of an epoch than of an individual. They do not, as a rule, publish separately the works of any special author, as we publish Chaucer, Spenser, and the rest. They publish anthologies of all the poetical works of an era. The *Man-yōshū*, or "Collection of a Myriad Leaves," was the first of these anthologies, and is therefore the most highly prized. It was compiled in the eighth century. The moderns have devoted a whole mountain of commentary to the elucidation of its obscurities. The *Kokinshū*, or "Songs Ancient and Modern," collected by Tsurayuki and including many of his own compositions, dates from the tenth century, a period whose style has remained the model which every later poet has striven to imitate. Other collections—all made by Imperial order—followed in the eleventh, twelfth, thirteenth, fourteenth, and fifteenth centuries. These, together with the "Songs Ancient and Modern," are known under the general name of the "Anthologies of the One-and-Twenty Reigns" (*Ni-jū-ichi Dai-shū*).

Until the time of the revolution of 1868, it was considered one of the essential accomplishments of a Japanese gentleman to be able to write verses. This was not so difficult as might be imagined; for nothing was then less honoured than originality. On the contrary, the old ideas had to be expressed in the old words, over and over again, plagiarism being held to be no crime, but rather a proof of wide read-

ing and a retentive memory: Japanese gentlemen also
composed Chinese verses, much as our school-boys compose Latin verses. As for the common people, they had,
and still have, songs of their own, conforming as far
as possible to classical models, but much mixed with
colloquialisms, and accordingly despised by all well-bred
persons. During the last ten years, young Japan, eager
for new worlds to conquer, has begun to turn its attention
to English versification. That the results still leave something to desire, will be gathered from the following specimen, entitled "Her Glee," which appeared in September,
1886, in the pages of a magazine in the English language
published by certain Japanese students at Tōkyō. So far
as we apprehend its obscurities through the mist of poetic
license, it would appear to be a dithyramb in praise of
woman, who is apostrophised as the cement of society, or,
to use the youthful poet's own words, " social glue."

### HER GLEE.

The purest flame, the hottest heat
  Is Woman's Power ever earth ;
Which mighty black and pale down beat,
  And made the Eden, place of birth.

Of what? of what? can thou tell me?
  A birth of Noble, High, value—
The station He destined for thee—
  Of woman, Mother, Social Glue.

Let her be moved from earth, to try.
  What dark mist overhelms human Race !
Let Lady claim with all the cry :—
  " Can you still hold and hold your peace ? "

How sweet, how mirthful, gay is Name!
What boon, thing, may exceed in kind?
Would She be praised, entolled—not Shame:
Tie Pale, of Both, to bound, to bind.

**Books recommended.** "The Classical Poetry of the Japanese."—"*Anthologie Japonaise*," by Léon de Rosny.—"*Altjapanische Frühlingslieder*," by K. Lange.—Also Aston's "Grammar of the Japanese Written Language," p. 197, *et seq.*, for details concerning prosody, and Chamberlain's "Handbook of Colloquial Japanese" for remarks on the more modern, popular poetry of Japan.—For the Nō or Lyric Dramas, see Article "THEATRE" of the present work.

**Porcelain and Pottery.** * At the end of the sixteenth
century after Christ, the Korean polity and civilisation
were ruthlessly overthrown by Japanese invaders. The
Korean art of porcelain-making then crossed the water. All
Japan's chief potteries date from that time, her teachers
being Korean captives. What had gone before was but preparatory—such things, we mean, as the coarse clay vessels
attributed to the eighth century saint, Gyōgi Bosatsu, the
black and chocolate-coloured tea-jars of Seto, which date
from the thirteenth century, and Shonzui's imitations of
Chinese blue porcelain, which date from the first half of the
sixteenth century. These early efforts may greatly interest
the antiquary; and the association of some of them with
the celebrated "tea ceremonies" (*cha-no-yu*) gives them a
*succès d' estime* in the eyes of native collectors. But they
are not art properly so-called. Japanese keramic art dates,
roughly speaking, from the year 1600. It reached its
zenith, also roughly speaking, between the years 1750 and
1830.

The chief styles of wares are Hizen, Kyōto, Satsuma,

* This article, as stated in the Preface, is from the pen of Captain Brinkley, R. A.,
the most learned authority on the subject. But the first paragraph and the paragraph
on pp. xli-), beginning "...which they were," have been added by the present writer

Kutani, Owari, Bizen, Takatori, Banko, Izumo, and Yatsu-shiro. Of these the most important is the ware of Hizen. It includes three principal varieties: (1) the Enamelled Porcelain of Arita, the "old Japan" of European collectors ; (2) the Enamelled Porcelain of Nabeshima ; and (3) the Blue and White, or Plain White, Porcelain of Hirado.

The earliest manufacture of porcelain proper in Hizen—and also in Japan, if we except the tentative and temporary productions of Shonzui Gorodayu—began in the closing years of the sixteenth century. The decoration was confined to blue under the glaze, and the ware offered no features of special merit. Not until the year 1620, do we find any evidence of the style for which Arita porcelain afterwards became famous, namely, decoration with vitri-fiable enamels. The first efforts in this direction were comparatively crude ; but before the middle of the seven-teenth century, two experts—Goroshichi and Kakiemon—carried the art to a point of considerable excellence. From that time forward the Arita factories turned out large quantities of porcelain profusely decorated with blue under the glaze and coloured enamels over it. Many pieces were exported by the Dutch, and some also specially manufactur-ed to their order for that purpose. Specimens of the latter are still preserved in European collections, where they are classed as genuine examples of Japanese keramic art, though beyond question their style of decoration was greatly influenced by Dutch interference. The porcelains of Arita were carried to the neighbouring town of Imari for sale and shipment. Hence the ware came to be known to Japanese and foreigners alike as *Imari-yaki* (*yaki*=any-thing baked; hence, "ware").

The Nabeshima porcelain—so called because of its

production at private factories under the special patronage of Nabeshima Naoshige, feudal chief of Hizen—was produced at Okawachi-yama. It differed from *Imari-yaki* in the milky whiteness and softness of its glaze, the comparative sparseness of its enamelled decoration, and the relegation of blue *sous couverte* to an entirely secondary place. This is undoubtedly the finest jewelled porcelain in Japan: the best examples leave nothing to be desired. The factory's period of excellence began about the year 1680, and culminated at the close of the eighteenth century.

The Hirado porcelain—so called because it enjoyed the special patronage of Matsura, feudal chief of Hirado—was produced at Mikawa-uchi-yama, but did not attain excellence until the middle of the eighteenth century, from which time until about 1830 specimens of rare beauty were produced. They were decorated with blue under the glaze, but some were pure white with exquisitely chiselled decorations incised or in relief. The production was always scanty, and, owing to official prohibitions, the ware did not find its way into the market.

The history of Kyōto ware—which, being for the most part faience, belongs to an entirely different category from the Hizen porcelains spoken of above—is the history of individual keramists rather than of special manufactures. Speaking broadly, however, four different varieties are usually distinguished. They are *Raku-yaki*, *Awata-yaki*, *Iwakura-yaki*, and *Kiyomizu-yaki*.

*Raku-yaki* is essentially the domestic faience of Japan; for, being entirely hand-made and fired at a very low temperature, its manufacture offers few difficulties, and has consequently been carried on by amateurs in their own

homes at various places thoughout the country. The
*Raku-yaki* of Kyōto is the parent of all the rest. It was
first produced by a Korean who emigrated to Japan in the
early part of the sixteenth century. But the term *Raku-
yaki* did not come into use until the close of the century
when Chōjiro (artistic name,* Chōryu) received from Hideyoshi (the Taikō) a seal bearing the ideograph *raku*, with
which he thenceforth stamped his productions. Thirteen
generations of the same family carried on the work, each using a stamp with the same ideograph, its caligraphy, however, differing sufficiently to be identified by connoisseurs.
The faience is thick and clumsy, having soft, brittle, and
very light *pâte*. The staple type has black glaze showing
little lustre, and in choice varieties this is curiously speck-
led and pitted with red. Salmon-coloured, red, yellow, and
white glazes are also found, and in late specimens gilding
was added. The *Raku* faience owed much of its popularity
to the patronage of the "tea clubs." The nature of its
paste and glaze adapted it for the infusion of powdered tea,
and its homely character suited the austere canons of the
" tea ceremonies."

*Awata-yaki* is the best-known among the keramic productions of Kyōto. There is evidence to show that the art
of decoration with enamels over the glaze reached Kyōto
from Hizen in the middle of the seventeenth century. Just
at that time there flourished in the Western capital a
potter of remarkable ability, called Nomura Seisuke. He
immediately utilised the new method, and produced many
beautiful examples of jewelled faience, having close, hard
*pâte*, yellowish white or brownish white glaze covered
with a network of fine crackle, and sparse decoration in

pure full-bodied colours—red, green, gold, and silver. He
worked chiefly at Awata, and thus brought that factory
into prominence. Nomura Seisuke, or Ninsei, as he is
commonly called, was one of Japan's greatest keramists.
Genuine examples of his faience have always been highly
prised, and numerous imitations were subsequently produced, all stamped with the ideographs *Ninsei*. After Ninsei's
time the most renowned keramists of the Awata factories
were Kenzan (1688-1740); Ebisei, a comtemporary of
Kenzan; Dohachi (1751-1763), who subsequently moved to
Kiyomizu-zaka, another part of Kyōto, the faience of which
constitutes the *Kiyomizu-yaki* mentioned above; Kinkozan
(1745-1760); Hozan (1690-1721); Taizan (1760-1800);
Bizan (1810-1838); and Tanzan who is now living. It
must be noted that several of these names, as Kenzan,
Dohachi, Kinkozan, Hozan and Taizan, were not limited to
one artist. They are family names, and though the dates
we have given indicate the eras of the most noted keramists
in each family, amateurs must not draw any chronological
conclusion from the mere fact that a specimen bears such
and such a name.

The origin of the *Iwakura-yaki* is somewhat obscure,
and its history, at an early date, becomes confused with
that of the *Awata-yaki*, from which, indeed, it does not
materially differ. To separate the two and describe their
slight distinctions, would carry us beyond the limits of the
space at our disposal.

In the term *Kiyomizu-yaki* may be included roughly all
the aience of Kiyōto, with the exception of the three varieties described above. The distinction between Kiyomizu,
Awata, and Iwakura is primarily local. They are parts of
the same city, and if their names have been used to de-

signate particular classes of pottery, it is not because the
technical or decorative features of each class distinguish it
from the other two, but chiefly for the purpose of identify-
ing the place of production.  On the slopes called Kiyomizu-
zaka and Gojō-zaka lived a number of keramists, all following virtually the same models with variations due to
individual genius.  The principal Kiyomizu artists were :—
Ebisei, who moved from Awata to Gojō-zaka in 1688;
Eisen and Rokubei, pupils of Ebisei ; Mokubei, also a pupil
of Eisen, but more celebrated than his master; Shuhei
(1790-1810), Kentei (1782-1820), and Zengoro Hozen,
generally known as Eiraku (1790-1850).  Eisen was the
first to manufacture porcelain (as distinguished from faïence) in Kyōto, and this branch of the art was carried to a
high standard of excellence by Eiraku, whose speciality
was a rich coral-red glaze with finely executed decoration
in gold.  The latter keramist also excelled in the production of purple, green, and yellow glazes, which he combined
with admirable skill and taste.  Some choice ware of the
latter type was manufactured by him in Kishū, by order of
the feudal chief of that province.  It is known as *Kairaku-
yen-yaki*, or "ware of the Kairaku park."

The principal potters of Kyōto at present are Seifu Yohei,
Tanzan, Taizan, Dōhachi, and Okamura Yasutarō.  Tanzan's *pâte sur pâte* decoration is the most remarkable thing
of his kind ever manufactured in Japan, but it is not pure
Japanese art.  Seifu's forte lies in reproducing the masterpieces of former times.  In this line nothing seems to baffle
him.  Spotted *céladon*, coral-red monochromes, jewelled
porcelain, everything in fact, lies within the compass of his
skill.  Taizan's work represents the genuine school of
Kyōto faience—beautifully manipulated ware, having yel-

lowish white finely crackled glaze, and elaborate decoration in green, red, yellow, blue, purple, and gold.

No phrase is commoner in the mouths of Western collectors than "old Satsuma;" no ware is rarer in Western collections. Nine hundred and ninety-nine pieces out of every thousand that do duty as genuine examples of this prince of faiences, are simply examples of the skill of modern forgers. In point of fact, the production of faience decorated with gold and coloured enamels may be said to have commenced at the beginning of the present century in Satsuma. Some writers maintain that it did actually commence then, and that nothing of the kind existed there before. Setting aside, however, the strong improbability that a style of decoration so widely practised and so highly esteemed could have remained unknown during a century and a half to experts working for one of the most puissant chieftains in Japan, we have the evidence of trustworthy traditions and written records that enamelled faience was made by the potters at Tatsumonji—the principal factory of Satsuma ware in early days—as far back as the year 1676. Mitsuhisa, then feudal lord of Satsuma, was a munificent patron of art. He summoned to his fief the painter Tangen—a pupil of the renowned Tan-yū, who died in 1674— and employed him to paint faience or to furnish designs for the keramists of Tatsumonji. The ware produced under these circumstances received, and is still known by, the name of Satsuma Tangen. But the number of specimens was small. Destined chiefly for private use or for presents, their decoration was delicate rather than rich, the colour chiefly employed being brown or reddish brown under the glaze, and the decoration over the glaze being sparse and chaste. Not until the close of the eighteenth century

did the more profuse fashion of enamelled decoration come
to be largely employed. It was introduced by two potters
who visited Kyôto, and there observed the ornate methods
so well illustrated in the wares of Awata and Kiyomizu.
At the same time, a strong impetus was given to the production of faience at Tadeno—then the chief factory in
Satsuma—owing to the patronage of Shimazu Tamanobu,
lord of the province. To this increase in production and
to the more elaborate application of vitrifiable enamels
may be attributed the erroneous idea that Satsuma faience
decorated with gold and coloured enamels had its origin
at the close of the eighteenth century. For all the purposes of the ordinary collector it may be said to have
commenced then, and to have flourished only for a single
life-time, since it practically came to an end about 1860;
but for the purposes of the historian we must look farther
back.          .

The keramic art in Satsuma owed much to the aid of a
number of Korean experts who settled there after the return
of the Japanese forces from Korea. One of these men,
Boku Heii, discovered (in 1603) clay fitted for the manufacture of white *craquelé* faience. This was the subsequently celebrated *Satsuma-yaki*. But in Boku's time and
indeed as long as the factories flourished, many other kinds
of faience were produced, the principal having rich black or
*flambé* glazes, while a few were green or yellow monochromes. One curious variety, called *Same-yaki*, had glaze
chagrined like the skin of a shark (in Japanese, *same*).
Most of the finest pieces of enamelled faience were the
work of artists at the Tadeno factory, while the best
specimens of other kinds were by the artists of Tatsumonji.

*Artists* they were—not manufacturers—and not only

artists, but clansmen faithful to their feudal chief. By him
they were fed; for him and for the love of their art they
worked. Pieces were made for special occasions—for presents, say, from their lord to the Shōgun at Yedo, or for
the trousseau of their lord's daughter. Time was no object.
There was no public of mediocre tastes to cater for. Nothing was made, as the vulgar phrase is, for the million.
The art was perfectly and essentially aristocratic. Hence
its distinction, the delicacy of its drawing, the subdued
harmony of its colouring. It is a mere piece of amiable
optimism to suppose it possible that such a tradition can
be kept up in the days which have produced that frightful
but aptly descriptive term, "art *manufacture*." What
we have here said of the aristocratic nature of the art of
Satsuma applies in a considerable measure to the other
schools. Indeed it is, generally speaking, true of Japanese
art in all its branches. The painter, the lacquer, the
worker in metal—all had in view the personal requirements
of a small and highly cultivated class of nobles. Money-
making was never their aim, nor were their minds dis-
tracted by the knowledge of the existence of numerous
styles besides their own.

The porcelain of Kutani is among those best-known to
Western collectors, though good specimens of the old ware
have always been scarce. Its manufacture dates from the
close of the seventeenth century, when the feudal chief of
Kaga took the industry under his patronage. There were
two principal varieties of the ware: *Ao-Kutani*, so called
because of a green (*ao*) enamel of great brilliancy and
beauty which was largely used in its decoration, and Kutani
with painted and enamelled *pâte* varying from hard porcelain to pottery. Many of the pieces are distinguished by

a peculiar creamy whiteness of glaze, suggesting the idea
that they were intended to imitate the soft-paste wares of
China. The enamels are used to delineate decorative subjects and are applied in masses, the principal colours being
green, yellow, purple, and soft Prussian blue, all brilliant
and transparent, with the exception of the last which is
nearly opaque. In many cases we find large portions of
the surface completely covered with green or yellow enamel
overlying black diapers or scroll patterns. The second
variety of Kutani ware may often be mistaken for "old
Japan" (i.e., Imari porcelain). The most characteristic examples of it are distinguishable, however, by the prepon-
derating presence of a peculiar russet red, differing essentially from the full-bodied and comparatively brilliant colour
of the Arita pottery. Moreover, the workmen of Kaga did
not follow the Arita precedent of massing blue under the
glaze. In the great majority of cases they did not use blue
at all in this position, and when they did, its *rôle* was essentially subordinate. They also employed silver freely
for decorative purposes, whereas we rarely find it thus
used on "old Japan" porcelain. Owing to various causes,
the manufacture of Kutani porcelain was discontinued
about the year 1750, and not revived for some thirty
years. The early wares of the second period of industry
followed the Arita fashions much more closely than any of
their predecessors. The beautiful *Ao-Kutani* was not
produced at all, the potters being doubtless deterred by the
difficulty of preparing and applying the rich transparent
enamels to which it owed its excellence. Not until 1843
did this characteristic variety re-appear, nor could it then
support comparison with choice specimens of the early
manufacture. Many examples of this second period of

*Ao-Kutani* are faience irregularly crackled, and having a peculiar, waxy, ivory-white glaze, easily distinguishable from anything previously produced. It is probable that numerous examples of this later ware have passed into the hands of Western collectors as "old Kutani."

About the time (1843) of the *Ao-Kutani* revival, a potter called Iida Hachiroemon introduced a style of decoration which subsequently came to be regarded as typical of all Kaga porcelains. Taking the Eiraku porcelains of Kyōto as models, Hachiroemon employed red grounds with designs traced on them in gold. The style was not absolutely new in Kaga. We find similar decoration on old and choice examples of *Kutani-yaki*. But the character of the old red differs essentially from that of the modern manufacture—the former being a soft, subdued colour, more like a bloom than an enamel, the latter a glossy and comparatively crude pigment. In Hachiroemon's time and during the twenty years following the date of his innovation, many beautiful examples of elaborately decorated Kutani porcelain were produced. The richness, profusion, and microscopic accuracy of their decoration could scarcely have been surpassed; but with very rare exceptions, their lack of delicacy of technique disqualifies them to rank as fine porcelains.

From 1863 to 1869 the manufacture of Kutani porcelain was again discontinued. At the latter date it was revived, expressly with a view to the demand of the foreign market. It was then that the porcelain so well-known in Europe and America as "Kaga ware" made its appearance. The technique mediocre, the decoration a profusion of designs of the red-and-gold type, it served chiefly for the manufacture of tea and coffee, dinner and dessert, services,

or big flashy vases.  The decoration is often of a high
character—miniature painting which for delicacy and accuracy leaves little to be desired.  But the perpetual glitter
of gilding and massing of red pigment pall upon the least
fastidious taste, and have never received the endorsemen·
of Japanese household use.  The potters themselves, apt
preciating the inevitable consequences of this monotony,
are now making resolute efforts to revive the incomparably
richer and more varied methods of the old *Ao-Kutani.*
Their work thus far gives earnest of ultimate success.

The province of Owari, or Bishū, though it stands at
the head of the keramic districts of modern Japan, cannot
claim great distinction for its ancient wares.  In the judgment of the Japanese tea clubs, however, this verdict would
not be admitted.  For it was at the little village of Seto,
some five miles from Nagoya, the chief town of Owari,
that the celebrated Katō Shirozaemon set up his kiln, about
the year 1230, and inaugurated the manufacture of the first
Japanese faience worthy to be considered a technical success.  Shirozaemon had spent some six years in China
studying keramic processes, and after his return he settled
at Seto, there producing dainty little tea-jars, ewers, and
other *cha-no-yu* utensils.  These, being no longer stoved
in an inverted position, as had been the habit before Shirozaemon's time, were not disfigured by the bare, blistered
lips of their predecessors.  Their *pâte* was close and
well-manufactured pottery, varying in colour from dark
brown to russet, and covered with thick, lustrous glazes,
black, amber-brown, chocolate, and yellowish gray.  These
glazes were not monochromatic : they showed differences
of tint, and sometimes marked varieties of colour, as
when chocolate brown passed into amber, or black

was relieved by streaks and clouds of grey and dead-leaf red. This ware came to be known as *Tōshiro-yaki*, a term obtained by combining the second syllable of "Katō" with the two first of "Shirozaemon." It obtained a wide vogue, and a genuine example of it is at present worth many times its weight in gold to Japanese dilettanti, though in foreign eyes it is little more than interesting. Shiro-zaemon was succeeded at the kiln by three generations of his family, each representative retaining the name of Tōshiro, and each distinguishing himself by the excellence of his work. Thenceforth Seto became the head-quarters of the manufacture of *cha-no-yu* utensils, and many of the tiny pieces turned out there deserve high admiration, their technique being perfect, and their mahogany, russet-brown, amber, and buff glazes showing wonderful lustre and rich-ness. Seto, in fact, acquired such a wide-spread reputation for its keramic productions, that the term "*seto-mono*" (literally, "Seto article") came to be used generically for all pottery and porcelain, just as "China" is in the West.

Seto has now ceased to be a pottery-producing centre, and has become the chief porcelain manufactory of Japan. The porcelain industry was inaugurated in 1807 by Tami-kichi, a local keramist, who had visited Hizen and spent three years there studying the necessary processes. Owari abounds in porcelain stone; but it does not occur in constant or particularly simple forms, and as the potters have not yet learned to treat their materials scientifically, their work is often marred by unforeseen difficulties. For many years after Tamikichi's processes had begun to be practised, the only decoration employed was blue under the glaze. Sometimes Chinese cobalt was used, sometimes Japanese, and sometimes a mixture of both. To Kawamoto

Hansuke, who flourished about 1830-1845, belongs the credit of having turned out the richest and most attractive ware of this class. But speaking generally, Japanese blues do · not rank on the same decorative level with those of China. At Arita, although pieces were occasionally turned out of which the colour could not be surpassed in purity and brilliancy, the general character of the blue *sous couverte* was either thin or dull. At Hirado, the keramists affected a lighter and more delicate tone than that of the Chinese, and, in order to obtain it, subjected the choice pigment of the Middle Kingdom to refining processes of great severity. The Hirado blue, therefore, belongs to a special esthetic category. But at Owari the experts were content with an inferior colour, and their blue-and-white porcelains never enjoyed a distinguished reputation, though occasionally we find a specimen of great merit. At present immense quantities are produced, all alike disfigured by the shallow, hard, garish colour given by European smalt, which pigment possesses that quality so essential in this manufacturing age, cheapness. The potter using smalt can be sure that, under fairly uniform conditions of temperature, his porcelains will emerge from the kiln neither blistered nor discoloured, whereas, when he employed Chinese cobaltiferous manganese, ninety per cent of his vases might be total failures. Of late years, the Owari decorators have added green and red to their palette for *sous couverte* painting, but they do not seem to have gained much by the innovation.

Decoration with vitrifiable enamels over the glaze, though it began to be practised at Owari about the year 1840, never became a speciality of the place. Nowadays, indeed, numerous examples of porcelains decorated in this

manner are classed among Owari products. But they
receive their decoration, almost without exception, in
Tōkyō or Yokohama, where a large number of artists,
called *e-tsuke-shi*, devote themselves entirely to porcelain-
painting. These men seldom use vitrifiable enamels,
pigments being much more tractable and less costly. The
dominant feature of the designs is pictorial. They are
frankly adapted to Western taste. Indeed, of the porcelain
it may be said that, from the monster pieces of blue-and-
white manufactured at Seto—vases six feet high and
garden pillar-lamps half as tall again do not dismay the
Bishū keramist—to tiny coffee-cups decorated in Tōkyō,
with their delicate miniatures of birds, flowers, insects,
fishes, and so forth, there is nothing that does not indicate
the death of the old æstheticism. Seto and the Tōkyō
*ateliers* constitute the Stoke-upon-Trent of Japan. Moreover, to such a depth of debasement had the keramic art
fallen in Owari, that before the happy renaissance of the
past three years, Nagoya discredited itself by employing
porcelain as a base for *cloisonné* enamelling. Many products of this vitiated industry found their way into the
collections of foreigners, disgracing Occidental taste and
parodying Japanese art.

In the pottery of Bizen are to be found the choicest
masterpieces of Japanese plastic skill. Pottery was produced
at several hamlets in Bizen as far back as the fourteenth
century, but ware worthy of artistic notice did not make
its appearance until the close of the sixteenth century,
when the Taikō himself paid a visit to the factory at Imbe.
Thenceforth utensils for the use of the tea clubs began to
be manufactured. This *Bizen-yaki* was red stone-ware,
with thin diaphanous glaze. Made of exceedingly refractory

clay, it underwent stoving for more than three weeks, and
was consequently remarkable for its hardness and metallic
timbre. Some fifty years later, the character of the
choicest *Bisen-yaki* underwent a marked change. It became slate-coloured or bluish brown faience, with *pâte* as
fine as pipe-clay, but very hard. In the *Ao-Bisen* (blue
Bisen), as well as in the red variety, figures of mythical
beings and animals, birds, fishes, and other natural objects,
were modelled with a degree of plastic ability that can
scarcely be spoken of in too high terms. Representative
specimens are truly admirable—every line, every contour
faithful. The production was very limited, and good pieces
soon ceased to be procurable except at long intervals
and heavy expense. The *Bisen-yaki* familiar to Western
collectors is comparatively coarse brown or reddish brown
stone-ware, modelled rudely, though sometimes redeemed
by touches of the genius never entirely absent from the
work of the Japanese artisan-artist. Easy to be confounded
with it is another ware of the same type manufactured at
Shidoro in the province of Tōtōmi.

The Japanese potters could never vie with the Chinese
in the production of glazes: the wonderful monochromes
and polychromes of the Middle Kingdom had no peers
anywhere. In Japan they were most closely approached
by the faience of Takatori in the province of Chikuzen. In
its early days the keramic industry of this province owed
something to the assistance of Korean experts who settled
there after the expedition of 1592. But its chief development took place under the direction of Igarashi Jizaemon,
an amateur keramist, who, happening to visit Chikuzen about the year 1620, was taken under the protection of the chief of the fief and munificently treated.

Taking the renowned *Yao-pien-yao*, or "transmutation ware," of China as a model, the Takatori potters endeavoured, by skilful mixing of colouring materials, to reproduce the wonderful effects of oxidisation seen in the Chinese ware. They did not, indeed, achieve their ideal, but they did succeed in producing some exquisitely lustrous glazes of the *flambé* type, rich transparent brown passing into claret colour, with flecks or streaks of white and clouds of "iron dust." The *pâte* of this faience was of the finest description, and the technique in every respect faultless. Unfortunately, the best experts confined themselves to working for the tea clubs, and consequently produced only insignificant pieces, as tea-jars, cups, and little ewers. During the eighteenth century a departure was made from these strict canons. From this period date most of the specimens best-known outside Japan—cleverly modelled figures of mythological beings and animals covered with lustrous variegated glazes, the general colours being grey or buff, with tints of green, chocolate, brown, and sometimes blue.

A ware of which considerable quantities have found their way westward of late years is the *Awaji-yaki*, so called from the island of Awaji where it is manufactured in the village of Iga. It was first produced between the years 1830 and 1840 by one Kajū Mimpei, a man of considerable private means, who devoted himself to the keramic art out of pure enthusiasm. His story is full of interest, but it must suffice here to note the results of his enterprise. Directing his efforts at first to reproducing the deep green and straw-yellow glazes of China, he had exhausted almost his entire resources before success came, and even then the public was slow to recognise the merits of his ware.

Nevertheless he persevered, and in 1838 we find him producing not only green and yellow monochromes, but also grayish white and mirror-black glazes of high excellence. So thoroughly had he now mastered the management of glazes that he could combine yellow, green, white, and claret colour in regular patches to imitate tortoise-shell. Many of his pieces have designs incised or in relief, and others are skilfully decorated with gold and silver. *Awaji-yaki*, or *Mimpei-yaki*, as it is often called, is generally porcelain, but we occasionally find specimens which may readily be mistaken for Awata faience.

Banko faience is a universal favourite with foreign collectors. The type generally known to them is exceedingly light ware, for the most part made of light gray, unglazed clay, and having hand-modelled decoration in relief. But there are numerous varieties. Chocolate or dove-coloured grounds with delicate diapers in gold and *engobe*; brown or black faience with white, yellow, and pink designs incised or in relief ; pottery curiously and deftly marbled by combinations of various coloured clays—these and many other kinds are to be found, all, however, presenting one common feature, namely, skilful finger-moulding and a slight roughening of the surface as though it had received the impression of coarse linen or crape before baking. This modern *Banko-yaki* is produced chiefly at Yokkaichi in the province of Ise. It is entirely different from the original Banko ware made in Kuwana, in the same province, by Numanami Gozaemon at the close of the eighteenth century. Gozaemon was an imitator. He took for his models the Raku faience of Kyōto, the master-pieces of Ninsei and Kenzan, the rococo wares of Korea, the enamelled porcelain of China, and the blue-and-white ware of

Delft.  He did not found a school, simply because he had nothing new to teach, and the fact that a modern ware goes by the same name as his productions is simply because his seal—the inscription on which (*Banko*, or "everlasting") suggested the name of the ware—subsequently (1830) fell into the hands of one Mori Yusetsu, who applied it to his own ware.  Mori Yusetsu, however, had more originality than Numanami.  He conceived the idea of shaping his pieces by putting the mould inside and pressing the clay with the hand into the matrix.  The consequence was that his wares received the design on the inner as well as the outer surface, and were moreover thumb-marked—essential characteristics of the *Banko-yaki* now so popular.

Among a multitude of other Japanese wares, space allows us to mention only two, those of Izumo and Yatsu-shiro.  The chief type of the former is faience, having light gray, close *pâte* and yellow or straw-coloured glaze, with or without crackle, to which is applied decoration in gold and green enamel.  Another variety has chocolate glaze, clouded with amber and flecked with gold dust.  The former faience had its origin at the close of the seventeenth century, the latter at the close of the eighteenth; but the *Izumo-yaki* now procurable is a modern production.

The *Yatsushiro* faience is a production of the province of Higo, where a number of Korean potters settled at the close of the seventeenth century.  It is the only Japanese ware in which the characteristics of a Korean original are unmistakably preserved.  Its diaphanous, pearl-gray glaze, uniform, lustrous, and finely crackled, overlying encaustic decoration in white slip, the fineness of its warm reddish *pâte*, and the general excellence of its technique, have always commanded admiration.  It is produced now in considerable quantities, but the modern ware falls far short of its predecessor.

In the province of Mino there is manufactured blue-and-white porcelain which, in respect of tenderness and lustre of glaze, delicacy of decoration, and purity of colour, is placed by some connoisseurs at the head of Japanese ware in its class. The maker is Katô Gosuke. Very beautiful ware of the same kind also comes from Aizu in the prefecture of Wakayama. Indeed, although the porcelain and faience now manufactured in Japan are generally inferior to the work of former times, it is impossible to suppose that this inferiority will be permanent when we look at the blue-and-white porcelain by Katô Gosuke of Mino and Higuchi of Hirado, the wonderful reproductions of Chinese masterpieces by Seifu of Kyôto, the *pâte-sur-pâte* faience by Tanzan of the same city, the *shadows* by Inoue Ryôsai of Tôkyô, the truly admirable monochromes by Takemoto, also of Tôkyô, and the "grains-of-rice" porcelain by Higuchi of Hirado. All these artists would have been renowned in any age, and there is every reason to hope that their efforts will yet restore to Japan the technical excellence which distinguished her productions in feudal times.

**Posts.** When Ieyasu, in A. D. 1603, brought Japan to a state of peace which lasted for two hundred and fifty years, a rude postal system spontaneously sprang up in the shape of private agencies, called *hikyaku-ya*, which under-took, for a low charge, but also at a low rate of speed, to transmit private correspondence from place to place both by land and sea. The official despatches of the Shôgunate were all sent by special government couriers, under the control of post-masters (*chiteishi*) at the various post-towns. Couriers belonging to the various clans carried the despatches of their respective *daimyōs* to and from the seat of government at Yedo.

The first approximation to a postal system modelled on that of the United States was made early in 1871, chiefly through the efforts of Mr H. Maejima, by the establishment of a government postal service along the Tōkaidō between Tōkyō, Kyōto, and Ōsaka. This was extended to the whole country, with the exception of certain parts of Yezo, in 1872. The 1 *sen* 6 *rin*, 8 *sen*, and 16 *sen* stamps of those early days have become extremely rare.

Concurrently with the Imperial Japanese post-office, American postal agencies continued to exist at the Treaty Ports until the end of 1873, and French and English agencies until the 1st April, 1879, on which date Japan was admitted into the International Postal Union with full management of all her postal affairs. Japanese letter-postage is now the cheapest in the world, because based on a silver standard which has depreciated in value. Inland letters go for 2 *sen*, that is, about two-thirds of a penny, post-cards for half that sum. The postage to China and America is 5 *sen* (less than twopence), that to all other countries of the postal union 10 *sen* (a little over threepence, though originally intended to be equivalent to fivepence).

**Praying-Wheel.** This instrument of devotion, so popular in Thibetan Buddhism, "is in Japan," say Messrs Satow and Hawes, "found only in connection with the mystic doctrine of the Tendai and Shingon sects, and its use differs slightly from that to which it is put in Thibet. No prayers are written on it; but the worshipper, attributing

to *ingwa* (the effects in this life of the actions in a former
state of existence) any sin of which he wishes to be rid,
or any desire that occurs to him, turns the wheel with the
simple request to Jizo[*] to let this *ingwa* duly run its course
—the course of *ingwa* resembling the perpetual revolutions
of a wheel." Praying-wheels (Jap. *rimbō*) are somewhat
rare in Japan. Visitors to Tōkyō will find three outside a
small shrine dedicated to the god Fudō close to the large
temple of Asakusa. They are mounted on low posts not
unlike pillar-post boxes.

The wheel which figures so frequently in Buddhist architectural design, is not the praying-wheel, but the so-called
*hōrin* (Sanskrit *dharmachakra*), or " wheel of the law," a
symbol of the doctrine of transmigration. Neither must
the praying-wheel be confounded with the " revolving
libraries " (*tenrinsō* or *rinsō*), sometimes met with in the
grounds of Buddhist temples. These " revolving libraries "
mostly contain complete or nearly complete sets of the
Buddhist canon ; and he who causes the library to revolve
lays up for himself as much merit as if he had read the
entire contents.

**Printing.** Printing reached Japan from China in the

---

* Jizō (Sansk. *Kshitigarbha*) is, say Messrs Satow and Hawes, in their "Handbook
for Japan," "the helper of those who are in trouble. Hence he is the patron of travellers,
and is frequently conceived into a sign-post. He is also a patron of pregnant women
and protector of children  His image is therefore often loaded with pebbles, which
serve in the other world to relieve the labours of infants, who are robbed of their
clothes by the Sō-dzu-baba hag (vulg. Shodzuka no baba), and then set by her to perform the endless task of piling up stones on the banks of that river [i.e., the river
Sō-dzu-kawa in the under-world]  He is usually represented with a pilgrim's staff in
one hand, and a ball, which represents wisdom, in the other."—We have given this
description of Jizō in full, because, though such a popular deity in Japan, he is little
heard of in other Buddhist lands. Need it be added that the similarity in sound
between Jizō and Jesus is purely accidental ?

wake of Buddhism. But it came somewhat later than the
other arts. The earliest example of block-printing in
Japan dates only from A. D. 770, when the Empress
Shōtoku caused a million Buddhist charms to be printed
on small slips of paper, for distribution among all the
temples of the land. Some of these ancient slips are still
in existence. The first notice of printed books occurs in
the tenth century, and the oldest specimen extant belongs
to a date falling somewhere between 1198 and 1211.

For about six hundred years after the introduction of
printing, Buddhist works—and those in scanty numbers—
seem to have been the only ones that issued from the press.
The Confucian "Analects," were first reprinted in Japan in
1364, from which time down to the end of the sixteenth
century Japanese editions of various standard Chinese
works, both in poetry and prose, were printed from time to
time. But the impulse to a more vigorous production was
given by the conquest of Korea at the end of the sixteenth
century, and by the Shōgun Iyeyasu's liberal patronage of
learning at the beginning of the seventeenth. The Japanese learnt from the vanquished Koreans the use of movable
types. These, however, went out of fashion again before
the middle of the seventeenth century, the enormous number
of types necessary for the printing of the Chinese written
character making the method practically inconvenient.

The first genuinely Japanese production to appear in
print was the *Nihongi*, or rather the first two books of the
*Nihongi*, in A. D. 1599. This work, which contains
the native mythology and early history, had been composed
as far back as A. D. 720. The collection of ancient poems
entitled *Man-yōshū*, dating from the middle of the eighth
century, was also first printed about the same time. From

that period forward, the work of putting into print the old
manuscript stores of Japanese literature went on apace,
while a new literature of commentaries, histories, poetry,
popular novels, guide-books, etc., kept the block-cutters
constantly employed. The same period saw the introduction of pictorial wood-engraving.

Since about 1870, the Japanese have adopted European
methods of type-founding. The result is that movable
types have again come to the fore, though without causing
block-printing to be entirely abandoned. All the newspapers are printed with movable types. A Japanese movable
type printing-office would be a strange sight to a European
printer. Provision has to be made for, not twenty-six characters, but ten thousand, which is approximately the number
of Chinese ideographs in common every-day use; and of
each character there must of course be different sizes — pica,
long primer, brevier, and so on. Needless to say that so
vast a number of characters cannot possibly fit in to one
small case within reach of a single man's hand and eye.
They are ranged round a large room on trays, in the order
of their radicals; and youths, supplied each with a page of
the "copy" to be set up, walk about from tray to tray,
picking out the characters required, which they put in a box
and then take to the compositor. As these youths, *more
japonico*, keep droning out all the while in a sort of chant
the text on which they are busy, the effect to the ear is as
peculiar as to the eye is the sight of the perpetual motion
of this troop of youths coming and going from case to case.

We have used the word "radicals" in the above description. For the sake of those who are unfamiliar with
Chinese writing, it must be explained that the Chinese
characters are put together, not alphabetically, but by the

combination of certain simpler forms, of which the principal
are termed "radicals." Thus 木 is the radical for "tree,"
or "wood," under which are grouped 梅 "plum-tree," 柳
"willow," 板 "a board," etc., etc. The radical for "water"
is 水, abbreviated in compounds to 氵, and under it
accordingly come 湖 "a lake," 油 "oil," 酒 "wine," 游 "to
swim," and hundreds of words having, in one way or
another, to do with fluidity. Of course Japanese printing-
offices also have to make provision for the native syllabic
characters, the so-called *Kana*. But as there are only
between two and three hundred forms of these, and as they
are generally used only for terminations and particles, they
are comparatively unimportant.

The ten thousand Chinese characters in common use are
cast in metal, according to one of the European processes.
When a rare character occurs in an author's manuscript,
it is cut in wood for the occasion. To keep on hand
types for all the seventy or eighty thousand characters of
the Chinese language would entail an expense too heavy
for even the largest printing-office to bear, and would
require too much room.

**Books recommended.** "On the Early History of Printing in Japan," in Vol.
X, Part I, and "Further Notes on Movable Types in Korea and Early Japanese
Printed Books," in Vol. X, Part II, of the "Asiatic Transactions," by Ernest Satow.
Our own remarks are chiefly founded on these two valuable essays.

**Proverbs.** Here are a few Japanese proverbs :—
Proof rather than argument.
Dumplings rather than blossoms.
· Breeding rather than birth.
Good medicine is bitter to the mouth.
A mended lid to a cracked pot. (*An assemblage of incap-
ables ; for instance, a drunken husband and an idiotic wife.*)

A cheap purchase is money lost.

A bee stinging a weeping face. (*One misfortune on the top of another.*)

Cows herd with cows, horses with horses. (*Birds of a feather flock together.*)

Not to know is to be a Buddha. (*Ignorance is bliss.*)

A man's heart and an autumn sky (are alike fickle).

Hate the priest, and you will hate his very hood.

Never trust a woman, even if she has borne you seven children.

The acolyte at the gate can read scriptures which he has never learnt.

To lose is to win.

Ten men, ten minds. (*Literally "ten men, ten bellies," the mental faculties being, according to popular belief, located in the abdomen.*)

When folly passes by, reason draws back.*

This last proverb is remarkable, as one of the few instances of personification which the language affords.

---

* Some persons may like to have the Japanese originals of these proverbs, which are given in the same order as that of the English renderings above :

Han yori shibe.

Hana yori dango.

Ushi yuri udachi.

Ryōyoku kari ni nigashi.

Warz-moby no boji-batu.

Yarz-momo-tai na toni-mkumi.

Naku tsura wo hachi ga sasu.

Ushi wa ushi-zure, uma wa uma-zure.

Shiranu ga Hotoke.

Otoko no kokoro to aki no sora.

Bōzu ga nikukereba, kesa made nikui.

Shichi-nin no ko wo nasu to mo, onna ni kokoro wo yurusu-na.

Monzen no kozō narawanu kyō wo yomu.

Makuru wa katsu.

Jū-nin tō-iro.

Mori ga tōreba, dōri hikkomu.

**Race.** There has been much strife among the learned on this question: to which race do the Japanese belong? Not scientific considerations only, but religious and other prejudices have been imported into the discussion. One pious member of the Scotch Kirk derives the Japanese from the Lost Tribes of Israel. An enthusiastic German professor, on the other hand, Dr. Wernich, takes up the cudgels to defend so charming a nation against "the reproach of Mongolism"—whatever that may be. The two greatest authorities on the subject, Baelz and Rein, say, purely and simply, that the Japanese are Mongols. We incline to follow Baelz in his hypothesis of two chief streams of immigration, both coming from Korea, and both gradually spreading eastward and northward. The first of these immigrations would have supplied the round or so-called "pudding-faced" type, common among the lower classes. The second would have supplied the aristocratic type, with its more oval outline, thinner nose, more slanting eyes, and smaller mouth—the type to which Japanese actors endeavour to conform when representing noblemen and heroes.

Be it remarked that *both* these types are Mongol. Both have the yellowish skin, the straight hair, the scanty beard, the broadish skull, the more or less oblique eyes, and the high cheek-bones, which characterise all well-established branches of the Mongol race. It is historically certain that *some* Mongols have come over and settled in Japan, namely, Koreans and Chinamen at various epochs of authentic Japanese history. Many guesses have been made concerning possible Malay immigrations from the South, by sea or *viâ* the Loochoo Islands. But there is no certain information, there are not even any legendary

traces, of such immigrations. The Ainos, who are not a
Mongol race, are indeed joint occupiers of the soil of
Japan with the Japanese, and much intermarrying has
gone on between the two peoples, and goes on still. It
has, however, been pretty well proved that this mixed
breed becomes unfruitful in the third or fourth generation—a fact which explains the scant traces of Aino blood
even in the population of the extreme north of the island. The two nations are as distinct as the whites
and the reds in North America.

*Books. "Die Körperlichen Eigenschaften der Japaner," by Dr. E. Baelz, pub-
lished in Parts 28 and 32 of the "German Asiatic Transactions."*

**Railways.** Strategical no less than business considerations have been taken into account by the Japanese government in constructing its lines of railway. The aim constantly kept in view has been to connect the two capitals,
Tōkyō and Kyōto. As a first step, work was begun on
the eighteen miles separating Tōkyō from Yokohama as
long ago as the year 1869, with the assistance of English
engineers, and the line was opened in the autumn of 1872.
Kōbe and Ōsaka were then connected, and other short pieces
followed, the inter-capital trunk line being delayed by
various causes. Japan is not naturally suited to railway
construction : the country is too mountainous, the streams—
mere beds of sand to-day—are to-morrow, after a heavy
rain, wild surging rivers that sweep away bridges and embankments. For these reasons the idea of carrying the
Tōkyō-Kyōto railway along the Nakasendō, or backbone
of the country, which would have been far better in time
of war, as being removed from the possibility of an attack
from the sea-side, fell through, the engineering difficulties

proving insuperable. The only alternative was to follow the Tōkaidō, the ancient highway of Eastern Japan, which skirts the coast along the narrow strip of flat country intervening between the foot of the hills and the Pacific Ocean. This work was completed, and the thousandth mile of railway opened, in the summer of 1889.

Japanese railway enterprise, although started by the government, is no longer exclusively in official hands. There are numerous companies—some private, others more or less under government shelter and patronage. Such, for instance, is the *Nippon Tetsudō Kwaisha* ("Japan Railway Company"), which owns the main line running north.

Reduced to its simplest expression, the Japanese railway system, when completed, will practically consist of one long trunk line from Aomori in the extreme north to Shimono-seki in the south-west, together with two large branches connecting each capital with the fruitful provinces of the west coast, minor branches to various points in the two metropolitan districts, and local lines in the island of Kyūshū, Shikoku, and Yeso.

Notwithstanding the natural obstacles to be overcome and the destructive climate, the Japanese lines of railways have been cheaply built, because labour is cheap; and they already pay fairly well. In round numbers, the cost to government since 1872 on construction and equipment has been six millions sterling. The net profits on the government railways for the financial year ending the 31st March, 1889, was a trifle over four per cent—a percentage which must have notably increased since the opening of the Tōkaidō line from Tōkyō to Kyōto, which is always full to overflowing. The total number of passengers carried during the same period of twelve months was 8,404,776; the total amount of goods carried was 616,913 tons.

We have alluded to the trouble caused by the capricious nature of Japanese rivers. Japan is perhaps the only country in the world where a railway may be seen to go under a river instead of over it. In the district between Kôbe and Ôsaka and near Lake Biwa, almost all the rivers tend to raise their beds above the level of the surrounding country, by means of the masses of sand and pebbles continually carried down by their rapid current. The river-bed thus stands athwart the flat strip of country between the mountains and the sea as a sort of wall or dyke, and the only thing to do is to take the line underneath it by a tunnel when the wall is of sufficient height to give headway for the train. Every now and then the bank bursts, the whole country-side is flooded, and the railway department is of course put to heavy expense.

Books recommended. The "Annual Report of the Imperial Railway Department."

**Religion.** Essentially an undevotional people, the Japanese have nevertheless accorded a certain measure of hospitality to the two greatest religions of the world—Buddhism and Christianity. Their own unassisted efforts in the direction of religion are summed up in Shintô. (See Articles on BUDDHISM, HISTORY AND MYTHOLOGY, MISSIONS, and SHINTÔ.)

**Rice.** Rice is believed by most persons to be the universal staple of food in Japan. This assumption is faulty, for it applies only to the towns. Wheat, barley, and especially millet, are the real staples throughout the rural districts, rice being there treated as a luxury to be brought out only on high days and holidays, or to be resorted to in case of sickness. We once heard an old beldame in a country village remark to another, with a grave shake of the head: "What! Do you mean to say that it has come to having to give her rice?"—the unexpressed inference being that the patient's case must be alarming indeed if the family had thought it necessary to resort to so expensive a dainty. But though the peasants do not eat much rice themselves, a great portion of their labour is devoted to growing it for other people to eat. The paddy-fields, as they are called, that is, the fields of rice standing in shallow water skilfully led on from field to field down the very gradual incline of a broad and fertile valley—these fields of vivid green, separated into squares by low mud dykes, form the most characteristic feature of the Japanese landscape. Some rice, too, is grown in the dry, but it is not so good as the other. The "paddy" rice is sown thickly in a comparatively small number of fields, which may be termed nurseries. In June, the young shoots are plucked up and transplanted at greater distances from each other. The generally silent fields may then be seen full of men and women standing knee-deep in the water and mud. The crops are gathered in about October. (See also Article on TRADE.)

**Roads.** Several of the chief highways of Japan are extremely ancient. Such are some of the roads near Kyōto, and the Nakasendō running the whole way from Kyōto to Eastern Japan. The most celebrated road of more recent origin, though itself far from modern, is the Tōkaidō, along which the *daimyōs* of the Western pro-

vinces used to travel with their gorgeous retinues to
the Shōgun's court at Yedo. The Ōshu-kaidō leading
north, and the Reiheishi-kaidō leading to Nikkō, are
other great historic roads. Many roads in Japan are
lined with tall cryptomerias and other trees. Shortly
after the introduction of telegraphy into the country, the
Japanese began to hew down these monumental trees in
their zeal for what they believed to be civilisation. The
telegraph-poles would, they thought, show to much better
advantage without such old-fashioned companions. A
howl from the foreign press of Yokohama fortunately
brought the official Goths to their senses, and after the
Tōkaidō had been partially denuded, the remaining avenues
were spared.

In too many of the newly built roads, though the
engineering selection is good, the execution is less so.
Roads are made of clay and dirt only. They run over
artificial embankments supported by mud foundations, there
is no sufficient provision made for carrying off water,
and the gradient of the hillside along which the road
itself is carried is left much too steep. Holes, ruts, and
landslips often attended with loss of life, are the result.
There is no idea of macadamising. As for mending, that is
done by new cart-loads of stones or earth, which effectually
supply travellers with dust during the dry weather and
a slough of despond whenever it rains. Sometimes twigs
of trees and even old cast-off straw sandals are utilised as
materials for road-mending.

**Samurai.** In the early Middle Ages—say, before the
twelfth century—the soldiers of the Mikado's palace were
said to *samurau*, that is, "be on guard" there. But when

feudalism came in, the word *samurai* was taken to denote the entire warrior class. "Warriors," "the military class," "the gentry," are perhaps the best English renderings of the word ; for it was of the essence of Old Japan that all gentlemen must be soldiers, and all soldiers gentlemen. The Japanese craze for altering names was exemplified in 1878, by the change of the historical and thoroughly native word *samurai* to that of *shizoku*, a Chinese term of precisely the same meaning. Under this new designation, the *samurai* still continue to exist as one of the three classes into which Japanese society is divided, the other two being the *kwazoku*, or "nobility," and the *heimin*, or "common people."

In the feudal times which lasted till A. D. 1871, the *samurai* lived in their *daimyōs'* castles, attended their *daimyōs* on all occasions, and received from them rations for themselves and their families—rations which were calculated in so many *koku*—that is, bags of rice—yearly. One of the early measures of the new Imperial Government was to commute these incomes for a lump sum, to be paid in government bonds. Optional at first, in December, 1873, the commutation was rendered obligatory by a second edict published in August, 1876. Since that time, many of the *samurai*, unaccustomed as they had been to business and to the duty of working for their livelihood, have fallen into great misery. The more clever and ambitious, on the other hand, practically constitute the governing class of the country at the present day, their former lords and masters, the *daimyōs*, having lagged behind in the race, and there being still a sufficient remnant of aristocratic spirit to render the rise of a plebeian to any position of importance a matter of considerable difficulty.

**Seismological Society.** See Earthquakes.

**Shampooing.** See Massage.

**Shintō.** Shintō, which means literally "the way of the gods," is the name given to the mythology and vague ancestor and nature-worship which preceded the introduction of Buddhism into Japan, and which survives to the present day in a somewhat modified form. Referring the reader to the Article on History and Mythology for a sketch of the Shintō pantheon, we would here draw attention to the fact that Shintō, so often spoken of as a religion, is hardly entitled to that name. It has no set of dogmas, no sacred book, no moral code. The absence of a moral code is accounted for, in the writings of the modern native commentators, by the innate perfection of Japanese humanity, which obviates the necessity for such outward props. It is only outcasts, like the Chinese and Western nations, whose natural depravity renders the occasional appearance of sages and reformers necessary; and even with this assistance, all foreign nations continue to wallow in a mire of ignorance, guilt, and disobedience towards the heaven-descended, *de jure* monarch of the universe—the Mikado of Japan.

It is necessary, however, to distinguish three periods in the existence of Shintō. During the first of these—roughly speaking, down to A. D. 550—the Japanese had no notion of religion as a separate institution. To pay homage to the gods, that is, to the departed ancestors of the Imperial Family and to the manes of other great men, was a usage springing from the same mental soil as that which produced passive obedience to,

and worship of, the living Mikado. Besides this, there
were prayers to the wind-gods, to the god of fire, to the god
of pestilence, to the goddess of food, and to deities presid-
ing over the saucepan, the cauldron, the gate, and the
kitchen. There were also purifications for wrong-doing,
as there were for bodily defilement, such as, for instance,
contact with a corpse. The purifying element was water.
But there was not even a shadowy idea of any code of
morals, or any systematisation of the simple notions of
the people concerning things unseen. There was neither
heaven nor hell—only a kind of neutral-tinted Hades.
Some of the gods were good, some were bad; nor was the
line between men and gods at all clearly drawn. There
was, however, a rude sort of priesthood, each priest
being charged with the service of some particular local
god, but not with preaching to the people. One of the
virgin daughters of the Mikado always dwelt at the ancient
shrine of Ise, keeping watch over the mirror, the sword,
and the jewel, which he had inherited from his ancestress
Ama-terasu, goddess of the sun. Shintō may be said, in
this its first period, to have been a set of ceremonies as
much political as religious.

By the introduction of Buddhism in the middle of the
sixth century after Christ, the second period of the existence of Shintō was inaugurated, and further growth in the
direction of a religion was stopped. The metaphysics of
Buddhism were far too profound, its ritual far too gorgeous,
its moral code far too exalted, for the puny fabric of Shintō
to make any effective resistance. All that there was of
religious feeling in the nation went over to the enemy.
The Buddhist priesthood diplomatically received the native Shintō gods into their pantheon, for which reason

many of the Shintō ceremonies connected with the court were kept up, although Buddhist ceremonies took the first place even in the thoughts of the converted descendants of the sun. The Shintō rituals (*norito*), previously handed down by word of mouth, were then first put into written shape. The term Shintō was also introduced, in order to distinguish the old native way of thinking from the new doctrine imported from India. But viewing the matter broadly, we may say that the second period of Shintō, which lasted from about A. D. 550 to 1700, was one of darkness and decrepitude. The various petty sects into which it then divided itself, owed what little vitality they possessed to fragments of cabalistic lore filched from the baser sort of Buddhism and from Taoism. Their priests practised the arts of divination and sorcery. Only at Court and at a few great shrines, such as those of Ise and Izumo, was a knowledge of Shintō in its native simplicity kept up; and even there it is doubtful whether changes did not creep in with the lapse of ages. Most of the Shintō temples throughout the country were served by Buddhist priests, who introduced the architectural ornaments and the ceremonial of their own religion. Thus was formed what is called *Ryōbu-Shintō*—a mixed religion founded on a compromise between the old creed and the new.

The third period in the history of Shintō began about the year 1700, and continues down to the present day. It has been termed "the period of the revival of pure Shintō." During the seventeenth and eighteenth centuries, under the peaceful government of the Tokugawa dynasty of Shōguns, the literati of Japan turned their eyes backward on their country's past. Old manuscripts were disinterred,

old histories and old poems were put into print, the old
language was investigated and imitated.  Soon the movement became religious and political—above all, patriotic,
not to say chauvinistic.  The Shōgunate was frowned on,
because it had supplanted the autocracy of the heaven-
descended Mikados.  Buddhism and Confucianism were
sneered at because of their foreign origin.  Shintō gained
by all this.  The great scholars Mabuchi (1697-1769),
Motoori (1730-1801), and Hirata (1776-1843), devoted
themselves to a religious propaganda—if that can be called
a religion which sets out from the principle that the only
two things needful are to follow one's natural impulses and
to obey the Mikado.  This order of ideas triumphed for a
moment in the revolution of 1868.  Buddhism was disestablished and disendowed, and Shintō was installed as the
only state religion—the Council for Spiritual Affairs (*Jin-
gikwan*) being given equal rank with the Council of State
(*Daijōkwan*), which latter controlled affairs temporal.  At
the same time thousands of temples, formerly Buddhist or
*Ryōbu-Shintō*, were, as the phrase went, "purified," that
is, stripped of their Buddhist ornaments, and handed over
to Shintō keeping.  But as Shintō had no root in itself—
being a thing too empty and jejune to influence the hearts
of men—Buddhism soon rallied.  The Council for Spiritual
Affairs was reduced to the rank of a department, the
department to a bureau, the bureau to a sub-bureau.  The
whole thing is now a mere shadow, though Shintō is still
in so far the official cult that certain temples are maintained
out of public moneys, and that the attendance of certain
officials is required from time to time at ceremonies of a
half-religious half-courtly nature.

The typical Shintō temple with its emblems is thus

described in the Introduction to Satow and Hawes'
"Handbook for Japan:"

"All that is visible to the eye of the worshipper is a
bundle of paper cuttings attached to an upright wand, or a
mirror, in the centre or back of an open chamber.  But
behind the grating in the rear is a sanctum, within which
not even the chief priest may intrude, except on rare
occasions, where the emblem of the god is kept enshrined
in box within box, and enveloped in innumerable wrap-
pings of silk and brocade.  Tradition alone informs us in
each case what this emblem, or *mi-tama-shiro* (representation of the august spirit), is—sometimes a mirror, or a
sword, a curious stone, or even a shoe, the mirror being
characteristic of the female, the sword of male deities.  A
possible explanation of the absence of images or pictorial
representations of the deity may be that in the earlier stage
of Shintō, and previous to the introduction of the arts in
conjunction with Buddhism, the Japanese people were
ignorant of sculpture and painting...............

"The architecture of a Shintō temple is in general
extremely simple.  The temple proper consists of a chapel
(*hon-sha* or *hon-den*) divided into two chambers.  That in
the rear contains the 'emblem' of the god, and is always
kept closed, while in the front part stands a wand from
which depend pieces of white paper cut out in a particular
form, and intended to resemble the offerings of cloth tied to
a branch of the Cleyera bush, such as in ancient times were
made at festivals, and probably left hanging all the year
round.  In recent years, by a reversion to the traditional
practice, it has become the fashion to offer strips of
coloured cloth.  The mirror which is seen in not a few
temples was borrowed from the Buddhists of the Shin-

gon sect, during the period of the predominance of Buddhism, and has nothing to do with Shintō. It is in no way derived from the mirror hidden in the recesses of the temple, as the 'emblem' of a deity. In front of the chapel there is usually a second building, sometimes separate, but more often connected with it by an ante-chamber. This is the oratory, or *hai-den*, and the ante-chamber is termed the *ai no ma*. A gong hanging over the entrance, for the worshipper to sound by the aid of a bell-rope, to call the attention of the god to his orisons, sometimes forms part of the furniture. In some cases, however, the oratory is a mere shed on four uprights; before this the worshipper bows his head, clapping his palms together, but not uttering an audible prayer. The brief ceremony concluded, he throws a few copper coins on the matted floor, and takes his departure. At all these temples the priests make an addition to their extremely small salaries by the sale of slips of paper imprinted with the title of the god, which are treasured as charms or find a place on the family altar as representative objects of worship. Washing the hands in a perfunctory manner, before worshipping, at a cistern placed in a convenient position near the temple is a practice common to Buddhism as well as Shintō. In the precincts of the main building frequently stands a row of smaller chapels dedicated to others of the numerous members of the Shintō Pantheon. These are distinguished as *sessha* or *massha* according to their degree of importance.

"The temple grounds are usually surrounded by a grove of trees, the most common among which is the cryptomeria, a useful timber tree. These plantations were originally intended to supply materials for the repair or re-erection of

the buildings, but in many cases their great antiquity causes
a sacred character to be attributed to the older trees, which
are surrounded by a fillet of straw rope, as if they were
tenanted by a divine spirit.   The distinctive character of
a Shintō temple is the *torii*, which always stands at the
entrance of the grounds, and may be repeated with greater
or less frequency at intervals until the space immediately
in front of the oratory is reached...............

  " Pure Shintō architecture does not admit of any external
decoration, as such, being applied to the temple in the
shape of carving or colouring.   It should preserve the
traditional form of the primeval Japanese hut, of which it
was, historically speaking, a mere adaptation.   The material should be wood, of the finest quality obtainable, *hi no
ki* being preferred, and it should be roofed with thatch or
bark."

  Mr. Satow furthermore says, speaking of the priesthood :
  " Shintō has scarcely any regular services in which the
people take part, and its priests (*Kannushi* or *Shin-shoku*)
are not distinguished by their appearance from ordinary
laymen.   Only when engaged in offering the morning and
evening sacrifices do they wear a peculiar dress of their
own.   This consists of a long loose gown with wide sleeves,
fastened at the waist with a girdle, and a black cap bound
round the head with a broad white fillet.   The Japanese
name for the former, which is frequently of brocade, is
*hita-tare*, and of the latter *eboshi*.   The priests are not
bound by any vows of celibacy, and are free to adopt
another career whenever they may choose.   At some
temples young girls fill the office of priestess, but their
duties do not appear to extend beyond the performing of
the pantomimic dances known as *Kagura*, and assisting

in the presentation of the daily offerings. They likewise
are under no vows, and marry as a matter of course when
their time comes. The services consist in the presentation
of offerings of rice, fish, fruits, vegetables, the flesh of
game, animals, and rice-beer, and in the recital of certain
formal addresses partly laudatory and partly in the nature
of petitions. The style of composition employed is that
of a very remote period, and would not be comprehended
by the common people, even if the latter were in the habit
of taking any part in the ritual."

*Books recommended.* "Shintō," p. 6r et seq. of the Introduction to Satow
and Hawes' "Handbook for Japan."—"The Revival of Pure Shintō," by Ernest
Satow, forming the Appendix to Vol. III; "The Shintō Temples of Ise," by the
same, in Vol. II; and "Ancient Japanese Rituals," by the same, in Vols. VII and
IX of the "Asiatic Transactions."—"Introduction to the *Kojiki*," forming the Supplement to Vol. X of the same.

**Shipping.** During the Middle Ages the Japanese were
distinguished among Eastern nations for their spirit of
maritime enterprise. Korea, China, Formosa, even the
distant Philippine Islands, Cambodia, and Siam saw the
Japanese appear upon their coasts, now as peaceful traders,
now as buccaneers. The story of one of these buccaneers,
named Yamada Nagamasa, *alias* Tenjiku Hachibei, who
ended by marrying a Siamese princess and becoming
viceroy of the country, reads more like a chapter from the
"Arabian Nights" than like sober reality. It is evident,
too, that the Japanese of the early part of the seventeenth
century were determined not to be left behind in the art of
shipbuilding. The English master-mariner Will Adams,
who came to Japan in the year 1600, built ships for Ieyasu,
the then Shōgun, one of which made voyages to Manila
and even to Mexico.

Suddenly all was changed. Alarmed beyond measure at the progress of Roman Catholicism, and fearing that in Japan, as elsewhere, the Spanish monk would be followed by the Spanish soldier of fortune, Iemitsu, the third Shōgun of the Tokugawa dynasty, issued an edict in the year 1636, whereby all foreign priests were expelled from the empire, foreign merchants were restricted to the two south-western ports of Nagasaki and Hirado, and all Japanese subjects were forbidden under pain of death to leave Japan. Drastic measures were resorted to in order the better to enforce the terms of this edict. All vessels of European form and even all larger vessels of native form were ordered to be destroyed, only such smaller junks as were sufficient for coasting purposes being allowed to be retained. The style of junk permitted was that still to be seen at the present day in Japanese waters. It is distinguished by a single square sail, and is so awkward as to render the vessel difficult to handle except when running before the wind. Thus, by a stroke of the pen, was Japan's shipping enterprise crippled for over two hundred years. The number of coasting junks no doubt remained large; for owing to the mountainous character of the country, communication by water was indispensable. What the actual amount of junk tonnage was at any period of the Tokugawa rule, or even at the beginning of the reign of the present Mikado, is unknown.

When the feudal government of Old Japan fell like a card palace, the restrictions on shipbuilding fell with it. The new Imperial government took a laudable interest in the development of a mercantile marine. The most efficacious of the measures adopted with this end in view is a notification which prohibits the construction of junks of over five hundred *koku* burthen." ·

Nor has everything been left to official initiative. Mr. Iwasaki Yatarō, the celebrated millionaire, started steamers of his own somewhere about 1870; and the company which he directed, known later under the name of the Mitsubishi† Mail Steam Ship Company, soon rose to be the most important commercial undertaking in the empire. It even influenced politics; for to the facilities which Mr. Iwasaki afforded for carrying troops at the time of the Satsuma rebellion, was due in no small measure the triumph of the imperialists in that their hour of need. Later on, another steam ship company of considerable importance, named the *Kyōdō Un-yu Kaisha*, was formed to run against the Mitsubishi.* But the rivalry between the two proving ruinous, they were amalgamated in the autumn of 1885 under the name of the *Nippon Yūsen Kaisha*, or Japan Mail Steam Ship Company. Numberless smaller companies have risen and fallen during the last two decades.

The following abstract of statistics is taken from the Annual Report of the Mercantile Marine Bureau for 1887 (published 1889):—

Number and Tonnage of all Japanese vessels on the 31st December, 1887. (With the Horse power of Steamers.)

---

*Article 1 of the " Regulations and Rules for the Measurement of Vessels' Capacity," published in 1888 by the Mercantile Marine Bureau of the Imperial Department of Communications, fixes the capacity of the *koku*, in vessels of Japanese build, as equivalent to ten cubic feet. Whether this was the precise value of the *koku* in earlier times, we cannot say. Probably not; for Old Japan knew little of exact computations, and, as a rule, each province was a law unto itself in questions relating to weights and measures.

† From *mitsu*, "three," and *hishi*, "lozenge-shaped," the crest of the company being three lozenges.

Including those belonging to *Government.* (Exclusive of Imperial Navy.)

*Of Foreign Form of Construction.*

Number ... ... ... ... ... ... ... ... ... 1,284.
Tonnage ... ... ... ... ... ... ... ... 133,297.
Horse-power ... ... ... ... ... ... ... ... 16,641.

The following table shows the dock accommodation of the Empire in 1889 :—

| | | Dry Docks, Pontoons, Patent Ships, etc. | | | | | |
|---|---|---|---|---|---|---|---|
| Port. | Names. | Extreme Length. | Breadth at Entrance. | Height of Ridge Sill above bottom of dock. | Depth of Sill at High Water. | Lifting power in Tons. | Remarks. |
| | | ft. in. | ft. in. | ft. in. | ft. in. | | |
| Kōbe | Pat. Slip No 1. | 900 | 36 | — | — | | Shears 83 Tons. |
| do. | — do — No 2. | 800 | 38 | — | — | 60 | |
| Nagasaki | Nagasaki Dockyard | 411 | 69 | 8. 11 | 23. 6 | | Shears 43 Tons. |
| do. | do. Pat. Slip | 320 | 30 | — | — | 900 | Vessels 298 ft. long have been taken up. |
| Yokohama | Yokohama No 1. | 391 | 82 | 3. 3 | 22.7 | ) | Floating derrick :— lifting power 20 Tons. |
| do. | — do — No 2. | 302.4 | 94.5 | 3. 3 | 38. 4 | } | Cranes 30 to 60 Tons. |
| do. | — do — No 3. | 308.4 | 43.3 | 3. 3 | 17. 10 | ) | |

**Shōgun.** The title of *Shōgun,* which means literally "generalissimo," and which was destined to play such a momentous part in Japanese history, seems to have been first used in A. D. 813, when one Watamaro was appointed *Sei-i Tai-Shōgun,* that is, "Barbarian-Subduing Generalissimo," to wage war against the Ainos in the north of the empire. The title was employed afterwards in similar cases from time to time. But Yoritomo, at the end of the twelfth century, was the first of these generalissimos to make himself also, so to say, Mayor of the Palace, and in effect ruler of the land. From that time forward, various dynasties of Shōguns succeeded each other throughout the Middle Ages and down to our own days. The greatest of these families were the Ashikaga (A. D. 1336-1570), and the Tokugawa (A. D. 1603-1867). A concatenation of circumstances, partly political, partly religious, partly literary, led to the abolition of the Shōgunate in the year 1868. The Mikado then stepped forth again, to govern as well as to reign, after an eclipse of well-nigh seven hundred years.

The practice of most modern writers on Japanese subjects—foreigners as well as natives—is to treat the Shōguns as usurpers. But surely this is a highly unphilosophical way of reading history. It is not even formally correct, seeing that the Shōguns obtained investiture from the Court of Kyōto as regularly as ministers of state have obtained their commissions in later times. We cannot undertake here to go into the causes that produced Japanese feudalism, with the Shōguns at its head. But if seven centuries of possession do not constitute a legal title, how many of the governments at present existing in the world are legitimate? And what test is there, or can there be, of the legitimacy of any government except the general acquiescence of the governed?

**Shooting.** No one is advised to come to Japan for sport. Deer and even bears do, no doubt, exist in the northern island of Yezo; pheasants, snipe, hares, and other small game in the Main Island. But "Treaty Limits," within which alone foreigners can obtain licenses to shoot,

are almost denuded of game, unless it be snipe and quail,
in consequence of having been shot over for a generation.
Shooting licenses may be obtained at the prefectural office
(*Kenchō*) of the various open ports, and at the *Tōkyō-Fu*
or city office in Tōkyō. The fee is $10. The shooting
season lasts from the 15th October to the 15th April.
These dates will seem late to English sportsmen; but it
must be remembered that the seasons begin later in Japan
than in England—spring as well as autumn.

**Siebold.** Philipp Franz, Freiherr von Siebold (A. D.
1796-1866), author of many books, both in Latin and
German, on the zoology, botany, language, and bibliography of Japan and the neighbouring lands, and best-known
by the magnificently illustrated folio work entitled "*Nippon, Archiv zur Beschreibung von Japan*," which is in
itself an encyclopædia of the information concerning Japan
which existed in his day, came of an old Bavarian family.
Like Kaempfer a century and a half before him, he judged,
and judged rightly, that the service of the Dutch East
India Company was the royal road to a knowledge of the
then mysterious empire of Japan. Appointed leader of a
scientific mission fitted out at Batavia, he landed at
Deshima, the Dutch portion of Nagasaki, in the month of
August, 1823. By force of character, by urbanity of
manner, by skill as a physician, even by a system of bribery
which fell in with the customs of the country, and which
surely, under the circumstances, no sensible man of the
world will condemn, he obtained an extraordinary hold over
the Japanese, suspicious and intractable as they then were.
Having, in 1826, accompanied to Yedo the Dutch embassy
which went once during the reign of every Shōgun to show

their respect and obtain favours by grovelling at His Highness's feet and entertaining him with pranks and songs, Siebold obtained permission to remain behind—the sole European in that great Asiatic capital, then absolutely sealed against the outer world. The excuse pleaded and accepted was that he would instruct the Japanese physicians and surgeons in the more recondite branches of their art. His leisure he utilised in multifarious scientific researches; and so well did he know how to ingratiate himself that some of the highest in the land willingly contributed to his store of knowledge. Suddenly a rumour got about that the chief Court spy—a very important official in those days—had sold him a map of the country. This was treason according to the old Japanese law. The spy was ordered to commit *harakiri*, and Siebold was cast into a dungeon, from which he emerged only on the 18th January, 1830, with strict orders never to return to Japan.

Arriving in Holland, he was created a baron and a colonel in the army by the king of that country, and spent the next twenty-nine years in writing his numerous works and arranging his scientific collections in the museums of Leyden, Munich, and Würzburg. More permanent even in their results than these learned labours was his activity in the field of practical botany. To him our western gardens owe the Japanese lilies, peonies, aralias, camellias, chrysanthemums, and scores of other interesting and beautiful garden plants with which they are now adorned.

Meanwhile, Commodore Perry's expedition had burst open Japan. Siebold, in his old age, returned as a semi-official ambassador to that same Yedo which he had quitted in chains so many years before. This mission was not altogether successful. The times were for war, not for

the peaceful negotiations of a man of science. Siebold's
proper field was not politics, but learning. It was, therefore
perhaps no loss to his reputation that a second half-politi-
cal expedition to Japan, which the Emperor Napoleon III
had thought of entrusting to him, was never carried out.
Judged by his scientific works and their practical results,
Siebold is the greatest of the many great Germans who
have contributed so much to the world's knowledge of
Japan, Kaempfer in the seventeenth century and Rein in
our own day being the other most illustrious names. If
small people may be allowed to criticise giants, we would
here note that the only weakness discoverable in the German school of investigators, as represented by Kaempfer,
Siebold, and Rein, is a certain insufficiency of the critical
faculty in questions of history and language. Surely it is
not enough to get at the Japanese sources. The Japanese
sources must themselves be subjected to rigorous scrutiny.
It was reserved for the English school, represented by
Satow and Aston to do this—to explore the language with
scientific exactness, and to prove, step by step, that the
so-called history, which Kaempfer and his followers had
taken on trust, was a mass of old wives' fables. Japan
being the land of contradictions, it is perhaps but natural
that the English and the Germans should here have
reversed their usual *rôles*. The Germans have roamed
abroad to collect facts. To the English, sitting quietly by
their fire-side, has belonged the field of minute historical
and philological criticism.

Books recommended. This sketch is founded on an obituary article by Ger-
hard Schirnhofer, translated in the "Japan Weekly Mail" for the 27th December,
1879. Siebold tells the story of his own earlier journeyings in his " *Nippon Arr&rs.*"

**Silk.** Silk is treated of from a commercial point of view in the Article on TRADE. Those whose tastes are literary and historical only, may be interested to learn that the silk-worm was still a rare novelty at the dawn of Japanese history—just imported, as it would seem, from Korea. The first mention of it is in the annals of the reign of the Emperor Nintoku, who is supposed to have died in A. D. 399. Up till then, the materials used for clothing had been hempen cloth and the bark of the paper-mulberry, coloured by being rubbed with madder and other tinctorial plants. Nintoku's consort, the Empress Iwa-no-Hime, was of such a jealous disposition—and if the chronicler is veracious she had ample reason for jealousy—that "the concubines employed by the Heavenly Sovereign could not even peep inside the palace;" for if they did, the Empress stamped with rage. Further levity on her husband's part drove her to such desperation that she retired to the house of a nobleman named Nurinomi who dwelt in another province, and when pursued, she caused the following excuse to be made :—

"'The reason of the Empress's progress is that there are some insects reared by Nurinomi—strange insects changing in three ways, once becoming creeping insects, once becoming cocoons, and once becoming flying birds— and it is only to go and look at them that she has entered into Nurinomi's house. She has no strange intentions.'— When they had thus reported, the Heavenly Sovereign said : 'That being so, I wish to go and see these insects, as I think they must be strange;' and with these words, he made a progress up from the Great Palace." *

**Singing-Girls.** The charms of the Japanese singing-girl

---

* "Kojiki," Section CXXIV. The translation is literal.

have been dwelt on so often that we gladly leave them to
her more ardent admirers.  Without her, Japanese social
gatherings would lose much of their vivacity and pleasing
*abandon*.  Of necessity endowed with more than the
ordinary share of personal attractions, elegant and accomplished in all the arts of a life of gaiety, it *is* little
wonder if she *is a* source of anxiety to staid elderly folks
of both sexes, and that amongst the other signs of the
times, a movement should be on foot to abolish her
altogether.  In official circles, the European banquet with
its familiar *salmis* and *aspics*, and its inevitable after-
dinner speeches, has well-nigh supplanted the native feast.
Waiters in swallow-tails replace the damsels of the guitar
and the wine-cup.

The training of a singing-girl, or *geisha*, as the Japanese
term her, which includes lessons in the art of dancing,
often begins when she is about seven years old.  She is
then practically engaged for a number of years, the career
once entered on being difficult to quit, unless good fortune
brings some wealthy lover able and willing to buy her out.

**Societies.**  The Japanese of our day have taken kindly
to societies and associations of all sorts.  They doubtless
feel that their nation has to make up now for the long
abstinence from such co-operative activity which was en-
forced during the Tokugawa *régime*, when it was penal
for more than five persons to club together for any purpose.

The four most influential societies at present are the
Sanitary Society of Japan with a membership of over six
thousand ; the Educational Society of Japan, with over
four thousand members ; the Society for the Promotion
of Commerce and Industry, and the Agricultural Society

of Japan. These, and not a few of those next to be
mentioned, publish Transactions and have branches in
the provinces. The Geographical Society of Tōkyō, the
Philosophical Society, the Engineering Society, the Medical Society, and the *Gakushikaiin*, an association with
aims kindred to those of the Educational Society, have
done excellent work. The Romanisation Society has made
a valiant, though not hitherto successful, effort to replace
by our simple European alphabet the endless complications
of the Japanese system of writing. We have, furthermore,
the Red Cross Association, under the immediate patronage
of the Empress, the Japanese Society of Arts, Judicial,
Anthropological, and various Scientific and Literary Societies, a Total Abstinence Society, a Temperance (*not* total
abstinence) Society, an Anti-Tobacco Society, a Young
Men's Christian Association, an Association of Buddhist
Young Men, and others of various hues and complexions,
not to mention political clubs, of which the number is
very great and constantly changing.

Some of the new Japanese societies have eccentric aims.
Thus, there is one which undertakes to dun debtors for
any one who chooses to apply. The dunning is put into
the hands of men who walk about in green coats and with
the society's name printed on their back. Another society
undertakes to get questions on every conceivable subject
answered by competent specialists, somewhat like our
"Notes and Queries." The object of a third small society
is punctuality. But the queerest society of all is surely
the Society for the Abolition of Present-Giving. We wish
failure and disaster from the bottom of our hearts to this
curmudgeonly league. In no country of the world do *les
petits cadeaux qui entretiennent l'amitié* play a more charm-

ing part than in Japan. Japan is becoming prosaic fast
enough in all conscience. Why ruthlessly pull up by the
roots the few graces that remain?

*Books recommended.* "The *Gakushikuan*," in Vol. XV, Part I, and "The
Japanese Education Society," in Vol. XVI, Part I, of the "Asiatic Transactions," both
by Walter Dening.

**Soroban.** See ABACUS.

**Sun, Moon, and Stars.** In the early Japanese mythology the sun is ruled over by a goddess, the glorious
Ama-Terasu, or "Heaven-Shiner," from whom is descended the Imperial Family of Japan. The Moon belongs
to her brother, the rough and violent god Susa-no-o.
According to the later Japanese poets, there grows in the
moon a cassia-tree (*katsura*), whose reddening leaves cause
its brighter refulgence in autumn. They also tell us of
a great city in the moon (*tsuki no miyako*), and the myth-
makers have brought down a maiden from the moon to
do penance on earth amidst various picturesque scenes.
But the genuinely popular imagination of the present
day allows only of a hare in the moon, which keeps
pounding away at rice in a mortar to make it into cakes.
The idea of the hare was borrowed from China; but the
rice-cakes seem to be native, and to have their origin in
a pun—the same word *mochi* happening to have the two
acceptations of "rice-cake" and "full moon." The sun is
supposed to be inhabited by a three-legged crow. Hence
the expression *kin-u gyoku-to*, "the golden crow and the
jewelled hare," is a periphrasis for the sun and moon.

The three great nights of the lunar year are the 26th of
the 7th moon, the 15th of the 8th moon, and the 13th of
the 9th moon, old calendar. These roughly correspond

to dates some five or six weeks later according to our calendar, and thus include the three moons of the autumn trimester. On the 26th night of the 7th moon, people in Tōkyō visit the tea-houses at Atago-yama or the sea-shore of Takanawa, and sit up till a very late, or rather early, hour to see the moon rise over the water, drinking *sake* the while, and composing verses appropriate to the sentimental character of the scene. The 15th night of the 8th moon, which is no other than our harvest moon at the full, is celebrated by an offering of beans and dumplings and of bouquets of eulalia-grass and lespedeza blossom. This moon is termed the "bean moon." The 13th night of the 9th moon sees offerings of the same bouquets, of dumplings, and of chestnuts. It is termed the "chestnut moon."

The stars are much less admired and written about in Japan than in Europe. No Japanese bard has ever apostrophised them as "the poetry of heaven." The only fable worth mentioning here in connection with the stars is that which inspires the festival named *Tanabata*. This fable, which is of Chinese origin, relates the loves of a Herdsman and a Weaving-Girl. The Herdsman is a star in Aquila. The Weaver is the star Vega. They dwell on opposite sides of the "Celestial River," or Milky Way, and may never meet but on the seventh night of the seventh moon, a night held sacred to them, strips of paper with poetic effusions in their honour being stuck on stems of bamboo grass and set up in various places. According to one version of the legend, the Weaving-Girl was so constantly kept employed in making garments for the offspring of the Emperor of Heaven—in other words, God—that she had no leisure to attend to the adornment of her person. At last however, God, taking compassion on her loneliness, gave her in marriage to the Herdsman who dwelt on the opposite bank of the river. Hereupon the woman began to grow remiss in her work. God, in his anger, then made her recross the river, at the same time forbidding her husband to visit her oftener than once a year. Another version represents the pair as mortals, who were wedded at the early ages of fifteen and twelve, and who died at the ages of a hundred and three and ninety-nine respectively. After death, their spirits flew up to the sky, where the Supreme Deity bathed daily in the Celestial River. No mortals might pollute it by their touch, except on the seventh day of the seventh moon, when the Deity, instead of bathing, went to listen to the chanting of the Buddhist scriptures.

**Swords.** The Japanese sword of ancient days (the *tsurugi*) was a straight double-edged heavy weapon some three feet long, intended to be brandished with both hands. That of mediæval and modern times (the *katana*) is lighter, shorter, has but a single edge, and is slightly curved towards the point. There is also the *wakizashi*, or dirk of about nine and a half inches, with which *harakiri* was committed. The four most famous Japanese sword-smiths are Munechika (tenth century), Masamune and Yoshimitsu (latter part of the thirteenth century), and Muramasa (latter part of the fourteenth century). But Muramasa's blades had the reputation of being unlucky. Towards the close of the fifteenth century arose schools of artists in metal, who made it their business to adorn the hilt, the guard, the sheath, and other appurtenances in a manner which is still the delight of collectors. But to the Japanese connoisseur, the great treasure is always the blade itself, which has been called "the living soul of the *samurai*."

Japanese swords excel even the vaunted products of Damascus and Toledo. To cut through a pile of copper coins without nicking the blade is, or was, a common feat. History, tradition, and romance alike re-echo with the exploits of this wonderful weapon. The magic sword, the sword handed down as an heirloom, figures as plentifully in the pages of Japanese novel-writers as magic rings and strawberry-marks used once upon a time to do in the West. The custom of wearing two swords is believed to date from the beginning of the fourteenth century. It was abolished by an edict issued on the 28th March, 1876, and taking effect from the 1st January, 1877. The edict was obeyed by this strangely docile people without a blow being struck, and the curio-shops displayed heaps of swords which, a few months before, the owners would less willingly have parted with than with life itself.

Japanese swords are made of soft, elastic, magnetic iron combined with hard steel. "The tempering of the edge," says Rein, "is carefully done in the charcoal furnace, the softer backs and the sides being surrounded up to a certain point with fire clay, so that only the edge remains outside. The cooling takes place in cold water. It is in this way that the steeled edge may be distinguished clearly from the back, by its colour and lustre. The backs of knives, axes and other weapons are united to the steel edge either by welding on one side, or by fitting the edge into a fluted groove of the back blade, and welding on both sides."

**Books recommended.** For a matter-of-fact description, see Rein's "Industries of Japan," p. 430. For historical and literary details, see McClatchie's "The Sword of Japan," in Vol. II of the "Asiatic Transactions."—There is a novel by L. Wertheimer, founded on the importance attached to the sword in feudal Japan, and entitled "A Muramasa Blade."

**Taste.** Japanese taste in painting, in furniture, in floral decoration, in all matters depending on line and form, may be summed up in one word—sobriety. The bluster which mistakes bigness for greatness, the vulgarity which smothers beauty under ostentation and extravagance, have no place in the Japanese way of thinking. The alcove of a Tôkyô or Kyôto drawing-room holds one picture and one flower-vase, which are changed from time to time. To be sure, picture and vase are alike exquisite. The possessions of the master of the house are not sown broadcast, as much as to say, "Look what a lot of expensive articles I've got, and just think how jolly rich I must be!" He does not stick up plates on walls;—plates are meant to hold food. He would not, whatever might be his means, waste £1000, or £100, or even £20 on the flowers for a single party;— flowers are natural things, simple things; it is incongruous to treat them like precious stones.

When will Europe learn afresh from Japan that lesson of proportion, of fitness, of sobriety, which Greece once knew so well? When will America learn it—the land our grandfathers used to credit with republican simplicity, but with which we of the present generation have come to connect the idea of a bombastic luxury, comparable only to the extravagances of Rome when Rome's moral fibre was beginning to be relaxed?

But it seems likely that, instead of Japan converting us, we shall pervert Japan. Contact has already tainted the dress, the houses, the pictures, the life generally, of the upper classes. It is to the common people that one must now go for the old tradition of sober beauty and proportion. You want flowers arranged? Ask your house-coolie. There is something wrong in the way the garden is laid out? It looks too formal, and yet your proposed alterations would turn it into a formless maze? Call in the cook or the washerman as counsellors.

' To tell the whole truth, however, Japan is only half-Greek. Her taste, faultless where line is concerned, deserts her whenever the appeal is to the ear. Not only is the music of the Japanese horrible beyond description;—they have little sense of proportion in language. The never-ending sentences of their authors meander over as many pages; a single romance will drag the reader through fifty volumes. Is it a question of lectures? Then they are not contented with less than half-a-dozen at a sitting; and if, as sometimes happens, the lecturers get into trouble, the audience will stay uncomplainingly in the silent hall for an hour or more, while negotiations are carried on with the police. The missionaries tell a similar tale; no sermon can be prolix enough to stay the insatiable appetite of their converts. The reason of all this is, that, as Sir Harry Parkes remarked long ago, the Japanese share in the inexhaustible patience of Orientals. Their tiresome books, their submission to officialdom, their theatres lasting from dawn to sunset—all these things flow from the same source, patience.

**Tea.** Tea is believed to have been introduced into Japan from China in A. D. 805 by the celebrated Buddhist saint, Dengyō Daishi. It had long been a favourite beverage of the Buddhists of the continent, whom it served to keep wakeful during their midnight devotions. A pious legend tells us that the origin of the tea-shrub was on this wise: Daruma, an Indian saint of the sixth century, had spent many long years in ceaseless prayer and watching. At

last one night, his eyelids, unable to bear the fatigue any
longer, closed, and he slept soundly until morning. When
the saint awoke, he was so angry with his lazy eyelids that
he cut them off and flung them on the ground. But lo!
each lid was suddenly transformed into a shrub, whose
efficacious leaves, infused in water, minister to the vigils
of holy men.

Though encouraged from the first by Imperial recom-
mendations, tea-culture made little or no progress in Japan
till the close of the twelfth century, when another Buddhist,
the abbot Myōe, having obtained new seeds from China,
sowed them at Toga-no-o, near Kyōto, whence a number of
shrubs were afterwards transplanted to Uji, which has
ever since been the headquarters of Japanese tea-growing.
Thenceforward the love of tea-drinking was engrained in
the Japanese court and aristocracy, and the cha-no-yu, or
tea ceremonies, became a national institution. But it is
doubtful whether the custom of drinking tea began to
spread among the lower classes till the end of the seventeenth century, which was also the time when our own
ancestors first took to it.

The tea drunk in respectable Japanese households generally costs about 25 cents a pound, while from 50 cents to
$1 will be paid for a better quality, fit to set before an
honoured guest. The most expensive Uji tea costs $6 per
pound. At the opposite end of the scale stands the so-
called bancha, the tea of the lower classes, 5 cents a pound,
made out of chopped leaves, stalks, and bits of wood taken
from the trimmings of the tea-plant; for this beverage is
tea, after all, little as its flavour has in common with
that of Bohea or of Uji. Other tea-like infusions sometimes to be met with are Kōsen, made by pouring hot

water on a mixture of various fragrant substances, such
as orange-peel, the seeds of the xanthoxylon, etc; *Sakura-
yu*, an infusion of salted cherry-blossoms ; *Mugi-yu*, an
infusion of parched barley; *Mame-cha*, a similar preparation of beans. *Fuku-ja*, or "luck tea," is made of
salted plums, sea-weed, and xanthoxylon seeds, and is
partaken of in every Japanese household on the last night
of the year. (See also Article on TRADE).

Book recommended. "The Preparation of Japan Tea," by Henry Gribble,
printed in Vol. XII, Part 1, of the "Asiatic Transactions."


**Tea Ceremonies.** Few things have excited more interest among collectors of Japanese curios than the *cha-no-
yu*, or tea ceremonies, of which so many of the highly
prized little "japanosities" in their collections are in one
way or another the implements. And as quarrelling with
other collectors is part of every true collector's nature, so
also has the battle raged round the Japanese tea-table—a
veritable and literal storm in a tea-cup. One set brands
the tea ceremonies as essentially paltry and effeminate, and
asserts that their influence has cramped the genius of
Japanese art, by confusing beauty with archaism and
making goals of characteristics worthy only to be starting-
points. The opposite school sees in these same ceremonies
a profoundly beneficial influence—an influence which has
kept Japanese art from leaving the narrow path of purity
and simplicity for the broad road of a meretricious gaudiness.

What, then, are these tea ceremonies? And first of all,
what is their history? Have their votaries at all epochs
been enamoured of simplicity and archaism to the degree
which both friends and foes seem to take for granted? If

our own slight researches into the subject prove anything,
they prove that these traits are comparatively modern.

The tea ceremonies have undergone three transformations
during the six or seven hundred years of their existence.
They have passed through a medico-religious stage, a luxurious stage, and lastly an esthetic stage. They originated
in tea-drinking pure and simple on the part of certain
Buddhist priests of the Zen sect, who found the infusion
useful in keeping them awake during the performance of
their midnight devotions. The first aristocrat whose
name is mentioned in connection with tea is Minamoto-no
Sanetomo, Shōgun of Japan from A. D. 1203 to 1219. He
seems to have been a youthful debauchee, whom the
Buddhist abbot Eisai endeavoured to save from the wine-cup
by making him try tea instead. As is still the custom of
propagandists, Eisai accompanied this recommendation by
the gift of a tract on the subject. It was composed by himself, and bore the title of "The Salutary Influence of
Tea-Drinking." In it was explained the manner in which
tea " regulates the five viscera and expels evil spirits," and
rules were given both for making the infusion and for
drinking it. The ceremonial which Eisai introduced was
religious. True, it included a simple dinner ; but its main
feature was a Buddhist service, at which the faithful
worshipped their ancestors to the beating of drums and
burning of incense. A tinge of the religious element
has adhered to the tea ceremonies ever since. It is still
considered proper for tea enthusiasts to join the Zen sect
of Buddhism, and it is from the abbot of Daitokuji
at Kyōto that diplomas of proficiency are obtained.

How long Japanese tea-drinking remained in this first
religious stage is not clear. This we know, that by the

year 1330, the second or luxurious stage had already been
reached. The descriptions of the tea-parties of those
days remind one of the "Arabian Nights." The *daimyôs* who daily took part in them reclined on couches
spread with tiger-skins and leopard-skins; the walls of the
spacious apartments in which the guests assembled were
hung, not only with Buddhist pictures, but with damask
and brocade, with gold and silver vessels, and swords in
splendid sheaths. Precious perfumes were burnt, rare
fishes and strange birds were served up with sweetmeats
and wine, and the point of the entertainment consisted in
guessing where the material for each cup of tea had been
produced; for as many brands as possible were brought in,
to serve as a puzzle or *jeu de société*—some from the
Toga-no-o tea-plantations, some from Uji, some from other
places. Every right guess procured for him who made it
the gift of one of the treasures that were hung round the
room. But he was not allowed to carry it away himself.
The rules of the tea ceremonies, as then practised, ordained that all the things rich and rare that were exhibited must
be given by their winners to the singing and dancing-girls,
troupes of whom were present to help the company in their
carousal. Vast fortunes were dissipated in this manner.
On the other hand, the arts were benefited, more especially when, towards the close of the fifteenth century, the
luxurious Yoshimasa, the Japanese Lorenzo de' Medici,
abdicated the Shôgun's throne in order to devote himself
altogether to refined pleasures in his gorgeous palace
of Ginkakuji at Kyôto, in the company of his favourites,
the pleasure-loving Buddhist abbots Shukô and Shinnô.
From this trio of royal and religious voluptuaries are
derived several of the rules for tea-drinking that still hold

kind called *koi-cha*, and a thinner kind called *usu-cha*. The former is used in the earlier stage of the proceedings, the latter towards the end. The tea is made and drunk in a preternaturally slow and formal manner, each action, each gesture being fixed by an elaborate code of rules. Every article connected with the ceremony, such as the tea-canister, the incense-burner, the hanging scroll, and the bouquet of flowers in the alcove, is either handled, or else admired at a distance, in ways and with phrases which unalterable usage prescribes. Even the hands are washed, the room is swept, a little bell is rung, and the guests walk from the house to the garden and from the garden back into the house, at stated times and in a stated manner which never varies, except in so far as certain schools, as rigidly conservative as monkish confraternities, obey slightly varying rules of their own, handed down from their ancestors who interpreted Sen-no-Rikyū's ordinances according to slightly varying canons of exegesis.

To a European the ceremony is lengthy and meaningless. When witnessed more than once, it becomes intolerably monotonous. Not being born with an Oriental fund of patience, he longs for something new, something lively, something with at least the semblance of logic and utility. But then it is not for him that the tea ceremonies were made. If they amuse those for whom they were made, they amuse them, and there is nothing more to be said. In any case, tea and ceremonies are perfectly harmless, which is more than can be affirmed of tea and tattle. No doubt, even the tea ceremonies have, if history libels them not, been sometimes misused for purposes of political conspiracy. But these cases are rare. If the tea ceremonies do not go the length of embodying a " philoso-

phy," as fabled by some of their foreign admirers, they
have, at least in their latest form, assisted the cause of
purity in art. Some may deem them pointless. None can
brand them as vulgar.

**Telegraphs.** The first line of telegraphs in this country
may be said to have been experimental; it was only 840
yards in length, and was opened for government business
in 1869. The following year Tōkyō and Yokohama were
connected by wire, and in 1871 a general telegraphic system for the Empire was decided upon, about 900 miles
being completed and opened for traffic in the same year.
The trunk line to Nagasaki was first constructed in order
to connect with the cables of the Great Northern Telegraph
Company, the engineers meeting with comparatively little
opposition from the people, but with a good deal of difficulty
from the unsettled state of the country, consequent on the
revolution of 1868 and the wretched condition of the roads
at that time.

On the introduction of telegraphy into Japan, a code was
devised on the basis of the well-known "Morse code,"
which admitted of internal telegrams being written and
transmitted in the vernacular. The new means of communication being thus placed within reach of the bulk of
the people, it soon became familiar and popular. In that
respect the Japanese system is unique among Eastern
countries. In India and China, for instance, telegrams
can be transmitted only when written in Roman letters
or in Arabic figures.

The first lines were surveyed, built, and worked under
foreign superintendence, with fittings principally of English
manufacture. But the rapid progress made by the Japanese

in technical matters has enabled them, in various directions, to dispense altogether with foreign experts.  With the exception of submarine cables and the most delicate electrical measuring apparatus, all kinds of material and instruments are turned out of the workshops attached to the Imperial Telegraph Department, while executively the system has been maintained solely by the native staff for some time past.  The principal cables are laid across the Straits of Shimonoseki, connecting the island of Kyushu with the Main Island, and across the Tsugaru Straits connecting the Main Island with Yezo.  Submarine cables connect Nagasaki with Shanghai on the one side and Vladivostock on the other.  A third submarine line— that between Japan, Iki, Tsushima, and Fusan (in Korea), is worked by the Japanese government.

The tariff for native messages was, for obvious reasons, originally framed on a very low basis, and with excellent results.  To-day it is probably under that of any other country in the world.  The rate for a single message of ten Kana characters to any part of the Empire is fifteen cents; for city local traffic it is only five cents or about twopence.  The names and addresses of the sender and receiver go free.  Telegrams in foreign languages within the empire are charged at the rate of five cents per word, with a minimum charge of twenty-five cents for the first five words or fraction of five words.  No charge is made for delivery within a radius of one ri from the telegraph office.

The number of offices open for public business at the end of 1889 was three hundred and eleven, including sixteen telephone offices.  Preliminary arrangements for the construction of telephone exchanges in the large towns have

just been concluded. The length of wire open at the end of 1889 was 16,808 miles. The number of messages conveyed was 3,149,170 in Japanese, and 63,364 in foreign languages.

The Telegraph Service was an independent section of the Ministry of Public Works until the abolition of that Department in 1885. It continued independent under the newly formed Ministry of Communications till March, 1887, when the Post and Telegraph Services were amalgamated.

**Book recommended.** "The Annual Report of the Director General of the Imperial Government Telegraphs."

**Theatre.** The Japanese theatre has a peculiar importance, as the only remaining place where the life of Old Japan can be studied in these radical latter days. The Japanese drama, too, has an interesting history. It can be traced back to religious dances of immemorial antiquity, accompanied by rude choric songs. An improvement was made in these dances at the beginning of the fifteenth century, when some highly cultivated Buddhist priests and the pleasure-loving Shōgun Yoshimasa took the matter in hand. Edifices—half dancing-stage, half theatre—were built for the special purpose of representing these Nō, as the performances were called; and though the chorus remained, a new interest was added in the shape of two individual personages who moved about and recited portions of the poem in a more dramatic manner.

The result was something strikingly similar to the old Greek drama. The three unities, though never theorised about, were strictly observed in practice. There was the same chorus, the same stately demeanour of the actors, who were often masked; there was the same sitting in

the open air, there was the same quasi-religious strain
pervading the whole. We say "was." But happily the
Nô are not yet dead. Though shorn of much of the
formality and etiquette which surrounded them in earlier
days, representations are still given by families who have
handed down the art from father to son for four hundred
years. There is no scenery, but the dresses are gorgeous
in the extreme. Even the audience, composed chiefly of
noblemen, is a study. They come, not merely to be
amused, but to learn, and they follow the play, book in
hand; for the language used, though beautiful, is ancient
and hard of comprehension, especially when chanted. The
music is—well, it is Oriental. Nevertheless, when due
allowance has been made for orientalism and for antiquity,
it has a certain weird charm. Each piece takes about an
hour to act. But the entire performance occupies the
greater part of a day, as five or six pieces are given in
succession, the intervals between them being filled up by
comediettas, whose broad fun, delivered in old-fashioned
colloquial, serves as a foil to the classic severity of the
chief plays.

From the Nô theatres of the aristocracy to the Shibai
or Kabuki theatres of the common people is a great descent,
so far as taste and poetry are concerned, though the interest
of the more vulgar exhibitions, viewed as pictures of manners—not in the world of gods and heroes, but in that
of ordinary Japanese men and women—will be greater to
most foreign spectators. The plays given at these theatres originated, partly in the comediettas just mentioned,
partly in marionette dances accompanied by explanatory
songs, called *jôruri* or *gidaiyu*. This explains the retention
of the chorus, although in diminished numbers and exiled

to a little cage separated from the stage. Hence, too, the peculiar poses of the actors, originally intended to imitate the stiffness of their prototypes, the marionettes. It was in the sixteenth century that this class of theatre took its rise. Oddly enough, though the founders of the modern Japanese stage were two women, named O-Kuni and O-Tsü, men alone have been allowed to act at the chief theatres, the female parts being taken by boys, as in our own Shakspere's age. It would seem that immorality was feared from the joint appearance of the two sexes, and in sooth the reputation of O-Tsü and her companions was far from spotless.

From the beginning, plays were divided into two classes, called respectively *jidai-mono*, that is, historical plays, and *sewa-mono*, or comedies of manners. Chikamatsu Monzaemon and Takeda Izumo, the most celebrated of Japanese dramatists, divided their attention equally between the two styles. It may be worth mentioning that both these authors belonged to the eighteenth century, and that both of them dramatised the vendetta of " the Forty-Seven Rônins." But Chikamatsu's most famous piece is one founded on the piratical adventures of Kokusen-ya who expelled the Dutch from Formosa in the time of Charles II. The Japanese *Kabuki* theatres are amply pro-vided with scenery and stage properties of every descrip-tion. One excellent arrangement is a revolving centre to the stage, which allows of a second scene being set up behind while the first is in course of acting. On the con-clusion of the first, the stage revolves, carrying away with it actors, scenery, and all; and something entirely different greets the spectators' eyes without a moment's waiting.

The *Nô* actors were honoured under the old *régime*,

whilst the *Kabuki* actors were despised. Indeed the very
theatres in which they appeared were looked down on as
places too vile for any gentleman to enter. Such outcasts
were actors at the time that, when a census was taken,
they were spoken of with the numerals used in counting animals, thus *ippiki, ni-hiki*, not *hitori, futari*. Those
to whom Japanese is familiar will appreciate the terrible
sting of the insult. Such actors formed the delight of the
shopkeeping and artisan classes alone. With the revolution
of 1868, these ideas and customs changed. Actors are
ostracised no longer. Since 1886, there has been a movement among some of the leaders of Japanese thought
towards the reform of the stage, Europe being of course
looked to for models. No tangible result seems, however,
to have been produced as yet. There is, it is true, a so-
called " Reformed Theatre " in Tōkyō. But to the naked
eye the performances there given differ little, if at all, from
those of the other theatres of the capital. For our own part,
though favouring the admittance of actors into Japanese
good society, if their manners fit them for such promotion,
we trust that the Japanese stage may remain, in other
respects, what it now is—a mirror, the only mirror, of Old
Japan. When our fathers invented railways, they did not
tear up the " School for Scandal," or pull down Covent
Garden. Why should the Japanese do what amounts to
the same thing? The only reform called for is one
which touches, not the theatre itself, but an adjunct, an
excrescence. We mean the tea-houses which serve as
ticket-agencies, and practically prevent theatre-goers from
dealing with the theatre direct. Engrossing, as these
parasitical little establishments do, a large portion of the
profits derived from the sale of tickets, they are probably

the main cause of the frequent bankruptcy of the Tōkyō theatres.

Talking of reform and Europeanisation, it fell to our lot a few years ago to witness an amusing scene in a Japanese theatre. The times were already for change. A small Italian opera troupe having come to Yokohama, a wide-awake Japanese *impresario* hired them, and caused a play to be written for the special purpose of letting them appear in it. This play represented the adventures of a party of Japanese globe-trotters, who, after crossing the Pacific Ocean, and landing at San Francisco, where they naturally fall among the Red Indians who infest that remote and savage locality, at last reach Paris and attend a performance at the *Grand Opéra*. Thus were the Italian singers appropriately introduced, Hamlet-like, on a stage upon the main stage. But oh! the effect, upon the Japanese audience! When once they had recovered from the first shock of surprise, they were seized with a wild fit of hilarity at the high notes of the *prima donna*, who really was not at all bad. The people laughed at the absurdities of European singing till their sides shook and the tears rolled down their cheeks, and they stuffed their sleeves into their mouths, as we might our pocket-handkerchiefs, in the vain endeavour to contain themselves. Needless to say that the experiment was not repeated many times. The Japanese stage betook itself to its wonted sights and sounds, and the Japanese play-going public was again happy and contented.

Books recommended. For the Nō dramas and comedietta, see "The Classical Poetry of the Japanese."—The *Kabuki*, or ordinary theatre, has not yet received thorough treatment at European hands. McClatchie's "Japanese Plays Versified" are, however, capital English pieces in "Ingoldsby Legend" style on

some of the chief subjects treated by the Japanese dramatists. There is also an
English translation of the *Chūshingura*, or play of "the Forty-Seven Rōnins," by
F. V. Dickins, and of two or three of the Nō comediettas by the Rev. Dr. Eby in a
magazine entitled "The Chrysanthemum."

**Time.** Japan is now quite European and commonplace
in her manner of reckoning time. Inquisitive persons
may, however, like to take a peep at her earlier and more
peculiar methods, which are still followed by the peasantry
of certain remote districts. Old Japan had no minutes, her
hours were worth two European hours, and they were
counted thus, crab-fashion :—

  9 o'clock (*kokonotsu-doki*), our 12 o'clock.
  8 o'clock (*yatsu-doki*),        „  2  „
  7 o'clock (*nanatsu-doki*),      „  4  „
  6 o'clock (*mutsu-doki*),        „  6  „
  5 o'clock (*itsutsu-doki*),      „  8  „
  4 o'clock (*yotsu-doki*),        „  10  „

Half-past-nine (*kokonotsu han*) was equivalent to our one
o'clock, and similarly in the case of all the other interme-
diate hours, down to half-past-four which was equivalent
to our eleven o'clock. But the hours were never all of exactly the same length, except at the equinoxes. In summer those of the night were shorter, in winter those
of the day. This was because no method of obtaining an
average was used, sunrise and sunset being always called
six o'clock throughout the year.

The week was not known, nor was there any popular
division roughly corresponding to it. Early in the present
reign, however, there was introduced what was called the
*Ichi-Roku*, a holiday on all the ones and sixes of the
month. But this arrangement did not last long. Itself
borrowed from our Sunday, the copy soon gave way to the

original. Sunday is now kept as a day of rest from official work, and of recreation. Even the modern English Saturday half-holiday has made its way into Japan. Sunday being in vulgar parlance *Dontaku*,* Saturday is called (in equally vulgar parlance) *Han-don*, that is, "half-Sunday."

But to return to Old Japan. Her months were real moons, not artificial periods of thirty or thirty-one days. They were numbered one, two, three, four, and so on. Only in poetry did they bear proper names, such as January, February, and the rest, are in European languages. The year consisted of twelve such months, with an intercalary one whenever New Year would otherwise have fallen a whole moon too early. This was about once in three years. Japanese New Year took place late in our January or in the first half of February; and that, irrespective of the state of the temperature, was universally regarded as the beginning of spring. Snow or no snow, the people laid aside their wadded winter gowns. The plum-blossoms, at least, were always there to prove that spring had come; and if the nightingale was yet silent, that was not the Japanese poets' fault, but the nightingale's.

Besides the four great seasons of spring, summer, autumn, and winter, there were twenty-four minor periods (*sekki*) of some fifteen days each, obtained by dividing the real, or approximately real, solar year of three hundred and sixty-five days by twenty-four. These minor periods had names, such as *Risshun*, "Early Spring;" *Kanro*, "Cold Dew;" *Shōkan*, "Lesser Cold;" *Daikan*, "Greater Cold." In addition to this, years, days, and hours were all accounted as belonging to one of the signs of the zodiac (Jap. *jū-ni-shi*), whose order is as follows:—

* A corruption of the Dutch *Zontag*.

| 1 *Ne,* * the Rat. | 7 *Uma,* the Horse. |
|---|---|
| 2 *Ushi,* „ Bull. | 8 *Hitsuji,* „ Goat. |
| 3 *Tora,* „ Tiger. | 9 *Saru,* „ Ape. |
| 4 *U,* „ Hare. | 10 *Tori,* „ Cock. |
| 5 *Tatsu,* „ Dragon. | 11 *Inu,* „ Dog. |
| 6 *Mi,* „ Serpent. | 12 *I,* „ Boar. |

The Japanese have also borrowed from Chinese astrology
what are termed the *jik-kan,* or "ten celestial stems"—a
series obtained by dividing each of the five elements into
two parts, termed respectively the elder and the younger
brother (*e* and *to*). The following series is thus obtained:—

    1 *Ki no E,*    ...   ...Wood —Elder Brother.
    2 *Ki no To,* ...   ...   Wood —Younger Brother.
    3 *Hi no E,*    ...   ...Fire   —Elder Brother.
    4 *Hi no To,* ...   ...   Fire   —Younger Brother.
    5 *Tsuchi no E,*...   ...Earth —Elder Brother.
    6 *Tsuchi no To,* ...   Earth —Younger Brother.
    7 *Ka † no E,*    ...   ...Metal —Elder Brother.
    8 *Ka no To,* ...   ...   Metal —Younger Brother.
    9 *Mizu no E,*    ...   ...Water—Elder Brother.
    10 *Mizu no To,*    ...   Water—Younger Brother.

The two series—celestial stems and signs of the zodiac—
being allowed to run on together, their combination produces the cycle of sixty years, as sixty is the first number
divisible both by ten and by twelve. The first year of
the cycle is *Ki no E Ne,* "Wood—Elder Brother, Rat;"
the second is *Ki no To Ushi,* "Wood—Younger Brother,

---

* *Ne* is short for *nezumi,* the real word for "rat." In like manner, *u* is for *usagi,* and *mi* for *hebi.* *I* is not an abbreviation of *inoshishi,* the modern popular name for a
"boar," but the old form of the word.

† Short for *kane,* "metal."

Bull;" and so on, until the sixtieth, *Mizu no To I*, "Water—Younger Brother, Boar," is reached, and the cycle begins again.

We said that Japan has quite Europeanised herself so far as methods of computing time are concerned. The assertion was too sweeping. Although the Gregorian calendar has been in force ever since the 1st January, 1873, she has not yet been able to bring herself to use the Christian era. Not only would the use of this era symbolise to the Shinto Court of Japan the supremacy of a foreign religion;—the fixing of the calendar from time to time, together with the appointing of "year-names,"* has ever been looked on in the Far-East as among the inviolable privileges and signs of independent sovereignty, much as coining money is in the West. China has its own year-names which it proudly imposes on such vassal states as Korea and Thibet. Japan has other year-names. The names are chosen arbitrarily. In China each year-name coincides with the reign of an emperor. This has not hitherto been the case in Japan, though an official announcement has been made to the effect that reigns and year-names, shall so coincide in future. Either way, the confusion introduced into the study of history may be easily imagined. Hardly any Japanese knows all the year-names even of his own country. The most salient ones are, it is true, employed in conversation, much in the same way as we speak of the sixteenth century or the Georgian era. Such are *Engi* (A. D. 901—923), celebrated for the legislation then undertaken; Genroku (1688—1704), a period of great activity in various arts; Tempō (1830—1844), the most brilliant time of the present century. But no one

---

* In Japanese, *nengō*.

could say off-hand how many years it is from one of these
periods to another. In the year 1872 an attempt was made
to introduce, as the Japanese era from which all dates
should be counted, the supposed date of the accession of
Jimmu Tennô, the mythical ancestor of the Imperial line;
and this system still has followers. Jimmu's reign being
held to have commenced in the year B. C. 660, all dates
thus reckoned exceed by the number six hundred and sixty
the European date for the same year. For instance, 1890
is 2550.

The following is a list of the year-names of the present
century:—

| | | | |
|---|---|---|---|
| *Kyōwa*, | 1801—1804* | *Ansei*, | 1854—1860. |
| *Bunkwa*, | 1804—1818 | *Man-en*, | 1860—1861. |
| *Bunsei*, | 1818—1830 | *Bunkyū*, | 1861—1864. |
| *Tempō*, | 1830—1844 | *Genji*, | 1864—1865. |
| *Kōkwa*, | 1844—1848 | *Keiō*, | 1865—1868. |
| *Kaei*, | 1848—1854. | *Meiji*, | 1868— |

The present year, 1890, is the twenty-third year of Meiji.
Astrologically speaking, it is *Ka no E Tora*, "Metal—
Elder Brother, Tiger."

**Book recommended.** "Japanese Chronological Tables," by William Bramsen.
This book has an elaborate introduction to the whole subject, and the tables are so
arranged as to show, not only the European year, but the exact day to which any
Japanese date, from A. D. 645 onwards, corresponds.

**Tobacco.** Tobacco seems to have been introduced into
Japan by the Portuguese about the year 1600. Its use was
at first strictly prohibited: but by 1651 the law was so far

* It may be asked: Why not take *Kyōwa* as equivalent to 1801—3. *Bunkwa* as equivalent to 1804—17, and so on in every case, instead of counting the final and initial
years of each period twice? The reason is that no new year-name ever came into
force on the 1st January. In most cases the year was well-advanced before the new
name was adopted.

relaxed as to permit smoking, though only out-of-doors.
Now there is hardly a man or woman throughout the
length and breadth of the land who does not enjoy the
fragrant weed; for, as an anonymous author quoted by
Mr Satow sarcastically remarks, "Women who do not
smoke and priests who keep the prescribed rules of
abstinence, are equally rare." The diminutive pipes of
modern Japan are but one among the innumerable instances
of the fondness of the Japanese for small things. To judge
by the old pictures that have been preserved, the first
Japanese pipes must have been as large as walking-sticks.

South recommended. "The Introduction of Tobacco into Japan," by Ernest
Satow, printed in Vol. II of the "Asiatic Transactions."

**Tōkyō.** This city, also called Tōkei* and formerly Yedo,
is of comparatively modern origin. Down to the Middle
Ages, most of the ground on which it stands was washed
by the sea or occupied by lagoons. On the seashore stood,
in the fifteenth century, the fishing hamlet of Ye-do
("estuary gate"), near to which a certain warrior, named
Ōta Dōkwan, built himself a fortress in the year 1456.
The advantages of the position from a military point of
view were discerned by Hideyoshi, who therefore caused
his general, Ieyasu, to take possession of the castle; and
when Ieyasu himself became Shōgun in 1603, he made Yedo
his capital. From that time forward, Japan thus practically
had two capitals—Kyōto in the West, where the Mikado
dwelt in stately seclusion, and Yedo in the East, whence
the Shōgun exercised his authority over the whole land.
On the fall of the Shōgunate in 1868, the Mikado came and
took up his abode in Yedo, and on the 13th September of

* Kei is pronounced nearly like the name of the English letter k.

the same year the name of the city was changed to Tōkyō or Tōkei, these being alternative methods of pronouncing the Chinese characters 東 京, with which the name is written. The meaning of the term *Tō-kyō* is "eastern capital." It was given in contradistinction to *Saikyō*, or "western capital," the name by which Kyōto was rechristened. Tōkyō has been burnt down and built up again many times, fires having formerly been as common in this wooden city as at Constantinople. At the present day it covers an immense area, popularly estimated at four *ri* in every direction, in other words, a hundred square miles. The population has been officially stated to be, in round numbers, 1,200,000. But this includes the whole metropolitan district (*Tōkyō-Fu*). The city proper has only about 900,000.

The principal sights of Tōkyō are the Shiba temples, with the tombs of the Shōguns of the Tokugawa dynasty, near which is the best *Kwankōba* or Bazaar; the *Enryōkwan*, formerly the summer palace of the Shōguns, and now used for the entertainment of distinguished visitors, in consequence of which it is not to be seen without special permit; the view over the city from the new tower on Atago-yama; the Shintō temple named *Shōkonsha*, erected to the memory of the loyal troops slain in battle against various rebels; the adjacent museum of military objects called the *Yūshūkwan*; Ueno Park, with tombs and temples similar to those of Shiba, and also some interesting museums; the popular Buddhist temple of Asakusa; the Monzeki or temple of the Monto sect in Tsukiji, to say nothing of such modern Europeanised buildings as the hotels, banks, government offices, asylums, etc., which will have an interest for some persons. In addition to these, according to the time of year, there are the cherry-blossoms of Mukō-

jima, Ueno, and Shiba, the irises of Horikiri, and the
wistarias of Kameido.   It is also worth while paying a visit
to one of the theatres, of which the *Shintomiza* in Tsukiji
is the best, and to the wrestling-matches held at the temple
of Ekôin and elsewhere.  But after all the chief sight of
Tôkyô to one fresh from home is Tôkyô itself—the quaint
little wooden houses, which brick structures in foreign style
have only partially replaced, the native dress which western
fashions and fabrics have not yet completely driven out,
the open air life of the people, the clatter of the clogs,
the *jinrikishas*, the dainty children—dressed, powdered,
and rouged for a Sunday outing—the indescribable grotes-
queness of the *soi-disant* European costumes of many of
the fine ladies and gentlemen of the middle class.

There are also the attractions of the shops, which make
Mr Percival Lowell truly observe that " To stroll down the
*Broadway* of Tôkyô of an evening is a liberal education
in every day art," for—as he adds—"Whatever these
people fashion, from the toy of an hour to the triumphs of
all time, is touched by a taste unknown elsewhere."  Mr.
Lowell, as an artist in words, does not add what we,
simple recorders of facts, are bound to do, that with so
much to appeal to the eye, Tôkyô also has not a little that
appeals to the nose.

The pleasantest excursions in the neighbourhood of
Tôkyô are to Ôji, famed for the incongruous mixture of
autumn tints and paper-mills; to Meguro with its temple of
Fudô; to Futago where the *ayu* or trout are caught; and
to Ikegami, the chief shrine of the Nichiren sect of Buddhists, with fine, though now decaying, temples standing
amidst gigantic trees.

**Books recommended.** For solid facts, Satow and Hawes' "Handbook to

Central and Northern Japan," pp. 1-44 ; "The Castle of Yedo," by T. R. H. McClatchie, in Vol. VI. Part I, and "The Feudal Mansions of Yedo, by the same author, in Vol. VII, Part III, of the "Asiatic Transactions." For picturesque descriptions and for "talky-talky," the pages of globe-trotters and book-makers innumerable.

**Topsy-turvydom.** It has often been remarked that the Japanese do many things in a way that runs directly counter to European ideas of what is natural and proper. To the Japanese themselves our ways appear equally unaccountable. It was only the other day that a Tōkyō lady asked the present writer why foreigners did so many things topsy-turvy, instead of doing them naturally, after the manner of her country-people. Here are a few instances of this contrariety :—

Japanese books begin at what we should call the end, the word finis (終) coming where we put the title-page. The foot-notes are printed at the top of the page, and the reader puts in his marker at the bottom.

Men make themselves merry with wine, not after dinner, but before. Sweets also come before the *pièces de résistance*.

The whole method of treating horses is the opposite of ours. A Japanese mounts his horse on the right side, all parts of the harness are fastened on the right side, the mane is made to hang on the left side ; and when the horse is brought home, its head is placed where its tail ought to be, and the animal is fed from a tub at the stable door.

Boats are hauled up on the beach stern first.

The Japanese do not say "north-east," "south-west," but "east-north," "west-south."

They carry babies, not in their arms, but on their backs.

In addressing a letter they employ the following order of words: "Japan, Tōkyō, Akasaka District, such-and-such a street, 19 Number, Smith John Mr," thus putting the general first, and the particular afterwards, which is the exact reverse of our method.

Many tools and implements are used in a way which is contrary to ours. For instance, Japanese keys turn in instead of out, and Japanese carpenters saw and plane towards, instead of away from, themselves.

The best rooms in a house are at the back. The garden too is at the back. When building a house, the Japanese construct the roof first; then, having numbered the pieces, they break it up again, and keep it until the substructure is finished.

In making up accounts, they write down the figures first, the item corresponding to the figures next.

Politeness prompts them to remove, not their head-gear, but their foot-gear.

Their needle-work sometimes curiously reverses European methods. Belonging as he does to the inferior sex, the present writer can only speak hesitatingly on such a point. But an English lady resident in Tōkyō tells him that the impulse of her Japanese maids is always to sew on cuffs, frills, and other like things, topsy-turvy and inside out. If that is not the *ne plus ultra* of contrariety, what is?

Men in Japan are most emphatically *not* the inferior sex. When (which does not often happen) a husband condescends to take his wife out with him, it is my lord's *jinrikisha* that bowls off first. The woman gets into hers as best she can, and trundles along behind. Still, women have some few consolations. In Europe, gay bachelors are apt to be captivated by the charms of actresses. In Japan, where there are no actresses to speak of, it is the women who fall in love with fashionable actors.

**Torii.** *Torii* is the name of the archways, formed of two upright and two horizontal beams, which stand in front of Shintō temples. As almost all visitors to this country seek for information concerning these characteristically Japanese structures, it may be well to quote what Mr Satow says concerning them in his essay on "The Shintō Temples of Ise," printed in Vol. II of the "Asiatic Transactions":—

"The *Torii*," writes Mr Satow, "was originally a perch for the fowls offered up to the gods, not as food, but to give warning of daybreak. It was erected on any side of the temple indifferently. In later times, not improbably after the introduction of Buddhism, its original meaning was forgotten; it was placed in front only and supposed to be a gateway. Tablets with inscriptions (*gaku*) were placed on the *torii* with this belief, and one of the first things done after the restoration of the Mikado in 1868 in the course of the purification of the Shintō temples was the removal of these tablets. The etymology of the word is evidently 'bird rest.' The *torii* gradually assumed the character of a general symbol of Shintō, and the number which might be erected to the honour of a deity became practically unlimited. The Buddhists made it of stone or bronze, and frequently of red-painted wood, and developed various forms."

It is perhaps right to add that this account, or rather the etymology given in it, has been disputed. Mr Aston, in his Japanese Grammar, derives *torii*, not from *tori*, "a bird," and *iru*, "to dwell," "to perch," but from *tōru*, "to pass through," and the same *iru*. Who would undertake to judge between two such authorities?

**Trade.** The value of Japan's foreign trade for the year 1889 was 136,000,000 silver *yen* (the Japanese *yen*, or silver dollar, being worth about 75% of the United States gold dollar, or 3/¼ sterling). Of this total, imports contributed $66,000,000, and exports $70,000,000. During the last ten years, the foreign trade of the empire has more than doubled itself: in 1879 it was estimated at only $66,000,000. The following are the chief articles of trade, with their respective values in 1889:—

IMPORTS.

| | |
|---|---|
| Textile fabrics ... ... ... ... ... | $30,831,900. |
| Arms, instruments, clocks, watches, and machinery ... ... ... ... | 6,515,900. |
| Sugar ... ... ... ... ... ... | 6,292,500. |
| Metals and metal manufactures... | 6,173,600. |
| Oils and wax ... ... ... ... ... | 4,814,600. |
| Drugs, medicines, dyes, and paints. | 3,012,900. |
| Provisions, wines, beer, and cigars. | 1,459,400. |
| Grain and seeds ... ... ... ... | 1,008,500. |
| Clothing and apparel ... ... ... | 956,900. |
| Books, paper, and stationery ... | 664,300. |
| Glass and glass ware ... ... ... | 436,500. |
| Sundry miscellaneous articles ... | 3,936,000. |
| | $66,103,000. |

EXPORTS.

| | |
|---|---|
| Raw silk ... ... ... ... ... ... | $26,220,151. |
| Waste silk and cocoons ... ... | 2,706,713. |
| Tea ... ... ... ... ... ... ... | 6,156,729. |
| Rice ... ... ... ... ... ... | 7,434,941. |

| Coal ... .. .. ... ... ... ... | 4,345,637. |
|---|---|
| Copper ... ... ... ... ... ... | 2,817,667. |
| Silk handkerchiefs and silk piece goods ... ... ... ... ... | 2,913,679. |
| Camphor and camphor oil ... ... | 1,432,364. |
| Watches ... ... ... ... ... ... | 1,137,952. |
| Porcelain and earthenware ... | 1,449,888. |
| Curios ... ... ... ... ... ... | 1,856,688. |
| Wheat, barley, rye, etc. ... ... | 343,269. |
| Tobacco ... ... ... ... ... | 197,020. |
| Dried fish ... ... ... ... ... | 149,528. |
| Fish oil and wax ... ... ... ... | 460,435. |
| Skins, hair, and shells ... ... ... | 243,758. |
| Antimony ... ... ... ... ... ... | 238,834. |
| Sundry miscellaneous articles ... | 9,956,746. |

$70,060,000.

SILK. This, the most valuable of Japan's exports, is
sent away to the European and American markets in
various forms—in its raw state as Filatures, Rereels and
Hanks, as Cocoons and Waste Silk; manufactured, chiefly
in the form of handkerchiefs. Of the description first
named—Filatures, Rereels, and Hanks—there were
exported from Yokohama 40,164 bales of 100 Japanese pounds (133¼ lbs English), valued, as stated in the
above table, at $26,220,152, between the 1st January and
the 31st December 1889. During the same period, 27,914
piculs (1 picul=133⅓ lbs) of Cocoons and Waste Silk,
valued at $2,706,713, and silk manufactured goods worth
$2,913,679 were also sent away to Europe and America.
In the year 1888, 6350 more bales of silk were exported
than during 1889, but the total value was less by $36,800.

The above figures will serve to give an idea of the importance of the silk industry of this country. With greater regularity in reeling, consequent upon improved manipulation, there is a hopeful outlook for the Japanese silk trade. Much has already been done, especially in the provinces of Shinshū, Kōshū, and Jōshū, where there are numerous spinneries worked after European models. The cocoon of Japan is but little inferior to its rivals of France and Italy, the present values being respectively :—

| | FRANCE. | ITALY. | JAPAN. |
|---|---|---|---|
| *Francs* | 63/65 | 62/64 | 60/61. |

Nor is there any reason for assuming that the Japanese cocoon may not, in the future, attain to the highest excellence. The central and north-central provinces of the Main Island are the chief silk-producing districts. The Japanese silk season begins on the 1st July, and ends on the 30th June of the following year. Export is made wholly from Yokohama, chiefly by foreign merchants. The Japanese, however, send away a certain quantity yearly on their own account.

TEA. Amongst the articles exported from Japan, Tea generally ranks as the second in value. Only in 1889 did it, from exceptional causes, give way to rice. During the season 1888/9, the total quantity exported was 40,400,000 lbs., and it is estimated that the figure of 41,000,000 will be reached at the close of the present season, 1889/90. Business commences about May, with the advent of the first pickings of the shrub, and continues throughout the year, no purchases of any magnitude being made, however, after the autumn.

The preparation of the leaf for native consumption differs

somewhat from the preparation for the foreign market. If
intended for Japanese use, the leaves are twice dried over
charcoal fires in paper covered baskets, before being sent
away for sale. This process of drying, or firing as it
is termed, is again gone through when the tea is purchased
by the dealer, and it is then ready for use.

In the case of teas destined to be sold at the treaty ports
for consumption abroad, the leaves are subjected to one
firing only, enough to preserve them while in transit.
The foreign merchants fire them in iron pans, heated by a
slow charcoal fire, the tea being continually kept in motion
by a coolie who stirs it about with his hands. Such colouring matter as may be required is then added, and the tea
after being sifted and picked over, is packed in boxes and
shipped to its destination abroad.

Japanese tea is not a favourite in Europe, where the
Chinese and Indian varieties are preferred; but in America
it is well liked, large quantities being annually consumed.
The following figures will serve to exemplify this statement :—

*Export of Tea from Yokohama in* 1889.
    United States     ...     ...     ...     ... lbs. 16,400,203.
    Canada     ...     ...     ...     ...     ...        6,729,960.
    Europe ...     ...     ...     ...     ...     ...        657,979.
                                                        _____
                                                        23,788,142

RICE. Japan produces annually about thirty-one million
*koku*\* of rice. Japanese rice, though not equal to the
Java and Carolina varieties, is of good quality, and
is more highly thought of in the European markets than

_____
\* The *koku* is equivalent to 5.3 bushels.

the ordinary kinds grown in India and Burma. The trade
is accordingly a considerable one, rice generally ranking second in value amongst Japanese articles of export. The
bulk of it is exported from Kōbe and the ports to the
south of Kōbe. The valuation set by the Imperial Customs on the quantity that was sent abroad in 1889,
partly by foreign merchants, partly by the government itself, is $7,434,941; but there are reasons for
thinking that this large figure will not be again attained
for several years to come. The government was formerly
accustomed to hold immense stocks of the grain. To the
recent discontinuance of this practice may be attributed the
impetus acquired by the operations of speculators, and
the consequent rapid fluctuations in value—fluctuations
formerly unheard of, when the market was steadied by a
knowledge of the supply always stored up in the government
warehouses.

GENERAL CONSIDERATIONS. The foreign trade of Japan
is in the hands of five countries, namely, Great Britain
(including British colonies and possessions), the United
States, France, China, and Germany. The amounts
taken by each of these countries are as follows :—

| | |
|---|---:|
| Great Britain ... ... ... ... ... | $55,498,530. |
| United States ... ... ... ... ... | 31,592,893. |
| France ... ... ... ... ... ... ... | 17,592,893. |
| China ... ... ... ... ... ... | 14,642,205. |
| Germany ... ... ... ... ... ... | 6,526,282. |

The chief centre of this trade is Yokohama; but Kōbe
is making such rapid strides that in the last ten years the
amount of its trade has trebled. As to the future prospects
of the Japan trade in general, there is every reason to

believe that the highest point has not yet been reached. Silk, the great staple export, is in a most flourishing condition. Tea holds its own fairly. Rice alone shows signs of having been overdone. Curios, the manufacture of which employs a great number of hands, are sent away in annually large quantities. Matches of Japanese manufacture and several descriptions of grain and seeds have also increased their export value. The recent construction of railways and the growing number of coasting steamers, the new silk filatures, the new rice and cotton mills—all these things are evidence of the industrial strides made by the Japanese during the last decade. As regards cotton, a considerable quantity of the raw material is now imported and worked up with good results. With the multiplication of factories, an increase in the import of this raw material and a consequent falling off in the importation of the manufactured article are bound to come about. It remains to be seen in what way the enlarged consuming power of the people may serve as a check on this decrease.

The figures quoted on the foregoing page show the marked preponderance of British interest in the Japan trade. Nevertheless, an assertion to the effect that the British mercantile community is not holding its own has been made and repeated in certain quarters. More especially clamorous was this assertion a few years ago, when the attention of business men in England was called, during a period of commercial slackness, to the "encroachments" of Germans in the foreign markets that had hitherto been exclusively in British hands. Figures were quoted to show that German trade in certain branches had grown in a larger ratio, and the conclusion was drawn that the Germans had

devised some new business methods, peculiarly adapted
to the requirements of their Japanese customers and likely
to end in driving British competition from the field.

A reference to the statistics published annually by the
Imperial Customs suffices to show that such a view has
no foundation in fact. The increase in the value of the
British import trade has been steadily maintained. The
total value of articles imported into Japan by British
merchants during the year 1887 was $19,000,000; the
total for 1889 was $26,000,000. During the same period,
Germany's import trade increased from $4,000,000 to
$4,900,000. If this is to be regarded as an ousting
of British trade from the field, words must have taken
some new sense with which we are not acquainted.
The alarm seems to have arisen from an unjustifiable
use of statistics. Judged by averages and percentages,
the advance from no share or from an utterly insignificant
share to a fair one will inevitably appear greater than the
advance from a large share to a larger still. The prosperity
or decline of a business must be gauged, not by such
deceptive percentages, but by actual amounts. That
Germany, long debarred by political circumstances from
participation in the trade of the East, should at last
have entered the field, is surely not a matter to cause any
reasonable business man either jealousy or alarm. The
articles of export in which Germany now takes the lead
are woollen yarn, flannels, aniline dies, iron nails, sheet
zinc, lamps, gunpowder, and certain kinds of chemicals.

A word now on the business habits of the Japanese.
Despised during long ages of aristocratic feudalism, hampered at every turn by vexatious restrictions, trade was
in a sorry plight when the ports were opened, and the

traders formed a class utterly unsuited to have the making
of their country's commercial prosperity. Of low caste
and doubtful probity, they were tricky rather than clever.
Favourable exceptions there were of course, and the
number of such exceptions has increased of late years,
owing to contact with the better business methods and
higher standard of business morality of foreigners. There
is still, doubtless, much room for improvement. - The Japanese merchant remains at bottom the petty trader. Commanding but scanty capital, he has never been able to or-
ganise a proper system of credit. His transactions with
foreign merchants are necessarily on a cash basis, because
even had he the will, he has scarcely the ability to fulfil a
contract should the market go against him. But the will
is often as conspicuously absent as the ability. The
largest dealer will not consider it derogatory to endeavour
to extricate himself from an engagement the fulfilment of
which might cause him the loss of a trifling sum. This
paltry spirit runs through all grades, the aims and am-
bitions of each Japanese business circle being smaller and
meaner than those of the corresponding class in Western
lands. The Japanese shopkeeper begins by asking a price
considerably beyond that at which he is prepared to sell,
and wastes hours in bargaining with his customers, who,
knowing that the first figure quoted is extortionate, endeavour to beat him down until their own estimate is
reached. Again, he admits of no such thing as a reduction
in price for a quantity. His view of the matter is that
if an article is worth so much when not in requisition,
its value must rise in proportion to the demand. Successful as a producer, the Japanese cannot yet be considered a good business man. At present, the assistance of

government is relied on *in* all large undertakings, a sure sign of want of individual enterprise.

**Treaty Ports.** The treaty ports, that is, those ports at which foreigners have acquired by treaty the right to reside and trade in Japan, are Yokohama, Kôbe, Ôsaka, Nagasaki, Niigata, Hakodate, and Ebisu-Minato in the Island of Sado. The low-lying portion of Tôkyô known as Tsukiji (literally, "made land") is included in the same category. The district surrounding a treaty port, within which alone, under the exterritorial system, foreigners have permission to travel without passports, is called TREATY LIMITS. The usual extent of treaty limits is ten *ri* in every direction, that is to say, about twenty-four and a half miles English.

**Treaty Revision.** This is at once the knottiest and the most infinitely wearisome of all Japanese questions. We leave the discussion of it to others, whose taste—and there is no accounting for tastes—inclines them to local politics.

**Tycoon.** The literal meaning of this title is "great prince." It was adopted by the Shôguns in comparatively recent times, in order to magnify their position in the eyes of foreign powers.

**Woman (Status of).** Japanese women are most womanly—kind, gentle, pretty. But the way in which they are treated by the men has hitherto been such as might cause a pang to any generous European heart. No wonder that some of them are at last endeavouring to emancipate themselves. A woman's lot is summed up in what are

allow men and women to sit in the same apartment, to keep their wearing apparel in the same place, to bathe in the same place, or to transmit to each other anything directly from hand to hand. A woman going abroad at night must in all cases carry a lighted lamp; and (not to speak of strangers) she must observe a certain distance in her relations even with her husband and with her brethren. In our days, the women of the lower classes, ignoring all rules of this nature, behave themselves disorderly; they contaminate their reputation, bring down reproach upon the heads of their parents and brethren, and spend their whole lives in an unprofitable manner. Is not this truly lamentable? It is written likewise, in the 'Lesser Learning,' that a woman must form no friendship and no intimacy, except when ordered to do so by her parents or by the 'middleman.'\* Even at the peril of her life, must she harden her heart like rock or metal, and observe the rules of propriety.

"In China, marriage is called *returning*, for the reason that a woman must consider her husband's home as her own, and that, when she marries, she is therefore returning to her own home. However low and needy may be her husband's position, she must find no fault with him, but consider the poverty of the household which it has pleased Heaven to give her as the ordering of an unpropitious fate. The Sage of old taught that, once married, she must never leave her husband's house. Should she forsake the 'way,' and be divorced, shame shall cover her till her latest hour. With regard to this point, there are seven faults, which are termed 'the Seven Reasons for Divorce:' (i) A woman shall be divorced for disobedience to her father-

\* See page 361.

in-law or mother-in-law. (ii) A woman shall be divorced if she fail to bear children, the reason for this rule being that women are sought in marriage for the purpose of giving men posterity. A barren woman should, however, be retained if her heart is virtuous and her conduct correct and free from jealousy, in which case a child of the same blood must be adopted; neither is there any just cause for a man to divorce a barren wife, if he have children by a concubine. (iii) Lewdness is a reason for divorce. (iv) Jealousy is a reason for divorce. (v) Leprosy, or any like foul disease, is a reason for divorce. (vi) A woman shall be divorced, who, by talking overmuch and prattling disrespectfully, disturbs the harmony of kinsmen and brings trouble on her household. (vii) A woman shall be divorced who is addicted to stealing.—All the 'Seven Reasons for Divorce' were taught by the Sage. A woman, once married, and then divorced, has wandered from the 'way,' and is covered with the greatest shame, even if she should enter into a second union with a man of wealth and position.

" It is the chief duty of a girl living in the parental house to practise filial piety towards her father and mother. But after marriage, her chief duty is to honour her father-in-law and mother-in-law—to honour them beyond her own father and mother—to love and reverence them with all ardour, and to tend them with every practice of filial piety. While thou honourest thine own parents, think not lightly of thy father-in-law! Never should a woman fail, night and morning, to pay her respects to her father-in-law and mother-in law. Never should she be remiss in performing any tasks they may require of her. With all reverence must she carry out, and never rebel against, her father-in-law's commands. On every point must she inquire of her

father-in-law and mother-in-law, and abandon herself to
their direction. Even if thy father-in-law and mother-in-
law be pleased to hate and vilify thee, be not angry with
them, and murmur not! If thou carry piety towards them
to its utmost limits, and minister to them in all sincerity, it
cannot be but that they will end by becoming friendly to thee.

"A woman has no particular lord. She must look to
her husband as her lord, and must serve him with all worship and reverence, not despising or thinking lightly of
him. The great life-long duty of a woman is obedience.
In her dealings with her husband, both the expression of
her countenance and the style of her address should be
courteous, humble, and conciliatory, never peevish and
intractable, never rude and arrogant;—that should be a
woman's first and chiefest care. When the husband issues
his instructions, the wife must never disobey them. In
doubtful cases, she should inquire of her husband, and
obediently follow his commands. If ever her husband
should inquire of her, she should answer to the point;—to
answer in a careless fashion were a mark of rudeness.
Should her husband be roused at any time to anger, she
must obey him with fear and trembling, and not set herself
up against him in anger and disputatiousness. A woman
should look on her husband as if he were Heaven itself,
and never weary of thinking how she may yield to her
husband, and thus escape celestial castigation.

As brothers-in-law and sisters-in-law are the brothers
and sisters of a woman's husband, they deserve all her
reverence. Should she lay herself open to the ridicule and
dislike of her husband's kindred, she would offend her
parents-in-law, and do harm even to herself, whereas, if
she lives on good terms with them, she will likewise rejoice

the hearts of her parents-in-law. Again, she should cherish, and be intimate with, the wife of her husband's elder brother,—yea, with special warmth of affection should she reverence her husband's elder brother and her husband's elder brother's wife, esteeming them as she does her own elder brother and elder sister.

" Let her never even dream of jealousy. If her husband be dissolute, she must expostulate with him, but never either nurse or vent her anger. If her jealousy be extreme, it will render her countenance frightful and her accents repulsive, and can only result in completely alienating her husband from her and making her intolerable in his eyes. Should her husband act ill and unreasonably, she must compose her countenance and soften her voice to remonstrate with him ; and if he be angry and listen not to the remonstrance, she must wait over a season, and then expostulate with him again when his heart is softened. Never set thyself up against thy husband with harsh features and a boisterous voice !

" A woman should be circumspect and sparing in her use of words ; and never, even for a passing moment, should she slander others or be guilty of untruthfulness. Should she ever hear calumny, she should keep it to herself and repeat it to none ; for it is the retailing of calumny that disturbs the harmony of kinsmen and ruins the peace of families.

" A woman must ever be on the alert, and keep a strict watch over her own conduct. In the morning she must rise early, and at night go late to rest. Instead of sleeping in the middle of the day, she must be intent on the duties of her household, and must not weary of weaving, sewing, and spinning. Of tea and wine she must not drink overmuch, nor must she feed her eyes and ears with theatrical performances, ditties, and ballads. To temples (whether Shintō or Buddhist) and other like places, where there is a great concourse of people, she should go but sparingly till she has reached the age of forty.

" She must not let herself be led astray by mediums and divineresses and enter into an irreverent familiarity with the gods, neither should she be constantly occupied in praying. If only she satisfactorily perform her duties as a human being, she may let prayer alone without ceasing to enjoy the divine protection.

" In her capacity of wife, she must keep her husband's household in proper order. If the wife be evil and profligate, the house is ruined. In everything she must avoid extravagance, and both with regard to food and raiment must act according to her station in life, and never give way to luxury and pride.

" While young, she must avoid the intimacy and familiarity of her husband's kinsmen, comrades, and retainers, ever strictly adhering to the rule of separation between the sexes ; and on no account whatever should she enter into correspondence with a young man. Her personal adornments and the colour and pattern of her garments should be unobtrusive. It suffices for her to be neat and cleanly in her person and in her wearing apparel. It is wrong in her, by an excess of care, to obtrude herself on other people's notice. Only that which is suitable should be practised.

" She must not selfishly think first of her own parents, and only secondly of her husband's relations. At New Year, on the Five Festivals,* and on other like occasions, she should first pay her respects to those of her husband's

* See page etc.

house, and then to her own parents. Without her husband's permission, she must go nowhere, neither should she make any gifts on her own responsibility.

" As a woman rears up posterity, not to her own parents, but to her father-in-law and mother-in-law, she must value the latter even more than the former, and tend them with all filial piety. Her visits, also, to the paternal house should be rare after marriage. Much more then, with regard to other friends, should it generally suffice for her to send a message to inquire after their health. Again, she must not be filled with pride at the recollection of the splendour of her parental house, and must not make it the subject of her conversations.

" However many servants she may have in her employ, it is a woman's duty not to shirk the trouble of attending to everything herself. She must sew her father-in-law's and mother-in-law's garments, and make ready their food. Ever attentive to the requirements of her husband, she must fold his clothes and dust his rug, rear his children, wash what is dirty, be constantly in the midst of her household, and never go abroad but of necessity.

" Her treatment of her handmaidens will require circumspection. These low and aggravating girls have had no proper education; they are stupid, obstinate, and vulgar in their speech. When anything in the conduct of their mistress's husband or parents-in-law crosses their wishes, they fill her ears with their invectives, thinking thereby to render her a service. But any woman who should listen to this gossip must beware of the heartburnings it will be sure to breed. Easy is it by reproaches and disobedience to lose the love of those, who, like a woman's marriage connections, were all originally strangers; and it were surely folly, by believing the prattle of a servant-girl, to diminish the affection of a precious father-in-law and mother-in-law. If a servant-girl be altogether too loquacious and bad, she should speedily be dismissed; for it is by the gossip of such persons that occasion is given for the troubling of the harmony of kinsmen and the disordering of a household. Again, in her dealings with these low people, a woman will find many things to disapprove of. But if she be forever reproving and scolding, and spend her time in bustle and anger, her household will be in a continual state of disturbance. When there is real wrong-doing, she should occasionally notice it, and point out the path of amendment, while lesser faults should be quietly endured without anger. While in her heart she compassionates her subordinates' weaknesses, she must outwardly admonish them with all strictness to walk in the paths of propriety, and never allow them to fall into idleness. If any is to be succoured, let her not be grudging of her money; but she must not foolishly shower down her gifts on such as merely please her individual caprice, but are unprofitable servants.

"The five worst maladies that afflict the female mind are: indocility, discontent, slander, jealousy, and silliness. Without any doubt, these five maladies infest seven or eight out of every ten women, and it is from these that arises the inferiority of women to men. A woman should cure them by self-inspection and self-reproach. The worst of them all, and the parent of the other four, is silliness. Woman's nature is passive (lit. *shade*). This passiveness, being of the nature of the night, is dark. Hence, as viewed from the standard of man's nature, the foolishness of woman fails to understand the duties that lie before her very eyes, perceives not the actions that will bring down blame upon

her own head, and comprehends not even the things that
will bring down calamities on the heads of her husband
and children. Neither when she blames and accuses and
curses innocent persons, nor when, in her jealousy of others,
she thinks to set up herself alone, does she see that she is
her own enemy, estranging others and incurring their
hatred. Lamentable errors! Again, in the education of
her children, her blind affection induces an erroneous
system. Such is the stupidity of her character that it is
incumbent on her, in every particular, to distrust herself
and to obey her husband.

"We are told that it was the custom of the ancients, on
the birth of a female child, to let it lie on the floor for the
space of three days. Even in this may be seen the
likening of the man to Heaven and of the woman to Earth;
and the custom should teach a woman how necessary it
is for her in everything to yield to her husband the first,
and to be herself content with the second, place; to avoid
pride, even if there be in her actions ought deserving
praise; and, on the other hand, if she transgress in ought
and incur blame, to wend her way through the difficulty
and amend the fault, and so conduct herself as not
again to lay herself open to censure; to endure without
anger and indignation the jeers of others, suffering such
things with patience and humility. If a woman act thus,
her conjugal relations cannot but be harmonious and
enduring, and her household a scene of peace and con-
cord.

"Parents! teach the foregoing maxims to your daughters
from their tenderest years! Copy them out from time
to time, that they may read and never forget them!
Better than the garments and divers vessels which the

fathers of the present day so lavishly bestow upon their daughters when giving them away in marriage, were it to teach them thoroughly these precepts, which would guard them as a precious jewel throughout their lives. How true is that ancient saying: 'A man knoweth how to spend a million pieces of money in marrying off his daughter, but knoweth not how to spend an hundred thousand in bringing up his child!' Such as have daughters must lay this well to heart."

**Writing.** The Japanese, having obtained their civilisation from China and Korea, were inevitably led to adopt the ideographic system of writing current in those countries. Its introduction into Japan seems to have taken place somewhere about A. D. 400, but the chronology of those times is extremely obscure.

According to this ideographic system, each individual word has its separate sign, originally a kind of picture or hieroglyph. Thus, A is "a man," represented by his two legs; A is "the moon," with her horns still distinguishable; A is "a horse"—the head, mane, and legs, though hard to recognise in the abbreviated modern form of the character, having at first been clearly drawn. Most characters are not so simple as these, but are obtained by means of combination, the chief element being termed the "radical," because it gives a clue to the signification of the whole. The other part generally indicates more or less precisely the pronunciation of the word, and is therefore called the "phonetic." It is much as if, having in English special hieroglyphic signs for such easy, every-day words as "tree," "horse," and "box" (a case), we were to represent "box-wood" by a combination of the sign for

" tree " and the sign for " box," " a box at the opera " by a combination of " house " and " box," and so on. Chinese, being unusually full of homonymous words, lends itself naturally to such a method. Names of plants are obtained by combinations of the character 艸, " herb," itself still to be recognised as a picture of herbs springing up from the soil. " The hand," 手, originally a rude picture of the outstretched fingers, helps to form hundreds of characters signifying actions. " The heart," 心, gives numerous abstract words denoting sentiments and passions. Similarly " the eye," " the mouth," " fire," " water," " silk," " rain," " metal," " fish," are parents of large families of characters. The study of this Chinese method of writing is most interesting—so curious is the chapter of the human mind which it unrolls, so unexpected are the items of recondite history which it discloses. But we can here do no more than allude to it thus briefly.

During the eighth and ninth centuries there came into use in Japan another system of writing, called the *Kana*, formed of fragments of those Chinese characters which happened to be most commonly employed. There are two varieties of it, the *Katakana* and the *Hiragana*. The invention of the former is popularly attributed to a worthy named Kibi-no-Mabi (died A. D. 776), and that of the latter to the Buddhist saint, Kōbō Daishi (A. D. 835); but it is more reasonable to suppose that the simplification—for such it really is, and not an invention at all—came about gradually than to accept it as the work of two particular men at any given moment.

Whereas a Chinese character directly represents a whole word—an idea—the *Kana* represents the sounds of which the word is composed, just as our Roman writing does.

There is, however, this difference, that the *Kana* stands for syllables, not letters. The following tables of the *Kata-kana* and *Hira-gana* will help to make this clear. We give the former in the order preferred by modern scholars, the latter in the popular order, called *I-ro-ha*, which has been handed down from the ninth century.

### THE KATAKANA SYLLABARY.

| a | ka | sa | ta | na | ha | ma | ya | ra | wa |
|---|---|---|---|---|---|---|---|---|---|
| i | ki | shi | chi | ni | hi | mi | | ri | (w)i |
| u | ku | su | tsu | su | fu | mu | yu | ru | |
| (w)e | ke | se | te | ne | he | me | (y)e | re | |
| o | ko | so | to | no | ho | mo | yo | ro | wo |

### THE HIRAGANA SYLLABARY.

| i | to | ha | ni | ho | he | to |
|---|---|---|---|---|---|---|
| chi | ri | nu | ru | wo | wa | ka |
| yo | ta | re | so | tsu | ne | na |
| ra | mu | u | (w)i | no | o | ku |
| ya | ma | ke | fu | ko | (y)e | te |
| a | sa | ki | yu | me | mi | shi |
| (w)e | hi | mo | se | su | | |

The order of the *I-ro-ha* bears witness to the Buddhist belief of the father of Japanese writing. The syllabary is a verse of poetry founded on one of the *Sûtras*, and so arranged that the same letter is never repeated twice. Transcribed according to the modern pronunciation, it runs thus :—

> *Iro wa nioedo,*
> *Chirinuru wo—*
> *Waga yo tare zo*
> *Tsune naran?*
> *Ui no oku-yama*
> *Kyō koete,*
> *Asaki yume mishi,*
> *Ei mo sezu.*

Which is, being interpreted :

"Though their hues are gay, the blossoms flutter down, and so in this world of ours who may continue forever? Having to-day crossed the mountain-fastness of existence, I have seen but a fleeting dream, with which I am not intoxicated."

In both syllabaries, consonants can be softened* by placing two dots to the right of the letter. Thus ﾊ is *ka*, but ﾊ is *ga*; ﾀ is *te*, but ﾀ is *da*, and so on. In this way the number of letters is raised considerably. There are various other peculiarities, Japanese orthography almost rivalling our own in eccentricity. Very few books are written in *Hiragana* alone—none in *Katakana* alone. Almost all are written in a mixture of Chinese characters and *Kana* of one kind or another, the Chinese characters being employed for the chief ideas, for nouns and the stems

---

* I. e., technically speaking, surds can be changed into sonants.

of verbs, while the *Kana* serves to transcribe the particles
and terminations. Add to this that the Chinese characters
are commonly written and even printed in every sort of
style—from the standard, or so-called "square," to the
most sketchy cursive hand—that each Chinese character is
capable of being pronounced in two or three different ways,
that each *Hiragana* syllabic letter has several alternative
forms, that there is no method of indicating capitals or
punctuation, that all the words are run together on a page
without any mark to show where one leaves off and another
begins—and the result is the most complicated and uncertain system of writing under which poor humanity has ever
groaned. Indeed an old Jesuit missionary declares it to
be evidently "the invention of a conciliabule of the demons
to harass the faithful."

But if Japanese writing is a mountain of difficulty, it is
unapproachably beautiful. Japanese art has been called
calligraphic. Japanese calligraphy is artistic. Above all,
it is bold, because it comes from the shoulder instead of
merely from the wrist. A little experience will convince
any one that, in comparison with it, the freest, boldest
English hand is little better than the cramped scribble of
some rheumatic old crone. One consequence of this
exceeding difficulty and beauty is that calligraphy ranks high
in Japan among the arts. Another is that the Japanese
very easily acquire our simpler system. To copy the
handwriting of a European is mere child's play to them.
In fact, it is usual for clerks and students to imitate the
handwriting of their employer or master so closely that he
himself often cannot tell the difference.

Book recommended. For the *Kana*, Aston's "Grammar of the Japanese
Written Language." There is no good manual of the Chinese characters as pronounced in Japan.

**Yedo.** See Tōkyō.

**Yeso.** Yezo, often incorrectly spelt Yesso, and officially styled the Hokkaidō or " Northern Sea Circuit," is the northernmost of the larger islands forming the Japanese archipelago. It lies, roughly speaking, between parallels 41¾' and 45½' of north latitude—the latitude of the part of Italy which stretches from Rome to Venice;—but it is under snow and ice for nearly half the year, the native Ainos tracking the bear and deer across its frozen and pathless mountains, like the cave men of the glacial age of Europe. It is asserted that Yoshitsune, the great Japanese hero, fled into Yezo and died there; but little attempt was made by the Japanese to colonise it until early in the seventeenth century, when the Shōgun Ieyasu granted it as a fief to one Matsumae Yoshihiro, who conquered the south-western corner of the island, establishing his capital at Matsumae, some sixty miles to the south-west of the modern port of Hakodate. His successors retained their sway over Yezo until the recent break up of the old feudal system. They treated the luckless Ainos with great cruelty, and actually rendered it penal to communicate to these poor barbarians the art of writing or any of the arts of civilised life. Frequent rebellions, suppressed by massacres, were the result. In the latter part of the eighteenth century, however, and in the first half of the nineteenth, a few Japanese literati made their way into the island. It is to their efforts—to the efforts of such men as Mogami, Mamiya, and Matsura—that our first scientific information concerning the land, the people, and the language of Yezo is due. The Imperial government has done all in its power to redress the wrongs of the hitherto down-trodden natives.

At one time, the Russians endeavoured to obtain a footing
in Yezo; but the opening of Japan nipped this encroach-
ment in the bud. Japanese statesmen eagerly plunged into
the task of developing the resources of the island. With
this end in view, they created a special government department, entitled the *Kaitakushi*, and engaged the services
of a party of Americans headed by General Capron. Large
sums were spent on model farms and other public works,
and a fictitious prosperity set in. The bubble burst in
1881, when the *Kaitakushi* was dissolved, and the administration of the island was assimilated, in the form of
prefectures, to that of the rest of the empire. It is
calculated that Yezo has cost the Imperial government
no less than thirty million dollars.

The chief towns of Yezo are Sapporo—the capital—and
the ports of Hakodate, Akkeshi, Nemoro, and Fukuyama
(the new name of the city of Matsumae, the seat of the
former *daimyō*, but now sadly decayed). It is, however,
not these that will attract the visitor. Rather will he seek
out the charming scenery of "the Lakes" near Hakodate,
whose Japanese names are Junsai Numa and Ōnuma, of
the volcano Koma-ga-take situated near the Lakes, and of
the shores of Volcano Bay, where the Aino aborigines
may conveniently be seen in their native haunts. Most
travelling in Yezo is done on horseback.

Yezo is interesting from a scientific point of view. The
great depth of the Straits of Tsugaru, separating it from
Japan proper, shows that it never—at least in recent geological epochs—formed part of Japan proper. The fauna of
the two islands is accordingly marked by notable differences. Japan has monkeys and pheasants, which Yezo has
not. Yezo has grouse, which Japan has not. Scientific,

or rather unscientific, management played a queer trick
with the city of Sapporo, if the local gossips are to be
credited.  The intention—so it is said—was to lay out the
city à l'américaine, with streets running due north and
south and due east and west.  The person entrusted with
the orientation of the plan was of course aware of the
necessity of allowing for the deviation of the compass ;
but being under the influence of some misconception, he
made the allowance the wrong way, and thus, instead of
eliminating the error, doubled it.  It is pleasant to be able
to add that the result was a practical improvement un-
dreamt of by the mathematicians.  The houses, having
no rooms either due north or due south, suffer less from
the extremes of heat and cold than they would have done
had they possessed some rooms on which the sun never
shone, and others flooded with sunshine all the year round.[*]

Books recommended.  "Japan in Yezo," by T. W. Blakiston.—"Reports and
Official Letters to the Kaitakushi," by General Capron and his Assistants.—Vol. II
of Miss Bird's "Unbeaten Tracks in Japan."

**Yoshiwara.**  When the city of Yedo suddenly rose into
splendour at the beginning of the seventeenth century,
people of all classes and from all parts of the country
flocked thither to try their fortune.  The courtesans were
not behind-hand.  From Kyōto, from Nara, from Fushimi,
they arrived—so the native authorities tell us—in little
parties of three and four.  But a band of some twenty or
thirty from the town of Moto-Yoshiwara on the Tōkaidō
were either the most numerous or the most beautiful,
and so the district of Yedo where they took up their

[*] A specialist in such matters calls our attention to the fact that the story has, as
the common phrase is, "not a leg to stand on," for the reason that the deviation of
the compass is so slight in this part of the world as to be practically insignificant even
when doubled.  We leave the story, however, as an instance of modern myth-making.

abode came to be called the Yoshiwara.* At first there
was no official supervision of these frail ladies. They were
free to ply their trade wherever they chose. But in the
year 1617, on the representations of a reformer named
Shōshi Jin-emon, the city in general was purified, and all
the libertinism in it—permitted, but regulated—was banished to one special quarter near Nihon-bashi, to which the
name of Yoshiwara attached itself. Later on, in A. D.
1656, when the city had grown larger and Nihon-bashi had
become its centre, the authorities caused the houses in
question to be removed to their present site on the
northern limit of Yedo, whence the name of Shin (i. e.,
New) Yoshiwara, by which the place is currently known.
Foreigners often speak of "a Yoshiwara," as if the word
were a generic term. It is not so. The quarters of similar
character in the other cities of Japan are never so called by
the Japanese themselves. Such words as *yūjobu* and
*kuruwa* are used to designate them.

Japanese literature is full of romantic stories in which the
Yoshiwara plays a part. Generally the heroine has found
her way there in obedience to the dictates of filial piety in
order to support her aged parents, or else she is kidnapped
by some ruffian who basely sells her for his own profit.
The story often ends by the girl emerging from a life
of shame with at least her heart untainted, and by
all the good people living happily ever after. It is to be
feared that real life witnesses but few such fortunate cases,

* The weight of authority is in favour of this account of the origin of the name.
According to others, the etymology is *yoshi*, "a reed," and *hara*, "a moor," and the
designation of "reedy moor" would have been given to the locality on account of its
aspect before it was built over. There is another Chinese character *yoshi* meaning
"good," "lucky;" and with this the first two syllables of the name are now usually
written (吉原).

though it is probably true that the fallen women of Japan are, as a class, less vicious than their representatives in Western lands—less drunken, less foul-mouthed. On the other hand, a Japanese proverb says that a truthful courtesan is as great a miracle as a square egg.

In former times, girls could be and were regularly and legally sold into debauchery at the Yoshiwara in Yedo and at its counterparts throughout the land—a state of things which the present enlightened government has hastened to reform. When we add that a weekly medical inspection of the inmates of all such places was introduced in 1874, in imitation of European ways, that each house and each separate inmate of each house is heavily taxed, that there is severe police control over all, and that, since 1888, the idea has been mooted of doing away with licensed prostitution altogether—a plan eagerly advocated by zealous Christian neophytes, but frowned on by the doctors—we have mentioned all that need here be said on a subject which could only be fully discussed in the pages of a medical work.

*Books recommended.—Mitford's "Tales of Old Japan," Vol I, pp. 57—69 in postscript to the story entitled "The Loves of Gompachi and Komurasaki."—A letter by Mr Henry Norman, entitled "The Yoshiwara." This appeared first in the "Pall Mall Gazette"—of what date we cannot say—and was reprinted in the "Japan Daily Mail" of the 5th November, 1888.*

**Zoology.** Japan is distinguished by the possession of some types elsewhere extinct, for instance, the Giant Salamander, and also as being the most northerly country inhabited by the monkey, which here ranges as high as the 41st degree of latitude, in places where the snow often drifts to a depth of fifteen or twenty feet. But in its main features the Japanese fauna resembles that of North China, Korea, and Manchuria—one indication among many that

the ancient land connection of Japan with the Asiatic continent must be sought in the North, not in the South.   The
Japanese fauna, both terrestrial and maritime, is unusually
rich.   To give a single example:—there are already a
hundred and thirty-seven species of butterflies known, as
against some sixty in Great Britain, and over four thousand
species of moths, as against some two thousand in Great
Britain.

The chief mammals are the monkey (*Inuus speciosus
Tem.*), ten species of bats, six species of insectivorous animals, three species of bears, the badger, the marten, the
dog, the wolf, the fox, two species of squirrels, the rat, the
hare, the wild-boar, a species of stag, and a species of
antelope.   Most of our domestic animals are also met with,
but not the ass, the sheep, or the goat.   Other missing
animals are the wild cat and the hedgehog.   No less than
three hundred and fifty-nine species of birds have been
enumerated.   We can only here call attention to the *uguisu*
(*Cettia cantans* T. and Schl.)—a nightingale having a different note from ours—to the copper and golden pheasants,
and to the cranes and herons so beloved by the artists of
Japan.   Of reptiles and batrachians there are but thirty
species.   Of these, the already mentioned Giant Salamander is by far the most remarkable, some specimens attaining to a length of over five feet.   There are also some
large, but harmless, snakes.   The only poisonous snake
is a small species of adder (*Trigonocephalus Blomhoffi*),
known to the Japanese under the name of *mamushi*.   The
country folk look on its boiled flesh as a panacea for many
diseases.

With regard to fish, Dr. Rein remarks that the Chinese
and Japanese waters appear to be richer than any other

part of the ocean. The mackerel family (*Scombsroidæ*), more particularly, is represented in great force, the forty species into which it is divided constituting an important element of the food of the people. But the fish which is esteemed the greatest delicacy is the *tai*, a kind of gold-bream. The gold-fish, the salmon, the eel, the shark, and many others would call for mention, had we the space to devote to them. Altogether, the number of species of fishes inhabiting or visiting Japan cannot fall far short of four hundred.

Insects are extremely numerous but, excepting the beetles, moths and butterflies, are not yet even fairly well-known, so that a rich harvest here awaits some future naturalist. There are two silk-producing moths, the *Bombyx mori* and the *Antheræa yama-mai*. Of dragon-flies the species are numerous and beautiful. There are but few venomous insects. The gadfly torments the traveller only in Yezo and in the northern half of the Main Island; the house-fly is a much less common plague than in Europe, except in the silk districts, and the bed-bug is entirely absent. On the other hand, the mosquito is a nightly plague during half the year in all places lying at altitude of less than 1500 feet above the sea; the *buyu* —a diminutive kind of gnat—infests many mountainous districts during the summer months, and the flea is to be found everywhere at all seasons.

The chief crustacea are fresh-water and salt-water crabs, together with crayfishes, which here replace the lobsters of Europe and are often erroneously termed lobsters by the foreign residents. One species of crab (the *Macrocheirus Kæmpferi Sbd.*) is so gigantic that human beings have been killed and devoured by it. Its legs are

over a yard and a half in length.   There is another species
—smaller than the *Macrocheirus*, but nevertheless formid-
able and hideous to look at—which is the subject of a
singular superstition.   The common folk call it *Heike-gani*,
that is, the Heike crab.   They believe these creatures to be
the wraiths of the warriors of the Heike or Taira clan,
whose fleet was annihilated at the battle of Dan-no-
ura in the year 1185.

Of mollusks, nearly 1200 species have been described by
Dunker, the best authority on the subject; and his enumeration is said by Dr. Rein to be far from exhaustive.   Of sea-
urchins 26 species are known, and of star-fishes 12 species.
The coral tribe is well represented, though not by the reef-
forming species of warmer latitudes.   There are also
various kinds of sponges.   Indeed, one of the most curious
and beautiful of all the many curious and beautiful things
in Japan is the Glass Rope Sponge (*Hyalonema Sieboldi*),
whose silken coils adorn the shell-shops at Enoshima.

**Books recommended.**  The above article is founded on Rein's "Japan." p. 157,
*et seq.*  Rein's treatment of the fishes is specially full, but a good résumé of the
other classes is given, together with references to the chief authorities on each.—See
also Blakiston and Pryer's "Catalogue of the Birds of Japan," printed in Vol. X,
Part I. of the "Asiatic Transactions;" Pryer's "Catalogue of the Lepidoptera of
Japan," in Vol. XI. Part II. and Vol. XII, Part II, of the same, with Additions
and Corrections in Vol. XIII, Part I; and the same author's beautifully illustrated
work entitled "*Rhopalocera Nihonica*."

# POSTSCRIPT.

Our article on Law had scarcely been printed when three new Codes appeared, namely, the Civil Code, the Code of Civil Procedure, and the Commercial Code. The new Civil Code, however, includes as yet but the law of things. Traditional Japanese usage still regulates such important matters as marriage, succession, adoption, and others belonging to the law of persons. The Code of Civil Procedure and the Commercial Code are to come into force on the 1st January, 1891. The Civil Code will not come into force till the 1st January, 1893.

## CORRECTION.

*In the second column of the table on page* 318, *for* Yokohama *read* Yokosuka.

# INDEX.

*(When several references are given, the most important is placed first.)*

INDEX. 399

THE END.

TŌKYŌ : PRINTED BY THE KAKUBUNSHA, I, MICHŌME, GINZA

# BY THE SAME AUTHOR.

"A Handbook of Colloquial Japanese," 1 Vol., 2nd. edit.

"The Classical Poetry of the Japanese," 1 Vol.

"A Simplified Grammar of Japanese" (Modern Written Style), 1 Vol.

"A Romanized Japanese Reader" (Modern Written Style), 3 Vols., viz. Vol. I, Japanese Text; Vol. II, English Translation; Vol. III, Notes.

"The Language, Mythology, and Geographical Nomenclature of Japan, Viewed in the Light of Aino Studies," 1 Vol. (Published as a Memoir of the Literature College of the Imperial University of Japan.)

"A Translation of the *Kojiki*, or Records of Ancient Matters, with Introduction and Commentary," 1 Vol. (Published in the Transactions of the Asiatic Society of Japan.)

"Aino Fairy-Tales" (illustrated).
- 1. "The Hunter in Fairy-Land."
- 2. "The Birds' Party."
- 3. "The Man who Lost his Wife."

In the "Japanese Fairy-Tale Series" (illustrated).
- "Urashima."
- "The Serpent with Eight Heads."
- "The Silly Jelly-Fish."
- "My Lord Bag-o'-Rice."

## IN JAPANESE.

"*Eigo Hensaku Ichiran*" (an elementary English Grammar), 2 Vols.

"*Nihon Shōbunten*" (an elementary Japanese Grammar), 1 Vol.

www.ingramcontent.com/pod-product-compliance
Lightning Source LLC
Chambersburg PA
CBHW030821110726
47900CB00006B/1697